CRITICS ARE RAVING ABOUT LEIGH GREENWOOD!

"Leigh Greenwood NEVER disappoints. The characters are finely drawn, the plots always created with just the right amount of spice to pathos and always, always, a guaranteed good read!"

—*Heartland Critiques*

"Leigh Greenwood remains one of the forces to be reckoned with in the Americana romance sub-genre."

—*Affaire de Coeur*

"Leigh Greenwood continues to be a shining star of the genre!"

—*The Literary Times*

"Greenwood's books are bound to become classics."

—*Rendezvous*

"What more could we want?"

—*Romantic Times*

TEXAS HOMECOMING

"Leigh Greenwood raises the heat and tension with *Texas Homecoming*. Few authors provide a vivid descriptive Americana romance filled with realistic angst-laden protagonists as this author can."

—*The Midwest Book Review*

A REAL MAN

"Has William told you that you have beautiful eyes? They're gray with flecks of silver."

Gray eyes weren't beautiful, flecked or not.

"They flash when you're angry," Owen said, his voice practically liquid heat, "but they're glowing now because you're feeling something quite different. Tell me what you're feeling."

She caught herself just in time to stop her treacherous tongue from telling him she liked being in his arms and wanted to hear more about her eyes.

"I'll bet William never did more than brush your hand. He's a fool. Anybody could tell him there's not a finer figure of a woman in Pinto Junction than you."

"Don't tell any more lies," she managed to say.

"I've heard more than one man say William doesn't deserve what he's getting. They say he'll never warm you up."

"I don't want to be *warmed up*," she said. "I want a husband who'll respect and admire me, one who'll treat me as an equal, who'll—"

"I'll bet he's never kissed you either."

Only one word could describe the feeling that flooded her. Panic.

"I can tell from your eyes I'm right. Well, I can't let you go into marriage without knowing what it's like to have been kissed by a real man at least once."

She struggled, not knowing what was coming, knowing instinctively it was dangerous. Then his lips touched hers, and she was lost.

Texas Bride

LEIGH GREENWOOD

LEISURE BOOKS   NEW YORK CITY

A LEISURE BOOK®

December 2002

Published by

Dorchester Publishing Co., Inc.
276 Fifth Avenue
New York, NY   10001

ISBN: 0-8439-5067-6

Printed in the United States of America.

Visit us on the web at www.dorchesterpub.com.

To Allison.
I couldn't have gotten through
the last two years without your help.

Texas
Bride

Chapter One

South Texas, 1867

Owen Wheeler wiped away the perspiration that ran down the back of his neck as he rode south toward the Nueces River. He took a swallow from his canteen and thought of his childhood home in the Appalachian Mountains. It seemed like a lifetime since he'd wandered their tree-covered slopes, drunk from the refreshingly cold water of sparkling streams. He hated southern Texas. It was unbearably hot and covered with brown grass and thorny plants that clawed, scratched, or tore at him as he rode by. It was so flat he could see for miles in any direction. If he had any sense, he'd be heading back to Virginia, not into some godforsaken, ramshackle town.

Pinto Junction. First, it wasn't a junction. There was nothing to connect. Second, a pinto was a brown and white horse. Everything in Pinto Junction was weathered

1

gray. But it was the biggest town between San Antonio and the Rio Grande River. And if his suspicions were right, it was the center of the rustling going on all over south Texas.

That's why he'd come. He'd heard Laveau diViere had turned to rustling, and he meant to hang Laveau for treason.

Owen entered the town from the north. He could tell immediately there wasn't much to this town that didn't owe its living to the cattle ranches that stretched for hundreds of miles in all directions, and from the looks of things, they weren't doing well. He saw one run-down hotel. The saloons didn't encourage him to hope he'd find more comfortable accommodations. He had money—his cousin Cade had divided the profits from the herd they'd taken to market—but he didn't plan to spend it. As far as people here would know, he was a would-be rancher with a penchant for gambling. His real trade, carpentry, wouldn't allow him to move around as freely as he wanted.

He carefully inspected each saloon he passed, guessing at the customers in each, calculating his chances of winning at poker while listening for the information he needed to hunt down Laveau. But first he wanted to find a room and change out of his worn denim pants and sweat-soaked shirt. He was certain that even in south Texas women wanted their men to smell as good as they looked. Owen knew he looked mighty good.

He paused before a house with a sign on the porch. ROOMS TO LET. He liked the look of the house. It was substantial, the largest in town, but not so big it would be like living in a hotel. He hoped the maid was pretty.

He got down off his horse and walked up to the house. The owner had made some effort toward a garden, but the killing heat had turned everything brown. Even the low fence that separated the yard from the road appeared to sag under the intensity of the summer heat. Owen was relieved to reach the shade of the porch. Several rocking chairs gave evidence it was sometimes cool enough to sit outside.

An attractive woman who looked a few years past the first bloom of youth opened the door.

"I'm Owen Wheeler," Owen said, slipping effortlessly into the smiling charm he used on every female he met. "I'm hoping you have at least one room still vacant."

"Yes, I have a room," the woman replied. She appeared confident and slightly aloof.

"May I come in and see it?"

"Wait here a moment." She closed the door and left him standing on the porch.

Owen didn't bowl over every female he met, but none had closed the door in his face once he'd put himself out to be charming, certainly not one buried so deep in the bottom of Texas she was never likely to run across a better-looking man. Before he could get curious, the door opened again. A young woman of more health than beauty said, "Miss Moody tells me you're looking for a room."

So the pretty one wasn't married. She seemed more promising than this tall, disapproving female. "That's right."

The woman neither smiled nor frowned, just watched him calmly out of amazing gray eyes apparently unimpressed with what she saw. She looked like a Quaker with her plain dress, hands folded in front, her coffee-brown hair captured in a bun at the back of her neck. But there was something about her that the prettier Miss Moody lacked, a kind of energy, an inner force or strength which even a stranger on first meeting couldn't miss. It didn't make her less plain, but somehow it made her plainness matter less. It also made her more interesting. More of a challenge to make her like him despite her obvious determination to do just the opposite.

"Wouldn't you be more comfortable at one of the saloons?" she asked.

"No, ma'am, I wouldn't," Owen said, beginning to be irritated. "I want to take a bath and change my clothes. I'm not used to this infernal heat."

"It's been a relatively cool summer."

"Not for anybody who wasn't born in this hell of southern Texas," Owen snapped.

"Miss Moody doesn't allow cursing."

"That wasn't cussing. When I cuss, you'll know."

"Are your boots clean?" She looked him over again before reluctantly opening the door.

"They haven't touched the ground since I stepped into the saddle this morning."

"Follow me. Be sure to take your hat off. Miss Moody is very particular about that."

Owen felt as if he'd stepped into a woman's bedroom rather than the parlor. He'd never seen so much chintz or so many frills and ruffles.

"Do you mind telling me your name?"

She didn't slow down or turn around. "Why will you be needing it?"

"I'll have to call you something. You'll be in and out of my room all the time."

She stopped then, turned to face him, her frown even more pronounced. "My name is Hetta Gwynne. I'll see you have little reason to use it." Not even a hint of flirtatiousness. She turned and started off once again.

Owen followed her up a stairway and down a narrow hall to a room that contained an iron-frame bed, a wardrobe, and a small table with a pitcher and basin. No chair and no curtains, only shades. The bedspread was a pale blue, the design on the wallpaper faded, and the pitcher and basin plain white.

"Rather stark, isn't it?" Owen asked.

"Most of our lodgers are men."

As though men were unable to appreciate color and variety. "Do you serve meals?"

"They'll be extra."

"Many restaurants in town?"

"Several."

"Any good?"

"Good enough for a man."

He wasn't used to being ignored by women, especially a plain one. His ego had been bruised. He would wring a response out of Hetta Gwynne if it was the last thing he did. "Where is the bathtub?" he asked.

"Outside. You have to pump your own water."

"You mean you expect me to take a bath in cold water?"

"The water is pumped into a cistern where it's heated by the sun. When you finish, you have to fill it up again. Laundry is an extra fifty cents a week. Leave your clothes in the bathhouse if you want them washed."

"Do you do the wash?"

Her gaze narrowed. "Why do you want to know?"

"Just curious. I wondered if Miss Moody did the washing."

"Miss Moody owns this house. She doesn't work."

"Do you do everything? Clean the rooms, wash the clothes, cook?"

"We don't have many guests."

"Aren't you afraid to be alone with strange men?"

"I keep a shotgun next to the bed. I shot a man a year ago. I haven't been bothered since."

Clearly a woman to avoid. "Where can I stable my horse?"

"The blacksmith has a barn. Ask him. If you need anything else, ring the bell on the table by the front door. Guests aren't allowed anywhere on the first floor except

5

the parlor and dining room. Miss Moody is most particular about that."

Owen had never met two more unlikely prospects to help relieve tedium. He considered looking elsewhere for lodgings.

"I'll try not to upset Miss Moody. I hope you won't have any more lodgers wanting a bath. I intend to use every drop of hot water."

"We don't get many people coming through."

"Of course, if *you* want to take a bath—"

"We change the sheets once a week," she went on, ignoring his insinuation. "Miss Moody likes to be paid a week in advance. Which meals do you want to take?"

"Supper." He dropped several coins into her outstretched hand. "I'll let you know about the rest afterwards."

Then she left him. Just closed the door and left.

"Ida Moody's uncle owns half the town," Myrl Henry was telling Owen. "She owns the other half."

The blacksmith had been happy to stable Owen's horse, but he had been as unwilling to talk to a stranger as Hetta Gwynne. The situation was the same at the first two saloons Owen entered. In the third he encountered Myrl, a broken-down cowboy more than willing to talk in exchange for free beer. In fifteen minutes he'd told Owen where to find the best whiskey, the best food, and the best poker games. He'd also warned him which saloons were the haunts of rustlers.

"You want to stay away from them," Myrl said. "If Ida finds out you been going there, she'll make you move out."

"Why?"

"She's afraid it'll give her place a bad name."

"Why? Is she courting?"

Myrl laughed. "Ain't nobody around here good enough for Ida."

"She and that maid ought to get along like gangbusters."

"Miss Ida's too good for any man. Hetta just doesn't like 'em. I'm surprised she didn't close the door on you. Of course, if you was homely, she'd be nice as an old maid aunt. Works like a slave for Miss Ida. She owns a ranch, but it's a ruin."

"What happened?" Owen asked. The saloon was the coolest spot he'd found. He was in no hurry to leave.

"Her pa liked catting around more than he liked working. He was a real looker, so he always found plenty of women who was willing. He let the place run down something awful. Then he went off and got himself killed in the war. Her ma died soon after. Then lightning struck the house and burned part of it. After rustlers ran off most of her stock, there wasn't much point in trying to work the place by herself, so she went to work for Miss Ida." Myrl leaned back in his chair, picked his teeth with a splinter. "What brings you to Pinto Junction?"

"I'm thinking about buying a ranch."

"Go someplace else. Rustlers will break you inside a year."

"What are folks doing to stop it?"

"What can we do? Can't be everyplace at once."

"You ought to organize."

"Nobody wants to listen to anybody else. And the merchants don't want to upset things too much. They're afraid the rustlers will turn on them."

Owen began to wonder if the information he'd gotten was dependable. He doubted there was room for more than one rustling operation in the area, but he couldn't see Laveau's ego allowing him to work *for* anyone.

But this wasn't the time to mention Laveau. According to Myrl, Laveau had the stamp of approval of the Reconstruction and the Union army. Anyone who touched him could end up with a rope around his neck, and Owen was determined the neck to stretch would not be his own.

Myrl finished up his beer and looked hopefully at Owen.

"I think I'll look around tomorrow," Owen said. "If I'm to buy a ranch, I'll want to know what my neighbors are like."

"Be careful," Myrl said. "People around here don't take kindly to outsiders."

Owen patted the gun at his hip. "That's what this is for." He'd used a rifle most of his life, but after a year in Texas he felt as if he'd been born with a gun at his waist. "How about you coming with me? You can smooth the way and answer the questions they won't. I'll stand you another beer."

Myrl grinned, and they shook hands. They got up and headed toward the doors. Before Owen's eyes had time to adjust to the bright sunlight, he heard gunshots from the street. Three men, one big and heavyset, another lean and mean-looking, and a third short and nearly as thick as he was tall, had circled a young man and were firing shots at his feet and shouting that they wanted to see how well a Johnny Reb could dance. The young man was unarmed and limping.

"Who are those men?" Owen asked Myrl.

"Newt Howren and his cronies," Myrl said. "Damn the bullies! Everybody knows Ben Logan's got a gimpy leg from the war."

"Did Newt or his friends fight?"

"They only fight when they're paid."

Owen's feet were moving before he realized he was walking into the middle of a fight that wasn't his. As he pushed his way into the circle, he knocked the lean man out of the way.

"You all right?" he asked the boy.

"So far." His eyes cut to the left, and Owen turned in time to see the lean man raising his gun. Owen threw himself to one side while drawing his own gun. His aim was off so badly the bullet went through the man's arm instead of his heart. Owen rolled up on his knees in time to see the short, fat man draw a bead on him. The man took time to aim.

Owen didn't, and the fat man screamed in pain.

Owen came to his feet, facing Newt. The big man stood staring at his two wounded companions. Owen thought he looked like a shell-shocked soldier after his first battle.

"Drop that gun," Owen said.

"Who the hell are you?" Newt bellowed.

"A Johnny Reb. If I ever hear of you bullying anybody again, I'll come after you. If it's another Johnny Reb, I'll kill you."

"You wouldn't be so brave without that gun."

"If you don't drop yours, you'll be dead, so it won't matter."

Newt let the gun fall into the dust. Owen fired a shot into it. The gun bounced up in the air and came apart. Owen looked up at Newt and grinned. "I think I broke it."

"You bastard!"

"At least I'm not a fat, cowardly slob who has to be backed by two worms before he has the guts to pick on a wounded soldier he outweighs by at least a hundred pounds."

"I'll kill you for that," Newt roared.

"Some other time," Owen said.

"I'm not done with you. Nobody wants anything to do with Newt Howren."

"Having met you, I can see why."

Owen collected the weapons of the two wounded men. "Where're you going?" he asked Ben.

"I was headed to the saloon. I thought I'd have myself a whiskey."

"Tell the bartender to give you one on me," Owen said. He glanced down at the boy's stiff leg. "I figure you earned it."

"You don't have to pity me," Ben said. "I got money."

"It's not pity. You got hit. I came through without a scratch. That could have been my bullet you caught."

Ben's expression relaxed. "Well, you'd better watch your back. I ain't aiming to catch any more bullets for you." He tipped his hat, turned, and headed toward the saloon.

Owen was startled to see the boardwalk full of people. "What's everybody staring at?" he asked Myrl.

"Nobody's ever stopped Newt. You're liable to be a hero."

The memory of a beautiful young girl dying exploded full-blown in Owen's mind, every horrifying detail etched in painful detail. He shuddered. "Let's get out of here." He walked away from the crowd.

"The sheriff'll want to talk to you," Myrl said.

"I'm not hiding."

"Maybe you'd better. Newt's never gonna forget what you did. He'll ambush you or shoot you in the back. Some people say he's tied in with the rustlers. He doesn't have a job, but he always has money."

"Anybody ask him where he gets it?"

Myrl looked at Owen like he was crazy. "Ain't nobody around here going to ask Newt a question like that."

"Why?"

"He's got friends."

"His kind always does. Don't forget to meet me tomorrow. I'm getting real curious about Newt and his friends."

"There's somebody else you ought to be curious about."

"Who?"

"Hetta Gwynne."

"Why should I be interested in a man-hating maid?"

"There's still cows left on her place."

"So?"

"A fella would think it would only take rustlers a couple of nights to round up what's left."

"If they bothered."

"They haven't, and she's got more cows than last year."

"I expect her cows had calves."

"What I'm trying to tell you is, rustlers have been especially bad this year, *but nobody is rustling Hetta's cows.* Now, don't you find that mighty curious?"

Chapter Two

There was no one in the dining room when Owen entered. He might have thought he'd mistaken the time, but the table had been set for two and several dishes were already out. "Naturally, Miss Ida would be late," he said aloud. "It would never do for a lady to be on time."

He walked over to a window covered with lace curtains and looked out. He felt a thousand percent better since his bath. He had worked hard this last year, but Cade allowed Owen and the other ex-Confederate soldiers to live at the hacienda. Owen had gotten used to a soft bed, cool walls on hot days, and good food. There were times when he regretted that his need for revenge had driven him from the comfort of the hacienda. But the longer he remained, the more his life seemed empty and pointless, the more this need tore at his temper.

Owen had put on a dark suit with striped pants, a cream-colored vest almost the shade of his thick blond hair, a white shirt, and a blue cravat held in place by a

12

gold tie pin. He'd exchanged his boots for soft-soled shoes. His cousin would have said he looked like a tenderfoot, but at least he didn't look like a Texan.

Hetta entered the room to set down a steaming bowl of beef stew. She gave him a brief glance. "You don't look like the same man who came to the door earlier."

"I'm glad you appreciate the difference."

"I didn't say I appreciated it," Hetta said as she turned to leave, "just that I noticed." She disappeared only to reappear moments later with a pan of biscuits and a lump of butter. "Miss Ida believes a man should dress for dinner."

Hetta had changed into another dress, but it was not a gown. She moved with the quick, efficient stride of a woman with no time to waste. She placed the last dish on the table and took her seat without waiting for Owen to seat her.

"Where's Miss Moody?" Owen asked.

"She's spending the evening with her uncle."

"I thought all ladies avoided being alone with a strange man."

"I'm not a lady."

He'd used the term generally, but it surprised him that Hetta didn't think herself a lady though she automatically accorded Ida that distinction.

"Of course you are."

"You have to be rich and pretty to be a lady."

She looked straight at him, her eyes wide and direct. She wasn't unattractive—there was a certain nobility to her features—but you couldn't call her pretty.

"I've always believed *lady* should be a title bestowed on a woman only after she's earned it," Owen said.

"That's not a very gallant attitude for a gentleman."

"I grew up in the Virginia mountains. I'm not a gentleman."

He thought he saw a flicker of interest in her eyes. "I

thought all handsome men wanted to be thought gentlemen."

"You think I'm handsome?"

"You know you are. You wouldn't dress up like a peacock otherwise."

Owen was irritated that his efforts appeared to have earned disapproval rather than admiration. "Like Miss Moody, I, too, believe a man should change for dinner."

"Maybe in your fancy cities back East, but I don't see much call for it out here."

"What do you see a call for, Miss Gywnne?"

"Call me Hetta." She turned back to her dinner, directing her attention to buttering a biscuit.

"You didn't answer my question," Owen said.

"Pretty people don't want to hear contrary opinions. They sometimes say they do, but they really don't."

A perceptive young woman regardless of her lack of social skills.

"You don't have to talk to me if you don't want," she said.

"Well, I do want to talk to you, and I want an answer to my question. What do you think is important in a man?"

"Character," she answered without looking at him.

"Everybody thinks character is important," Owen said, a bit impatiently. "I'm talking about the things about a man that make a young woman swoon."

"Any young woman who swoons over a handsome man is in no position to judge prudently."

Owen was beginning to be irritated. "Why do you keep talking about *handsome men* like it's an affliction?"

Hetta put her fork down, wiped her mouth with her napkin, and turned toward Owen. "It has been my experience that handsome men are too much concerned with their looks and their effect on women. They waste what time and money they do possess on their pleasure rather than use it for their families. Because they've been catered to all their lives, they think their looks entitle them to things less handsome men must work for or do without. They seldom develop character or values with any but the most shallow roots. And they have a tendency to pontificate on all manner of subjects even when they possess only the most superficial knowledge."

Owen took a deep breath. "You're certainly comprehensive in your opinions."

"You asked."

"I hope you don't mean to include me in that characterization. Why, just this afternoon, at great peril to myself, I rescued a crippled man from harm."

"I know what you did for Ben."

He'd only mentioned Ben in a halfhearted attempt at humor. Her knowing about it made it seem like he was bragging, and that annoyed him.

"While I approve of what you did, I don't approve of men who go around shooting guns in the street."

"You have a mighty detailed account of what happened."

"Strangers are rare in Pinto Junction. People remember everything they do."

"I'll have to remember that."

"I don't approve of gambling or drinking," Hetta said.

Owen had never pretended to take criticism well, and Hetta Gywnne was pushing the limits. "Have you ever heard of not passing judgment until you know a person?"

"I know what I see."

"What if I did the same thing?"

"You already have. You've decided I'm plain, that you'll never be interested in a woman like me, and you're wondering if Miss Moody will be at dinner tomorrow."

Not exactly, but close enough to make him squirm.

"I did wonder if my presence had driven Miss Moody away. As for you, you're not beautiful, but your face has strength and character. Yet I don't know if I want to get to know you. Your mind is closed on too many subjects."

"Those are opinions I have reached by observation. I won't change them until I see changes in the men I observe."

"But men like Newt and me make you doubt you ever will."

"I don't put you in the same class as Newt."

"I suppose I should feel fortunate."

"I don't know why you're so angry."

"I suppose you would be happy if I criticized everything about you within hours of setting eyes on you."

She started to say something, then apparently changed her mind. When she finally selected an answer, her expression was very much like that of a child preparing to take a dose of bitter-tasting medicine.

"All the men of my acquaintance fit the description I've just given you, my father closest of all. I will be quite pleased if you should prove to be the exception." She smiled, but it was an unsuccessful effort. "A woman can't afford to be wrong about a man. If she is, she pays for that mistake the rest of her life."

"You have a home here with Miss Moody, and you own a ranch. I'd say you were safe enough."

"Ida was kind enough to give me a job when my house burned."

"Did you like the ranch?"

For the first time that evening he saw signs of happiness in her face. "It's the only home I've ever known, the only one I want. I even love the work, the roping, branding—"

"What the hell did your father mean by letting you do that? You could have been killed!"

"Miss Moody doesn't allow cursing."

"I'll make sure I don't cuss in front of Miss Moody. So you had to do the work or it wouldn't have been done?"

16

No wonder she had such a bad opinion of men.

"My father took the admiration of women as his due. My mother would have done anything for him."

"Are you back to me and Newt again?"

"Newt is a bully who feels that anything he can get away with is okay."

"And you think I'm like that?"

She shrugged her shoulders. "You've forced me to be quite candid, Mr. Wheeler."

"Call me Owen."

She ignored his interruption. "It has been my experience that men who have been endowed with exceptional size, attractiveness, or courage depend far too much on those traits. They foolishly rush into ill-considered undertakings. When they're successful, they're heros and those who failed to follow them are cowards. When they are big and strong, they take what doesn't belong to them. Men who are blessed with looks trade on them, turning foolish women like my mother into blind slaves."

Owen had listened to her initial remarks with only mild irritation, but her comments about women allowing themselves to be turned into slaves caused mild irritation to become simmering anger.

"What makes you think men are the only ones to trade on their looks?" he asked.

"I'm sure they're not, but women have a greater love of home and family, a greater sense of responsibility and fairness, better understanding of the damage they can do by—"

"You don't know what you're talking about!" The words burst from Owen. "I don't know what your father did, but no man can cause so much pain or be so destructive as a beautiful woman who can't think of anything except how to please herself."

"I know women who—"

"You live in a thorn patch too far from civilization to know what a woman of great beauty and a depraved soul can do. Men are driven hard by their physical needs, needs so strong no woman can understand them, needs that drive them like helpless lambs into the slaughterhouse of a female determined to use that weakness for her own pleasure."

"Are you a weak man, Mr. Wheeler?"

"No."

"Are you driven hard by these *needs* that are so terrible no woman could understand them?"

"No."

"Then I must congratulate you on your success."

He started to tell her he was pleased himself, but he realized in that moment he was angry. He liked women. He enjoyed flirting, but the driving force behind his obsession with women was anger at his mother and what she had done to his father. It was his way of proving he wasn't the pliable, gullible, spineless fool his father had been. No woman was going to manipulate him, humiliate him, laugh at him, treat him with contempt.

But his behavior made him angry because in toying with women's emotions while remaining uninvolved, he was doing the same thing his mother did. That made him even more angry, more determined to get back at her by flirting even more heartlessly. He'd found himself on a merry-go-round, unable to get off.

"I'm glad to say no woman has made a fool of me," Owen said.

"That's very important?" Hetta asked.

"Wouldn't it be for you?"

"Women can't afford to be as proud as men. Our lives depend on them too much."

As far as he could see, beautiful women pretty much called the tune. Even after they were married, they seemed to have a wanton streak that drove them to destroy the very home they worked so hard to create. If a man didn't control his wife, he couldn't blame anyone but himself if she made a strumpet of herself.

"You're lucky you live so far from civilization," Owen said. "I'd hate to see all your illusions shattered."

"That can happen in Pinto Junction, too," Hetta said, getting to her feet. "Do you want anything else?"

He'd been so involved in their conversation, he hadn't realized they had finished eating. He couldn't recall whether he'd enjoyed the food or not. "I'd like some coffee."

She picked up her plate. "I'll bring it when I come back for your plate."

"I can wait until you finish clearing the table."

"That's not necessary."

"It is if you're going to have coffee with me."

"I'd rather not."

"Are you afraid of me?"

"Certainly not."

"Does Ida object to you using the parlor?"

"I'm not a slave."

"But you're a servant. We never had servants, so I don't know what they can and can't do."

"I'm paid to do my work, but Miss Moody treats me like her equal."

"Then why don't you call her Ida?"

She paused.

"You don't call her Ida because you don't feel her equal."

"I do."

"Then put down those dishes and let's have our coffee in the parlor."

Hetta called herself an idiot at least a dozen times as she dropped the coffee into boiling water. She must be, to agree to have coffee with Owen Wheeler. It didn't matter that she always had coffee in the parlor with Ida. It didn't matter that they often invited guests to join them. What mattered was that she had let precisely the kind of man she most distrusted talk her into doing something against her will

She wasn't worried that he would misbehave. She wasn't pretty enough. Even if her mirror hadn't told her she was plain, she would have had no doubt. As far back as she could remember, her father had told her she and her mother were plain, that they were lucky to have such a handsome man as husband and father.

Her mother had responded by treating her husband like a minor god. Hetta had rebelled. She'd been particularly angry that her father made no attempt to be discreet about his unfaithfulness, but her mother said a plain woman couldn't expect to hold the interest of such a handsome man all the time. He always came back home when his other women got tired of his shiftless ways. Hetta had actually been glad when he went off to the war.

He'd died at Shiloh. Unable to endure the shock of losing the man she adored, her mother had died less than a year later. Hetta was still angry at her mother for taking the easy way out and leaving her to wrestle with the ranch alone. It hadn't been a long battle. Bandits had raided with impunity, the house had burned, and she'd had to look for a way to support herself. She'd counted herself fortunate when Ida gave her a job.

Hetta was thankful for her good fortune, but each day increased her longing to return to her ranch. That had seemed impossible until Mr. diViere rented her land. She would soon have enough money to repair the house, buy more cows, and hire someone to help her.

She'd never expected to marry. She was too plain and too poor. So she'd been surprised when William Tidwell, who worked in his father's hardware store, began to show an interest in her. She couldn't doubt William's in-tegrity—he was as plain as she—and his sense of duty and responsibility were beyond question.

But Hetta knew she wasn't in love. She felt vaguely disappointed that she didn't feel more passion for Wil-liam, but she also felt relieved that she could approach their relationship without any of the distortion of her mother's idolatry. Theirs would be a marriage based on common sense and mutual respect.

William had nothing of his own and couldn't marry without his parents' permission, but his mother was jeal-ous of her only child. She thought he was too young, that no woman was good enough for him. But William had assured Hetta that his mother would love her once she got to know her. Hetta wasn't so certain, but she hoped William would ask his mother soon. Ida Moody was the best friend anyone could have, but Hetta wanted a home of her own.

She wanted her ranch.

But this was no time to start thinking about William. The coffee ready, she poured it into Ida's china coffee pot. She put everything on a tray and started toward the parlor.

It was a shame that Owen had to be like her father. She didn't know why she was attracted to him when other men had left her cold, but there was something about him that made him different. He was just a little taller, better looking, a little more confident, a little more intelligent. . . . He seemed to have more of everything than anybody Hetta had ever met. And Hetta was honest enough to admit that that extra made a difference.

But there was something else about Owen that at-tracted her. There was a kindness about him that was unexpected. Courage, too. No one in Pinto Junction would have risked his own safety to protect Ben from Newt. Certainly not a man like her father.

"I was starting to think I'd have to come after you," Owen said when she entered the parlor. He held the door for her, cleared a place for the tray on the table, waited for her to settle herself on the sofa before he took a seat.

She tried not to think his courtesy was anything special. Everybody knew that Virginia men grew up knowing how to make a woman feel special, probably even men from the mountains. He was just too handsome. She expected that Ida's cousin Jonas would soon be ordering a suit exactly like Owen's. Jonas considered himself the best-dressed man in Pinto Junction, but he couldn't begin to compare with Owen.

"I never like to rush coffee," Hetta said. "It sometimes comes out tasting burned."

"I spent four years in the war and one working as a cowhand. My only requirements are that it be wet, hot, and black."

"I take it you don't want sugar."

"I couldn't call myself a man if I did."

Hetta smiled as she bent forward to pour the coffee. Despite his fancy clothes, Owen wanted to be considered as rough and tough as the next guy. She looked up to hand him his coffee and nearly dropped the cup. He'd gotten up from his chair and come across the room. Their faces were only inches apart.

She had never before let herself get this close to a man who was so handsome. His good looks nearly made her stop breathing. She was aware that a smile was merely the result of muscle movement, that it had nothing to do with the heart, mind, or soul, but surely a smile as wonderful as his couldn't be entirely false.

Hetta forced herself to look away. The man was merely being polite. His smile didn't mean anything one way or the other. She received another shock when he sat down on the sofa next to her.

"You don't mind, do you?" he asked. "This way I won't

have to get up when I want a second cup."

He left plenty of room between them, but she felt as though they were practically touching.

"You're not still afraid of me, are you?"

"I was never afraid of you."

"Good. So what do you do for entertainment around here?"

Chapter Three

Chapter Three

Hetta wasn't quite sure how to answer him. Except for the July picnic and an occasional dance, the women of Pinto Junction spent their evenings finishing up all the tasks they hadn't completed during the day. The men spent theirs in the saloon.

"I don't suppose we have much of what you'd call entertainment," she said.

"Not even after cattle drives or when the branding is done?"

"We've never had a cattle drive," she said.

"Don't you take your cows to market?"

"What market?" She'd heard of some people taking their cattle to St. Louis or New Orleans, but she didn't know anybody who'd done it.

"How about harvest?" Owen asked. "Christmas? The Fourth of July?"

"Folks around here don't go to parties much."

"No wonder you're so unhappy."

"I'm not unhappy."

"You act like smiling would break your face. You walk around me like I was a panther and you weren't sure the rope was strong enough to hold me."

There was something panther-like about him. He was sleek and sinewy and languorous, as if he knew he had nothing to fear.

"We're not used to strangers. We like to get to know people before we make them bosom friends."

"I'm just talking about having a little fun."

"Folks down here are real careful about their fun."

"What you mean is folks down here are boring."

"You don't have to stay if you dislike us so much."

Why on earth would she say something like that? she wondered. It was obvious that a man like Owen would never stay in Pinto Junction, but strangely enough, she'd imagined he would. Which just went to show the folly of looking a handsome man in the eye.

"It's none of my concern what you do," she said and started to get up, but he put out a hand to restrain her.

"Don't run away."

She couldn't move. She'd been touched by men before. The contact had left her indifferent, irritated, or merely eager to get out of their reach. But nothing had ever made her feel as though her bones had melted, as though she couldn't get up off the sofa if the house were on fire. It was absurd. The way she felt reminded her strongly of how her mother said her husband made her feel—foolish, unable to move, unable to think clearly, lacking the desire to think at all, willing to do anything to enjoy his nearness for a lifetime.

She looked down at his hand on hers. He hadn't exerted any pressure, yet his hand anchored her to the sofa as surely as if it weighed a ton. How could an ordinary hand affect her so strongly? His nails were clean, his fingers were long and slim, but that could describe the hand of several men she knew.

She couldn't stay where she was, not so close, not with him touching her. She didn't dare look up. She was certain that would destroy any strength she had. She busied herself in transferring everything from the table to the tray.

"I'm not running away, but the dishes have to be done."

"You just said you have nothing to do all evening. What's the rush?"

"I don't like leaving work. It just makes it harder when I get around to it. And thinking about it ruins my pleasure in what I'm doing."

"Then you do find pleasure in my company. I was beginning to think you equated me with a dose of bad medicine."

Hetta felt the heat rise in her face. She started to assure him she hadn't received even the slightest pleasure in his company, but that wouldn't have been the truth. No woman could dislike the undivided attention of a handsome, charming man. The danger came in thinking he meant anything by it.

She forced herself to look at him now. He had a smile that transformed his features, made them seem perfect. She wasn't experienced with men. She couldn't tell if his smile was genuine, but it drew her like a honeybee to the first spring flower.

She couldn't understand why he should want to smile at her. She wasn't pretty, or entertaining, and didn't enjoy flirting. She could only assume he was being polite. If so, Virginians really ought to warn people. Young women unfamiliar with their ways could develop quite unrealistic expectations.

But Hetta wasn't foolish, and she hadn't developed any expectations at all. "I was speaking in general."

"Be specific."

"Mr. Wheeler—"

"Call me Owen."

"I'm aware you're new in town and have nothing to do with your evening, but I have far too much work to spend time in this senseless bandying of words. You know you're not interested in me."

"But I am interested in you."

Hetta felt the room go still around her. He couldn't mean what he said. Not the way she meant it. "You don't know anything about me."

"I know you have a ranch. I've been thinking about buying one."

Hetta was shocked to find her heart beating twice as rapidly as normal. She didn't know how she'd allowed herself to get caught up so quickly in the aura that surrounded Owen. He was like a physical force impossible to be around without being affected, but she couldn't afford to let herself be affected, not even for a single evening.

"I'm told you're not bothered by rustlers," Owen said. "I'd like to know how, so I could protect any ranch I might buy."

She didn't like the feeling of disappointment. She hated to know she'd been foolish enough to expect something else. Owen was exactly the kind of man she'd warned herself against her whole life.

"If that's all you wanted, you could have asked."

"I didn't say it was all, just one of the things."

She didn't know why he'd come to Pinto Junction, but she was absolutely certain it had nothing to do with her. Yet when he looked at her like that, spoke to her in that tone of voice . . . it was foolish, absurd, impossible!

"Another rancher is using my property until I'm able to manage it again. In exchange he takes care of my herd."

27

"But how does he protect it from the bandits?"

"I don't know that he does. We haven't had a roundup, so no one knows."

She couldn't understand why talking about the ranch should interest her so little. She'd been thinking about it all the time lately. The only explanation was that she was disappointed that Owen hadn't been interested in her. Personally.

But despite his kindness, courage, and beautiful manners, she wouldn't allow herself to be disappointed over anything to do with Owen. She didn't think it was the same, but this could be the way her mother had felt about her father. Yet she didn't feel like falling down at his feet. She didn't think the sun rose and set in him. She didn't believe that his every word was gospel. She didn't feel so miserable that she wanted to sit in the corner and cry her heart out. Except for the strangeness of it, she felt quite good.

Still, this way was madness, and she had no intention of going mad. "More coffee?" she asked.

He held out his cup. "You ready to close up shop?"

"I need to finish in the kitchen."

"And leave me to finish my coffee alone?"

"I'm sure you've drunk hundreds of cups of coffee without my help."

"But I didn't drink them alone."

"Try. I promise it isn't hard."

"But it's no fun."

"You can't expect fun all the time."

"Why not?"

He was the most stubborn man she'd ever met. She stood and reached for the tray. He put his hand on her wrist. His touch was light. It was clear he was only playing, but her temperature seemed to have spiked.

"Tell me about this rancher you have a deal with," Owen said.

"There's nothing to tell. I had a ranch I couldn't run. Mr. diViere had a herd—"

"Who did you say?"

The change in him was instantaneous. One moment he was smiling, flirtatious. In the next he looked angry enough to commit murder.

"Mr. diViere."

"What's his first name?"

"I don't remember."

"Is it Laveau?"

"I think so. I'm sure Ida's uncle called him by that name."

"Where is he now?"

"I don't know."

"This is a small town. People don't just disappear."

"He's not in Pinto Junction." She'd been so surprised by the change in him, she'd forgotten he still held her wrists. She pulled, but he didn't release her.

"Where did he go?"

"He said he was taking some cattle to market."

"Where?"

"He didn't say."

"Did you ask?"

"No."

"You'll never make a success of your ranch if you don't learn everything you can about the cattle business. And the most important thing is where you can sell at a good price."

He stood, but he still held her wrists.

"I'll learn when the time comes. Now if you'll—"

"When is he getting back?"

"I don't know."

"He just comes and goes on your ranch and you don't ask why or what he's doing?"

"He pays me for the privilege of *coming and going*."

"Where do the cattle come from?"

29

"If you want to know, you'll have to ask him."

"I intend to, the first chance I get. Why would you hook up with a man like Laveau?"

"I didn't *hook up with him*. He offered me a business proposition, and I took it." She didn't understand his attitude. "Everyone in Pinto Junction likes Mr. diViere. We know he fought for the Union, but he's a Texan and he's kept the army away from us. We've heard what drunken soldiers have done in other towns."

She didn't understand Owen's expression. The anger was easy to see, but the rest of it was hidden in the depths of his enormous dark blue eyes. They reminded her of the color of the sky before a storm.

"How could you trust someone like Laveau?" Owen asked.

"He found my father wounded and dying. Knowing he was a fellow Texan, my father entrusted his sword to him, asked him to take it back to his family."

"Where did your father die?"

"Shiloh."

"Laveau was never at Shiloh."

"He must have been. He brought me letters, mementos."

"Then he stole them. Laveau never fought at Shiloh."

"You don't know. You don't even—"

"I rode with Laveau diViere for three years in a Confederate troop of Night Riders. He betrayed us. Twenty-four men died because of him."

"I can't believe that's true. Nobody likes it that he fought for the Union, but he's been good to us."

"Laveau diViere is a coldhearted villain who wouldn't hesitate to cut your throat if it served his purpose. I intend to hang him."

She stared at him, unable to believe what she'd heard. "Even if he did what you say—and I don't believe it for one minute—you can't go around threatening to hang people. Now, I don't want to hear any more of your mad ravings. And I'd just as soon you let me go."

She raised her arm, trying to break his grip. He merely released it and quickly caught her in a different grip, pressing her arms close to her body, bringing her closer to *him*.

"The only person who's mad is Laveau. I won't stop until I bring him to justice." He pulled her closer until she could feel his breath on her skin. "You don't have to help me. Just don't get in my way."

Hetta was about to assure Owen she didn't intend to interfere in his business in any way when the parlor door opened. She turned to see Ida in the doorway, a shocked expression on her face. Right behind her, looking equally stunned, stood William Tidwell.

"Get your hands off that woman," William thundered, pushing Ida aside to stride into the room, his face deep red.

Hetta had never seen William in the grip of strong emotion. She couldn't believe she was the cause of this incredible transformation in the man she considered the most dependable, even-tempered, predictable person she'd ever known. She went so limp with shock and embarrassment, she was relieved that Owen didn't immediately release her arms.

"Who are you?" Owen asked.

"It doesn't matter who I am," William thundered back. "Get your hands off that woman."

Owen didn't move a muscle. "This woman has a name."

"A name you're not fit to use."

Hetta suspected that William's actions had made Owen furious, but she guessed he was embarrassed to have been caught treating her in such an ungentlemanly fashion. When he released her and stepped back, she was certain of it.

"I meant Hetta no harm."

William stepped between them. The two men made Ida's parlor seem almost too small to contain them.

"Just putting your hand on her is an insult."

"William, he wasn't—"

"We don't allow strangers to handle our women."

"William!"

"If you touch her again, you'll have me to deal with."

"If I touch Miss Gwynne again, it'll be with her consent. If you attempt to interfere then, you'll have *me* to deal with. Good night," Owen said, turning to Hetta. "I apologize for causing the evening to end on a sour note. What time is breakfast?"

"Seven," Hetta replied.

"You can't stay here," William said. "Ida will give you your money back."

"I don't want it back. Now, unless you want me to forget that your outrage is in defense of a woman, you'll turn your attention to Hetta." He turned and left the room.

"You can't let him stay here," William said, turning to Ida.

"Of course she can," Hetta said. "He's already paid. She can't throw him out without a reason."

"You don't call manhandling you a reason?"

Hetta found it nearly impossible to believe that she, plain Hetta Gwynne, could have been the cause of two men nearly getting into a fight.

"He wasn't manhandling me," she said. "Something I said, a person I mentioned, caused him to become agitated. I'm not even sure he was thinking of me."

"Who did you mention?"

"Mr. diViere. He said he'd fought with him in the war, that he was a thief and a traitor, that he intended to hang him."

"He's crazy," Ida said. "I'll tell him to leave tomorrow."

"I can't say I like diViere," William said, "but he has kept the Army away from us."

"And he's renting Hetta's ranch."

But he hadn't yet paid her. She didn't believe Owen's accusation, but she was glad she'd asked Ida's uncle to send a letter reminding diViere that he hadn't paid her.

"I expect he'll have forgotten all about it in the morning," Hetta said. "Good-looking men say a lot of things to impress women foolish enough to believe them."

"I'll make some fresh coffee," Ida said and winked at Hetta. "I promised William a cup if he'd walk me home."

"Thank goodness you don't believe him," William said to Hetta. "You never know what a man like that will do. Did you hear what he did today?"

"You've got to hear William tell it," Ida said as she prepared to leave the room. "He's spellbinding."

"It happened in front of our hardware store," William said, looking pleased with himself. "I saw the whole thing."

Hetta had a strong suspicion, confirmed by Ida's wink, that she'd *accidentally* run into William so she'd have an excuse to invite him in. Ida was always looking for chances to throw them together. She really was a wonderful friend.

But as William told a story she already knew, Hetta absentmindedly massaged her arms and wondered what Owen Wheeler was doing in Pinto Junction. Was he telling the truth about Mr. diViere? And why could she still feel the imprint of his hands where he'd touched her?

Owen walked to the dark end of Ida's porch. He forced himself to take one deep breath after another until his insides stopped churning. Why couldn't he forget Rachelle Ginter? She was like a poisoned cloud hanging over him. He'd tried to pay for his crime. The last year of the war he'd fought like a fool, taken insane risks, volunteered for any mission, no matter how dangerous. He'd had three horses shot from under him, but not once had a bullet so much as ripped his clothing.

He'd sworn he'd never flirt with a decent woman again, yet here he was flirting with a woman who wasn't even beautiful. It was in his blood. He'd tried like hell to stop going from one woman to another, but it was bred into him. He couldn't do anything else. He couldn't *be* anything else.

Damn you, Ma! I hope you burn in hell!

"He just wanted some company while he drank his coffee," Hetta told Ida for the tenth time. Even though they'd discussed the whole evening in detail, Ida wouldn't let it drop. "Men that handsome and good with a gun aren't used to being left alone."

"That's exactly what you must do," Ida said, her expression serious. "I never expected I'd come home to find you in the arms of a stranger."

"I wasn't *in his arms*," Hetta said, her temper becoming frayed by this endless interrogation.

She was feeling increasingly claustrophobic in Ida's house, increasingly angered by the need to explain her actions, by the expectation that she would mold her behavior to fit Ida's ideas of decorum. She appreciated Ida's friendship, her effort to encourage William's attentions, but being a servant, no matter how it was dressed up, was still being a servant. It grated on her sense of independence, her sense of who she was. She needed to get back to the only kind of life she knew, the only kind she'd ever wanted. She *needed* to get back to her ranch. She was also tired of Ida acting like her mother. Hetta was only two years younger than her friend. "It felt more like I was in his clutches," she said.

"Which is all the more reason for you to stay away from him."

"I intend to, but I refuse to let any man think I'm afraid of him. He wasn't threatening me."

"I should hope not," Ida said, giving Hetta a look she didn't like, "but I wouldn't trust him."

"I don't. I don't even like him."

"Good."

But she was attracted to him. It would have been one thing if it were just that he was attractive. Women always liked pretty things, from china to lace to jewelry, but Hetta had always been immune to attractive men. She'd sometimes wondered if her universal dislike of men wasn't a prejudice that was as blind as it was rigid.

She couldn't say that any longer. For whatever reason, she was strongly attracted to Owen Wheeler. And if she gave herself half a chance, she might even start to like him. Though why she should be so perverse, she was hard pressed to say. Her heart was generally a very dependable organ. Up to this point, it had been in complete agreement with her mind, and her mind said William Tidwell would be the best possible husband for her.

"Do you think he's going to stay in Pinto Junction very long?" Ida asked.

"He said he was thinking about buying a ranch, but he doesn't look like a rancher to me."

"Not the way he dresses. You can't get clothes like that anywhere in Texas except San Antonio."

"He said he came from Virginia. Maybe he got them there."

"I met a Virginian in New Orleans last spring. We were on the same river boat for a week. No, those clothes came from Texas."

"Then maybe he does want to buy a ranch. He was asking me about the arrangement I have with Mr. diViere. He says people are saying the bandits don't bother my cows."

"I don't think that's a suitable subject for a woman,"

35

Ida said, "but I do know that being alone with Mr. Wheeler is not good for a woman's reputation. It certainly won't make William happy."

"There wasn't much I could do, with you spending the evening with your uncle."

"Well, I won't be spending evenings there again soon. Aunt Agatha is in another one of her moods, and I refuse to be in the same house with her until she recovers herself."

Hetta knew that saying Aunt Agatha was in *another one of her moods* meant the woman was a harridan, and no one could stand her when she went on a tirade.

"I'll ask him to leave as soon as he comes down," Ida said.

Hetta didn't understand why that made her feel slightly guilty. It was his behavior that was at fault, not hers. He had no one but himself to blame if he couldn't find an equally suitable place to stay.

"You don't have to do it for me," Hetta said, not making eye contact with Ida.

"He's a gunman."

"We don't know that. We only know he's good with a gun. Besides, I'm glad someone had the gumption to stop Newt and his thugs from picking on poor Ben."

"They say Ben can't hold a job, that he's in the saloons every night."

"Nobody will *give* him a job. That's why he drinks."

"I wouldn't know about that," Ida said as she handed Hetta her cup. "I'm not acquainted with his family." She was silent while Hetta washed and dried the cup and saucer. "Do you think Mr. Wheeler really wants to buy a ranch?"

"I don't know, but I doubt we have anything fancy enough for him."

"I don't know what brought him to Pinto Junction, but I don't think it's ranches."

36

"Why do you say that?" Hetta asked.

"Ranchers are dull, married, and have a bunch of kids."

"Not all."

"The others are young, foolish, and go broke inside a year. That man doesn't fit into either category. I think he's a spy."

"Who could he be spying for in Pinto Junction?"

"Mexico."

Hetta had been forced to listen to Ida's conspiracy theories before. Ida believed that Cortina and his bandits were just an advance force to weaken Texas before the Mexican army invaded to recapture Texas.

"William said Mr. Wheeler spent nearly half an hour talking to some *vaqueros* outside his hardware store."

"If he's looking for a ranch, it makes sense to talk to cowhands."

"He was talking to them *in Spanish*!"

"Nearly everybody in Texas speaks some Spanish."

"He's from Virginia. How would he know Spanish unless he's working for the Mexican army?"

"I have no idea. Did you tell William your theory?"

Ida's expression turned petulant. "He said he thought Mr. Wheeler was here for some other reason."

"Did he have any idea what that reason might be?"

"No."

"Then maybe we ought to accept his explanation that he's here to buy a ranch."

"We'll see," Ida said, turning to leave the kitchen. "But I think I won't ask him to leave, after all."

"Why not?" Hetta asked, dismayed at the sudden quickening of her heartbeat.

"If he's a spy, somebody's got to watch him. I'll organize a committee of women to watch his every move, but I can't ask just anybody. It wouldn't do if he got wind of our suspicions."

37

"No, it wouldn't," Hetta said, certain he'd laugh rather than get angry. What could an ex-soldier have to fear from a phalanx of women?

"I won't offer him a key. You'll have to open the door so we'll know what time he comes in."

Hetta wasn't looking forward to having her sleep broken. "I don't see what good that will do if we don't know where he's been."

"That'll be easy. A stranger can't do much of anything in Pinto Junction without half the town knowing. I expect he'll be out rather late. I doubt he'll be wanting breakfast any earlier than noon."

Hetta was surprised when Owen returned before she locked the front door. She listened to his footsteps as he walked along the hall overhead. She could hear him as he moved about his room. Much to her dismay, she found herself imagining him as he undressed for bed. She tried to drive the images from her head, but to no avail.

She could easily see his broad shoulders and strong arms bare of clothing. She imagined him washing his upper body with meticulous care. First his hands. She liked his hands. They were strong without being thick and hairy, elegant without being unmanly. She knew they were powerful. She could still feel his hands around her wrists.

They had felt rough. She had expected them to be soft and smooth. He didn't appear to be the kind of man to do hard work, though he had the body of one who did. He didn't have to be without a shirt for her to see the breadth of his shoulders or sense the power in his arms. She had become acutely aware of both when he gripped her arms and drew her close. She could feel the heat pouring off him, the magnetism that made it impossible for her to lump him with other men. He was different. He was—

She was grateful for the knock on her door. She didn't know what Ida wanted, but anything that distracted her from her incredible preoccupation with Owen was welcome. She didn't put on her robe before she opened the door. The sight that met her eyes left her bereft of speech.

Owen stood before her, naked to the waist. "You forgot to leave me any soap."

Chapter Four

Hetta couldn't believe Owen Wheeler was standing outside her doorway naked to the waist. Nor could she believe she was staring at his chest. She tried to shift her gaze to her feet, the ceiling, Owen's face—anything!—but she couldn't move. A man's naked flesh was only inches away from her, and she was standing there as if she were hypnotized.

His chest was broad, his stomach flat, and his shoulders well muscled. His skin was unblemished, the sprinkling of blond hair almost invisible. His nipples formed small, brown peaks on the swells of muscle. He looked perfect, as though created from some woman's imagination. Not hers. She'd never imagined what a man looked like naked.

Hetta was shocked to find she wanted to reach out and touch Owen's body, to see if his skin was warm and soft, if the muscles would quiver under her touch, if the sudden warmth that filled her body like a burgeoning flame would grow hotter still. She felt the muscles in her arm tighten, her hand begin to lift.

She was so shocked at her own reaction, she said the first thing that came to her mind. "You don't look dirty."

The moment she realized what she'd said, she wanted to vanish into thin air.

"I had a bath, but I like to wash up before I go to bed," Owen said, a faint smile on his lips. "Don't you?"

Hetta didn't know why his harmless words should have formed a link in her mind between their bodies, but the jolt that went through her from head to toe was undeniable. She'd never had this kind of reaction to a man, and she didn't want it.

"I'm sure I put soap in your room," she said, forcing herself to concentrate.

"I guess I took it with me when I had my bath."

They stood there, looking at each other, waiting.

"You're not going to make me go outside to get a used cake of soap, are you?"

"No." Her mind wasn't working well enough for her to require him to do anything.

"Are you going to get me another cake of soap, or are you going to send me to bed unwashed?"

"I'll get you another cake, but you'd better put some clothes on. If Ida sees you, she'll faint."

"You didn't."

"I wasn't raised like Ida, but I'm still not accustomed to men being so brazen."

"You think I'm brazen?"

Conversation had enabled her to gather what was left of her scattered wits. "You know you are. If you'll wait in the hall, I'll get your soap."

"I'll go with you."

"That's not necessary." She needed to get away from him.

41

"I'm sure William wouldn't want you wandering about in the dark by yourself."

"He'd want me wandering about with you even less."

She'd almost forgotten what William had told her about the gunfight. Owen was a dangerous gunman, and she was wandering about a dark house with him completely unafraid. She wouldn't be surprised to wake tomorrow and discover she'd imagined half of it.

But she hadn't imagined Owen, his bare chest, or its effect on her. She went back into her room to get her robe, but not even that enveloping garment made her feel protected from Owen's nakedness.

"Please, wait for me in the hall."

"You really don't like me, do you?"

She ought to dislike him. She did disapprove of him, but she couldn't stop thinking about him. "I don't know you well enough to like or dislike you. Now, either wait for me in the hall or go outside and retrieve your soap from the bathhouse."

"You're a hard woman, but I'll wait."

She picked up her candle, lit it from his, and left her room. Owen followed close behind, his bare feet padding softly on the floorboards. She breathed a sigh of relief when she closed the kitchen door between them. So much tension left her body, she felt weak. It took only a moment to find the soap. It took a physical effort to make herself open the door and enter the hall. She wanted to stay where it was safe. She kept telling herself she'd be safer in her bedroom after Owen got his soap. She was still repeating that under her breath when she reached the front hall.

"Here," she said, holding out the soap. "Do you need anything else?" Why had she asked that question?

"No." He reached out and took the soap from her outstretched hand, his fingers brushing against her palm.

"Sorry to be such a bother. I'll remember to bring my soap back next time."

He flashed one of his brilliant smiles and started up the steps to his room. She stood there as he disappeared from sight, as she heard his steps down the hall. The closing of the door to his room brought her out of her trance. She hurried to her own room and slammed the door. Yet she still didn't feel safe. The attraction to Owen was just as strong as ever.

"I wouldn't have opened the door to him," Ida was telling Hetta.

"I thought it was you. None of your other lodgers have ever done that."

"What can you expect of a man who shoots people in the street?"

"Defending Ben isn't exactly *shooting people in the street.*"

"Why are you defending him?" Ida flushed guiltily when Owen entered the dining room.

"Do you have room for one more?" he asked.

He wore a yellow shirt with thin red stripes under a black vest. His well-worn pants were a dull brown, made of some heavy material. His boots were worn and scuffed, the handkerchief around his neck a faded blue, and the hat in his hand flat-crowned with a wide brim. Except for being unbearably handsome and clean-shaven with neatly combed blond hair, he looked like a working cowhand.

"What do you want for breakfast?" Hetta asked.

"Just coffee."

"You won't get much work done on an empty stomach," Ida said.

"I'm just looking at ranches today," Owen said.

"What kind are you looking for?" Hetta asked, hoping

to ward off any questions Ida might have about spying for Mexico.

"I don't know yet," Owen replied as he accepted a cup of coffee. "I'm planning to spend the next couple of weeks looking to see what appeals to me the most."

"You could see three counties in that time," Ida said.

"I want to know the area thoroughly."

"There are a lot of people around here who speak only Spanish."

"No problem. I picked up Spanish working for a friend of mine."

Ida looked at Hetta with obvious triumph in her eyes. "And where in Mexico was his ranch?"

"It's outside of San Antonio," Owen answered. "His wife's grandmother inherited it. Some sort of Spanish grant. You might have heard of the family. The name's diViere."

Hetta felt her stomach cramp into a tight knot, but Owen's expression showed none of the anger of last night.

"That's the name of the man who's renting Hetta's ranch," Ida said, "but he's French."

"Laveau is French, Spanish, and English, but he'll fight for the side that offers him the most," Owen said. "He entered the war fighting for the South, then went over to the Union side. He's a traitor."

"That can't have anything to do with us," Ida said.

"It has everything to do with you if you're protecting him."

Ida had started to look frightened. "My uncle said he has excellent credit."

"He should have. He stole thousands of dollars from a man he fought with for three years."

Hetta hadn't especially liked diViere when she'd first met him. He was too suave and good-looking for her comfort, but since everyone in town quickly accepted him, she decided she'd judged him unfairly. Her opinion had remained positive until months went by without his paying for the use of her ranch. She'd finally become so worried she'd had Ida's uncle write Mr. diViere to ask for her money.

"People in Pinto Junction like Mr. diViere," Hetta said. "You won't make yourself popular by spreading rumors."

Owen's expression remained cold and hard. "Laveau diViere is a traitor and a thief. Sooner or later, everybody in Pinto Junction is going to find that out. I just hope you don't have to pay too big a price for that information."

"What do you mean?" Ida asked.

"I'd bet my last dollar Laveau's stealing from this town."

"That's impossible," Ida said. "Nobody fools my uncle."

"He fooled men he ate with, slept next to, rode with, and fought alongside for three years. You'll keep believing him until it's too late. Is supper the same time every night?"

"*Dinner* is served at seven o'clock," Ida said.

"I'll be back." He turned to go.

"Where are you going?" Hetta asked, appalled at the question the moment the words were out of her mouth.

"I'll let Myrl decide. Once I've decided which ranches are the best, I'll look at them a second time."

"You're mighty thorough," Ida said.

"I don't like to make mistakes. Ladies," he said with a slight inclination of his head before he left the room.

"Why should he make up such an outlandish story about Mr. diViere?" Ida asked. "I'll speak to my uncle about Mr. Wheeler."

"Please, don't," Hetta said.

"Why not?" Instant suspicion showed in Ida's face.

Hetta didn't know why she was going out of her way to protect Owen Wheeler. He hadn't offered any proof to back up his accusations. He probably thought his word was enough, but it wouldn't be in Pinto Junction. People didn't like it when strangers caused trouble.

"Nobody will believe him. Besides, he'll probably be gone in a few days, and everybody will forget he was ever here. I don't see any point in getting everybody upset over nothing. Everybody's already worried enough about the rustling and Reconstruction."

"And well they ought to be," Ida said, her mind diverted. "Only last month Uncle Fred was saying . . ."

Hetta knew Uncle Fred's worries by heart. She was worried about Owen, and upset with herself for worrying about him. She shouldn't care about his attempts to sully Mr. diViere's reputation, about whether he wanted to buy a ranch or spy for Mexico, about what the townspeople might do to him. She most certainly shouldn't have noticed that his working clothes were even more attractive on him than his fancy suit. The sooner she put him out of her mind, the better.

But she reluctantly admitted that for reasons completely beyond her, Owen Wheeler had insinuated himself into her consciousness, and she couldn't get him out. And he'd done so without even trying.

"I think I'll go out to the ranch today," Hetta announced as she stood up to begin clearing away the breakfast.

"What for?" Ida asked.

"I haven't been there in a long time. I ought to see how things are doing, talk to Tom Manly."

"What's he going to tell you?"

"He promised to make a count of my cows."

"There aren't enough to rebuild your house."

"There may be with what Mr. diViere pays me for the ranch."

"Has he paid you yet?"

"No, but I asked your uncle to write to him and demand payment. I'll take my ranch back if he doesn't."

"Uncle Fred doesn't know when to expect him back."

"I don't care if he comes back or not. I just want my money."

"I'm sure you'll get it. Uncle Fred has great faith in him."

Owen's accusations were making Hetta wonder. Mr. diViere had said he'd try to get the army to drive the bandits back into Mexico, but the army hadn't come and the bandits were worse than ever. "I'm going out to the ranch and look around."

"I'm sure nothing's changed," Ida said.

"I'm feeling restless," Hetta said. "I feel like I've got to go to the ranch or bust."

"Do you expect me to get my own lunch?"

That kind of treatment usually made Hetta angry, but this morning she felt her anger slide away. Ida was a very lonely woman. It had to be difficult to be the richest woman in town and think no one was good enough for you. She was a prisoner of her privilege. At least Hetta was only a prisoner of poverty.

"I'll leave you a cold lunch," Hetta said.

"Seen anything you like?" Myrl asked Owen.

"Not yet," Owen answered.

"This is some of the best grazing land in Texas."

They had stopped under the shade of a pecan and cottonwood grove along a dry creek bed. Owen had wanted to keep going, but he realized Myrl needed to rest. The old cowboy's presence was the reason ranchers had given Owen permission to ride anywhere he wanted.

The open plain stretched before them, mile after mile of grassland broken up by a few clumps of trees along stream beds or a ribbon of woodland bordering the Nueces River and its tributaries. An incredible variety of unfriendly plants—cactus, mesquite, catclaw, dwarf oak, huajillo, black brush, and others—covered the plain, sometimes in impenetrable thickets.

"I don't see enough cows," Owen said.

"What makes you say that?"

"I worked on a ranch long enough to know how many cows a piece of land can carry. I ought to see twice as many as we've seen today."

"I told you we had rustlers."

"Cortina hasn't been in this part of Texas in more than a year. It's not anybody coming over the border from Mexico. You've got rustlers right here."

"Who do you have in mind?"

"Laveau diViere."

"Tell that story in town, and you're liable to find yourself in a fight."

"So you're saying Laveau has set himself up as some kind of local savior."

"Something like that."

"Everybody buying into it?"

"As long as he keeps the Reconstruction out."

Owen knew he was up against a clever man, but he hadn't imagined just how cleverly Laveau would use his affiliation with the Union army. Owen knew the army wouldn't come this far inland, so Laveau must have hired some soldiers to help him carry off the deception. Owen would have expected Texans to turn on Laveau the moment they heard he'd fought for the Union, but they were even more angry at the treatment they were receiving at the hands of the army of occupation. Army tribunals had replaced civil courts. Union soldiers seemed to take an almost sadistic pleasure in demeaning or ridiculing Texans. Many had lost virtually everything they owned. Yet they were not only denied services paid for by their own state taxes, but also often publicly humiliated when they came hat in hand to beg some favor. Owen was beginning to realize that the truth might not be enough to hang

Laveau. That realization only served to make the thirst for revenge burn more hotly inside him.

"There's rustling going on, and it's not Cortina's bandits. I followed Cortina's trail from San Antonio, and he hasn't been within a hundred miles of Pinto Junction the whole time."

The old man seemed to sag. "I've had a suspicion something was wrong."

"What's the name of the ranch we're coming up on next?" Owen asked.

"The Gwynne spread."

"Hetta Gwynne?"

"Yep. DiViere uses it to hold the herds he's moving to Mexico. He says he's a cattle buyer, which is why he's gone all the time," Myrl added.

"Let's mount up," Owen said, heading for his horse. "I want to see this ranch."

"Tom Manly don't like nobody poking around."

They rode out. The sun beat down on them mercilessly. Owen looked forward to the coming of winter, relief from the sun, rain to nourish the parched land. The only streams with water in them were spring fed.

"He probably doesn't want anybody knowing the ranch has the best water in the county," Myrl said.

"How did it go to ruin?"

"Pure neglect. Patrick Gwynne spent anything he made on liquor and women. Wouldn't have had anything to spend if Hetta hadn't learned to do half his work for him."

Owen's lingering irritation at Hetta faded. He knew what it was like to have a worthless parent. He could only imagine what it was like to be a young girl left to do difficult and dangerous work. Maybe he couldn't blame her for jumping at Laveau's offer, but he could blame her for becoming a willing accomplice to his thievery.

49

But maybe she didn't know Laveau was a thief. He'd fooled the rest of the town. Why couldn't he have fooled a young woman forced to work as a maid to have food to eat and a roof over her head?

Owen told himself it was a foolish waste of time to feel sympathy for Hetta. She disliked him, distrusted everything he said, and had a fixed prejudice against *men like him*. Not that Owen was interested in her. She had a nice figure and he liked her spunkiness, but she wasn't pretty enough to hold his attention for more than a few minutes.

"Hetta said she wants to rebuild her place, live on the ranch again one of these days," Owen said.

Myrl harrumphed. "Not if she marries William Tidwell. He'll never live out here."

"Why not?"

"He's worked in his parents' store practically from the time he could walk. He doesn't know how to do anything else."

"Maybe she'll marry someone else."

"She'd better take William, dull as he is. She's too plain to catch another man."

Owen felt an urge to tell Myrl that Hetta wasn't all that plain, that the young men of Pinto Junction could do a lot worse, but he was too surprised that he even *wanted* to go to Hetta's defense to say anything.

"I thought Laveau was paying her to use her ranch."

"He is. If he can remember to do it."

Maybe Laveau's scorn of anyone he considered beneath him would provide Owen with a vulnerability he could exploit. If there were enough people who'd been treated badly, he might get Ida Moody's uncle to start asking questions.

"Tell me more about Hetta's ranch."

"You can forget buying it. She wouldn't sell if she was down to her last nickel."

"I don't want to buy it. I just want to know why Laveau wanted it instead of one of the others."

It took a while and repeated questions before Owen got his answer. It wasn't the water or the grass, though they were some of the best in the area. It wasn't even the size. It was the position. The Gywnne ranch, following a stream that flowed to the Nueces, was long and narrow and cut all the way through the county.

It provided a perfect escape route to Mexico for cattle rustled from ranches in the north and east.

He wondered how much Hetta knew about her ranch. If it had been any other woman, he'd have said little or nothing, but Hetta had worked her ranch in her father's stead. Owen wasn't interested in Hetta, but he was beginning to respect her too much to want to see her involved with Laveau.

"Do you come this way often?" Owen asked Myrl.

"Nobody comes this way often. Tom Manly has made it clear he doesn't want people poking around."

"That's an odd way to treat your neighbors." Owen pointed to a horse grazing close to the half-burned ranch house. "Does he live in the house?"

"Nobody lives in it."

"Then why would he be here?"

"You can ask him just before he orders us off the place."

Owen was curious about the Gwynne ranch, but he didn't plan to challenge Manly if the fellow refused to let him ride through. He'd ask Hetta for permission. She wouldn't want to give it, but she would, just to prove she wasn't afraid of anything he might find out.

A couple of well-used trails connected a few of the ranches to Pinto Junction, but there wasn't anything like a road between the ranches. Owen and Myrl rode through the grass, flushing out sparrows, an occasional hawk, and causing small animals—mice, rabbits, and a young gray fox—to scurry out of their path. But he didn't see any cows. He was beginning to wonder if Laveau had fooled Hattie, offering to protect her ranch when he really meant to rob her of everything she had.

No, that didn't seem right. If he was using this as a passageway for his stolen cattle, the last thing he'd want would be for Hetta to start asking questions. If he had set up an elaborate rustling operation, he would make certain all the important cogs stayed in place.

But if that was the case, where were the cows?

There were hoofprints everywhere. At some time in the recent past a large number of cows had been held on this ranch.

"Grass has been grazed down low," Myrl observed.

Owen nodded. "I wonder what Hetta would say about that."

"Why don't you ask her?"

Owen looked in the direction Myrl pointed. Hetta had just appeared on a rise a little distance behind the ranch house.

Chapter Five

Hetta wished she hadn't come out to the ranch. It hurt every time she had to look at the ruin of her home, knowing she couldn't do anything to change it. She was becoming more impatient with her exile in town, with her position as Ida's friend—and servant. She supposed it was her independent nature, which had been fostered by years of being on her own, but she was finding it more and more difficult to appear to be content, thankful.

Maybe that was part of the reason she'd been so irritable with Owen. He had the freedom she wanted, and seeing him waste it made her angry. She didn't know what he was doing, but she doubted he wanted to buy a ranch. He was probably using that as an excuse to gamble and flirt for a while before moving on. Consequently, she wasn't the least bit happy when she saw Owen and Myrl riding toward the house. She was even less glad of the feelings that sprang up unbidden.

There was no rational explanation for it, but she experienced a flush of pleasure. And excitement. Could she have been hoping she would meet up with him? Surely she couldn't be that stupid!

As Owen and Myrl walked their horses toward her, they had plenty of time to see every part of the ruined house, the neglected outer buildings, the thorn-covered bushes that had grown up in what had once been her mother's yard. Hetta felt the heat of embarrassment burn her cheeks, and that made her angry.

"You shouldn't be out here alone," Owen said when he reached her. "It's not safe."

His comments caught her off guard. She didn't know what she'd expected, but not concern for her safety.

"This is my ranch," she said, her ire beginning to deflate. "I'm safe enough here."

"No woman is safe by herself."

"Do you think I'm so weak that—"

"You don't even have a gun. What would you do if you ran into bandits?"

It was difficult to remain put out at a man who seemed genuinely concerned for her safety. Not even William had been so worried about her. She didn't understand why Owen should be different.

"Tom Manly is around somewhere," she said.

"Somewhere's not here, but you're safe now. Tell me about your ranch. You don't have to worry I'll to try to buy it," he said when she hesitated. "Myrl said you wouldn't sell. So you can come down off that potato hill and show me around."

"This isn't a potato hill."

"It looks like the ones we had in Virginia."

"This isn't Virginia."

"I know. Virginia was never this hot. And not every plant comes equipped with thorns."

"It's how they keep from being eaten," she said.

"I don't want to eat them."

She repressed a bubble of laughter. "Longhorns do."

"I'm not surprised at anything those miserable creatures do."

"You can't hate longhorns and want to buy a ranch."

"Why not? If I wanted to have a rattlesnake ranch, would I have to like them?"

Only an insane person would want to raise rattlesnakes. "Why would you do that?"

"I wouldn't. But if I did, I wouldn't like them."

He'd obviously been in the sun too long. "There's really nothing to see except the remains of the house."

"Lightning?"

She nodded. Nearly all the damage was confined to the roof, but it might as well have been everything. It was impossible to occupy a house without a roof.

"I was just about to ride back to town" she said. The less she saw of him, the better.

"Can't you stay a little longer?"

"I left Ida a cold lunch. I owe her a hot supper."

"Dinner," Owen reminded her. "You and I have supper. Ida has *dinner.*"

Ida's little pretensions had often irritated Hetta, but it made her angry that Owen would use them to make fun of Ida. Hetta moved off the small mound—she had no idea why it was there—and started toward her horse. "I have to be going. Myrl can tell you anything you want to know. He was riding over this land before there were any ranches."

"Where's your horse?" Owen asked.

She pointed to a buckskin.

"It doesn't have a sidesaddle."

"Have you ever tried to rope a steer from a sidesaddle?" she asked.

He grinned, and her stomach did a rapid somersault. Why did the miserable man have to be so handsome?

55

"I learned to ride astride from the moment I got on a horse."

"How do you manage to mount up wearing a dress?"

"I wear pants underneath," she said, lifting her hem far enough to expose one pant leg. "And I mount up when no one's watching."

"You're out of luck this time."

"I don't need your help."

"Is she always this sweet?" he said, turning to Myrl. Owen had dismounted, but Myrl had remained in the saddle. The difference between Texas and Virginia, she supposed.

"Naw. Sometimes she's downright snippy."

"Warn me if you see a snippy mood coming on. I don't think we poor Virginia boys are tough enough to handle Texas snippy."

Hetta's mind didn't know what to make of Owen, but she was dismayed that her heart—or whatever she should call the undependable part of her that controlled her emotions and feelings—apparently had decided it wanted all this nonsense to mean that Owen liked her.

Her mind rejected the notion as absurd, laughable, but the other part of her saw something appealing and was going after it. She decided her only recourse was a hasty retreat. Owen's actions might mean many things, but serious interest wasn't one of them.

Hetta walked to her horse and stooped to remove the hobbles.

"Let me do that." Before she could stop him, Owen had dropped to his knees and untied the hobbles. "You'll get your dress caught on the thorns."

"Then I'll just have to get it uncaught." How did he think she'd survived until he got here?

"Always take advantage of a man's offer of assistance, Hetta. It makes the man happy and makes you look gracious and ladylike."

That was unfair. There was no way she could look gracious or ladylike. She had grown up as a cowhand and would go back to being one as soon as she could return to her ranch.

"Thank you," she said with exaggerated politeness. "I couldn't have done it without you."

"See. It's not hard when you try."

She was certain he was mocking her, but he had a way of smiling that took the sting out of his words. No matter how often she got mad at him, she couldn't stay angry. There was just enough doubt to keep her wondering. But not hoping. That would be foolish. "I'm not used to depending on anyone," she said.

"You're depending on Laveau."

Whenever he mentioned Mr. diViere, everything about him changed in a way she didn't like.

"He offered me a business deal. I accepted. That's no different from what anyone else does."

"Except you're hand-in-glove with a traitor and a thief."

"I'm not *hand-in-glove* with anybody." She took hold of the reins, put her foot in the stirrup, and mounted in one swift, practiced move. "Now, if you will excuse me," she said with exaggerated politeness, "I have to be going."

"Wait—"

But she had already started her horse down the trail that led from her ranch into town, the same trail her father had traveled so many times. It was difficult to remember she'd ever loved him, ever looked forward to his coming home. Laveau said her father had died a hero's death, leading a charge against the enemy, so she supposed she should be able to forgive him.

She wondered if he'd done it intentionally, if he knew he'd ruined his life and that all he had left was to die courageously.

But dying was a coward's way out. It took courage to

live, to face problems. But her father had never faced the consequences of his actions. He'd often come home smelling of whiskey, sometimes so unsteady he could hardly—

"It's not polite to ride off and leave a gentleman caller behind."

His following her was so unexpected, she blurted out the first thought that came to her mind. "Stop making fun of me. I know I'm not pretty enough to have a gentleman caller."

Suddenly she wanted to cry, and that made her madder than ever. She didn't cry. Ever. She'd faced the facts of her life long ago, had come to terms with them. No crying. No feeling sorry for herself and looking for someone to blame.

She spurred her horse into a canter, but Owen stayed alongside. "I'm not rich enough to make men forget my plainness."

"A good man looks for a great deal more in a woman than money and a pretty face."

She turned to him. "Are you trying to tell me that you're a good man, that you can see beyond my lack of face and fortune?"

"I've never been a good man, but I know that anyone attempting to judge you on face and fortune alone would be making a grave mistake."

She couldn't believe what he was saying about her, but his opinion of himself stunned her. "Why do you say you aren't a good man?"

He didn't answer her question.

She wondered if he'd referred to something he'd done during the war. She didn't know much about wars, but she doubted that people followed rules too closely. Still, he didn't strike her as the kind of man to castigate himself for things he'd done in the past. She'd assumed that in his own way, Owen was as impervious to taking blame as her father had been.

"What did you mean by saying people would be making a mistake if they only looked at my face and fortune?"

She wasn't asking because she expected a compliment. He was an unusual man, and she was certain he'd say something unexpected.

"Beauty fades, and war can destroy a fortune like that—" He snapped his fingers. "Any man looking for a wife should look for what will remain after all the trappings are stripped away."

"Is that what you're doing?"

"I'm not looking for a wife," he said, seeming to snap out of a dark mood. "I'm just looking to enjoy life, have a little fun, meet pretty women, dance, maybe sing a few new songs."

"I figured looking for a ranch meant you wanted to settle down."

"Money doesn't last unless you put it to work."

Suddenly she realized Myrl wasn't with them. "What happened to Myrl?"

"He said he was too old to be chasing after pretty girls. He's leaving that to young fools like me."

Myrl hadn't meant to hurt her feelings, but nobody chased after her, not even young fools. And though she'd steadfastly denied it, she now realized she wanted to be courted and flattered and told she was wonderful. She wasn't greedy, but just once she wanted to experience the thrill of knowing that a man wanted her, would put himself out to please her.

"Myrl is a broken-down old cowhand who can't think clearly even when he's sober," she said.

"He knows when to make himself scarce."

Owen was probably so used to spouting flattery, he wasn't aware of the words that came out of his mouth. He certainly didn't look like a young fool in love.

"Are you going to tear your house down and start over again?"

It was a fair assessment of the situation, but it wasn't what she was going to do.

"It's my home," she snapped. "It may not be much by Virginia standards, but—"

"I grew up in a log cabin."

Hetta whipped around to face him, certain he was lying, but his expression was serious.

"I'm a mountain boy. We did a little hunting to trade for the things we couldn't grow. There was nothing left when the war was over, so I came to Texas to work for my cousin."

"But . . ." She stopped before she could ask any of the questions that filled her head.

"Where did I get enough money to buy a ranch?" He grinned. "Seven of us worked ourselves to exhaustion for eight months rounding up and branding cows. Then we spent four months on the trail to St. Louis fighting Indians, white men meaner than Indians, and farmers determined to drive us out of the state. But we got more than a thousand steers to St. Louis, where they sold for almost thirty-two dollars each."

That meant he had over four thousand dollars! That made him rich by anybody's standards.

"During the war I got to see how rich people lived, what they ate, how they dressed. I don't have a grand house, and I don't much care what I eat, but I like to dress well. It makes me feel good. Why do you disapprove?"

"I don't." She thought he looked wonderful.

"That's not the feeling I get."

She didn't like being on the defensive. "Tell me what I did, and I'll try to stop it."

"I think you disapprove because you think it makes me like your father."

"I don't know you that well."

"That's not what you said last evening, and you'd only met me a couple of hours earlier."

It was hard to believe he'd been in Pinto Junction less than a day. What was it about him that made it seem as if she'd always known him? None of this made sense. She needed to get away from him, to have some time to think, to try to figure out what he was doing to her.

"You do remind me of my father," she said. "I can forgive my father for many things, but not for the pain he caused my mother. I guess that's why I acted as I did. I shouldn't have. I'm sorry."

"You don't have to apologize. You're probably right to make the comparison."

"You don't mind?"

"I didn't say that. Why did you decide to work for Ida Moody?"

The question was unexpected, but she welcomed the change of subject. "She needed someone to live with her, and I needed a job and a place to stay. It's a perfect situation for both of us."

"What will you do if she gets married?"

"I may get married first."

She shouldn't have said that, but she was tired of everybody thinking she would be the last one to be asked.

"I forgot William. He appears to be a dependable young man. Boring but dependable."

"He didn't hesitate to stand up to you when he thought you had mistreated me. You may find that boring, but I think it's wonderful."

"That's one lesson I never can remember."

"What?"

"It's stupid to criticize a man to the woman who's engaged to him."

"I'm not . . ." She'd almost said she wasn't engaged. "We haven't announced anything yet."

61

"Why the hell not?"

"Because not everybody goes around being an outrageous flirt and saying dozens of things they don't mean."

"I've never told any woman I loved her, but you can be sure that if I did love someone and wanted to marry her, I'd keep her the hell away from men like me."

"Are you so dangerous?"

"Hell, yes."

"You don't seem proud of it."

"I'm not."

She didn't understand him at all. "Why are you so angry at yourself?"

"Who said I was?"

"I did."

"What do you know?"

"Enough to tell you're very angry, but not at me."

"I'm plenty mad at you."

"No, you're not."

He brought his horse alongside hers, appeared ready to reach out toward her.

"Are you going to grab my wrists again? It won't change anything."

"I hope William knows he's getting a nag for a wife."

"I'm not nagging you."

"Take it from me, you're nagging."

"I'll stop if you tell me what has made you so angry."

"What right do you have to know?"

"None, but maybe you'll feel better if you tell somebody."

"Somebody knows."

"Then that somebody also thinks you're guilty."

His gaze bored into her like a drill. "What are you, some kind of witch?"

She didn't understand why she seemed to have an intuitive feeling about him. She'd often worried because she didn't know what William was thinking, how he was going to react to something she said or did.

"I've observed a lot of people. I can tell when someone is carrying a load of guilt."

He remained silent.

"If you're not going to talk, you might as well go back to looking at ranches and let me get on home."

"I can't let you go by yourself."

"I won't be by myself. That's William coming for me now."

Chapter Six

Owen didn't know whether to be angry or relieved that William's presence kept him from telling Hetta about Rachelle. Despite what he said, he had been on the verge of telling her. Of one thing he was certain. He couldn't understand why Hetta would want to marry William. The man might have courage, but he had the face of a bull-dog and a personality to match.

"He shouldn't have let you come out here by yourself," Owen said.

"He works in his father's hardware store. He can't take off every time I want to come out to the ranch."

"When was the last time you came?"

"A little while ago."

"How long ago?"

"Since the last winter rain."

"Your fiancé can't take a couple of hours once a year to make sure you're safe? What the hell kind of fiancé is that?"

Hetta blushed furiously. "First, he hasn't asked me to marry him."

"What's he waiting for?"

"Secondly, I'm perfectly capable of taking care of myself."

"If you were my woman, I'd damned well make sure you didn't have to."

"Then it's a good thing I'm not *your woman*. Now stop arguing. I don't want William to get upset again."

Owen was tempted to tell her that William ought to be the one worrying about her getting upset but decided to wait until he heard what William had to say. It amused Owen when William placed himself between Owen and Hetta.

"You shouldn't have come out here alone," he said to Hetta, after casting an angry glance at Owen.

"That's what I told her," Owen said, "but she insisted she was perfectly safe."

"No woman is perfectly safe alone."

"I told her that, too, but she said she could take care of herself."

"I would have come with you if you'd asked."

"I suggested that, but she said you were too busy."

"Do you mind if I have a conversation without you interrupting?"

"We've already covered that stuff. I was just trying to save time."

"If you want to *save time*, you can go about your business. Miss Gwynne doesn't need your escort any longer."

"I'm not escorting her. I'm going back to town."

It was obvious that William wanted to get rid of him, so Owen decided to ride back with them.

"You shouldn't be riding with a stranger," William said to Hetta.

"He's not a stranger," Hetta said. "He's rooming at the house."

65

"He's only been there one night, during which time he laid hands on you."

"I've already explained that."

"Even if it was exactly as you say, I don't approve."

"What do you mean, *even if it was exactly as you say?*" Owen asked. "Don't you believe she's telling the truth?"

"Of course I do."

"Then say so."

"Owen, go find Myrl, look at another ranch, do anything you like, just leave us alone," Hetta said.

"This is the man you're planning to marry—"

"Owen!" Hetta practically screeched.

"—and he doesn't believe you're truthful."

William looked from one to the other. "I do believe she's truthful. . . . We haven't talked about marriage. . . . If you would just leave. . . . That's a very big step."

"It's more like leaping a chasm," Owen said. "But if you hesitate, you'll fall in."

William looked perplexed. "What's he talking about?" he asked Hetta.

"I think he means—"

"I mean if you don't know what the hell you're doing, you'll make Hetta miserable."

"He's too kind and thoughtful to make anyone miserable," Hetta said.

"If that's what you think, you've got a lot to learn."

"If you insist upon riding back to town with us," William said to Owen, "I'd appreciate it if you could refrain from talking to Miss Gwynne. It's not good for her character to be associated with a man like you."

"What makes you so wonderful, other than the prospect of inheriting your father's hardware store?"

"Don't answer that," Hetta said. "He's just baiting you."

"I don't mind answering him," William said to Hetta in what Owen thought was a patronizing manner. "It might even be instructive to him."

"I'm sure he doesn't want to be instructed," Hetta said.

"But I do. I want to know how to be—"

"Did any of the ranches you saw today interest you?" Hetta interrupted.

William looked puzzled. "Don't you know the ranches he saw?"

"I didn't ask."

"But I thought—"

"Maybe someone told him we rode out together," Owen said, "or warned him we might meet."

"They were right to warn me," William said.

Hetta turned on William. "Do you mean you came because you thought I might be with Owen, not because you thought I might be in danger?"

Owen was amused to realize the young fool didn't see the approaching thunderclouds.

"Ida said I ought to make sure you were safe. I said I couldn't leave when Ma and Pa were depending on me, but when I learned Ida hadn't thrown *him* out after all, I couldn't take a chance he might find you alone."

"Myrl was with him," Hetta said.

"Where is he now?" William asked.

"I expect he went back to a saloon," Owen said. "You don't approve of saloons?" he asked when William scowled.

"They encourage drunkenness, gambling, and low company," William said.

"But Myrl likes drinking, gambling, and low company. I do, myself, from time to time."

"That's what makes you unfit to accompany Miss Gwynne."

"What makes you fit company for Hetta?"

"Please refer to her as Miss Gwynne."

Owen flashed his imp-of-mischief grin at her. "Hetta," he said, "you all right with me referring to you as Miss Gwynne?"

The look on her face was thunderous.

"*Address* her as Miss Gwynne, too," William said.

"Oh, you didn't say—"

"I don't care what anybody calls me," Hetta said.

"That's not very thoughtful," Owen said. "You can see it matters a great deal to William."

"Well, it's my name, so I will decide how it's used. Call me Hetta. Everyone does. It would be stupid for you to go about addressing me as Miss Gwynne."

"I don't think that fits William's notion of the respect due the woman who will some day be his wife."

"Owen Wheeler, it you say that one more time, I'm going to—"

"I forgot. It's a private matter, but it seems everybody in town is talking about it. Maybe you'd better consider getting the private part over with."

"Thank you," Hetta said, really angry now. "You can't know how much I appreciate your taking the time to give us your advice."

"I expect I do," he replied. "I'll drop back a bit, give you a little privacy."

He slowed his horse until they were about a half dozen lengths in front of him. He could hear enough of their conversation to know that William was lecturing Hetta on the impropriety of being in the company of men like Owen. The man had to be a fool not to know that independent women didn't like to be lectured, especially when they were wrong. But Owen suspected that William really didn't understand that Hetta was an independent woman. Circumstances had forced her into a subservient position, but she wouldn't be treated as subservient by any man, especially her husband.

He considered for a moment abandoning her to her fate, but he couldn't let her get tied up with Tidwell. There were times when he flat out didn't like Hetta, but he'd have to be completely hardhearted not to feel some

sympathy for her. She had endured the same kind of prof-
ligate parents he had. They'd come through the experience in different ways—he didn't trust any woman
enough to marry her, and she was determined to marry
a man as different as possible from her father—but he
still felt a bond with her.

He realized that if he wanted to get rid of William, he
would have to be more subtle.

"I hope you're through exchanging confidences," he
called out. "I'm tired of talking to myself. I already know
what I'm going to say."

William's displeasure at Owen rejoining them was obvious, but Owen thought he detected a trace of relief in
Hetta's expression.

"Tell me about the ranch business around here," Owen
said to William. "You ought to be in a position to know
how people are faring."

William didn't appear happy at Owen's interruption,
but he was pleased to be asked for his opinion. "Everybody would be a lot better off if we could stop the rustling."

"I thought Laveau—Mr. diViere—was supposed to get
the army to do that."

"He said he'd try, but all he could promise was to keep
the Reconstruction people away from Pinto Junction."

"Do you have any idea who's behind the rustling?"

"No. The cows just seem to disappear."

"Got many new cowhands about?"

"A lot have drifted in since the end of the war."

"Who're they working for?"

"Everybody. Several of them are employed on Hetta's
ranch."

"I hear her cows aren't being rustled."

"I'm not surprised. The place isn't worth bothering
with. I can't wait for her to sell it. Do you want to buy it?"

Owen decided he wouldn't have to convince Hetta to

dump William. The fool was going to manage that all by himself.

"I knew that man would find some way to meet up with you," Ida said after William and Owen had left. "I'm glad I sent William to get you."

Hetta's nerves were rubbed raw and her temper was in shreds. She was furious at Owen for baiting William and at William for being so wrapped up in his own good opinion of himself, he couldn't see what Owen was doing.

"What made you think I couldn't take care of myself?"

"No woman can take care of herself with a man like that. He's so good-looking it's easy to forget he's a spy."

"Good Lord, Ida, have some sense. The man is not a spy."

"You don't know," Ida said, reddening.

"As for Owen's harming me—"

"That's exactly what I mean!" Ida said triumphantly. "He's already got you calling him by his name."

"And he calls me Hetta, but that doesn't mean he's a danger to me, or I'm in danger of succumbing to his fatal attraction."

"What did William say about it? Was he angry? Possessive?"

Hetta appreciated Ida's efforts to throw her and William together, but she wished Ida would let well enough alone. Ida believed that William would talk to his parents sooner if he saw so much of Hetta, he couldn't wait to get married. Hetta wasn't so sure, even if his mother gave her blessing. William was as obsessed with his store as she was with the ranch. It would be a problem. "He was just as het up over it as you."

"Wonderful! I knew he would be as soon as he thought another man was interested in you."

Hetta laughed, but not in amusement. "Owen's not interested in me. He's just a flirt looking for a way to pass the time."

"Maybe, but women don't always do what's best when it comes to a man like that."

"Maybe other women don't, but I do."

"Good, but I'd rather you didn't socialize with my lodgers."

"I'm not socializing with him. He and Myrl happened to come by the ranch when I was there. He rode back with William and me because he was done for the day."

"It may be as you say—"

"It *is* as I say."

"—but people are going to think differently if they keep seeing you together."

"They've only seen me with him once, and then I was accompanied by William. If they think I'm that easily duped, they're going to think, like father, like daughter."

"I'm sure they won't. You're hardworking, practical, and sensible."

Hetta wondered why that description left her feeling as though she'd been insulted.

"Has William talked to his mother yet?" Ida asked.

"No."

"People are taking it for granted you're engaged."

"So Owen said."

"How would he know?"

"A flirt has to be aware of community feeling or he might find himself in danger."

"Well, he'll cause quite an uproar if his interest in you gets out."

"He's not interested in me."

"Maybe not, but he has shown you more attention than one would expect."

Hetta was certain that Owen wasn't interested in her. If he was, he had a peculiar way of showing it. Insulting her and accusing her of being in league with a rustler—

he hadn't said that exactly, but it was what he'd implied—were not ways to her heart. But she supposed that really handsome men didn't have to work all that hard to get women to fall in love with them.

"I'll do my best to make sure I'm not alone with him again," Hetta said. "Whenever you decide to go to your uncle's for dinner, I'll tell him he has to eat in the restaurant."

"Good. Now I'll leave you alone so you can start dinner." Ida stood. "I hope we're having something good. I feel unusually hungry tonight."

Not even preparations for dinner could stop Hetta from wondering what Owen was doing in Pinto Junction. His desire to hang Laveau seemed genuine. His interest in rustling was sensible if he was really considering buying a ranch, but she couldn't help feeling that something was wrong.

And where did she fit into this picture? She had no illusions. Owen wasn't interested in her in any romantic sense, but he was showing an interest she couldn't explain. Was he flirting merely to pass the time or to make William jealous?

It was a shame he wasn't an honorable man. Maybe then she wouldn't feel so guilty about liking him in spite of herself.

Owen didn't know what to make of Hetta's attitude during dinner. He could have understood if she'd been angry with him because of his needling William, or if she'd refused to sit down to the table with him and Ida, but she acted as though nothing had happened. She said almost nothing.

"Uncle Fred told me this morning the rustling was beginning to have a serious effect on his business," Ida was saying. She had talked virtually nonstop all evening. "People can't raise much in the way of crops in this part of Texas, but they always had cows to sell when they needed extra cash. Uncle Fred says nobody needs to do any work to raise longhorns. They thrive where other animals die. Leave them alone and they'll keep right on multiplying. Then when you need some money, you go out and get yourself a few."

"That's work," Owen said.

"Uncle Fred says all you have to do is chase them in the direction of the tallow factories. You just have to follow to make sure nobody else claims them before you get your money."

Either Uncle Fred was telling his niece only what he thought a gently bred young woman should know about ranching, or he was a complete fool.

"Is that what you did?" Owen asked Hetta when she continued to eat her dinner in silence.

"No." She didn't amplify her answer.

"Of course Hetta didn't do anything like that," Ida said. "Texas men don't expect their women to have anything to do with cows. They're nasty, dangerous creatures. Uncle Fred says they'll attack a man just as readily as a wolf or a bear. Of course I've never seen a bear—or a wolf, either. Uncle Fred does have a bearskin rug in his office. Aunt Agatha hates it and won't enter the room—I think that's why Uncle Fred keeps it—but the teeth must be this big." She held her hands nearly a foot apart.

"I worked with a man from California," Owen said. "He said he saw a bull get into a fight with a bear. The bull was so torn up they had to shoot him, but he killed that bear."

Ida's eyes grew wide. "I've heard there's so much gold in California lying around to be picked up, a man can make himself a fortune in one afternoon. Uncle Fred has talked about going to California and opening a bank, but every time he mentions it, Aunt Agatha has one of her fits."

Owen knew Ida wasn't stupid, but she chattered and smiled at him so much he wondered briefly if she was trying to attract his attention. He ultimately decided that Ida was trying to protect Hetta from his *wolfish* advances. That caused him to smile. Hetta Gwynne was completely safe from him.

"You must tell me everything your friend said about California," Ida said, turning her biggest smile on Owen.

"Rafe doesn't talk much," Owen replied.

"Rafe. What an interesting name. Much more so than Fred or Ben or Tom."

"Or Owen," Owen added.

"Your name *is* rather ordinary."

"So is Ida," Hetta said, breaking her silence.

"It's no more so than Henrietta," Ida said, a tinge of spite in her voice.

Owen turned to Hetta.

"My father didn't want a girl. He wanted to name me Henry."

Owen wished Hetta's father had survived the war just so he could have had the pleasure of knocking some sense into his head. His mother had been monumentally selfish, but she'd been too interested in indulging herself to have any time to be cruel to her children. Patrick Gwynne had been sadistic as well as self-indulgent. It was a miracle Hetta wasn't bitter.

"I like Hetta," he said. "It suits you." Their conversation was disturbed by a knock at the front door.

"I'll go," Owen offered. "It's dangerous for a young woman to open the door at night."

"Hetta always answers the door," Ida said.

That was what Owen had expected, but he hadn't expected to see William when he opened the door. "What do you want?" Owen asked.

"That's for Miss Ida to ask, not you," William announced as he marched himself inside. "Where is she?"

"In the dining room."

William didn't wait for Owen to show him the way.

"Mr. Moody said he's got to see you right away," William said to Ida when he entered the dining room. "He sent me to fetch you."

Owen could tell from the stiffness of William's face and the surprise on Hetta's that this was an unusual circumstance. As far as he knew, Ida had gotten herself home alone the night before. Owen wondered what was different about tonight.

Ida appeared more upset than either of them. "I wonder what he can want," she said. "I hope nothing's happened to Aunt Agatha." She stood.

"You shouldn't be left alone with this man," William said to Hetta. "You come along, too."

Ida immediately seconded William's invitation.

Hetta looked from William to Ida to Owen, then back to Ida again. "I've got the washing up to do," she said.

"But I can't leave you with him," Ida said.

"Why not?" She turned to Owen. "You won't attempt to take my virtue, will you?"

Chapter Seven

There were a lot of things in the world Owen didn't understand, but he did know women. "You know what's happening, don't you?" he said the minute the door closed behind William and Ida.

"I imagine her uncle wants some help with her aunt." Hetta rose and started to gather the plates.

"Sit down and listen to me," Owen said, but she continued to stand, undecided. "The dishes won't go anywhere. And if it's really a problem, I'll help."

"You!"

"I'm a lousy cook, so for four years I probably washed more dishes than you did."

She stared at him in disbelief.

"We didn't have servants on the battlefield. Now sit down."

She sank into her chair.

"Somebody doesn't want you to marry William, and I think it's Ida."

Hetta smiled and started to get up. "You're wrong. Ida wouldn't—"

Owen reached out, took her by the wrist. "Ida is a woman who's always had what she wants. If she decides she wants your fiancé, she won't hesitate to go after him."

Hetta looked down at his hand on her wrist. He released her. She sat back down. "I trust Ida and William completely."

"You can never trust a man when a pretty woman sets her cap for him."

Hetta cast him a pitying smile. "Ida has been *helping* me with William. She got him to walk her home the other night so he could be with me. She sent him out to the ranch so we could be alone together."

"He should have come after you on his own."

"You can't understand a man like William. He has responsibilities—"

"I can't understand any man who thinks more of his store than the woman he's going to marry. No woman should be left alone with another woman's man." Hetta would have understood if she'd known his mother.

"Ida and I have been best friends all our lives. We look out for each other. Women do that, you know."

"Until a man comes between them."

Hetta was silent for a moment. "Ida was raised to believe that no one in Pinto Junction was good enough for her. I expect she'll move to San Antonio or Galveston when she's ready to look for a husband."

"She'll never leave. She's the queen here. She'd be just another attractive woman with a little money in San Antonio or Galveston. How long has she been getting William to escort her home?"

"She doesn't."

"He came home with her last night."

"She brought him here for me."

"Nonsense."

"She sent him out to the ranch to protect me from you."

"It gave her a reason to talk to him and look good in his eyes."

"Women aren't like men. They don't—"

"I know a lot more about women than you think. My mother made herself a whore to the whole county."

Hetta looked stunned. He didn't know whether she didn't believe him or couldn't believe he would tell her such a thing.

"I *know* what a beautiful woman can do when she wants something. I also know that even a man of strong principles doesn't stand a chance when she goes after him."

"I trust William," she said, but her voice was a mere thread.

"My father trusted my mother. Wives all around us trusted their husbands. My mother made fools of them all. Not a single man she set her sights on ever escaped her trap. She finally got the rich husband she wanted, but I don't know if she's faithful to him."

"I'm so sorry. If I'd known—"

Owen brought his balled-up fist down on the table so hard, the silverware rattled. "Can't you see what's in front of your face?"

"Ida Moody is the best friend I've ever had. I would never be so disloyal as to suspect her of trying to steal William."

"If this were poker, I'd say your pair was up against Ida's royal flush."

"I don't play cards. I don't know what you're talking about."

"I'm saying Ida's got all the advantages. She's got money, her own house, a rich uncle, and she's pretty."

"Whereas I have no money, my house burned, I have no rich uncle, and I'm as plain as a stick."

"I agree with all but the plain-as-a-stick part. So you see—"

"Don't patronize me. I know what I look like."

"But you don't know how others see you."

"Yes, I do. I've heard the whispers for years. *It's such a shame she didn't get her father's looks.*"

"So knowing your disadvantages, what are you going to do to protect yourself?"

It clearly did no good trying to explain to Owen that not all people were as unprincipled as his mother or as suspicious as he was. "What would you have me do?" It might be fun to learn what kind of strategy he would devise.

"I'd have gone with him and Ida, even if it meant I'd be doing dishes after midnight. Are you in love with him?"

She looked uncomfortable, began playing with her fork. "That's not a proper question for you to ask."

"Then don't tell me, but you've got to answer it for yourself."

"You know so much about women. Why don't you tell me?"

"I think you've always thought you were so unattractive, no man would want to marry you. You settled on William because you thought he probably felt the same way. He's probably a nice enough guy, but like all unattractive, dull men, he's susceptible to flattery—"

"I never flattered him."

"—and he found your interest in him very flattering. You've talked yourself into believing you're in love with him because he's precisely the kind of man you think you want for a husband."

"Has anyone ever told you you're rude, arrogant, and full of yourself?"

Owen laughed. "My cousin. All the time."

"I'd like to meet your cousin."

"You wouldn't like him. He's always sure he's right. And he usually is."

"I'm surprised you're not bosom friends."

"We disagree all the time."

"Well, you're wrong this time, too. Even if Ida were trying to steal William from me, which I'm certain she would never do, he wouldn't be so untrustworthy."

"Okay, have it your way." Owen stood and picked up his plate and glass.

"You don't have to do that."

"I know."

"I don't understand you," she said, looking at him like she was trying to see behind some mask. "What are you doing here? What do you want?"

"I've already told you."

She picked up her plate and headed toward the kitchen. "I know what you said. Now I want the truth."

"You can't see through a woman you've known all you life, but you can see through me after less than two days."

She put her dishes in the sink before turning back to him. "My father was like you. He used his charm to distract people from looking closely at what he was doing, to persuade them to do things they didn't want to do."

"You don't like me at all, do you?"

"Whether or not I like you isn't the issue," she said as she brushed past him to return to the dining room. "We're talking about character, not charm."

Owen waited until she returned with Ida's dishes. "So you're saying I have a rotten character."

She put the dishes down before she faced him. "I'm saying you've used your looks and charm to get what you want. I might like you—one can't always control one's likes and dislikes—but I can't respect you."

Owen didn't like it when his cousin made him face the truth about himself. He didn't like Hetta doing it any better. An old demon raised its head, the demon that wanted to captivate Hetta just to prove her wrong. It didn't matter that he didn't want to seduce her, that he never wanted to get married. She'd attacked him, and his impulse to retaliate was strong.

That was what his mother would have done.

Which was why Owen didn't speak until he had himself under control.

"William is a dull man who will bore you to death inside of six months, but I hope he and Ida prove worthy of your faith. I even hope I don't turn out to be quite as black as you paint me. But in the event you're right, I think I'll head on over to the saloon and make a few objectionable friends. Maybe meeting someone as awful as myself will inspire me to reform."

"I didn't mean—"

"Don't worry. You haven't said half of what I've heard before."

He left before his good intentions melted away, before the smile on his face hurt so much it cracked.

Damn you, Ma. She doesn't even know me, and she can see you in me. Damn you to hell!

Hetta was so mad at Owen, she was tempted to follow him to the saloon. And do what? She'd told him he was wrong, so what was the point of telling him again? Still, she wanted to do something to him for forcing her to doubt William and Ida for even one second. And the later the hour grew, the harder it was to ignore his accusations.

There was nothing unusual about Ida needing an escort. William had escorted her a dozen times during the past year, along with other men, married and unmarried, and Hetta had never felt a twinge of doubt. Now she sat in the parlor, waiting impatiently, imagining any number of things she knew to be quite impossible.

All because of Owen Wheeler.

She couldn't understand how the arrival of one man

81

less than two days ago could have affected her life so powerfully. She shouldn't talk to him several times a day or even be aware of him except at the table. She most certainly shouldn't have shared confidences. She couldn't imagine what had caused her to behave in such an uncharacteristic manner.

Owen was much more adroit, more clever than her father had been. He argued with her, criticized her and her friends, and still managed to make her think of him constantly. Maybe she couldn't blame it on him. Maybe— probably—much of the fault lay with herself. She had allowed her common sense to be seduced by the appearance he gave of genuine interest. She kept forgetting he probably thought of her as a piece of furniture, there to make use of, though the next piece of furniture would do just as well. There was no reason to remember furniture.

Now she got angry at herself for being so self-critical. She wasn't a beauty, but she was intelligent, a capable conversationalist, and honest. She was willing to work hard for what she got. She was a loyal and dependable friend, a patriotic Texan, and a foe of thieves and bullies. And she had every reason to believe that William was only waiting to announce their engagement until he could talk to his parents.

When he had first appeared to show an interest in her, she'd thought she was mistaken, that it was folly to expect him to want to marry a woman like her. But his interest had lasted so long, people in town were aware of it.

There was no reason for her to allow Owen to upset her. Nevertheless, she experienced a tremendous feeling of relief when she heard footsteps on the porch. She jumped up and nearly ran to the front door. The smile on her lips froze, the greeting caught in her throat, when the door opened and Owen entered the hallway.

"I can tell by your face they haven't returned."

"I was just surprised to see you back so early."

"You were *shocked.*" He closed the door and followed her to the parlor.

"I thought you'd be home much later and in an un-suitable condition." His clothes smelled of whiskey and cigar smoke. She turned when she heard him laugh.

"I enjoy having a drink, but I hate being drunk."

"That's an admirable attitude."

"But not enough to redeem me in your sight."

She didn't know why his wanting her to think well of him, and her not being able to, should bother her.

"You'll leave soon," she said. "After a couple of weeks you won't remember my name."

He hadn't entered the parlor but leaned against the door frame. When she resumed her seat and looked up, she found him regarding her in a manner she found vaguely uncomfortable.

"I may leave, but I'll never forget you."

"You sound quite sincere."

"I am." His expression grew even more indecipherable. "And I'm just as surprised as you."

Hetta didn't see how he could look and sound so genuine and be lying. Maybe he meant something altogether different from what she was thinking. She heard a woman's laughter, and a man's voice in response. Then footsteps on the porch. Owen stood away from the door frame.

"I'd better be going."

"Don't. I mean, you're staying here," she added when the words came out sounding like a plea.

"Why? None of you are comfortable with me around."

"We'll have to learn to be if you buy a ranch in the area, won't we?"

She didn't know why she was talking such nonsense, but the front door opened and she was spared having to explain herself. Or face Owen's uncomfortably penetrating gaze.

"It was sweet of you to wait up for me," Ida said as she came in.

"You didn't remember to take your key."

Ida laughed. Hetta couldn't tell if it sounded coquettish or embarrassed.

"William would have had to go around the back and knock on your window."

William flushed, and Hetta found herself feeling impatient at his unnecessary modesty.

"It's a good thing you didn't," Owen said. "It would probably have ended up terrifying her."

"Men don't normally go around knocking on women's windows during the night," William said. "She would know it was some kind of emergency."

"Like Ida's having to rush off to her uncle's house tonight," Owen said.

"Uncle Fred wanted to talk business," Ida said. "He knows I don't understand commerce, so he wanted William to explain things to me."

"The rustling has gotten so bad, hardly anyone can pay their debts," William said. "We're better off than most, but Pa says things weren't this bad during the war. He said it might be worth putting up with the Reconstruction if it means the army would get rid of the rustlers."

"You could get rid of the rustlers yourself," Owen said.

"We've already tried," William said.

"What did you do?"

"If you're going to discuss rustlers, I'm going to bed," Ida announced. "Come on," she said to Hetta. "Mr. Wheeler can lock up after William leaves."

"I can't stay," William said. "Mother can't sleep until she knows I'm home."

"She's such a sweet woman," Ida said. "No wonder you love her so much."

Beulah Tidwell had many strong points. She was hard-working, dependable, efficient, had a mind for detail, and could remember who'd bought nearly every item that had passed through the Tidwell stores, but no one could call her sweet. She tolerated no familiarity and was always too busy to gossip over coffee or help with the church social.

William muttered something about it being late, about being tired after a long day, and left.

"I'm surprised to see you home so early," Ida said to Owen while looking inquiringly at Hetta.

"I thought Miss Gwynne might be lonely enough to accept even my poor company," he said, casting an amused glance at Hetta.

"I'd prefer that you not seek Hetta's company when I'm not at home," Ida said. "It's not suitable for a woman about to be married."

"He just came home, Ida. He wasn't *seeking me out*."

"It's still not good for your reputation."

"How can sitting in a formal parlor talking with a lodger damage her reputation?" Owen asked.

"No woman is entirely safe with a stranger. Besides, it worries William to know you're here."

"He said that?" Hetta asked, angry that he would say something like that to Ida rather than to her.

"Not exactly," Ida admitted, "but I can see it in his eyes. He's such a thoughtful man. Now I'm tired, so I'm going to bed."

"Very good," Owen said to Hetta when the door closed behind Ida.

"What do you mean?" Hetta asked.

"I was beginning to think you were either stupid or gutless. Glad to see I was wrong on both counts."

"I don't know what you're talking about, and I don't want to know." She turned the key in the lock and put it on the hook. "Now *I'm* going to bed."

Owen laughed softly.

"What are you laughing at?" she asked.

"You. You're really quite charming. It's not a conventional charm, but it's charm nevertheless."

"I never thought anyone could talk more nonsense than my father, but you've got him beat by a mile. Go to bed and dream of your new ranch."

His smile died. "I'd rather dream of hanging Laveau diViere."

That thought sent shivers down Hetta's spine. She had let his smile, his attention, cause her to forget his harsh intention. That alone was reason to dislike him.

Why didn't she?

The farm was like so many others they'd stopped at over the last three years. The genuine though uneasy welcome was no different from their welcome yesterday and the day before. But the oldest daughter was the prettiest he'd seen in a year. She could hardly wait to tell him she was seventeen, that she didn't have to blush and hold back around the soldiers, not even soldiers with such a fearsome reputation as the Night Riders. He asked about the coolest spot to bed down. She told him it was the orchard. He asked her to show him the way. She said he was a handsome flirt. He grinned and agreed. Cade had given strict orders that they go to sleep immediately, but the girl was too pretty, too vivacious and entrancing.

"What's your name?" he asked as they rounded the corner of the stone farmhouse and headed toward an orchard of peaches, apples, pears, and cherries. A grape arbor looked very inviting, but several men were already asleep in its deep shade. Trellises of several kinds of berries were placed on the far side of the orchard.

"Rachelle," she replied. "Do you like it?"

"It's very pretty. Like you."

He'd never met anyone so full of laughter. She was like

*sunshine itself. He knew he shouldn't do anything to touch
her heart, but he couldn't resist her any more than a bear
could resist honey.*

"I bet you tell every girl you meet the same thing."

"Just the pretty ones."

She skipped ahead, turned around to face him. "Mama
warned me about men like you."

"What did she say?"

"That I was to run."

"Are you going to run away?"

She laughed again. It was an intoxicating sound.

"Not yet. I want you to tell me about the places you've
been, the things you've seen."

"Why do you want to know?"

"I've spent my whole life on this farm. I feel like I don't
know anything, that there's all kinds of wonderful things
out there I know nothing about. Tell me about them."

He thought of the war and the ugliness that it had
brought to so many people; it seemed to have left her miraculously untouched. It wouldn't hurt if he painted a glorious picture for her, made her believe the world outside
her valley was as wonderful and magical as a mythical
kingdom. After the war, she'd marry some farmer, settle
down, and live her whole life without leaving the valley.

"What do you want to know?" he asked.

"Tell me about the clothes beautiful ladies wear."

"Clothes. I wish they didn't, but they do."

She swatted him playfully and laughed. "You're awful."

"I know. Isn't it wonderful?" He would do virtually anything to make her laugh. No sound had ever made him
feel so good, so at peace with himself.

"My friend went to Alexandria last year. She described
the most wonderful dresses."

Owen couldn't imagine any farmer's daughter catching
so much as a glimpse of the really wealthy women. "I'm

sure there are even more wonderful things than what she saw."

"Tell me. Please, tell me."

He opened his mouth to describe a dress of his imagination, but a curse came out instead. His cousin was headed toward him, and he didn't look pleased.

"What's wrong?" Rachelle asked, her smile gone.

"That's my commanding officer," he said, pointing to the man coming toward them. "He disapproves of flirting."

"He should. It's wrong."

"Do you hate it so much?" He chucked her under the chin, and grinned until she laughed again.

"Not when you talk about clothes."

"You're supposed to be resting up for our ride tonight," Cade said, "not trying to seduce every female within reach."

Rachelle blushed and turned away. Owen reached out to take her by the wrist, his face tight with anger. "You don't have to worry about me," he said to Cade.

"I have to worry whether we'll be less welcome than the Yankees if you can't keep your hands off every woman in the valley."

Rachelle succeeded in breaking away. She picked up a fallen, partially rotten peach, threw it at Owen, then started running toward the house, her laugh as joyous as her eyes were bright.

"I don't need your sanctimonious preaching," Owen shouted at Cade.

"You're part of my command, and as such—"

At that moment, a cannonade of gunfire broke out all around them. Men on horseback crashed through the orchard. Owen looked up to see Rachelle throw up her hands and fall to the ground.

"You son of a bitch!" Cade shouted as he propelled Owen toward the cover of the barn. "You got that girl killed."

Chapter Eight

Owen jerked awake, his nightshirt soaked with sweat, his soul filled with guilt and horror at what he'd done, his mind reeling with the picture of Rachelle lying on the ground, her bright yellow dress just visible through the tall grass.

He sat up and dropped his head into his hands. He was weary of the dream, weary of the guilt, weary of the self-loathing. He had never intended that girl any harm, but he couldn't ignore an attractive woman.

However, something was different this time. He had turned his attention to Hetta rather than Ida. Maybe it was because he felt Hetta was somehow involved in Laveau's rustling.

He didn't want her to be involved. That was different, too. Usually he didn't want a woman to have a particularly good character, but he didn't feel that way about Hetta. He even wanted to save her from marrying William!

Then why had he spent half the evening trying to get Hetta to fight Ida for William? Because he couldn't stand to lose a woman to another man, or to lose at anything. *Even if he didn't want what was at stake.* He had to be top dog, and anybody he liked had to be top dog. He liked Hetta, so he couldn't stand to see her be so blinded by friendship that she'd let Ida steal William away from her. If she married William, she'd have a husband who could support her comfortably and give her the solid, dependable life she craved.

Yet though he couldn't stand to watch Hetta lose William to another woman, he couldn't accept the idea of her marrying him either. This was crazy, and he knew it. He had no business interfering in Hetta's life. He didn't know why he should care so much, but he did. It was as if she was his sister and he was looking out for her.

But it didn't *feel* like that. He could only conclude he was interested in Hetta as a person. That had never happened before, and he didn't know what to make of it. They had nothing in common. They argued over everything.

Did her plainness make him think about her differently from other females? Maybe, but he didn't think she was all that plain. She didn't have a bow-shaped mouth, dimpled cheeks, or peaches-and-cream skin, but there was a certain attractiveness in her strength. He liked the way she faced him directly, her gaze open and forthright.

At least he *thought* that was the way he felt. It all depended on whether she was in cahoots with Laveau. How could she be? She believed so strongly in the good in everybody, she wouldn't have seen the evil in Laveau unless somebody pointed it out.

As he got up to change his nightshirt, he decided to put Hetta out of his mind. He had work to do, and he couldn't afford any distraction. But even as he went back to sleep, he found himself wishing Hetta wasn't so trusting. She'd already had more than her share of bad luck. And unless he did something, she was in for more.

"You talk too much," Lester Benham complained. "Just play cards."

"I did," Owen said, pointing to his discard. "I'm waiting for you."

For the last three days Owen had spent most of his time in the saloon, playing poker and trying to gather information about the rustling. He'd acquired a reputation as a cheerful companion and a good poker player, capable enough to win more than he lost, clever enough to keep his winnings from being too large.

"There he is," Myrl said.

"There who is?" asked Lester, still trying to decide which card to play.

"Tom Manly," Myrl said. "Owen's been wanting to look over the Gwynne place, but Tom was never around."

Owen didn't like what he saw. Manly was wearing two guns, and bullets were missing from some of the loops on his gun belt.

"He had a big herd on the place earlier in the summer," Lester said, still debating his next move. The others had dropped out, leaving only him and Owen.

"What happened to it?"

"Don't make it my business to know what Manly's doing."

"You ranchers ought to know as much as you can about each other. You ought to work together to stop the rustling."

Lester placed his bet, Owen raised, and Lester called. He was not happy to find Owen's three deuces beat his two aces and two queens.

"Manly says he doesn't have any rustling," Lester said, throwing his cards down in disgust.

"I'd like to know why," Owen said.

"Well, there's Manly at the bar. Nothing's stopping you from asking him."

Owen figured he'd have a better chance if he got Hetta to tell Manly to show him around. Newt Howren entered the saloon and went straight to Manly. They took their drinks, retired to a corner, and were soon in earnest conversation.

"You lost your chance," Lester said to Owen. "Newt hates your guts."

"Is Newt Manly's boss?"

"Naw. Newt works for Manly from time to time, though."

"When he's gambled away all his money," Myrl said.

"He likes to gamble?" Owen asked, wondering if this could be the opening he needed.

"Once he sits down, he hardly ever gets up until he's broke."

"Tell him I've got money and nobody to play with."

"He's a terrible loser."

"Maybe he can get Manly to join us."

Myrl wasn't exactly eager to talk to Newt and Tom, but he got up and shuffled off.

"What are you up to?" Lester asked Owen.

"Just trying to buy a ranch."

"You wouldn't be asking all these questions if you weren't up to something else."

"I can't see much sense in settling here if somebody's going to make off with my stock."

"So what's the point in gambling with Newt and Tom?"

"I hear nobody rustles from the Gwynne place. Since Tom is the foreman and Newt works for him, it seems like a good idea to talk to them."

"It makes sense when you say it that way, but I'd be careful."

"Why?" Owen asked, giving Lester a friendly grin. He'd been receiving hints for days but nothing concrete.

"You just said it. Nobody rustles Tom. We wondered, too, but we can't find nothing going on at his place."

"Then he shouldn't have any reason not to let me ride over the ranch."

"What ranch are you talking about?"

Owen looked up to see Newt standing at his shoulder.

"The Gwynne place. I'm looking to buy a ranch."

"Miss Gwynne ain't interested in selling," Newt said. "You want to gamble, or you going to talk?"

Owen gestured at the pile of coins in front of him. "I'm looking to gamble until my luck runs out. Or your money."

"If our money runs out first, your luck will be out at the same time," Newt said.

"Stick around," Owen said to Myrl and Lester. "I don't want anybody thinking I got aces up my sleeves."

Myrl grinned and dropped into a chair next to Owen. "You couldn't run me off," he said. Lester looked undecided before nodding his agreement.

"You want me to move?" Lester asked Newt. He was sitting between Newt and Manly.

"I don't care where you sit as long as you keep your mouth shut," Newt growled.

Owen shuffled the cards. "High card deals first, winner after that. Okay?"

Newt and Manly nodded as they settled into chairs. Owen won the cut with a king. "I'll let Myrl deal for me," he offered. His opponents nodded, their expressions grim. Owen decided this wasn't going to be an easy night.

Two hours later Owen conceded he'd understated the case. Neither man was a good loser. They weren't good poker players, either. Owen had learned to judge the strength of Newt's hand by the increase in his cussing. Manly was more difficult to read, but Owen noticed that his eye twitched when he thought he might have a winning hand. Owen had won more than twenty-five dollars from each of them.

"I'm tired," Owen said.

"You can't quit a winner," Newt said.

"We can play again tomorrow night."

"Keep on playing."

"I'm sure you can find somebody here—"

"They're all yella-bellied cowards. None of 'em will take a hand with me."

"It's because you beat them up if you lose," Manly said.

"They cheat," Newt said.

"I hope you're not accusing me of cheating," Owen said.

"Can't be," Myrl said. "Lester and me watched everything you did."

Newt looked stymied. "You sure won an awful lot."

"That's because I fold when I know I'm going to lose." Newt played every hand.

"Well, I'm folding," Newt said and tossed down his cards. He had a single pair.

"How about you?" Owen asked Manly.

"I'm thinking."

"Suppose I offer a different bet," Owen said.

"Like what?" Manly asked.

"Let me ride over the Gwynne place."

Manly's eyes grew hard. "I told you she ain't selling."

"From what I hear, nobody's made an offer. If I like what I see, maybe I can talk her into it."

"It's a waste of time."

"It's my time and money. You got something you don't want me to see?"

Tension held the group as still as statues.

"Like what?" Manly asked, his eyes harder then ever.

"I don't know," Owen said with a self-deprecating smile. "I haven't seen the place yet. I'll raise you ten against your showing me about."

Owen didn't like the way Manly stared at him. He wasn't afraid of the man in a fair fight, but Manly looked like the kind who'd make certain the fight *wasn't* fair. Manly laid down three jacks. He showed virtually no reaction when Owen laid down three queens.

"When do you want to come out?" Manly asked.

"How's Tuesday?"

"Fine."

Manly pushed his chair back, got up, and left without any comment. Newt got up and went over to the bar. Owen heard him order a whiskey. A couple of men who'd been watching the games came up to the table. "Mind if we sit?" one asked.

"I'm about ready to leave," Owen said.

"We just wanted to know why you're thinking about buying a ranch when there's so much rustling."

"Because I intend to stop it."

"How?"

"All of us working together to organize a system of watches. Let your men ride with other crews."

The men didn't appear to like that idea.

"Don't you trust your men?"

"Sure."

"You trust your neighbors?"

"Yeah."

"What's going on here?" Newt asked from behind Owen's shoulder.

"We're organizing to catch the rustlers," Owen said.

"How're you going to do that?"

"Work out a system where the cowhands work on different ranches."

"And who's going to work out this *system* of yours?"

"Anybody can, but I was going to offer."

"Maybe we don't like some stranger coming in here accusing us of rustling."

"I didn't accuse anybody of rustling."

"You accusing me of lying?"

"Are you?"

Newt charged him, but Owen sprang out of his chair and drew his gun.

"You wouldn't have the guts to call me a liar if you didn't have that gun in your hand."

"I haven't called you a liar," Owen said. "But if I do, I'll do it without this gun."

"I ain't letting you organize no ranchers," Newt said.

"I think that's up to them."

Newt turned to the three men at the table, placed his hands on the table, and stared straight at them. "I say he ain't organizing nobody. Anybody here say different?"

The three men looked as if they'd swallowed their tongues. "See," Newt said, turning back to Owen, "nobody wants you to organize nothing."

"It sounds like a good idea to me," Lester said.

"Well, it sounds like a bad idea to me," Newt said, whipping back around. "And I won't have it."

"Seems like it's about time you boys decided who runs this town," Owen said to the men.

"They know Newt will round up some of that wild bunch he runs with and shoot up their places," Myrl said.

Newt turned to Myrl, but he stopped when he heard the click of a cocked hammer.

"You touch that old man, and I'll put a bullet between your eyes," Owen said.

"You're such a big man with that gun in your hand. How big are you without it?"

Owen didn't know if he could beat Newt, but he could tell from the looks around him that the men didn't expect him to back down from this challenge. "Looks like it's about time somebody taught you some manners," Owen said.

"You going to try?" Newt said with a sneer.

"Looks like I'm the only one volunteering." He handed

his gun to Myrl. "Make sure he stays off me until we get outside."

Myrl pointed the gun at Newt. "I been itching for a chance to do this for nigh onto a year."

Owen tossed his gun belt on the table. "Come on, before I get sick just thinking about fouling my hands on carrion like you."

Owen figured Newt was used to winning his fights by intimidation. If he could get Newt really mad, he'd probably just charge in, depending on his size to carry him. Owen hoped so. Though he'd survived hundreds of fights—mountain boys fought just to keep from being bored—he could use every advantage.

"Hurry up, fat boy," he called over his shoulder. "You're not hanging back because you're scared, are you?"

He slammed the saloon door in Newt's face. The street was quiet, but he knew that as soon as the fight started, it would be thronged with people. Newt came charging into the street.

"Hold up," Owen said. "I don't want to mess up my clothes. Do you think people would mind if I took off my shirt?"

Newt's answer was colorful enough to make a barmaid blush.

"What was your mother, some kind of cheap whore?" Owen asked. "She should have taught you better."

Newt was so mad he charged Owen like an angry steer, head down, fists working like pile drivers.

Owen stepped aside, whirled, and planted a fist in Newt's soft belly. A pain-filled grunt told him not even a hundred pounds of fat could protect Newt from a hard punch.

The fight proceeded in the same manner, Newt charging furiously, Owen dodging and landing punches. Newt would yell obscenities and Owen would say something else to keep him so angry he couldn't control himself. After being staggered on the sixth charge, this time by a blow to the temple, Newt turned, stopped, and stared at Owen.

His chest heaved as he gasped for air. He seemed unsteady on his feet. "Why don't you stand and fight like a man?"

"Because you're a snake, Newt. And a thief. I think you're working with the rustlers. I think you ride away from this saloon and steal from the men you drink with."

"You're a dirty liar," Newt howled, but he didn't charge Owen this time. He approached carefully as he looked for an opening that would allow him to get in close.

"You're a lousy poker player, too."

Newt charged but turned quickly this time, almost catching Owen as his fist connected with Newt's neck. Owen had been landing solid blows, but Newt showed no sign of stopping. Deciding to take a chance, Owen charged Newt head down. The force of his attack knocked Newt down, but Newt was able to get a grip on Owen's arm.

Newt caught Owen in a bear hug, apparently planning to squeeze the wind out of him. Owen brought his knee up into Newt's abdomen at the same time as he butted Newt's face with his head, smashing his nose and bloodying his mouth. The big man roared in pain and fury.

Newt struggled for a grip that would enable him to keep Owen from pummeling him with his fists, head, and knees. The big man got Owen in a body hold, determined to crack his ribs against his own body. A sharp, vicious jab to Newt's throat sent the fat man to the ground gasping for air.

"You want some more, or have you had enough?" Owen's body felt as if it had been in a vise. He was sure he had at least one broken rib, maybe several.

"He's done for," Lester said.

"I want him to promise he won't get his friends to come after us once we organize."

Newt didn't answer.

"Promise to leave these ranchers alone or stand up and fight," Owen said.

Newt tried to get to his feet, but he fell back.

"Promise?" Owen asked. When Newt didn't respond, Owen grabbed him by the hair and jerked his head back. "Promise?"

"Yeah." The sound was barely audible.

"Everybody heard. If you go back on your word, I'll come after you with my gun."

Owen turned to retrieve his clothes and found himself face to face with Hetta.

Chapter Nine

It disgusted Hetta to see men fighting in the middle of the street. She didn't see why they couldn't settle disagreements without fists or guns. She hated the way every man and boy in the town had gathered around the combatants, shouting and cheering. She felt less angry and more apprehensive when she saw that one of the combatants was Newt Howren. She'd like to think someone could take that bully down a notch, but he was too big, too mean, and the men who should have been the ones to stand up to him made a point of staying out of his way.

Pinto Junction wasn't a big town, but there were enough people in the dusty street to block the fighters from her view. She walked up to a very tall man who lived on the street behind Ida and tapped him on the shoulder.

"Who's Newt fighting?" she asked, not the least bit surprised when he didn't turn to look at her.

"I don't know the fella's name. He's new in town."

Owen? It couldn't be.

"Never thought I'd see it, but the new fella's winning," the man said.

The crowd shifted position, and Hetta got a brief glimpse of the fighters. Owen! There could be no mistake. She started elbowing her way through the crowd.

She caught sight of Newt. Horrified by the amount of blood on his face, she expected to see Owen's handsome face battered nearly beyond recognition. Elbowing her way to the inner ring, she found herself next to Myrl. "Why didn't you stop him?"

"Can't nobody stop that man once he makes up his mind to do something."

Then she saw Owen, stripped to the waist, his face unbloodied and as handsome as ever. "Haven't they started to fight yet?"

"How do you think Newt's face got to look like a piece of raw meat?"

"Owen did that?" Nobody had ever bloodied Newt's face.

The last climactic moments of the fight left Hetta with her mouth hanging open and her stomach feeling as if she was going to throw up. She had no business feeling proud of Owen, yet she was. He had managed to defeat a bully no one else in Pinto Junction dared challenge.

Finding herself face to face with Owen surprised her as much as it surprised him.

"Put your clothes on," she said. "You're making a spectacle of yourself."

She had no idea why she'd said that. It was one thing to show up at her bedroom door naked to the waist asking for soap. It was quite another to be naked in the street. Not that either was acceptable, but . . .

She couldn't believe the thoughts going through her head. Maybe it was the fight that had caused her mind to cease functioning intelligently. She had to pull herself together, stop acting like a brainless female.

She had plenty of time to regain her equilibrium as she watched every man and boy in the crowd shake Owen's hand and give him a hearty slap on the back.

"I think I'd like a bath first," Owen said to Hetta when he'd accepted his last congratulations and had his hand wrung one last time.

"A good, long soak will do you good," Myrl said. "You'll have aches and pains all over."

"Not to mention a few broken ribs," Owen added.

"You've got to see the doctor," Hetta said. "He doesn't live very far."

"I spent the last year working next to one of the best doctors to survive the war," Owen said. "He'd tell me to wrap it tight and go back to work."

Hetta couldn't imagine any doctor who would be so unfeeling.

"Now if you're ready, I'll escort you home," Owen said to Hetta.

She found it impossible to imagine herself walking through the middle of town accompanied by a man who was *naked to the waist*. Her face felt warm just thinking about it. "Put your shirt on."

"It'll get sweaty."

"I'll wash it."

Owen's gaze narrowed. His smile grew. "You're embarrassed to be seen with me, aren't you? Don't deny it. I can see it in your face."

"If you're so sure you know what I'm thinking, why bother asking me?"

"I'm just surprised, that's all."

"I have my reputation to worry about. Now put your shirt on and come with me." She turned and started home. She refused to bandy words with him in front of a dozen amused onlookers.

"I can find my way," Owen said when he caught up with her. "I'm not a child."

"All men act like children. That's why they get into fights."

She was annoyed with herself. If he wanted to get into fights and walk down the street naked, it shouldn't bother her. Just the thought of Owen naked sent chills up and down her spine.

"You don't know why I had to fight Newt," he said, the smile gone from his eyes.

"Nobody *has* to fight."

"Newt challenged him," Myrl said, working hard to keep up with them. "He had to fight or pack up and leave town."

"That might be a good thing," Hetta said. "Nothing's been the same since you arrived."

Owen's mesmerizing smile was back. "You can't know how pleased I am to hear that."

"I wasn't talking about myself. Not even Ida's the same, and she disapproves of you tremendously. She thinks you might be a spy."

What was it about this man that made her say things she didn't want to say? His grin was wider than ever, his chest just as bare. Why was it that handsome men never did what you wanted them to do?

"Tell me about myself. I sound terribly interesting."

"Ida doesn't think you're here to buy a ranch. She thinks a man who gambles and dresses so well has no place in a town like Pinto Junction."

"I dress well because I gamble."

"She thinks you're spying for Mexico, that there's an army across the border ready to invade."

"What am I doing, helping them capture Pinto Junction? What a strategic victory that would be."

"She was just stating a possibility. We can't know the real reason you're here."

"To buy a ranch."

"He's going to organize the ranchers to stop the rustling," Myrl put in.

"How are you going to do that?"

"Organize the ranch crews to work together to watch each other's land *and each other*."

Hetta stopped abruptly, turned to face Owen. "You think one of us is doing the rustling?"

"It's not Cortina's bandits. They can find a lot more cows in east Texas."

"They'll kill you."

"A million Yankees spent four years trying. I figure I'll survive a few rustlers."

She searched his face for any sign of foolish bravado but saw nothing but calm confidence. After his having proved himself with his fists as well as his gun, she expected most of the ranchers would fall in with his plans. She started walking again. "I hope you're right. I'd hate to have to write your family."

"The only one who cares is my cousin, and he'd find out on his own."

She stopped and turned again. "I'm sorry."

"My father headed west after the war. I don't know where he is. My mother wouldn't care." They neared the house. "You going to tend my wounds?"

"I'll help bandage your chest. Myrl can help you with your bath."

She nearly burst out laughing at the old man's sputtered reaction. She was relieved to see Owen's smile break through. She liked it better when he smiled.

The house was empty when she entered. She'd hoped Ida would be home. Anything to take her mind off Owen. It didn't matter that she kept thinking of ways to get him to leave town. She shouldn't be thinking of him at all. It was too soon to start preparations for dinner, and she'd washed and put everything away after breakfast. She had nothing to do but gather material to bandage Owen's chest.

That made things even worse. She couldn't touch a pin or unfold strips of cloth to go around Owen's chest without seeing a vivid image of Owen, his broad chest heaving, his face alive with excitement, his body far more imposing than William's.

There was no physical side to her relationship with William. They'd never so much as held hands. They'd known each other all their lives, so their relationship had progressed almost imperceptibly from lifelong friends to something much warmer. They'd gone to a couple of parties together and a dance in the spring. She'd enjoyed being with William, but he hadn't tried to kiss her good night, and she hadn't planned to let him. After her father's exploits, she didn't intend for sex to be part of their relationship except to have children.

She knew instinctively that wouldn't be the case with Owen. No matter who he married, whether he loved her or married her because she was beautiful, sex would be a vital part of the relationship. Maybe that was why she was acutely aware of him at all times. She was horrified to find herself thinking about Owen's relationship with his future wife. It made no sense, especially since she disapproved of him in almost every way.

Well, maybe not in that many ways. He traded on his looks, but it hadn't bothered him that she wasn't impressed. She had to give him credit for not being afraid to face danger. She didn't know what he could do about the rustlers, but she felt certain he would organize the ranchers as he'd said he would. And he'd stood up for Myrl and Ben, people who weren't able to stand up for themselves.

That impressed her most of all.

Most men like Owen were totally self-centered. They usually allied themselves with the strong, the rich, the beautiful, and the popular, with whom their mixture of looks and charm was most effective and where there was the most to gain. It was a shame his looks had ruined him for people like her.

She told herself not to be foolish. She had been ruined for people like Owen long before. She was plain, she had no money, and lived in the backside of Texas. She wanted nothing more than to settle on her ranch for the rest of her life.

Anyone could see that Owen was destined to live in a city, go to parties, dance with beautiful women, and marry someone rich and beautiful.

The sound of the front door opening scattered her thoughts. Ida was returning. She would feel more comfortable with a barrier against any kind of intimacy with Owen. Her relief fled when Owen walked into the parlor, still naked to the waist.

"Where's Myrl?" she asked, grabbing at straws.

"He doesn't dare go near water. There's nothing but dirt and dried sweat holding him together."

He looked at her, and a slow smile spread across his face. She was suddenly aware that she'd jumped to her feet when he entered the room. Now she stood clutching the bandages to her bosom as though they formed some kind of protective barrier. She was angry at him for laughing at her, but she couldn't blame him. She was behaving foolishly.

"I'm making you uncomfortable," Owen said.

"I'm not used to half-naked men, but if you stay with us much longer, I probably will be."

"I hope not. You blush delightfully. I'd hate for you to lose that innocence."

"I can't afford to be innocent. A woman alone—"

"You've told me. Do you know how to bandage cracked ribs?"

"No."

"Just do what I tell you."

"How do you know so much about it?"

"This isn't my first time. Wild steers don't like being rounded up. And when you brand them, they try to kill you."

"I know all about working cattle. Sit down. Tell me if I get the bandage too tight."

But the moment Owen sat down next to her, every feeling except acute awareness of his nearness fled.

"Turn your back to me," she said.

"Then I won't be able to see you blush when one of your fingers accidentally touches my skin."

She dropped her hands to her lap. "If you're going to make fun of me—"

"I like seeing you blush."

"Well, I don't like doing it. It makes me feel stupid."

"Why? Every young beauty I ever met keeps a blush as part of her arsenal of charms."

"I'm not a young beauty, and I have no intention of attempting to collect *an arsenal of charms*. I'd look foolish trying to employ them."

"No young woman looks foolish when she's being charming."

"I'm not charming, either. So I'd appreciate it if—"

Owen reached out, took her chin in his hand, and forced her to look at him. "Don't disparage yourself. You have character. That's important."

She removed his hand from her face. "You are a great beauty and you have no character. Look at which of us is the more successful." The look in his eyes stunned her. It was hurt. It was so unexpected, she hardly trusted her judgment. "Sorry. I shouldn't have said that, but you upset me. I know what I look like."

"Does your stiff-necked fiancé ever tell you you're beautiful?"

"William's not given to telling lies."

"Not even small, harmless ones for your sake?"

"I prefer the truth."

"No woman prefers the truth when it comes to how the man she loves sees her."

"I'm beginning to doubt you have any cracked ribs. You're too eager to tease me to be suffering."

His patently false anguished moan caused her to smile. "You are hopeless. If my father behaved as you do, I begin to see why women were always acting like idiots over him."

"Why do you say that?"

"You're not hurt, and I've been worried about you. You're telling me bald-faced lies, and I'm allowing you to sit in Ida's parlor without a shirt. Who else but an idiot would do that?"

"A woman in love."

"Since I'm not in love with you, that still doesn't answer my question."

"Well, put your dainty hands all over my body, and I'll try to think up an intriguing answer."

Hetta looked at the hands clenched in her lap. They had handled ropes, a plow, washed dishes, and scrubbed floors. How could he even suggest they were dainty?

They really weren't all that large. And the calluses had disappeared. They looked a little rough from so much hot, soapy water, but they were rather small for a woman of her size. Looked at in that light, a person *might* be able to consider them dainty. But putting them all over Owen's body was quite another matter.

"If you don't stop provoking me, I'll send you to Myrl."

"I promise to be more prim than a Puritan."

She nearly giggled. The notion of Owen as a Puritan was almost too much for her.

"I don't think you could stand the strain. How about just not talking?"

"I'll try, but only because I'm scared of you."

She did giggle, but she stifled it quickly. She knew it would just prompt him to say something else outrageous. She held one end of the folded strip and handed him the rest. He placed it across his chest and handed it to her on the other side. She placed it across the loose end and handed it to him again. They did this twice more.

"Is it tight enough?" she asked.

"Just right," he replied.

She fastened it with one of those new safety pins Ida had brought back from New Orleans. She'd just handed him the next bandage when the door opened and Ida and William walked into the parlor.

Chapter Ten

Why should William come to the house the one time when, though it was quite easy to explain the situation, it was *impossible* to make it appear innocent?

"You're just in time to inspect Hetta's handiwork," Owen said, apparently not the least bit upset by the situation.

"I heard you took Newt's stack apart brick by brick," William said. He favored Owen with an admiring look. "I wish I'd seen it."

"I don't approve of fighting," Ida said.

"I don't either," Owen said, "especially when it's my ribs getting broken."

"It's barbaric," Ida said.

"It depends on who's winning," Owen said, his good humor unimpaired.

"I can't believe you would be alone with him in his state of undress," Ida said to Hetta.

"I tried to get her to come to my room," Owen said, "but she refused."

"You didn't do any such thing," Hetta said, "so stop trying to make trouble."

"I tried to get Myrl to bandage me up," Owen admitted, "but he said he'd rather drink beer and talk over the fight at the saloon."

"A few cracked ribs is nothing compared to the condition Newt's in," William said.

"You will not admire him for brawling in the street," Ida said, every inch of her patrician nose in the air.

"I admire anyone who can beat Newt Howren," William said, giving Hetta an opportunity to be pleased that he had the backbone to stand up to Ida, "but Hetta should have sent you to a doctor."

"She tried," Owen said, "but I got used to doing without them during the war."

"Where did you fight?" William asked.

"In Virginia."

"Were you in any important battles?"

"William!" Ida exclaimed. "I will not stand here listening to you discuss battles. Uncle Fred sent us to get Daddy's records."

"Deeds," corrected William.

"I know nothing about business papers," Ida said irritably. She turned to Owen. "Since you appear to be thoroughly bandaged, I would suggest you retire to your room. I will need the parlor to look through Daddy's papers. Uncle Fred insists I pay attention to my business affairs." She sighed, still irritated. "It will probably take William weeks to make me understand the simplest things."

"I'll be happy to help," Owen said.

"I'm sure William can teach me all I need to know."

Hetta and Owen left the room together, his expression

saying *I told you so* as clearly as if he'd spoken the words. She still had faith in William's constancy, in Ida's friendship. Ida really did hate business. She even let Hetta pay the bills, and it was obvious that William would have liked to hear more about the fight.

"Are you sure there's nothing else I can do for you?" Hetta asked Owen. "Of a medical nature," she added when she saw the beginning of an impish grin.

"Why don't I break in on them and get William thoroughly enthralled with stories of some of the biggest battles of the war?"

"Did you actually fight in any battles?" Owen was flirtatious, irreverent, and easygoing. It was hard to envision him as a hard-bitten soldier willing to kill anyone wearing the wrong uniform.

"Only the last year. Before that, I was part of a special mounted troop that carried out night raids on Union convoys, ammunition dumps, and payroll shipments."

"Is that where you met Mr. diViere?" She was sorry she'd mentioned the topic even before she'd finished saying his name. She didn't like the way Owen changed.

"That's the troop he betrayed. More than twenty men died."

She wanted to ask what had happened, but she still couldn't make herself believe that the man she'd met could have been responsible for so much horror.

"I'd better go," he said. "If Ida finds me here, she'll take it out on you."

"I don't know why she dislikes you so. She normally enjoys her lodgers."

"She's angry because I like you better than her."

He couldn't have said anything that would have shocked Hetta more. Nobody *ever* liked her more than Ida. Ida was a charming hostess and knew how to please men. It was absurd that anybody would like Hetta better.

"How can you say such a thing and expect me to believe it?"

Owen flashed one of those smiles she was sure he had practiced before a mirror until he achieved easy perfection. "Maybe because you don't believe anything I say, do your best to drive me away, and continue to prefer the company of that barely animated stick to me."

She had to smile. "You mean I've piqued your vanity."

"Something like that."

She was relieved. That was an explanation she could believe, because it was exactly how her father would have reacted.

"Then I will take great pleasure in continuing to turn my back on you," she said.

"Or maybe I like you because you're an interesting woman. I've never met anyone quite like you."

That answer scared Hetta. She didn't know how to handle a man like Owen liking her. It had never happened. She couldn't think of any reason why it should happen now.

"It's a good thing I don't believe anything you say. I could easily make a fool of myself."

"I doubt you'll ever do that, not even if you marry William."

"What do you have against William? And don't start on about him not being exciting or handsome or full of fancy words."

"That's pretty much it."

"It's pointless to discuss anything with you. You refuse to see any side but yours."

"You do the same thing."

"That's because I'm right."

She'd expected a spirited retort. Instead he smiled, a little wistfully, she thought. "Maybe you are. My cousin thinks I'm wrong all the time, too."

"I don't see how he can say that. Why, you . . ." She

didn't know what stopped her, his slow grin or the realization that she was about to defend him.

"Caught yourself before you said something good about me, didn't you?" He actually had the nerve to chuckle. "Careful. Next thing you know, you'll be trying to convince Ida I'm not a spy. Who knows where *that* could lead?"

"Even if I did feel obliged to defend you—and I don't think you're a spy—you'd soon make me so angry I wouldn't do it."

Owen put on his shirt. "I think I'll go back to the saloon. After this tongue-lashing I need to bask in a little bit of glory to heal my wounded spirit. Still, set the table for three," he said as he buttoned his short. "Ida will invite William to stay for dinner."

"He always eats with his parents."

"We'll see." All the bantering disappeared from his voice and expression. "Don't let him break your heart. He's not worth it."

Hetta stood rooted to the spot, unable to believe Owen was genuinely worried that William might hurt her. William was as dependable as the sun in the morning and the moon at night. But Owen was ephemeral, here one moment and gone the next, serious until you started to take him seriously, and then he'd start joking. He would defend an ex-soldier or fight a bully, then deny any concern for anybody at all.

It was impossible to believe anything he said, because he was so full of contradictions. Sometimes she could almost believe he *did* like her. He could be very convincing, but that was the stock in trade of a flirt.

No man was going to break her heart, not even William. She would cherish her husband, be faithful and loyal, support him in whatever he wanted to do, but she wouldn't give him her heart. She had no intention of suffering the same fate as her mother.

*   *   *

Hetta had never been so excited. Mr. diViere had paid her for the use of her ranch. She finally had enough money to start rebuilding her home. She had managed to talk William into going with her to the ranch to discuss what materials to buy.

"Are you certain you want to spend all your money on this place?" William asked as they surveyed the charred ruin.

"I'd rather spend it to purchase stock, but I've got to have somewhere to live."

"You can live with Ida."

"I can't run my ranch from Ida's house."

"You can't run it from anywhere as long as you don't have any stock."

"I'll buy some when Mr. diViere pays me again in a few months."

"I don't see why you can't stay with Ida."

"Because I don't want to be a servant."

"Ida doesn't think of you like that. You're the only real friend she has."

It was impossible to explain to William that she couldn't live in someone else's house as an equal.

"I appreciate everything she's done for me, but I can't wait to have my own home again."

"Do you mean live out here?"

"Of course. What did you think I meant?"

"I thought you meant you needed someplace to stay when you didn't want to drive back that night." William had insisted they use a buggy. He disapproved of a woman riding a horse.

"This is my home."

"It won't be after we're married."

This was the first time he'd mentioned marriage in weeks. She felt herself grow tense.

This was what she'd been waiting for since he had

115

invited her to their first dance. It was practically the same as announcing their engagement. At least that was what women whispered to Hetta. She realized she'd fallen into believing what she'd been told. But did she really want to get married right now?

The mere fact that she would ask herself such a question shocked Hetta.

"We're not married yet." She avoided meeting his eyes. "Now tell me what I'll have to buy and how much it'll cost."

Hetta had always known William was a town person. Even in Texas, there was a difference between people who liked the comfort of living in a community and those who liked a little more breathing space. But she hadn't realized just how much of a difference it was until William started to criticize the way the two different parts of the house had been joined, the way it had been constructed, and the way it would have to be rebuilt. When he said it wouldn't be worth the cost for the tenth time, Hetta would have lost her temper if Tom Manly hadn't ridden up.

"What are you doing?" he asked her without getting down from his restless horse.

"Figuring out how much it'll cost to rebuild my house."

"Why would you want to do that?"

"So I can live in it."

"Mr. diViere is paying to use this place. He doesn't want anybody living out here."

Hetta had never had much contact with Tom Manly, but she'd always considered him a pleasant person. He wasn't acting that way now.

"He didn't say that when he asked to use the place," Hetta said. "I wouldn't have let him have it if he had."

"This is no place for a woman," Tom said.

"I lived here until my mother died." The house had burned the same week. She had been relieved to have somewhere to go—the death of her mother and the destruction of the house coming so close together had made her feel especially vulnerable—but she'd been gone too long now. She needed the feeling of roots. She needed her own home.

"There's rustlers about," Tom said.

"You can protect me."

"Mr. diViere doesn't keep cows here all the time," Tom said. "He only uses it as a base for cows he's selling."

"Maybe you shouldn't move out here," William said.

"Rustlers are after cows," Hetta said, exasperated. "They're not interested in carrying off American women. They've got plenty of their own."

Tom clearly didn't mean to give up, but she couldn't understand why he cared what she did. He stayed in town or camped out when he had cows. It wasn't as if he'd been using the house. Tom became so insistent, she was on the verge of demanding to know the real reason behind his objections when he suddenly looked up and cussed. She squinted against the sun to see who was riding down the dusty, weed-choked track toward her house.

Owen.

She hadn't told him she'd finally received her money. She didn't like the change in him whenever she mentioned Mr. diViere.

Besides, she'd been uncomfortable around Owen ever since he said he liked her for herself. She didn't know how to take the things he said. She'd felt sure of her ground when she thought he was nothing but an insincere flatterer. But if he really did like her for herself, if he thought she was interesting, then maybe she'd had everything wrong from the beginning.

It was a puzzle she couldn't figure out, so she gave up trying. He would leave soon, and none of it would matter. In any case, she was certain he'd agree with William and

Tom that she should stay with Ida. He would probably consider independence a character fault.

Still, for reasons she didn't understand, she smiled at him. He would probably interpret it as a welcome, which it was in a way. Besides, it was always a pleasure to look at him.

What was wrong with her? She had seen what that kind of thinking had done to her mother. But she wasn't in danger of falling in love with Owen. Neither was she in the habit of denying the truth. He was handsome. It was a pleasure to look at him, but it was the same kind of pleasure she got from looking at a pretty dress or a beautiful sunset or a handsome horse. There was nothing emotional about it.

"What are you doing here?" William demanded when Owen rode up.

"Tom promised to show me the ranch."

Hetta didn't know what to make of that, but she didn't trust Owen. He might seem to be amiably aimless, but she knew better.

"I know why Tom and I are here," Owen said. "What about you two?"

Hetta didn't feel she owed him an explanation, but she wanted him to know that diViere had lived up to his promise.

"Mr. diViere paid me for the use of my ranch. Tom and William have given me their opinions about rebuilding my house. You might as well give me yours."

Owen dismounted, walked over to the house, looked at it for about ten seconds before he turned and said, "Burn the rest of it and start over again."

That was just the kind of remark she'd expected him to make, but there was one important difference. He hadn't said she shouldn't rebuild.

"Do you think it's okay for me to live here?"

"Why not? It's your place."

"It's not safe for her to be out here by herself," William said.

"She won't be living out here *by herself* after you marry her," Owen said.

Hetta found herself wishing she had come alone. Owen was supporting her, but he was also embarrassing her.

"You don't think it would be too dangerous for me to live out here?" she asked him.

"Nobody's going to bother a lady like you."

Okay, that was laying it on a bit thick, but she didn't mind. "You don't think it's improper?"

"You ought to find out who's saying stuff like that," Owen said to William. "You've got to defend your future wife."

"This has nothing to do with whom I marry," Hetta said.

"Once a man puts his brand on a woman, he can't let anybody impugn her virtue," Owen said.

Hetta unclenched her fingers from the fist she longed to plant right in the middle of Owen's mouth. He'd said *brand* because he knew it would rile her. That was how her father had felt.

"I'm asking for myself," Hetta said, forcing herself to speak calmly, "without consideration of a husband, fiancé, or even a male relative."

"If you want to live here, I don't see why you shouldn't."

"Since I'm *not* going to burn down the rest of the house, how do you suggest I rebuild?"

"Ask your fiancé," Owen said. "I'll help when it comes to buying breeding stock."

She was going to kill him. If he called William her fiancé once more, she was going to take his gun and shoot him dead.

"Thank you. Since you have nothing helpful to say, you can go back to town."

"I came out to look at the ranch."

"I'm not selling."

"I know, but I want to look at it anyway."

She bit her lip to keep from responding. He was taunting her, testing her, plaguing her, and she didn't know why, out of all the women in Texas, he had to choose her.

"What did William say about the house?" Owen asked.

"Tell him," Hetta said to William.

She was only half listening until she realized Owen knew a lot about building a house. He not only disagreed with William about how much of the old structure could be saved, but also brought William around to his point of view.

"How do you know so much?" Hetta asked Owen.

"One of the men I worked with is an engineer."

She was beginning to suspect this group of people Owen had *worked with*. It seemed to contain every kind of expert one might need.

"You don't want to keep any damaged wood," Owen said, drawing her a little away from William and Manly.

"I can't afford a lot." There were few trees in their part of Texas. Wood for building houses had to be carted in at great expense.

"Then rebuild only what you can afford." He glanced toward William. "Your husband can pay for the rest after you get married."

Hetta looked daggers at him. "We'll live in what I can afford to build."

"You'll need more than that for all his children," Owen said. "I'm sure he'll father a dozen."

"He may, but I won't be the mother of all of them." Why did she let Owen goad her into making such crazy statements? "Do you think you can stop provoking me long enough to tell me what I need?"

"If you'll stop provoking *me*. This is such a waste. You're worth more."

"I'm content with the value," she said.

"Liar."

He said the word softly, but the impact on her was explosive. How dare he make such an accusation! He had no right to say such a thing. He didn't even have the right to think it. He wasn't her friend.

"You have no right—"

"I know, but you're still lying to yourself."

She wouldn't listen to him. From the first moment she'd met him, he'd done nothing but attempt to seduce her with his smile and charm. She didn't know why she even spoke to him.

Yes, she did. In spite of everything, she liked him. She didn't quite understand that, since they were always arguing, but it was true. Maybe that was the stock in trade of all philanderers. Even though you knew they were leading you into hell, you couldn't help enjoying the trip.

But even as she stewed in her indignation, a corner of her heart turned cold with the fear that she could never love William enough to marry him, that she'd just talked herself into liking him because she wanted it to be true, that maybe she couldn't love any man even if she wanted. She was flattered to have a man show a romantic interest in her, but had her desire for a solid and dependable husband caused her to confuse appreciation with love?

"I'm sorry you have so little faith in me—"

"It has nothing to do with faith. I deal in facts. And Ida's a *fact* you'd better face before you lose your insipid fiancé."

"I've told you over and over that William is not my fiancé. Besides, what could Ida possibly have to do with—"

Owen took her by the shoulders and spun her around. She saw a buggy coming down the track. Ida was driving.

121

Chapter Eleven

Hetta refused to acknowledge Owen's cynical smile when William hurried over to help Ida down. He was distrustful of everyone else because that's the kind of person he was. She smiled and walked over to greet Ida.

"Whatever possessed you to drive all the way out here? I'm surprised you didn't get lost."

"I did, twice," Ida said, managing to look and sound helpless and irate at the same time. "I'd still be wandering around if some child hadn't pointed me in the right direction."

"You shouldn't have driven out alone," William said. "There are bandits and rustlers running loose."

"Yet your fiancée plans to live out here," Owen pointed out.

"That was my decision," Hetta said, unable to stop herself from elbowing Owen in the ribs.

"You wouldn't be living out here alone if you were *my* fiancée," Owen said.

"We won't find out, will we?" she said with all the sweet insincerity she could muster.

"I thought you weren't telling anyone until William spoke to his parents," Ida said.

"Owen is just trying to see how much trouble he can cause."

"What's he doing here?"

"Helping me figure out what I need to rebuild my house."

"I'm sure his offer was well meant." Ida's expression said just the opposite.

"He knows as much as I do about building," William said.

Ida didn't appear to like having William disarm the barb she'd aimed at Owen. "I'm sorry to interrupt, but William's father has taken ill, and his mother needs him immediately."

"What's the matter with Pa?" William asked. He was an only child and close to his parents.

"Something about his stomach"—she waved her hands in a helpless kind of way—"I never was good with medicine."

"I can't leave Hetta."

"She'll come with us," Ida said. "Mr. Wheeler can give her his estimates this evening."

"I'll see that Miss Gwynne gets back to town safely," Owen said.

"I'd rather depend on Tom," William said.

Manly had retreated to the shade of a cottonwood to smoke a very thin cigar.

"She's coming back with us," Ida said.

Hetta was angry at the elder Mr. Tidwell for getting sick, at Mrs. Tidwell for being so demanding, at Ida for her clumsy attempts to throw her together with William and protect her from Owen, at Owen for just being Owen, and at herself for caring. "I don't need anybody to babysit me. Go with Ida," she said to William. "Owen can help me finish figuring up the lumber. I'll let you check over the figures. Tom Manly can see me safely back to town."

"I can't leave you alone with two unmarried men," Ida wailed.

"I was alone with three before you arrived."

"But William was here."

"There's no danger to me or my reputation," Hetta said to William. "Go to your mother."

William hesitated. "Are you sure you won't come back with us?"

"I'd only have to come out again. I'll be fine. I'm sure your mother will feel much better once she has you by her side."

"She has nobody but me and Pa."

I have no one at all, but I'm expected to carry on as though nothing was wrong. That was a selfish thought, and she was glad she hadn't said it aloud, but it was the way she felt.

William left with Ida, and Hetta turned back to Owen. "We'd better hurry up if Tom's going to show you around."

"I'm not letting you drive back to town alone," Owen said.

"Tom can ride with me."

"Particularly not with Tom."

Manly still lounged against the trunk of the cottonwood, but he was listening to their conversation.

"Do you remember when I said Laveau was a thief and a traitor?" Owen asked.

"I refuse to listen to—"

"He's a rustler, too. That's why I came to Pinto Junction. I followed his trail here. He's rustling cows up north, bringing them down here, and using your ranch as a holding area."

His accusations almost took her breath away.

"I don't for one minute believe—"

Owen whirled, his gun appearing in his hand with a suddenness that stunned Hetta. Tom was standing away from the cottonwood, his hand reaching for his gun.

"I'd drop my hand to my side if I were you," Owen said.

"I don't like you accusing Mr. diViere of stealing."

"I don't like that he's stealing," Owen said. "Why don't you work with me to put a stop to it?"

"I'm not working with you on anything."

"Is that why you don't want me to see the ranch?"

"You can see anything you want, but I ain't going to show you nothing."

Tom walked over to his horse, mounted up, and rode away without a word.

"I hope you're satisfied," Hetta said.

"I am, actually. Ida hauled off weak-willed William and I drove off mendacious Manly. I've protected the fair maiden from the dragons for another day."

"You're crazy, you know that?"

"You'll thank me when Laveau and Manly are exposed as rustlers."

"Tom can't be. It would be insanity to hold steers rustled from my neighbors on my ranch."

"I imagine those particular herds are taken to another staging point. Laveau is smarter than I gave him credit for."

"You never give up, do you?"

"Twenty-five people died because of his treason, including a girl so innocent she didn't know I was flirting with her. She was running back to her house, laughing because she was happy, when some son of a bitch shot her in the back. My cousin dragged me away, or I'd have attacked the soldiers with my bare hands. Laveau is responsible for that girl's death. *And so am I.*"

Hetta had wondered what drove him so hard, but

125

she'd never imagined it was anything so terrible.

"Do you know what she wanted me to tell her? Not that she was beautiful or her eyes reminded me of stars. She'd never seen a really pretty dress. She wanted to know what one was like. I killed her because I couldn't pass a pretty woman without trying to attract her attention."

"You shouldn't blame yourself for—"

He grabbed her shoulders so hard it was painful. "She wouldn't have left her house if it hadn't been for me. There's nobody I can blame except myself." He released her abruptly and backed away. "And Laveau," he added in a much softer voice. "I blame Laveau."

He turned and walked away with an angry, ground-swallowing stride. He stopped when he reached what was left of the old corral.

Finally she believed what he said about Laveau. The agony in his face and eyes couldn't be faked. Whatever else might be the truth, a girl had died, and Owen held himself and Laveau responsible.

Maybe he had coaxed the girl to go with him to the orchard, but even an innocent female could tell Owen was a flirt. The way his eyes lit up when he saw a woman, the smile that curved his lips, his insouciant attitude were there for everyone to see. Whatever his sins, he didn't hide them. He was honest, at least.

Except when he said he might like her for herself.

Still, maybe he *did* like her. His only friends in town were a broken-down cowboy and a crippled ex-soldier. Maybe he just wanted somebody to talk to, somebody he could be himself with. She often felt that way herself. Despite her friendship with Ida and her relationship with William, she never felt that she could be entirely herself with them. They expected something of her.

Owen didn't.

She wanted to put her hand on his shoulder and comfort him, but she knew men didn't like women to see their weaknesses. If only they knew women would like them better for knowing they were human, but men had this image they had to maintain. They had to prove that nothing could touch them, that they could survive anything life threw at them.

She wondered if Owen ever got tired of being strong. Did he ever want to bend his head, drop the sword, let someone else step forward to slay the dragon? She wondered where he had heard about dragons.

Owen turned and started back toward her. She didn't know whether to pretend to be looking at the house or to turn away. In the end she simply stood there, watching.

"We'd better finish up. I imagine you want to get back to town." He had himself under control now.

Thirty minutes later she said, "I have all I need to know. I've got to find somebody to do the work before I do anything else."

"Do you know anybody?" he asked as he walked with her to her buggy.

"I'll ask William."

"I wouldn't depend on him to answer more than a few questions before Ida comes to fetch him for his mama or papa."

She whirled on him. "I see nothing wrong with his attachment to his parents. I'd have been much happier if my parents had loved me as much."

"I was talking about his willingness to turn his back on his fiancée every time someone beckons."

"If you don't stop calling me that, I'm going to do something violent."

"I thought you wanted to be his fiancée."

"I do, but I don't want you talking about it all the time."

"Why do you want to marry such a spineless worm?"

She had to clench her teeth to keep from screaming

at him. "From now on, don't talk to me about William. Don't even mention his name."

He held out his hand to help her into the buggy. It would have been pointless for her to attempt to refuse.

"Look at anything on the ranch you want, but I'm not selling." She picked up the reins.

"I'm riding back to town, too."

"I'm perfectly capable of driving myself." She snapped the reins and clucked to the horse. "I'll see you at dinner."

She should have known it wouldn't be that easy to get rid of him. In less than a minute he was alongside her buggy.

"It would be a lot easier to talk if I were riding in the buggy with you."

"I don't want to talk to you."

"Of course you do. I'm a handsome flirt, remember? All women like to talk to men like me."

"Not me. I like boring clods."

"I'm trying to break you of the habit."

"Why? So you can take his place?"

She couldn't believe she'd said anything so ridiculous.

"I don't think you love him," Owen said. "I'm just trying to make you face the truth."

"Why? So I can live alone for the rest of my life? What's so terrible about marrying a man you don't love? Most men and women settle for something far short of the ideal. What's wrong with respect, companionship, trust?"

"There ought to be passion between a man and a woman. If not, they might as well remain single."

"A man can go anywhere he wants, do anything he wants, become anything he wants. If a woman wants to be respectable, she has to stay where she was born and live with family or work as a servant. You can't blame a woman if she decides to settle for something short of the man of her dreams."

"You're too good to settle for less."

"Why do you care whom I marry?"

"I don't. I just don't want it to be William."

Did he believe she had a great number of choices? Even in a city, she imagined a woman met only a few men she might marry. In a place like Pinto Junction, she was lucky to find even one. It was only the greatest luck when that candidate preferred her as well.

"You'll be gone soon, so what I do won't matter. I doubt you'll remember us for more than a day or two."

"I may stay."

"And do what, settle down and get married?"

"I might."

"Men like you never *settle down*. It's not in your blood. You can't resist trying to make every woman you meet fall in love with you."

"You don't really know what I'm like."

"Maybe not, but there's no point in trying to find out."

"We could be friends."

At least he had the grace to hesitate before making such an outrageous statement. "That's impossible."

"Why?"

"It just would be."

"Don't give me that. Either you have reasons, or you're afraid of me and don't want to admit it."

"What could I be afraid of?"

"Being seen with me, maybe having people think we're friends."

"We never could be friends—we're too different—but if we were, I wouldn't be afraid of being seen with you anywhere."

"I bet you wouldn't have dinner with me tonight because you think the community wouldn't approve."

"You haven't asked me to have dinner with you. Which would be absurd, since I have to cook dinner for Ida."

"You won't have to cook if she's not at home."

"You aren't the least bit interested in having dinner with me. You only want to prove you're right and I'm wrong."

"All I'm asking is that you have dinner with me if Ida's not home. It will save you hours of cooking and cleaning up. Why should you care why I ask?"

"Because women do care about things like reasons and appearances and feelings, and—you'd never understand. Men don't."

"Explain it to me over dinner."

"Ida will be home."

"If she's not."

"She will be."

"You're scared."

"I'll have dinner with you," she nearly shouted, "on one condition."

"What's that?"

"That you stop pretending you care what I do or what happens to me."

"You have to admit that a leisurely walk to the restaurant is much better than spending two hours over a hot stove," Owen said.

"It was shorter."

Hetta could have kicked herself for letting Owen goad her into having dinner with him just to prove a point. And she could have strangled Ida for not being at home. Things didn't get any better when the waitress came to take their order.

Pearly Norris had never been a pleasant woman during the best of times, but the loss of her husband in the war had made her bitter. "What are you doing here with him?" she asked when she came to the table.

"Having dinner," Hetta answered.

"Why aren't you cooking it like you ought to?"

"Miss Moody is out for the evening," Owen said. "I offered to buy Miss Gwynne dinner in appreciation of all the meals she's cooked for me."

"It's not proper for a lady to accept gifts from strange men," Pearly said, giving Hetta what could only be described as an evil eye. "Especially when she's as much as engaged to marry somebody else."

"William's father is ill," Hetta said. "He has to stay with his mother."

"Which is where you ought to be," Pearly said. "A woman's first duty is to her family."

"William's parents aren't my family," Hetta said. "I can't force myself on them."

"When did showing Christian charity get to be forcing?"

"I'm sure it hasn't," Owen said, "but it's not Christian charity to keep hungry people waiting for their dinner."

"We only serve *supper* here," Pearly snapped. "If you want dinner, you'll have to have Hetta cook it for you." She looked very pleased with her snide remark.

"I'd like the pork loin," Hetta said, determined to give Pearly no more opportunities to embarrass her, "with the baked apple and potatoes."

"I'll have the same," Owen said, "with coffee and pie for dessert. Don't you want some pie?" he asked Hetta.

"I don't know yet."

"Decide now," Pearly said. "There won't be any later."

"Then I'll have pie and coffee, too."

"I thought you'd want beef," Pearly said to Owen. "Yankees always do."

"He's from Virginia."

"That's close enough." With that she turned and walked off.

"I'm sorry," Hetta said, embarrassed.

"Forget her and enjoy yourself. It's got to be more pleasant to eat a meal when you know you don't have to clean up afterwards."

"You know it is, so stop crowing over your victory. It isn't gentlemanly of you."

"You said I wasn't a gentleman."

"No, you said it. I always thought you were."

A flirt, maybe something of a con man, definitely untrustworthy, but he had all the manners and thoughtfulness of a gentleman. He behaved perfectly all evening. He was charming without being flirtatious. He listened to her when she spoke, without making silly comments about her lips or eyes or hair. There were moments when she felt they might truly become friends, but she knew these days were just a momentary digression in their lives. Tomorrow or the day after, things would get back to normal.

Still, she couldn't help wishing they wouldn't. She wasn't fool enough to fall in love with Owen, but her life had been more fun since he'd arrived. It was enjoyable to have such a handsome, charming man pay attention to her.

She enjoyed the envious glances thrown her way, but wasn't so happy with the questioning and disapproving ones. This was her home. She hated to upset people.

"No Wheeler is a gentleman," Owen said. "All you have to do is ask my cousin's grandmother-in-law. What she says about us would curl your hair."

"I could use a little curl." Her ordinary brown hair had been as straight as a stick from birth. She'd always envied Ida's curls. "When can I meet her?"

"She refuses to leave her room until Laveau comes for her. He's her grandson, and she adores him."

"Mr. diViere is your cousin's wife's brother?"

He nodded.

"And you're planning to hang him."

"Do you think that will make things a little awkward?"

"You'll never be able to visit your cousin again."

"Oh, he wants to hang him, too."

Hetta wondered if madness was hereditary in the Wheeler family. Hoping to change the subject to something safe, she said, "Tell me about the kind of ranch you're looking for."

But at that moment, Ida Moody entered the restaurant accompanied by William Tidwell.

Chapter Twelve

"Well, well, what do we have here?" Owen said.

Ida turned slightly pale when she saw Hetta and Owen, nudged William, and headed straight for their table.

"Don't say a word," Hetta said.

"How can you be so blind?" Owen said.

"They're my friends. I trust them."

"I don't think the public does."

"What do you mean?"

"Look at the way people are staring."

"They're coming over here. They have nothing to hide."

"Fine. Make a doormat of yourself."

"I'm not a doormat."

"Then stand up to that woman."

That was exactly what Hetta intended to do. It was time William got his mother to announce their engagement. But no sooner had Hetta opened her mouth than she realized she wasn't about to allow herself to be put in that position. If William really wanted to marry her, he'd speak to his parents without her prodding. Owen was proof that a man could like her for herself. And even if he was often obnoxious, he had given her confidence in herself in a way no one else had. If William let her get away, that was his loss.

"I don't intend to fight over any man," she said to Owen. "If William wants to marry me, he'll have to go the rest of the way on his own."

"Atta girl," Owen said. "Now you're showing some sense."

Hetta wasn't so sure.

"What are you doing here with him?" Ida asked as soon as she reached the table.

"Why aren't you with your father?" Hetta asked William.

"Mrs. Tidwell is too upset to think of dinner," Ida said. "She said she didn't have the heart to sit down to the table knowing her poor husband couldn't eat anything."

"We'll take her a plate," William said. "I'll convince her to eat something later."

"I'm sure you will," Ida said. "Though I can understand how she must feel, seeing her beloved husband so ill."

Hetta knew Ida was being kind because of William, but she had an almost uncontrollable urge to remind Ida of some of the things she'd said about Mrs. Tidwell a few days earlier.

"We'll join you," Ida said. She sat down next to Owen, forcing William to sit next to her. "Hetta, you must be looking forward to eating a meal without having to cook it first."

"I don't know, since the food hasn't come yet, but I'm told I'm a better cook than Mr. Robinson."

"Who told you that?"

"I did," Owen said.

"I can't say that I agree," Ida said.

135

"I didn't ask you to."

Owen's gaze locked in on Ida in a way she clearly wasn't used to. "I am entitled to my opinion," she said.

"We're all entitled to make mistakes."

Ida wasn't good at verbal sparing. No one ever dared do it with her. She looked at William. Hetta could have told her she was on her own.

"We need to order quickly," Ida said. "I'm sure Mrs. Tidwell would be delighted to have you sit with her for a while," she told Hetta.

"Mama doesn't like anybody to sit with her when she's upset," William said. "She only puts up with Ida because she can talk business."

"Does she often talk business with Ida?" Owen asked.

"She says Ida's got too much money sitting idle. She thinks I ought to talk her into putting it to work."

"And what to you think?" Owen asked him.

"I told Ida the same thing weeks ago. I even thought up a plan, but she won't let me tell her about it."

He looked more animated than Hetta had seen him in weeks.

"I don't like business," Ida said. "I told him to talk to Hetta. She gets excited about running that ranch of hers."

"This is nothing like running a ranch," William said. "This takes brains, not brawn."

"And you think Hetta has only brawn?" Owen asked.

"She has both," William said. "I'm going to try to get her to sell that ranch so she can come in with Ida and me."

Pearly, her eyes alive with curiosity, chose that moment to come over to the table to get the new orders. Hetta had to swallow her response. William had never said anything to her about investing with him and Ida. Everybody knew she meant to rebuild her house and start ranching again.

She was also upset that he'd been talking to Ida about

an investment before mentioning it to her. She, not Ida, was going to be his wife. He should have talked to her first.

"How's your father's store doing?" Owen asked William as soon as Pearly left.

If there was anything William loved almost as much as his parents, it was the store. He could talk about it for hours.

"I don't consider business a proper subject for conversation during dinner," Ida said.

"If I'm going to buy a ranch around here, I would like to know about the local business climate," Owen said

"Then you ought to ask William's father or my uncle."

"William represents the future, and that's what I'm interested in."

"I don't approve of change."

"Why don't we ask William what he thinks?"

"There has to be a lot of change soon if we're going to survive," William said. "My father and Ida's uncle don't understand that."

They didn't leave the restaurant until more than an hour later. William had talked almost the entire time about reestablishing supply lines after the war, finding markets in the North for Texas beef, and the need to bring Reconstruction to an end.

"You did that intentionally," Hetta said to Owen. She had sent Ida back with William. She knew Mrs. Tidwell didn't like her very much, and she wasn't in any mood to put up with Mrs. Tidwell's whining self-pity. The woman was as weak and clinging at home as she was hard and miserly in the store.

"I wanted his opinion," Owen said. "He's going to be a rich man."

"You think he's that smart?"

"About business, but he doesn't know the first thing

about people. He didn't even notice Ida was listening to him."

"That surprised me."

"Ida's scared. I think she knows her uncle has made some serious miscalculations. She's reevaluating William."

"William will be happy to give her all the advice she wants."

"I doubt it would suit Ida's sense of propriety to put her affairs in the hands of a man who isn't her husband."

"If Ida married him, she would change him."

"She would try. But when she realized he didn't see or hear her half the time, she'd give up and enjoy her wealth."

"That's all beside the point. He still prefers me."

"He may prefer you, but he'll marry Ida. He doesn't have the will to resist his parents."

"What have his parents got to do with it?"

"Don't be naive. The Tidwells and Moodys are the only families with money in this town. One has a son, the other a daughter. What's more natural than that they should join forces, especially since things aren't going well for either of them now?"

"Are you sure about that?"

"Why do you think Uncle Fred has been wanting to see William so much recently? The rustling has hit everyone hard, and Reconstruction is taking business out of the hands of people who fought for the South and giving it to carpetbaggers."

"But Mr. diViere promised that wouldn't happen."

"Laveau couldn't stop it even if he wanted. Now, I'm tired of talking about William. Do you know what I like about Texas?"

"No." She never knew what was in his mind.

"The sky. Especially at night. It seems endless."

Hetta wasn't used to looking at the sky. Stars twinkled,

the moon shone, the night air was cool. There was nothing especially worth noticing.

"When I was working for my cousin, I used to lie in my bedroll at night and stare at the sky. It taught me to never put limits on myself. No matter when we think we've reached a boundary, there're always more places to see, more things to do. There's no end to it."

"But that's the sky."

"But it's like life, isn't it? There are no limits to what we might accomplish as long as we believe in ourselves."

"You never say anything serious unless you're trying to tell me something I don't want to hear."

"You've limited yourself by thinking the best you can do is William. He's a choice, not a limit."

"I don't understand you," she said. "If you were an ordinary man, I'd say you were trying to get me to marry you. But since I know—"

"You should never marry me. I'm the worst possible choice."

"Since you haven't asked me, I don't have that choice."

"I'll never get married."

"Why?"

She couldn't be sure—she couldn't see well in the dark—but something had penetrated the armor he kept around himself.

"Why settle for one woman when there's a whole world full of them."

"Is this part of your theory of not limiting yourself?"

"Why shouldn't it be?"

"Because there's no point in having growth without a foundation, morals, a set of beliefs that are fundamental. Without a foundation, anything you accomplish will fall apart."

"What a weighty conversation we're having for a moonlit night."

"We don't really know each other. What other kind of

conversation can we have without talking nonsense?"

"I guess we're lucky to be talking at all," he said, then started talking about the sky again.

Thoughts kept revolving in her mind. They didn't know each other. They didn't like each other. He'd probably disappear soon. She found herself wishing he wouldn't, and didn't understand because they really didn't have a thought in common. What was it about him that she would miss?

His belief in her. He thought more of her than she did of herself, more than anybody else had in her whole life. Yes, that's what she'd miss.

"I don't know why you don't ask Hetta to marry you," Ida said to William as they walked back to his home.

"Ma says I can't afford to get married now. I'll have to live at home unless I marry a rich wife."

Ida hadn't been friends with Hetta all their lives without realizing Hetta could never live in the same house as Mrs. Tidwell.

"Hetta's rebuilding her ranch house. You can live there."

William turned so quickly he almost knocked the covered plate Ida was carrying out of her hands. "I was hoping you could talk her into selling the ranch. Your uncle says Mr. diViere will buy it. Then she could invest with us."

Ida had always considered William quiet, boring, unattractive. She had come to realize he was quiet because he was thoughtful, boring because he was preoccupied with the store. He wasn't handsome, but he was tall and strong. He would make Hetta a good husband if he could overcome his dependence on his parents.

"But you could live on the ranch," she suggested.

"I don't know anything about ranching."

"Hetta knows plenty."

"I can't have my wife running a ranch," he said. "It wouldn't be proper."

"I don't think Hetta would like working in a store."

"My wife won't do that, either. I want her to be a lady like you."

Ida was flattered, but she didn't think Hetta would care for that kind of life.

"Ma doesn't like Hetta," William said.

"Why?" That did surprise Ida. Everybody liked Hetta.

"She says she's not good enough for me."

"No mother thinks any woman is good enough for her son."

"She says you are. I keep telling her that Hetta's as good as you because you've been best friends forever."

"Let me talk to your mother." Ida hoped she hadn't taken on too much. Trying to throw Hetta and William together was one thing. Acting as a mediator between her friend and Mrs. Tidwell was quite another.

"If you really want to help, talk Hetta into selling that ranch. Ranching is not a good way to make money. If I had the cash from the sale, I could double and triple it in a couple of years."

Ida felt her pulse quicken. "That fast? Are you sure?"

Her uncle had said business would rebound after the war, but the war had been over for more than a year and her income was still shrinking. Her world of wealth and privilege was threatening to collapse around her, and it was scaring her badly.

"Things don't look good right now, but they'll improve. Soon ranchers are going to figure out how to get their cattle to Northern markets. When that happens, places like Pinto Junction will be knee-deep in cash money. You watch Owen Wheeler. If he decides to buy a ranch here, it means he thinks he can turn a profit even with the rustlers."

They reached the Tidwell home, and the next several

minutes were spent listening to William's mother detail nearly every breath his father had taken in their absence and her certainty it would be his last.

"If I could just see William settled with a wife and children," she said to Ida when Ida had coaxed her to sit down and eat some dinner, "his father and I could die happy."

"Hasn't he mentioned Hetta Gwynne?" Ida asked.

"Why should he mention a maid?"

"Hetta isn't exactly a maid."

"She cooks and cleans, doesn't she?"

"Yes, but—"

"Then she's a maid. I want William to marry someone like you. He talks about you all the time. Just yesterday he was saying what he could do if he could get you to invest with him."

"But that's business, not—"

Mrs. Tidwell pushed aside her plate, grabbed Ida's hands, and pulled her forward.

"I know he likes you. All you'd have to do is let him know you're interested. I'd take care of the rest. I'd—"

"William doesn't want to marry me," Ida said, looking straight into Mrs. Tidwell's eyes. "He wants to marry Hetta."

Mrs. Tidwell looked at her as if she had lost her mind. "Nonsense."

"He's been seeing Hetta for almost a year."

"Has he asked her to marry him?"

"No, but—"

"There! That proves it. He's only seeing Hetta so he can get close to you. He's been in love with you since he was a little boy."

Ida was certain William wanted to marry Hetta, but the idea that a man would have harbored a secret love for her since boyhood thrilled her. Many men had admired her or schemed to get her money, but no one had ever loved her.

The whole time she was growing up, her mother had told her how beautiful she was, how men would fight over her, how she deserved only the most handsome and richest husband. But her one attempt to make a life for herself in San Antonio had been a failure. She'd fled back to Pinto Junction and the safety it offered.

In her flight she'd left behind her dream of romance. Now Mrs. Tidwell was offering it to her again.

But William was in love with Hetta. "You're wrong," Ida said.

"Don't tell me I don't know my own son. I know everything about him. He likes that Gwynne gal well enough, but it's you he's set his heart on. He's been happier than I've ever seen him since you've been talking with him."

"We talk about my investing some money with him."

"You ought to marry him and give him all your money. He'll make you a rich woman."

"William doesn't—"

"He adores you. He'd work his fingers to the bone for you."

"Hetta's my best friend. I couldn't—"

"It's you he wants. Has he never told you he dreams about you?"

"That would be most improper."

"But it's not improper for me to tell you. He says—"

"I don't want to know," Ida said as she jumped to her feet. "I have to be getting home. I don't like for Hetta to be in the house alone with Mr. Wheeler."

"That gal can take care of herself."

"If you would just talk to her, get to know her, you'd see—"

"She'll never be William's wife. You will be."

"Hetta's my best friend. I couldn't betray her even if I wanted to, which I don't."

"She'll never have him, so you might as well. He'll keep you rich. Remember that. He'll keep you rich."

Ida hurried home, wondering how the things she did with the best of intentions nearly always turned out to be mistakes. Her aunt had told her not to go to San Antonio. Her uncle had told her to stay out of Hetta and William's relationship. But if William liked her instead of Hetta . . .

She'd been jealous that Hetta had an admirer when she didn't. But William wanted to marry Hetta—she'd heard him say so with her own ears. Mrs. Tidwell didn't know her son as well as she thought.

But if she did?

Ida didn't let herself think about that. She liked William better than she'd expected, but she didn't love him. And even if she did, she couldn't betray Hetta. Not even to remain rich.

"Do you really think we'll catch any rustlers?" Myrl asked Owen.

"Maybe not. But I know we wouldn't have just sitting in the saloon."

Owen's patrols had been in operation for a week. There hadn't been any confirmed cases of rustling in that time, and already the ranchers were complaining about the waste of time and lack of sleep.

"I could use a drink right about now," Myrl said.

The country they rode over was a mixture of grassland and tangled brush. Small trees and bushes were gradually taking over where overgrazing had thinned the native curly mesquite, bluestem, grama, and wheat grasses. Owen used the cover these thickets provided to survey the open savannahs. Their horses' hooves made a swishing sound as they walked though the dry grass. The night was warm, the sky clear, and the moon very bright.

"I still don't see why you're so interested in clearing out the rustlers," Myrl said.

"I told you. I'm looking to buy a ranch."

"You don't look like a rancher. Don't act like one, either. You live in a rooming house, dress like a tenderfoot, gamble like a professional, and use a gun like you growed up with it."

"Chalk it up to my Virginia heritage."

Myrl didn't appear convinced. "Folks are suspicious of you. They say you don't look like a man who's likely to settle in a place like this."

"I can settle anywhere as long as I find what I want."

But did he know what he wanted?

He'd been running from his mother, his father, even himself, for so long he didn't know what he was running toward. He'd been looking over his shoulder, never ahead. He judged everything by the way it affected the demons that tormented him. He didn't know what he'd do if he ever managed to outdistance them.

He didn't know what he would do if he didn't.

How could he have reached the age of twenty-six and have no more idea what he wanted than he had when he was six? No, he had been more certain at six. He'd wanted food, safety, and parents he could depend on. About all he knew now was that he didn't want to be weak like his father or wanton like his mother.

"Ain't any females around here for you to marry, either," Myrl said.

"What about Ida?"

"She won't marry no stranger."

"There's Hetta."

"If she don't marry William, she'll end her days an old maid."

"She'd make some man a wonderful wife."

"She don't like men. Everybody was surprised when she took up with William."

"Probably because he doesn't resemble a man."

"Why don't you like that boy?"

145

"I don't dislike him. I just think he's boring." That wasn't exactly right. He thought William was too boring *for Hetta.*

"How could he run a mercantile and not be a bore?" Myrl asked.

Owen started to answer, but the smell of a mesquite fire quivered in his nostrils. "Smell that?" he asked Myrl in a loud whisper.

"Yeah. Somebody's cooking."

"No, somebody's branding steers."

Chapter Thirteen

"Keep under cover," Owen cautioned Myrl, "and don't make so much noise."

"How am I supposed to ride through this tangle of trees and vines without making any noise? I'm too old to be crawling through brush trying to get the jump on men young enough to be my sons."

"Then what the hell are you doing out here?"

"I didn't count on running into rustlers. I thought you'd be so grateful to me for keeping you company, you'd buy me a couple of beers."

Owen laughed silently. "You mean to tell me you were so desperate for a beer you took a chance on running into rustlers?"

"Sounds downright stupid when you say it that way."

"It's stupid any way you say it. Now, either you buck up and come with me or go back and wait."

Owen headed off through the brush. He wondered why no one had found any signs of rustling during the last week. Maybe the rustlers were lying low until they figured out his system. Only they ought to know by now he didn't have a *system*. Not even he knew what he was going to do until the last minute. Maybe the rustlers had gotten tired of waiting. After all, they had to keep stealing to pay for their drinking, gambling, and women.

Especially their women. Females never came cheap. His mother had cost two men everything they had.

Hetta wouldn't be like that. She was one woman who wasn't afraid of work. Or being on her own. He couldn't understand why she wanted to marry William. She wasn't in love with him. She probably thought they'd be comfortable together, be able to work together, have a peaceful life together, that William would never get close to her because he loved his store better than any human. There wouldn't be any sex. It would be the same as living with a good friend.

There was nothing really wrong with William, but Hetta was too warm-blooded, too vital, too alive to marry a man who would spend his life devoting his attention to his ledgers. William would never adjust to living on a ranch any more than Hetta would adjust to living in town.

It would be better for both of them if she let Ida steal him away.

The sound of voices broke in on his thoughts. He couldn't see the men. They were hidden in a dry wash, but the firelight reflected off nearby trees. Owen dismounted, ground-hitched his horse, and crept forward on foot to where three men were gathered around a fire. This was no fly-by-night operation. They were using a branding iron rather than a cinch ring or a running iron.

They were rustling mavericks. Once the animals were branded, it would be impossible to prove they were stolen.

He heard something crawling through the brush and turned as Myrl crept up next to him. "It's rustlers, all right," the old man said when he got a good look at what was going on.

"Tom Manly is one of them. Ever seen the other two?"

"They look like a couple of men I've seen with him in the saloon."

"How good are you with a gun?"

"Decent, but I'm hell on wheels with a rifle." He grinned as he pulled his rifle up next to him.

"Good. Stay here. If anybody tries to get away, put a bullet in him."

Owen worked his way through the tangled, thorny brush along the wash. He had nearly reached a spot on the bank opposite the men when he heard the ominous sound of a rattle.

No, several rattles.

He'd disturbed a nest of rattlesnakes. He couldn't see them, but he could hear their dry scales brushing against rocks as they slithered out of the nest to look for the enemy that had attacked them. Gathering his muscles, Owen threw himself into the wash . . . away from the snakes but almost into the middle of the rustlers.

All hell broke loose.

A bullet smashed into the sand next to Owen's face, throwing dust in his eyes. Half blinded, he fired in the direction of the gunfire. He heard additional gunfire as well as the pop of a rifle.

Then almost as quickly as it had started, the gunfire stopped. The only sound to break the stillness was of a horse galloping away.

"Owen, you okay?"

Myrl. Owen still couldn't see for the dust in his eyes. He was afraid to move in case the rustlers were still there.

"Yeah," Owen replied as he tried to clear his eyes. "Where is everybody?"

"Two of them are dead. One got away."

"Manly?"

"I aimed for his shoulder, but he moved."

Owen cleared the last of the dust from his eyes, to find himself looking into the eyes of a dead man he didn't know. Manly lay less than ten feet away, the branding iron on the ground next to him, a gun still in his hand.

"I promised you a rustler," Owen said, his tone harsh. "I keep my promises."

"I wish it hadn't been Manly," Myrl said.

"He was a rustler."

"People won't believe it. They'll be afraid diViere will go back on his promise to keep the army and Reconstruction away."

"Laveau has no control over the army. Reconstruction, either."

"Ain't nobody going to believe you. They're going to want your hide."

"What do you suggest I do, leave his carcass here for the coyotes?"

"Tell everybody Tom was helping us. You got one rustler and a branding iron to show somebody's rustling."

"And planning to do more." Owen dusted himself off. He bent down and picked up the branding iron. "Ever seen this brand before?" he asked Myrl.

"Nope."

He hadn't expected Myrl would. He was almost certain the calves would be held at some distant ranch—one very much like Hetta's—until the rustlers collected enough to drive them to Mexico.

He stared down at Manly's body. It went against the grain to pretend that a crook was innocent, but maybe this was the best way. If he exposed Manly as a rustler, Laveau would never come back to Pinto Junction. But with Manly dead, Laveau would have to return to hire a new foreman. That was when Owen would expose him for the murderous traitor he was.

"Help me load up the bodies," Owen said to Myrl. "And

think up a good reason for Manly to have joined us. Everybody knows he didn't leave town with us."

"Everybody was just about to give up," Hetta said to Owen.

"I knew it was only a matter of time before we caught somebody."

They were seated in the parlor. Hetta had been checking the list of materials for her house. She was worried she couldn't afford to purchase enough materials to repair the whole house and still have money to buy necessities like food. But she couldn't continue working for Ida. Every time she cooked a meal or made a bed, her servitude chafed a little more until she could hardly control her temper. Now that Manly was dead, there was nothing to keep her from moving back to the ranch.

"I was surprised Manly was riding with you," she said to Owen. "I thought you two didn't like each other. At least, now you know he had nothing to do with the rustling. That means Mr. diViere doesn't, either."

"I—"

"I know you don't like Mr. diViere, but he's been good to Pinto Junction."

"Would you be quiet long enough for me to get a word in!"

Hetta jerked back as if she'd been slapped. She hadn't realized she was talking so much or that she kept interrupting Owen. It was just that ever since they'd had dinner in the restaurant, she was uncomfortable around him.

From the tales Pearly was spreading, people were speculating that she was interested in Owen, that Ida had gone to get William so he could defend his woman. Just being called any man's woman was enough to make her spitting mad, but the injustice of the gossip made her so angry she had failed to control her tongue on at least two occasions. As one matron said, "You wouldn't be getting so upset if there weren't some truth in it."

Hetta figured people would change their minds in a few days, but in the meantime, she avoided Owen as much as possible. She should have stayed in her room, but the more she thought about her being punished while Owen had the run of the town, the angrier she got.

Ida usually acted as a barrier between them, but she had spent the afternoon with her uncle. Hetta knew that money was tight when Ida said she might leave the ROOMS TO LET sign up all the time.

"Sorry. What did you want to say?" Hetta asked Owen.

"Manly wasn't riding with me and Myrl. He was one of the rustlers. The leader, I imagine."

She set her work aside and directed her gaze full on Owen's face. "You told everybody he was riding with you."

"I know, but—"

"Why did you do that?"

"If you'll stop interrupting, I'll tell you."

He got out of his chair, stalked across the room, and bent over her. She stood. She wasn't about to be bullied just because she was a woman. She stared back at him, eye to eye, practically nose to nose. His eyes opened wide, and his breathing paused before resuming its normal pattern.

She'd never actually looked into Owen's eyes. Now, with their faces only inches apart, she could see that his eyes were such a dark blue that from a distance they almost looked black. For the first time, she realized his eyebrows were several shades darker than his hair, almost a light brown. His skin was fair, his nose straight, his lips full, his jaw prominent—even more so now as he clenched his teeth. All of which proved what she already knew.

Owen Wheeler was one devilishly handsome man.

With a major effort of willpower, Hetta turned away from Owen and walked to the window that faced the street. The heavy lace curtain made it difficult to see out, impossible to see in. "I promise I won't interrupt you again," she said, then turned to face him.

"Myrl said people in town wouldn't like me saying Manly was a rustler."

He paused, but Hetta didn't say anything.

"I was going to use his being a rustler to prove Laveau was behind the rustling, but Myrl says people won't believe me, that they'll be angry I'm trying to ruin the reputation of a man who's protected them from the Union army as well as from Reconstruction. You going to say anything?" he asked when Hetta nodded her agreement.

"Was that your only reason?" she asked.

"No. I realized if I exposed Laveau, he'd never come back."

"What makes you think *I* believe he's a rustler?"

"I just told you Myrl and I caught Manly and two of his friends trying to brand yearlings."

"Why did you tell me?"

"Because I wanted you to know the truth."

"Where is your proof?"

She didn't understand why he should tell everybody one story and her another. She didn't like the feeling in the pit of her stomach. She kept thinking about his blue eyes and firm lips. She couldn't ignore the impact of his presence in the room or its effect on her, no matter how hard she tried.

"Would you believe it if William had told you?"

She hesitated, but she had to be honest. She would have asked questions, but she'd have believed William. "Yes."

"Just like that? No questions?"

"I'd have asked questions, but I'd believe him."

"Why?"

"I've known him all my life. I trust him not to tell me lies."

"Do you trust everybody you've known all your life?"

"No."

"Then why William?"

"Because he wants to marry me."

"That's no reason. If he wanted to marry you enough, he'd lie his head off to get you to agree."

"William would never do that."

"But I, on the other hand, have no compunction about telling you any old lie that comes into my head. I lie for the fun of it, to make you distrust your friends, to turn you against anybody willy-nilly."

"I never said that."

"You've got all those preconceived notions about me," he said, advancing toward her. "I'm a stranger who dresses too well and flirts too much, so I must be lying about wanting to buy a ranch."

"I—"

"I've said Laveau—another stranger, I might point out—is a traitor and a rustler, and you think I must be lying. I tell you the truth about Manly, and you think I must be lying. I don't know what you think I've got to gain in all of this, but it must be mighty important to warrant all these lies." He was so angry, he had backed her halfway across the room. "Yet you'd believe William, a man who doesn't know anything about ranches or rustling, just because you've known him ever since you can remember."

"It's not just that."

"Then what is it?"

He had caught her between the sofa and the doorway.

"I'm not letting you sneak away until you give me an answer," he warned.

"I'm not sneaking anywhere," she replied, angrily trying to break his hold on her hand. "I'm not afraid of you."

"I don't want you to be afraid of me. I just want to know why you can't believe anything I say. And don't give me that tired old tale about your father."

He pulled her closer.

"What has William done to make you trust every word out of his mouth?"

He was much too close. She could practically feel the heat pouring off his body, sense the tension that filled him, smell the spices that told her he'd shaved recently. She didn't understand why everything should feel so much more intense, so much more real, than it did when she was with William. She didn't understand why she felt attracted and repelled at the same time, why she wanted to run away but was powerless to move. She didn't know why she wanted him to prove to be untrustworthy at the same time as she wanted him to be even more wonderful than he seemed. She didn't understand why he had the power to disturb her peace of mind in ways no one else could. She didn't understand anything about him or his effect on her. She just wished he'd go away and let her life get back to normal.

But no sooner had that thought raced through her mind than she knew it wasn't so. It might be stupid, it might even be dangerous, it certainly didn't make any sense, but she wanted him to stay.

"He hasn't done anything," she managed to say.

"He must have done something. He's practically inarticulate unless he's talking about his store. His looks are ordinary, and he has absolutely no idea what to do with a woman."

"And you do?"

He drew her so close their bodies brushed against each other. Her heart pounded so fiercely she couldn't understand why it wasn't painful. She told herself she wanted to pull away, to break his hold on her, leave the room, but her muscles wouldn't move.

"None better," he said, his voice suddenly losing its sharp edge and becoming soft, almost smoky with desire.

He pulled her closer until their bodies touched from breast to thigh. She gasped for breath, and her body turned rigid.

"Does William ever hold you so close you feel like your bodies are about to melt into one?"

Nobody had ever held her close. She put her hands on Owen's chest to push him away, but she wanted to keep her hands on his chest. She wanted to explore the muscles that moved so smoothly beneath his skin, which enabled his arms to hold her in an embrace with the power of iron.

"Has William told you that you have beautiful eyes? They're gray with flecks of silver."

Gray eyes weren't beautiful, flecked or not.

"They flash when you're angry," Owen said, his voice practically liquid heat, "but they're glowing now because you're feeling something quite different. Tell me what you're feeling."

She caught herself just in time to stop her treacherous tongue from telling him she liked being in his arms and wanted to hear more about her eyes.

"I'll bet William never did more than brush your hand. He's a fool. Anybody could tell him there's not a finer figure of a woman in Pinto Junction than you."

"Don't tell any more lies," she managed to say.

"I've heard more than one man say William doesn't deserve what he's getting. They say he'll never be able to warm you up."

"I don't want to be *warmed up*," she managed to say. "I want a husband who'll respect and admire me, one who'll treat me as an equal, who'll—"

"I'll bet he's never kissed you, either."

Only one word could describe the feeling that flooded her. Panic.

"I can tell from your eyes I'm right. Well, I can't let you go into marriage without knowing what it's like to be kissed by a real man at least once."

She struggled, not knowing what was coming, knowing instinctively it was dangerous. Then his lips touched hers, and she was lost.

No one had ever held her close, admired her, kissed her, but she was absolutely certain that if it had happened dozens of times, none of them could have compared to being in Owen's arms and being kissed by him in a way that made her feel she was the most desirable woman in the world, even the *only* woman in the world.

Unfamiliar feelings rushed through her, plunged into the depths of her heart, raced along every nerve in her body, penetrated her brain and paralyzed it, disoriented her so thoroughly she hardly knew where she was, consumed her strength to the point she was certain she couldn't stand without help. She did the only thing a sensible woman could do.

She kissed Owen back.

She was breaking every promise she'd ever made to herself, but she'd never felt so wonderful. She felt transformed. Re-created. Nothing about her life would ever be the same. She was standing in a man's embrace, her body shamelessly pressed against his, her arms around his neck—she didn't know when that had happened— kissing him with every fiber of her being.

No man had ever kissed her, but she had no difficulty responding to the pressure of his lips on hers. She wasn't the least bit confused when his tongue invaded her mouth. She tightened her hold on his neck, stood on tiptoe, and dived into the kiss with all the fervor and breathlessness of a woman afraid that something this wonderful might never happen to her again, something so wonderful she didn't hear the parlor door open.

Ida's outraged voice thundered in her ears.

"Henrietta Gwynne! What do you think you're doing?"

157

Chapter Fourteen

The sound of Ida's voice brought Hetta face to face with the enormity of what she'd done. She wanted to fling herself across the room as far from Owen as possible, to deny what had happened, to say it was just a trick of the imagination. She wanted to vanish so she'd never have to face Owen or Ida again. She wanted to say the sheer excitement of being held tightly by a man who thought gray eyes were beautiful was too much for her common sense.

But she knew that nothing could explain what she had done.

"I was kissing her," Owen said, as though they hadn't been caught doing anything more improper than sitting too close together.

"How could you betray William?" Ida demanded of Hetta.

"It was just a kiss," Owen said, "not a declaration of eternal devotion."

Ida ignored Owen. "William loves you more than his life," she said to Hetta.

"If he did, he'd have convinced his mother to announce our engagement before now," Hetta said.

She wished she could have swallowed her words. She'd never stated—or even thought to herself—that William might not love her. But as soon as the words were out of her mouth, she knew they were true. She didn't think William loved her the way she wanted, *needed*, to be loved. But there was one thing about which she was certain.

She didn't love William.

"How can you say that?" Ida demanded. "He loves his parents very much and doesn't want to hurt them."

"How would marrying Hetta hurt his parents?"

Owen's question appeared to throw Ida into some confusion.

"They think he's too young. And now his father is ill."

"Which seems to me the perfect time to get married. Then William would have someone to help out."

"I think it's time you looked for other lodgings."

"You're throwing me out?"

"This is ridiculous, Ida," Hetta said. "Owen's not in love with me, and I'm not in love with him."

"Then what were you doing?"

"As usual, he was trying to prove I was wrong and he was right."

"And how was kissing you supposed to do that?"

Hetta didn't know. Once Owen had taken her in his arms, she had lost the thread of any logic that could have made sense of what she was doing.

"I wanted to know why she would believe anything William told her while she questioned everything I said."

"Because William is a man of character. He's dependable, loyal, quiet, hardworking—"

"And dull," Owen said. "I wanted to see if a little excitement might make her change her mind."

"I don't want your kind of excitement in my home, Mr. Wheeler. Nor your methods of persuasion. Please remove yourself and your belongings immediately."

"Really, Ida, this is not necessary. It was only foolishness," Hetta said.

"It certainly was, but I don't intend to discuss it until Mr. Wheeler has left the room."

"If you mean to discuss me, I'd rather stay."

Hetta was mortified to be the cause of such a brouhaha. She hated it when people got angry at each other. She had rarely argued with her father, and never with Ida. When they'd disagreed, she'd held her tongue for the sake of harmony.

But today was too much.

"You were wrong to throw Owen out," she said as soon as Owen had left the room.

"I find him kissing you, a woman engaged to another man," Ida said in amazement, "and you say I shouldn't throw him out?"

"William said he was going to talk to his mother about us, but he never actually said he wanted to marry me."

"So you thought you'd round up a second fiancé in case the first one didn't come up to scratch."

"Don't be ridiculous!"

"You dare call me ridiculous?" Ida's voice rose higher in pitch.

"I do if you think I'm trying to get Owen to marry me. He can't help trying to convince every woman he meets that he's the object of her dreams."

"Then why isn't he flirting with me? I'm prettier."

Hetta tried not to show how much that hurt. Why did everything have to come down to how pretty a woman was? "I suppose because I told him that first night what I thought of men like him. He's been trying to change my mind ever since."

"So you thought if he was handing out free kisses, you might as well have a few. No harm in that, especially not when your fiancé was hard at work trying to come up with new ways to make more money for the two of you."

"It's your money he's using, not mine."

"It could be your money if you'd sell the ranch."

"Did he ask you to tell me that?"

"No, but I know he wants it."

"What if I want him to sell the store?"

"He loves that store."

"I love my ranch."

"Whatever you do, you can't be seen with Owen again. I can hardly believe the gossip I've been hearing since you had dinner with him last week."

"I had dinner with you and William as well. What kind of gossip could there be?"

"People are wondering why you would be seen with him when you're engaged to William."

"Why didn't they wonder why *you* were with William?"

"They know I was sitting with his mother."

"I thought maybe you were sitting with William instead. You haven't talked about anyone else."

"If I was sitting with him, it was to talk about you, tell him how wonderful you are, encourage him to get his mother to announce the engagement."

Hetta didn't want to appear ungrateful, but hearing that made her furious. If William didn't think enough of her to talk to his parents without Ida's urging, she didn't want to marry him. "I wish you'd stay out of this, Ida. William will talk to his mother when he's ready. I don't want you bringing him home so we can be together."

"Don't worry. I won't. You always seem to be with Owen."

"I won't be since you've thrown him out."

"I don't see how you can prefer him to William."

"I don't."

"He had his hands on you the first day he got here. Now I find you in his arms, kissing him like you were a ...a ..."

"Like a what, Ida? And you'd better be careful what word you choose."

"I can't believe you'd do that to William. He's so sweet and innocent and trusting."

"Are you sure you're not more worried about William than about me?"

"How can you say that? We've been friends all our lives. I'd do anything to help you find a husband."

"Because you don't think I can find one on my own."

"It never hurts to have someone else—"

"—point out things William might have missed."

"It's better than trying to make him jealous by carrying on with Owen Wheeler."

"I'm not carrying on with him!"

"It sure looked like carrying on to me. It's indecent, and I won't have it in my house."

Something snapped inside Hetta. "I don't want to be responsible for bringing ill repute on your house. I'll move out immediately."

"No! You can't do that! I didn't mean—"

"You think my behavior was indecent. Who knows when I might do it again? I might be immoral like my father and start letting Owen kiss me any time the mood strikes. You've never said anything, but I always knew you were afraid I might be like my father."

"I don't. You know I didn't trust Owen from the start."

"It doesn't make any difference, Ida. I'd better go. I'm so stubborn, I'm liable to kiss Owen just to prove that neither you nor William can stop me. You wouldn't be happy, and quite frankly, I wouldn't feel comfortable here anymore."

"You can't go. What would I do without you?"

"Why don't you ask William?"

*   *   *

"You can't stay in this hotel," Owen said to Hetta. "It's not a decent place."

"It's better than bedding down in the street."

"You ought to go back to Ida's. She won't know what to do without you."

"She'll have to learn."

Hetta had packed only enough for the night. She'd collect the rest of her things when she moved to the ranch. She wasn't sure the log room was habitable, but she couldn't afford to spend money staying in a hotel.

Ida had tried to talk her out of leaving. She insisted she hadn't meant to accuse Hetta of wanting to let Owen kiss her. She admitted it was probably impossible to have a man such as Owen kiss you and not feel compelled to kiss him back. She'd even promised to let Owen move back, but Hetta knew it was time she got back to her ranch. Now that she'd finally made the break, she was relieved.

It had taken someone like Owen to shake her out of her old ways of thinking, to force her to admit she didn't love William, to prove to her there should be a lot more between a man and a woman than dependability. His touch, his kiss, had shown her there was an entire world of feelings and sensations she didn't know anything about.

"Then why did you leave?"

"That's none of your business."

"Since I was the cause of it, I think it is."

"Okay, I left because I didn't feel she trusted me anymore. She accused me of using you to try to make William jealous."

"Why not? His mama's got him tied to her apron strings with some big, strong knots."

"But she does love him. She depends on him in the store."

"Have it your way, but you can't stay in this hotel."

"It's the only one in town."

"Which means the rustlers stay here as well as the preachers."

"Will you be serious?"

"I am. I'm worried about you."

That was too much. From the moment he'd laid eyes on her, he'd bedeviled her, annoyed her, tried to drive a wedge between her and William, generally done nearly everything in his power to make her life miserable.

"Why don't you let me worry about myself? I was doing pretty well before you got here."

"No, you weren't. You let yourself get bamboozled into doing all the work around the ranch so your pa could waste his time and money on sinful women. You got yourself practically engaged to a mama's boy who can't see beyond his ledgers. Your house burned down. Your ranch went to ruin. You let Laveau hoodwink you. Then you ended up playing nursemaid to a selfish woman masquerading as your best friend. I'd say you were in a desperate situation."

Hetta nearly choked. "Please go away and leave me alone."

"I can't. I'm in the room next to yours."

She should have expected something like that. It was a small hotel.

"If you won't go back to Ida's house, let me sleep in the room with you. To protect you," he added.

It took Hetta a moment to realize he was serious. She had thought she knew something about men, but she was learning he had a kind of brass, a sense of self-worth, that went beyond anything she'd thought possible.

For a moment she envied him that freedom. She'd spent so much of her life being made acutely aware of her limitations. She had struggled to acknowledge them and accept them, even grow comfortable with them.

Then Owen had ruined it all.

She had refused to believe him when he said she shouldn't marry William, but now she had an annoying suspicion he was right. Then he'd made things worse by saying he liked her and wanted to be her friend, to watch out for her. Nobody did that.

Then he'd kissed her. You wouldn't have thought that would be such a problem. A man forces himself on you. You either burst into tears and drive him away with great, sloppy, hiccupping sobs, or you slap him as hard as you can and stalk out of the room. Instead, showing a complete lack of presence of mind as well as no sense of proper conduct, she had kissed him back. And that had destroyed her hopes for the future, because she'd realized there was much more to the relationship between a man and a woman than William would ever understand.

"I can't let you sleep in my room, even for protection. There'd be no end to the gossip."

"Don't you value your life more than gossip?"

"I'm tempted to say yes, but sometimes gossip can destroy a life. Since I don't believe my life is in danger, I'm declining your generous offer. I find it amazing you would want to protect me."

"I feel responsible for what happened. If I hadn't been showing off—"

She smiled at him, surprised and pleased that he seemed genuinely sorry. "You can't meet any woman without trying to prove she can't resist you. Well, you made your point. You're a tremendously handsome man, charming, entertaining, and virile. I also believe there's a sweet, kind person somewhere inside you. Maybe you'll find the right woman to bring it out, someone so beautiful you'll consider yourself plain in comparison with her. You'll never find what you're looking for here. Now it's late and I'm tired. I'll lock the door and put a chair against it. You ought to do the same. After catching the rustlers, you might be in more danger than I am."

"Does that mean you believe Manly was rustling?"

She sighed in defeat. "I guess I always did. I just didn't want to. Let's not talk about it anymore. Tomorrow I'm going out to my ranch, and you're going back to San Antonio."

"What if I don't?"

"All you want from Pinto Junction is Mr. diViere, and he's not here. Make it easier on everybody. Go look for him somewhere else."

Hetta entered her room and leaned against the door as she closed and locked it, but she didn't move for a long time. She felt like crying, and she knew exactly why. It was that damned kiss. Until then she'd considered herself lucky to have a man like William. Now she knew William was a mirage.

He might think he was in love with her, but he really wasn't or he would have spoken to his parents long ago. He would have visited her without Ida having to arrange *accidental* meetings. He'd have held her hand, put his arms around her, kissed her the way Owen had.

But William had done none of this, and Owen Wheeler had come along. Pushing his way into her life, challenging her opinions, knocking down her prejudices, forcing her to question her own experiences. But it was the kiss that had changed her completely. She no longer wanted the quiet, safe life a man like William offered. Despite the danger, the almost certain heartache, she wanted the excitement a man like Owen Wheeler could offer.

Tears ran down her cheeks because she knew she would never have it.

She cursed Owen Wheeler. She was just someone who had caught his interest for the short time he would be in Pinto Junction. He would go away and forget he'd ever known her. She would never forget him. He would haunt her for the rest of her life.

She pushed herself away from the door, put her suitcase on a chair, and dropped onto the bed. She fell back and put her hands over her eyes. Was she going to end up like her mother, loving some man so much he could treat her like dirt and she'd still worship the ground he walked on?

Tears rolled down her cheeks. Tears of regret that she'd lost her chance for happiness. Not the delirious, heaven-storming kind implied in Owen's kiss, but the dependable, lifelong commitment. Now she was faced with wanting the impossible and knowing she couldn't have it.

She cursed Owen.

She never wanted to set eyes on him again.

Owen stared at his untouched beer.

"You going to drink that?" Myrl asked.

"Doesn't look like it," Ben Logan said. "I've finished two, you've had three, and he's still staring at his first."

"If you're not going to drink it—"

Owen pushed the beer over to Myrl.

"What's eating you?" Ben asked. "No use pretending it's nothing. You don't drink, you refused to play cards, you hardly open your mouth. If you didn't look so healthy, I'd say you were taking sick."

"Woman trouble," Myrl said. "He just got kicked out of Ida's house. Must have been some dustup behind that."

"He's not interested in Ida," Ben said.

"You saying it was over Hetta?" Myrl asked.

"Why don't you ask Owen?"

"You going to tell us?" Myrl asked.

"Don't feel like it," Owen said.

"Your privilege," Ben said, "but would it have anything to do with the fact that Ida and William just went past, Ida bending his ear something awful?"

"Where are they headed?" Owen asked.

"Can't say."

"Git up and find out," Myrl said. "Even with that gimpy leg, you can move faster than I can."

"They went into the hotel," Ben said when he came back. "Do you know what they want?"

"Yes," Owen said getting up from the table, "and I mean to see they don't get it."

Chapter Fifteen

Owen had been feeling guilty ever since Hetta closed her door in his face. He wondered if his compulsive need to prove his attractiveness came from being ignored by his parents most of his life. He felt a kinship with Hetta, yet he couldn't conquer the impulse to prove he was irresistible to her. He could tell himself he'd done it because William wasn't worthy to be her husband, but he had no reason to care who Hetta married.

Yet he couldn't stop himself from practically running down the boardwalk to the hotel and up the stairs inside. He reached the landing in time to see Ida and William standing outside the door to Hetta's room. He kept hidden from their view and listened.

"What are you doing here?" Hetta asked from inside the room.

"I couldn't let you stay here," Ida said. "When you wouldn't listen to me, I asked William to see if he could talk some sense into you."

"I'm not sensible, or I wouldn't have let Owen kiss me."

"That was Owen's fault."

"I forgive you," William said. "Men like Owen Wheeler prey on guileless young women who can't resist them."

"Ida resisted him," Hetta said, "but I didn't. You can't put all the blame on him. Maybe I'm like my father after all."

"Don't be ridiculous," Ida said.

"Your irreproachable behavior is one of the reasons I admire you so much," William said.

"Maybe I'm tired of being irreproachable. Maybe I want to be wild."

"You're too sweet and kind to ever do anything like that."

"What if I wanted you to tell me I was beautiful, that you couldn't do without me?"

Owen nearly laughed at the bewildered expression on William's face.

"I know what's really upset you," William said. "Ida's convinced me I've been wrong to wait so long to talk to my parents. I'll speak to them as soon as my father's better."

"I told you he was just waiting for the right time," Ida said.

"Maybe he waited too long."

Yes! Owen said to himself. *Stand up to him. Tell him what a fool he's been. Throw him out.*

"You're upset. You can't mean that," Ida said.

"I am upset, but I know something is wrong."

"It's Owen Wheeler," William said. "A man like him can turn any woman's head."

"Why? Are women so weak they can't know their own minds?"

"All women are weak," William said. "That's why they need husbands to guide them when they go astray."

*Much more of this and Hetta won't need any encour-
agement from me to throw you out.*

"Women are just as capable as men of knowing their
own minds," Hetta said. "But I'm not at all sure of my
own mind right now. I need time to think, to figure out
how I feel."

"That's why it's important for you to come back home,"
Ida said.

"Meanwhile, she can keep cooking and cleaning,"
Owen said, stepping forward, "waiting for William to
work up the courage to talk to his parents."

"What are you doing here?" William asked.

"Spying," Ida said.

"I'm staying here. My room is next to Hetta's."

"I insist you go back home with Ida," William said to
Hetta.

Hetta stepped out into the hall. "Couldn't you stay
away a little longer?" she asked Owen.

"This is a hotel. Anybody staying here has a right to
use the hall any time."

"Do you want me to throw him out?" William asked.

Owen felt his temper begin to rise. "I was in the wrong
before, but I'm not this time."

"Don't try to make him leave," Ida begged. "He might
shoot you."

"For Pete's sake, Ida, people don't go around shooting
off guns just because they wear one," Hetta said.

"He's shot two men already."

"Only because nobody in Pinto Junction had the guts."

"I can't believe you're defending him."

"I'm not. I'm just using common sense."

"Then you'd better marry William and let him do your
thinking for you."

The look Hetta gave Ida brought pure joy to Owen's
heart.

"If my life has to be ruined, I want to know I wasn't

171

spineless enough to let somebody else ruin it for me."

"I don't understand you," William said.

"I don't understand myself," Hetta said, "but I will. Now both of you go home. I'm tired. I want to go to bed."

"But it's not safe here," William said.

"I'll see that no harm comes to her," Owen said.

"I wouldn't trust you to guard a dead cow, much less a woman I hold dear," William said.

"Normally you'd be wise to feel like that," Owen said, "but I've already caused her enough trouble."

"I don't want you to have anything to do with her," Ida said.

"That's up to Hetta."

"Go home, both of you. I'll lock my door."

Ida and William looked at Owen. He knew they wanted him to disappear. He started to stand his ground but changed his mind.

"I left a beer unattended," he said. "Make sure the chair isn't on a rug," he said to Hetta. "It'll slip."

"You would know something like that," Ida said.

Owen was pleased that Hetta had had the courage to stand up to Ida and William. It had to be hard, living in a small town with no money and no way to make a living, to turn down the help of the two richest, most influential young people in town. He'd always known she was stubborn and opinionated, but now he knew she had courage. He wasn't too fond of stubborn and opinionated— he had too much of that in his own makeup—but he had great respect for courage.

He stopped when he reached the street. Pinto Junction wasn't really much of a town. He could see practically every building by turning in a circle. He couldn't imagine what would make anyone want to stay, but there must be something that kept Hetta and William here, brought Ida back from San Antonio, Ben Logan home from the war.

Maybe he'd try to figure out what they saw that he didn't. It would also give him a better chance of understanding Hetta. The more he learned about her, the more he wanted to know.

"I won't let you come," Hetta said to Owen. "I didn't need your help last night, and I don't need it today."

"It's crazy to think you can live out at your ranch by yourself. Besides, you need a foreman."

"I'll hire one."

"You'll do it faster and better with my help."

They'd been arguing like this for the last hour as they rode their horses toward her ranch. Hetta had opened her door to find Myrl sleeping outside. When she'd asked him why he didn't sleep in his own bed, he had told her he was giving Owen a chance to get some rest. Apparently, Owen had stood guard at her door during the night. She was so stunned, she didn't point out to Myrl that sleeping on the job probably wasn't what Owen had in mind. It had never occurred to her that he would care that much. William hadn't offered to stand guard at her door.

Her mood had been almost conciliatory when Owen caught up with her just as she was leaving town. She'd conceded that she might have misjudged his character. His telling her she'd pegged him right did nothing to change her mind. He was a much nicer man than she'd given him credit for.

But her temper had become frayed when he listened to her every argument, even agreed with some, and still didn't change his mind about going out to the ranch with her. She had tried to control her tongue—how could she be rude to a man who had stood guard outside her door all night?—but there was only so much a woman could endure, and Owen Wheeler always went over the limit.

173

"You can't stay out there by yourself. Even old stick-in-the-mud agrees with me there."

"Don't refer to William by that name."

"Would you rather I call him mama's boy?"

"I would prefer that you not speak of him at all."

"At last we're in agreement on something. Since I'll be at the ranch with you, I might as well be your foreman. Some people say bandits have stolen all your cows. Others say nobody rustles your cows. I think it's time we found out the truth."

"I can do that without your help."

"If you ran into rustlers, they'd kill you. I'm sure you know how to use a gun, but women tend to feel that if they could just *talk* to a rustler, they could get him to have a change of heart. Meanwhile, the rustler has pulled his gun, shot you, and made off with the cows."

"You don't have a very good opinion of women, do you?"

"I love women."

"No, you don't. They're the enemy you have to conquer. I don't think you even *like* women."

"I've had firsthand knowledge of how treacherous they can be."

"I don't know what your mother did, but she didn't cause two dozen men to die. Nor did that girl who haunts you still."

"You can't know."

"You can't take all the responsibility for her death. You encouraged her to go into the orchard, but she went because she wanted to spend some time talking to a handsome and exciting man. Then there was the soldier who was so green or frightened he shot a woman. It wouldn't surprise me if he, too, remembers it and agonizes over it."

"You're not going to make me feel less responsible."

"Maybe not, but you'll get no sympathy from me if you

174

continue to blame yourself. Or your mother. You've got looks, intelligence, and the will to get on with your life. Forget Laveau. Go back to San Antonio, or Virginia, and build a life for yourself."

"Are you going to take your own advice?"

"Yes."

"Does that mean you won't marry William?"

"It means I've decided I want a lot more out of marriage. If I don't believe I can get it, I won't marry William even if it means I never marry anyone."

"Good. Don't sell yourself short."

"I'm not selling myself short. I know exactly what I look like."

"But you don't know what you look like to others."

She turned in her saddle. She'd given up trying to please anybody and was riding astride. "If you dare to tell me I'm beautiful, I'll shoot you with your own gun."

"Someday you'll have sons and daughters who will think you're beautiful. Will you shoot them?"

"Don't be absurd."

"I'm not. People will see different things in you because they aren't looking for the same thing. You said William's looks didn't matter to you because you thought his character was admirable. Isn't that true?"

"Yes, but that didn't blind me to what he looks like."

"After a while it would. You'd see in his face all the kindness, the love, the gentleness, the thoughtfulness you valued. You'd know he made you feel loved, cherished, even beautiful. You would grow to love those features so much that one day they *would* be beautiful in your eyes."

Hetta didn't know what had taught Owen that truth, or even if he believed what he said, but it made her feel more kindly toward him. He'd given her hope of being beautiful in a way that time could never change.

But she'd never thought that even William could love her enough to make her plain face beautiful to him.

"Okay, I'll stop thinking I'm plain if you'll try to stop taking all the blame for that girl's death. You've got to try," she said when she could see him begin to withdraw, "or you'll never find anyone to love you like you want to be loved."

"I don't want anybody to love me."

"Everybody wants to be loved. It's human nature."

"Some men can do without love as long as they have enough money and sex. The stuff you women want—togetherness, faithfulness, children—all that is a noose around those fellows' necks."

She wanted to disagree, but she'd seen too many men who were only too anxious to turn their backs on women who loved them, children who wanted little more than to see their faces before going to sleep at night. Most women were willing to settle for a man who was faithful, kind, and dependable. She'd had that and had thrown it way. Maybe she didn't want any man at all.

But that wasn't right, either. She would welcome a family and responsibility. Her husband just had to be the right man. She had found excitement and sexual attraction in Owen, but she'd never marry a man like him. She had found dependability and faithfulness in William, but he didn't make her pulses thunder the way they did when Owen kissed her. Why couldn't she want one or the other? Why did she have to have both?

She felt emotionally bruised and sore. Maybe after a few weeks on the ranch she'd have a better idea of what she wanted. In the meantime, she and Owen had to hammer out some ground rules.

"It'll be a tight squeeze," Owen said as they rode into what had been the ranch yard.

"You're not sleeping in the house."

"There's not enough to call it a house."

"Why don't you see if you can find Manly's old camp?

Once you've settled on a bed ground, I'll meet you there when I need to."

Owen looked at her with a grin full of irony. And challenge. "You're not going to banish me to some thorn patch, force me to cook over a campfire, and ignore me for days at a time."

"I didn't ask you to come."

"Let's get something clear right from the start. We work out the rules together. I'm sleeping where I can see and hear you. We'll eat at the same time. When you ride out, I'll ride out."

"Doesn't look like you've left me many rules to make."

"Oh, there's lots more. You get to decide whether I can kiss you again. I'd like to do that, maybe more than once."

Hetta found that her breaths weren't coming nearly as easily as they ought. "There will be no kissing. You just did that to prove something."

"What was I proving?"

"See, you can't even remember."

"Oh, yes, I can. What about touching?"

"No touching either."

"I'm not sure it can be avoided, like when we're working together, maybe riding the same horse—"

"I never ride double!"

"—when we're sitting next to each other in front of a fire in the evenings. We could also go for walks if you were of a mind. People usually hold hands when they walk. I could lift you across streams—"

"The washes are dry in the summer."

"—help you climb up on a rock or into a tree to escape a rattlesnake."

"I shoot rattlesnakes."

"Suppose there's rustlers about and you don't want them to know you're watching."

"Then I'll let the snake bite you. That ought to finish off the poor critter."

"You think I'm poison?"

"Not to me. You're not even a bad rash."

"What am I?"

"I haven't decided. I thought you were awful at first, but there are some occasional flashes of decency."

"Tell me and I'll get rid of them immediately."

"You're making fun of me again."

"I'm just trying to get you into a good mood before we discuss the last rule."

"What's that?"

"Where we sleep. You see, I figure—"

"I'll go back to the hotel before I let you share my bedroll," she said, interrupting him.

"I wasn't going to suggest that, but if you're considering it—"

"I'm not."

She was a fool to think he would want to sleep with her. Her father had told her no man would bother a gal as homely as she was.

"It did cross my mind, but if you're dead set against it—"

"I am."

"—I guess I'll have to go with my second plan."

She wanted to know why he was teasing and friendly again. She needed to know because his behavior was having an unexpected effect on her. She was having difficulty remembering he was the enemy, that she shouldn't believe anything he said. Lately he'd been acting like a friend, but he must want something. She didn't know what that might be, but she couldn't imagine he was doing this out of pure friendship or even guilt.

"What's your second plan?"

They had reached the ruins of the ranch house. The roof on the kitchen and porch had been completely destroyed. Charred beams arched across the parlor—if the lowly room could justify such a name—and the bedroom. But the log room hadn't been damaged. She could use it as her bedroom.

"Were you planning for me to sleep outside?" he asked.

"Why not?"

"I did more than enough of that during the war."

"There's only room for one person."

Owen dismounted and walked over to the house. He walked straight through the ruins to the log room. That irritated Hetta. That was her room. By entering it he invaded her privacy. Not that she thought he concerned himself much with privacy. But this wasn't like being in the army and working with a group of men. Just her staying at the ranch with him would be enough to start everyone in Pinto Junction speculating. She had to convince him to set up his own camp, or she might as well announce she was a loose woman.

Owen emerged from the cabin. "There's room enough for two. We can share."

Chapter Sixteen

"I can't sleep in the same room with you."

"Do you think I'm going to attack you?"

"No, but what would everybody think? I don't have to ask. I know. They'd think I was a strumpet."

"Are you?"

"Or course not!"

"Then don't pay them any attention."

She slid out of the saddle. "Maybe you're used to ignoring what people think, but I'm not."

"I developed a thick skin. You can probably guess some of the things people said about my mother."

Damn him! Here she was preparing to scold him for being indifferent to her reputation, and he had to throw something like that at her. It hadn't been easy having a father like hers, but she was certain it was nothing compared to having a mother like his. Men and women were held to different standards when it came to immoral conduct.

"My reputation will be in shreds overnight."

"I can't protect you if I can't see you."

"I don't need your protection."

"You can't be sure."

"I am."

"I'm not, and since I'm bigger than you, what I say goes."

Damn him! Why did he think he could get away with things just because he was big? "If you touch me, I'll shoot you."

"I plan to touch you a lot. I might even kiss you if I can talk you into it, but I won't dishonor you."

"If you sleep in the same room with me, nobody will believe that."

"We'll worry about that when the time comes. For now, let's figure out what we're going to do first. When does your lumber arrive?"

"I don't know. William said Reconstruction has made it nearly impossible to predict schedules."

"Then we might as well see if you have enough cows to worry about."

As he began to unbuckle the straps that held his bed-roll and bulging saddlebags, she realized she was about to make a decision that would change her life forever. If she stayed here with Owen, she could never go back to town. But that was merely symbolic. The important changes, the changes in her mind and heart, had already made it impossible for her to go back to being the person she used to be. Where she lived was incidental. It didn't matter that she would have to sleep on the floor, cook over an open fire, wash wherever she could. The only thing that *really* mattered was that she had decided what to do with the rest of her life. What unnerved her was the possibility that Owen might have something to do with that decision.

"Want me to help you unpack?" Owen asked.

She was startled out of her distraction. Owen had taken everything from his horse and stowed it in the log room.

She hurried to loosen the straps and carry her bags into the log room. It looked smaller than she remembered, much too small to give her the space she needed to feel safely separated from Owen. But that really had nothing to do with the size of the room. She hadn't felt safely separated from Owen in Ida's house, and they had occupied rooms on different floors. They'd passed the point where awareness of each other had anything to do with space. She couldn't separate herself from him or the ideas and emotions he'd planted in her head and heart.

Nobody else had ever made her feel special. That applied to William as well. She hadn't done anything to make him feel special, either. She wondered why.

Because she'd never expected feeling special to be part of a relationship.

Owen had changed all that. From the very first evening, he'd talked to her, argued with her, even shouted at her, but their awareness of each other was almost tangible. He hadn't been stupid enough to tell her she was beautiful, but he'd convinced her that a man who truly loved her would grow to love her features, to think she was beautiful because of the love he felt for her, because of who she was.

No one would ever feel that way about her, but Owen had made it impossible for her to settle for less.

"You're not exactly rich," Owen said to Hetta, "but you've got a fair amount of stock."

They were riding back after a day spent counting cattle.

"I don't understand it. Where did they come from?"

"Well, mama cows get together with daddy cows—I won't explain exactly how because I don't want to offend

GET UP TO 4 FREE BOOKS!

You can have the best romance delivered to your door for less than what you'd pay in a bookstore or online. Sign up for one of our book clubs today, and we'll send you **FREE* BOOKS** just for trying it out...**with no obligation to buy, ever!**

HISTORICAL ROMANCE BOOK CLUB

Travel from the Scottish Highlands to the American West, the decadent ballrooms of Regency England to Viking ships. Your shipments will include authors such as CONNIE MASON, CASSIE EDWARDS, LYNSAY SANDS, LEIGH GREENWOOD, and many, many more.

LOVE SPELL BOOK CLUB

Bring a little magic into your life with the romances of Love Spell—fun contemporaries, paranormals, time-travels, futuristics, and more. Your shipments will include authors such as KATIE MACALISTER, SUSAN GRANT, NINA BANGS, SANDRA HILL, and more.

As a book club member you also receive the following special benefits:

- **30% OFF** all orders through our website & telecenter!
  (Plus, you still get 1 book FREE for every 5 books you buy!)

- **Exclusive access** to special discounts!

- **Convenient** home delivery and **10 days to return any books you don't want to keep.**

There is no minimum number of books to buy, and you may cancel membership at any time. See back to sign up!

*Please include $2.00 for shipping and handling.

YES! ☐

Sign me up for the **Historical Romance Book Club** and send my TWO FREE BOOKS! If I choose to stay in the club, I will pay only $8.50* each month, a savings of $5.48!

YES! ☐

Sign me up for the **Love Spell Book Club** and send my TWO FREE BOOKS! If I choose to stay in the club, I will pay only $8.50* each month, a savings of $5.48!

NAME: _____

ADDRESS: _____

_____

TELEPHONE: _____

E-MAIL: _____

☐ **I WANT TO PAY BY CREDIT CARD.**

☐ VISA ☐ MasterCard. ☐ DISCOVER

ACCOUNT #: _____

EXPIRATION DATE: _____

SIGNATURE: _____

Send this card along with $2.00 shipping & handling for each club you wish to join, to:

**Romance Book Clubs
1 Mechanic Street
Norwalk, CT 06850-3431**

Or fax (must include credit card information!) to: 610.995.9274. You can also sign up online at www.dorchesterpub.com.

*Plus $2.00 for shipping. Offer open to residents of the U.S. and Canada only. Canadian residents please call 1.800.481.9191 for pricing information. If under 18, a parent or guardian must sign. Terms, prices and conditions subject to change. Subscription subject to acceptance. Dorchester Publishing reserves the right to reject any order or cancel any subscription.

your innocence—but pretty soon you have bunches of little cows."

"Will you stop talking to me like I'm an idiot?"

She pretended to be angry, but her smile peeped through. Owen didn't know whether she was smiling because she had hundreds of cows instead of dozens, or because she was back in the saddle on her own land. He didn't care as long as she was happy.

"Where did you learn so much about cows?" she asked.

"My cousin's ranch. For every hundred cows you have, he has a thousand."

She pummeled him with questions about himself, Virginia, the war, his cousin, even the Randolphs. She'd particularly enjoyed the stories about Hen and Monty Randolph, the twins who were seasoned warriors at seventeen.

"When we took the herd to St. Louis, it was almost like the war again."

"How?"

"Some farmers didn't want us in Missouri. They thought we would either destroy their crops or infect their cattle with tick fever. Others tried to steal our herd or demanded a cut in exchange for letting us through. We had a few gun battles along the way, but we didn't give up a single steer. I'm not sure we'd have made it without those Randolph twins. They were hell on wheels. I was scared of them myself."

She laughed. "You attacked three men by yourself, and you're trying to tell me you were afraid of teenagers?"

"Always be a little bit afraid," he said. "It keeps you careful."

They were riding across one of the grassy savannahs that punctuated the dense tangle of trees and thorny plants where longhorns hid during the day. Owen couldn't understand why he was starting to like this part of Texas. It was as flat as a saucer and hotter than any battlefield he'd ever been on. There were no hills to offer a view, nothing to see if there had been. No greens so rich and deep they looked almost blue. No meadows covered in a carpet of yellow or blue flowers so thick you could hardly see the plants that bore them. No singing birds or buzzing bees. It was a quiet land, slumbering, waiting, stunted.

Yet there was something here that drew him. Maybe it was the openness. After growing up in the mountains where every vista was blocked by another mountain, the ability to ride for miles in a straight line fascinated him. It was wild, free, untamed, and much to his surprise, he was finding he liked that very much.

He couldn't explain his fascination with Hetta, either. When she made it plain she held no liking for his sort of man, he'd determined to make her eat her words. A totally unexpected change had occurred in him. He wanted to be different so she would be wrong.

He'd never meddled with engaged women, so why had he broken the pattern with Hetta? Maybe his fascination with her was a result of their common background; they'd both grown up with one parent lacking moral fiber, the other lacking the backbone to do anything about it. Great! A friendship whose only basis was two badly scarred lives. Well, friendships had been founded on less.

"You know I can't pay you to work for me," Hetta said.

"We can barter, I give you something you want, you give me something I want."

She eyed him much like a bird would a snake crawling up a tree toward its nest. "And just what might that be?"

"Right now I'd settle for you smiling a few times a day and not distrusting every word I say."

"After that?"

"See, that's exactly what I mean. You think I'm going

to ask for something you don't want to give."

She seemed a little embarrassed, but she didn't back down.

"Let's just say I'm helping you so I have a reason to stay in Pinto Junction a little longer."

"Why would you want to do that?"

"Because sooner or later, Laveau will come back. I mean to be here when he does."

"Do you really plan to hang him?"

"I know you don't think he's guilty—"

"I believe he betrayed your troop, but he betrayed them to the Union. If you hang him, they'll hang you."

"That ought to make you happy."

"I may not agree with you about a lot of things, but I don't want to see you hanged."

"I wonder if William feels that way."

"Why do you care what he thinks?"

"I don't, but there he is at the ranch house." He pointed ahead. "My guess is he's come to take you back to town."

Owen didn't want Hetta to leave the ranch. They'd been more at ease with each other today than at any other time. He felt that they might become real friends. He wanted her to like him. To approve of him, too.

Right now he wanted to separate her from William Tidwell forever. William wasn't a bad person. He was just the wrong man for Hetta. He would try to turn her into the *grande dame* of Pinto Junction. That would be fine for Ida Moody, but it would suffocate Hetta. Still, he'd had his say, played his cards. It was time for Hetta to make her decision.

But he would stay close by, just to make sure William didn't take unfair advantage. Hetta had a kind heart. He wouldn't allow anybody to take advantage of her.

Hetta was surprised by how irritated she was at William's appearance. She wondered whether his coming was Ida's idea or his.

"I don't want you to say anything," she said to Owen. "Let me do the talking."

"Believe it or not, that's exactly what I'd intended to do. I'll unsaddle our horses, give them a rubdown, and then find a good place to picket them for the night."

Hetta dismounted and watched Owen lead their horses away. Somehow she felt deserted. Maybe it was because she and Owen were in agreement for a change, and she knew she and William wouldn't be.

She looked at him now, pacing back and forth next to his buggy. He hadn't changed one iota from what he'd always been, but it was as if she was seeing him for the first time. No, William hadn't changed. She'd been the one to change. Owen had made her realize she wasn't in love with William, only in love with the idea of being married.

No, that wasn't right. She'd been afraid no one would ever want to marry her. So when the most eligible man in Pinto Junction showed an interest in her, she'd been anxious to believe she was in love. Looking back, she could see that having lost her father to the war, her mother to a broken heart, her cows to rustlers, and her home to fire had probably played a big part in her feelings so.

Then Owen had kissed her. It was like waking up, coming out of a trance, a dream that didn't exist. Now she saw things as they really were.

"I expected to find you at the hotel," William said when she reached him.

No "hello," no lover's greeting, not even a smile. In fact, he looked hot, peeved, and out of temper.

"Come out of the sun. You must be burning up," she said.

"When I found you'd left the hotel, I was certain you'd gone back to Ida's. I didn't realize you had come out here until she came by the store."

He hadn't cared enough to find out for himself. He'd only left his precious store when Ida told him she wasn't at home. It was as though he couldn't think of her without Ida being there to prod him, to remind him of her existence. *Not* the signs of a man in love.

"I told you I was coming out here."

"I didn't believe you. I certainly had no idea you would come out here with him." He pointed to Owen, who was unsaddling the horses under a shed a few feet from the house.

"I tried to make him stay in town, but he insisted I needed protection."

"And who's going to protect you from him?"

"I don't need protection from Owen."

William paced agitatedly. "What if he tries to kiss you again?"

"He won't."

"Ida said he forced you."

"The next time I kiss her, it'll be because she wants me to."

Neither of them had heard Owen approach.

"I need my curry comb," he said, taking the item out of his saddlebags. "Horses love it." He sauntered off as if he didn't know he'd dropped a bomb into their conversation.

"What does he know about cows?"

"A lot, as it turns out."

"You still can't stay here with him."

"Somebody's got to help me. I can't work this place by myself."

"You shouldn't be trying. You don't even have a place to live," William said, gesturing to the house. "It's nothing but a burned-out ruin."

"I can live in the log room. The fire didn't touch it."

"And where is he going to sleep?"

She hoped she didn't blush. "Why do you want to know? Don't you trust me?"

"Of course I do," he said, visibly ruffled by her question, "but I don't trust him."

"Did you know he stood guard outside my hotel room door last night?"

William looked shaken. She'd have given a lot to know whether he was sorry he hadn't thought of it or embarrassed someone else had.

"I suppose he's the one who told you."

"No, Myrl told me. He was watching early this morning so Owen could get some sleep. I nearly stumbled over him."

"Do you think I should have stood guard?" William was clearly defensive.

"No. I just told you about Owen so you'd stop thinking I wouldn't be safe. He's much more of a gentleman than I would expect of a man who's so attractive and charming."

"I wondered how long it would take you to notice that."

He seemed so petulant, she couldn't help laughing, even though she knew it was the one thing she shouldn't do. "I'm not blind, William."

"I suppose you're acting cold to me and moving out of town because I'm not charming and attractive."

Now she'd hurt his feelings. She felt a spurt of impatience, but she'd been spurned far too often not to understand how much it hurt. She put her hand on his arm. "Neither one of us is charming. You're not handsome and I'm not beautiful. You're an honest, dependable, intelligent, fine man. Once you give your word, I know you'll keep it. You'll make a wonderful husband and father, a pillar of the community, a man others will look up to and respect."

"They won't respect me if my wife never does anything I want."

That was the first time he'd actually referred to her as his wife. It was also the first time she wished he hadn't. "We're not engaged, William. You haven't even talked to your parents."

"Things are too unsettled. Business is bad. With Pa being in such poor health, I don't want to upset them."

"Then it's a good time for me to turn my attention to my ranch. That will allow you to devote all your time and attention to your parents and the store. Once everything is better and you know what you want—"

"I know what I want. I want—"

She put her hand over his mouth. "Don't say it. For the next few weeks, don't even think about me."

"Don't you want to marry me?"

She wondered if he was upset because she might be rejecting him or just having trouble coping with a new idea. "It's the wrong time for both of us. You need to devote your attention to your work and getting your father well. I need to brand my calves and try to rebuild my ranch."

"I'm finished with the horses," Owen said. The sound of his voice, his sudden appearance, broke the tension between her and William. For once she was relieved to have Owen around.

"I guess we have to starting thinking about fixing supper," she said.

"You're not coming into town to eat?" William asked.

"It's too far to ride there and back every time I get hungry."

"But you don't have a kitchen."

"We didn't have kitchens during the war," Owen said, "but we managed to muddle through."

"Hetta doesn't have to *muddle through*," William said angrily. "I was planning to take her to dinner."

"That's sweet of you," Hetta said, "but you can't do it every night."

"I hope not," Owen said. "I'm a terrible cook. I'm counting on her keeping me from starving."

"I don't imagine you've ever starved," William said with something close to a sneer.

"We fought the war over the same territory for so long, there wasn't anything left, even for civilians. Some people were reduced to eating vermin. Thousands of soldiers went for weeks with nothing but rotten meat and wormy bread sold to the army by merchants who got rich off the misery of their fellow countrymen. It made some of us sick, but we ate it because we had nothing else."

Owen had rarely spoken of the privations and hardships of war. It horrified her to think that fellow Southerners would make fortunes out of the misery of others.

"I'm sorry," William said, stiff and angry, "but that has nothing to do with Hetta. She's coming with me."

"William, I've just told you I can't."

"I won't have my fiancée eating her supper sitting on the ground with a cowboy nobody knows."

Hetta was so surprised, she almost waited too long to respond. "I'm not your fiancée. You've never asked me to marry you."

"You know I want to."

"If you wanted to marry her so much, why haven't you asked her before now?" Owen asked.

"That's none of your business," William said.

"Hetta is my friend, and friends look out for each other."

"Owen, you don't have to—"

"It's not right for a man to call a woman his fiancée when he hasn't gotten his parents' permission to marry her."

"I don't have to have my parents' permission."

"Then why haven't you asked her?"

"Owen, for God's sake—"

"You've taken her for granted like you would an employee."

"Owen, will you stop it!"

"I've never taken her for granted."

"Then prove it. Grab your clothes and move out here with her."

"We're going to live in town," William said. "Hetta's going to sell the ranch."

Chapter Seventeen

Hetta had never made a secret of the fact that she intended to rebuild her ranch as soon as she was able or
that she intended to work it herself. But she and William
had never talked about it. Now that she thought about it,
she realized they'd hardly talked about anything. Until
Owen came along and upset everything, she'd been too
insecure, too afraid something might cause William to
change his mind, to talk about the future.

Looking back on it now, she was ashamed of herself.
She'd always thought she was independent, so strong-
willed that she could go it alone if she must. All the while
she was just as terrified as her mother of being deserted
by a man.

"I told you I wasn't going to sell my ranch," she said
to William.

"I thought you said it just so you could feel independent. I was sure you'd stay with Ida. You had a perfectly
good home."

"I had a *job*, William. Ida's house was never my home. This is."

"But you can't ride back and forth every day."

"Of course she can't," Owen said. "She'll soon have babies to take care of."

"Why don't you stay out of this?" William said to Owen.

"I'm hungry. You two aren't close to settling this, so let me see if I can help. You expect Hetta to move into town, live in your mother's house, work with you in the store. Is that right?"

Having Owen draw the picture with such stark clarity was a shock to Hetta. She had no more intention of living in the same house with Mrs. Tidwell than, she was certain, Mrs. Tidwell had of allowing her to move in.

"It doesn't make sense to buy a second house," William said. "There's plenty of room for us and children."

"But Hetta wants to live on the ranch and rebuild her herd. She expects you to ride into town each day while she stays here."

"I can't live this far from the store," William said, apparently surprised anyone would make the suggestion.

"I'll see about rounding up some firewood," Owen said to Hetta. "Shouldn't take me more than a few minutes."

Hetta knew Owen was leaving to give her an opportunity to send William away.

"You can't really mean to live out here," William said.

"Your mother would never allow me to set foot in her house."

"Of course she would."

"Well, it's not something we have to settle now. We both have a lot to do before we start making plans for the future."

"But I thought—"

"Apparently we were both wrong. Now you'd better get back to the store. I know you don't like to leave it for long."

"You refuse to go back with me?"

"It has nothing to do with refusing to go back with you. I want to live in my own house."

"It sounds like a refusal to me." He looked sullen, stubborn. "What am I going to tell Ida?"

"Why should you tell her anything?"

"I promised I'd bring you back with me."

Hetta felt anger fly all over her. What made him think he could make such a promise? "You forget Ida thought I was trying to seduce Owen behind your back."

"She thought it was the other way around."

"Either way, I couldn't stay in her house after that."

"She didn't—"

"If Ida has something to say to me, let her say it herself. As for Owen, I'm as safe now as I was then."

"We all know you're only a momentary diversion he'll forget when the first pretty female comes along."

Hetta had told herself the same thing, but it sounded brutal coming from the man she'd hoped to marry. "William, get back in your buggy and leave before you say something I'll find truly unforgivable."

William looked taken aback, but Hetta didn't feel she could explain. "Tell Ida not to worry about me. I hope your father is feeling better." She turned and left before he had a chance to say another word.

"Don't ever go near that man if he has a gun," Owen said, coming from around the side of the log room. "If he handles it as badly as he handles words, somebody will get killed."

"It's all your fault," Hetta burst out. "Everything was fine before you got here."

"Nothing was fine. I just helped you realize it. Now stop trying to get mad at me and decide what you're going to cook. I really am hungry."

*   *   *

"I never cooked over an open fire before," Hetta said to Owen.

"You did remarkably well for a beginner."

She'd been trying to get angry at him all evening, but she'd finally given up. She did cook, but he'd gathered the wood, built the fire, carried the water, and washed up afterwards.

Hetta tried to account for her feeling of peace and well-being but couldn't. Here she was virtually camping out on a broken-down ranch ten miles from town, with no house to stay in, no riding stock, no chickens or cow. She'd given up the best job she was ever likely to have, moved out of the most luxurious house she'd ever lived in, maybe lost her best friend, and had effectively broken off with the only man who'd ever wanted to marry her. She didn't want Mr. diViere to keep using her ranch, but she didn't have enough money to rebuild her ranch house or enough cows to survive on her own. And she was facing the prospect of having to work with the most irritating, troublesome man she'd ever met.

Yet she liked him. She wasn't exactly sure she was safe from him, but she was certain she was safe from anyone else. She laughed silently. He'd protected her right out of a job, a home, and a potential husband. Yet a weight had been lifted from her shoulders. She'd been freed from restrictions that had been threatening to choke the life out of her. She'd forgotten what it was like to have no employer to please, no would-be husband to fret over. She was free.

Free to be a disastrous failure. Yet even that prospect didn't dispel the feeling that things just might be right in her world.

There was much more to like about Owen than looks and manners. Except for his preoccupation with hanging Mr. diViere, he had a strong sense of right and the courage to back it up with his guns, his fists, or his brains. He also had an odd habit of gravitating toward people whom society would consider of marginal value—Myrl, Ben Logan, and herself—of lifting them up by the mere fact of his friendship.

"We need more horses if we're going to brand calves," Owen said, dropping to the ground next to her.

"Manly was using our horses," she said. "They're probably running loose around here somewhere."

"What do you say to hiring Ben and Myrl?"

"How are we going to get any work done using a cripple and a drunk?"

Owen leaned back until he lay flat on the ground. He looked up at the moon rather than at her. "You have too little faith in people."

"I didn't say they wouldn't *want* to help. I just don't understand how they can."

"Myrl can take care of the fire and the branding irons. Ben is still capable of working from a saddle."

"I don't have any money to pay them."

"I do."

"I can't take money from you."

"You'll pay me back."

"How?"

"When you sell your first steers."

"There aren't enough for a drive to Mexico."

"We'll drive them north to my cousin so he can take them to St. Louis. How many steers do you think we saw today—ones big enough to go to market, I mean?"

"About seventy-five."

"They'll bring more than two thousand dollars. Not a fortune, but enough to keep you going for another year."

Hetta had trouble getting her breath. Two thousand dollars seemed like a fortune to her.

"We'll probably find a few more when we start branding."

Hetta pulled in her burgeoning dreams of a thriving

and expanding ranch. "I still can't take your money."

"You don't have any other choice." He chewed on a piece of grass. "Look at that sky. Isn't it beautiful?"

She didn't understand this man at all. He ought to be in some big city spending his money on beautiful women. Yet he was planning to spend at least six months working his butt off *and* paying to support her ranch. Instead of discussing financial terms like a sensible businessman, he wanted her to look at the sky with him.

"It's like a limitless canopy, dotted with twinkling stars, a sliver of a moon, and just enough wispy clouds to keep it from being the same all over. Have you ever studied the stars?"

"No."

"I never had until the war. We used to ride across country at night. It was fun to see if I could guide by the stars."

"Could you?"

"I never got the chance. Cade always had maps. He's got no sense of adventure."

"Wasn't it better to have maps when you had enemy soldiers all around you?"

Owen sat up, turned to face her. "Haven't you ever wanted to go someplace you've never been, not make any plans, just see what would happen?"

She couldn't categorize his expression. He looked a little like a man who thinks there's something better just over the next hill. But stronger than that was the feeling he knew that things probably weren't any better over that next hill, but he wanted to go anyway because not taking a chance would make him feel cheated.

Yet the Owen Wheeler she was coming to know was a rational man who could size up a situation, see what needed to be done, and do it, a man who didn't like to fail.

"I've had more than enough uncertainty in my life,"

she said. "I'd be happy if things could stay the same forever."

"Is that why you were going to marry William?"

The question shocked her because she had a terrible feeling he'd put his finger on a truth she'd never suspected.

"No."

She thought he would argue, but he lay back down, resumed chewing on the blade of grass, and stared at the sky. Everything about his actions said he knew she was lying.

"I never knew when Papa would come home or what he would do," she said. "It never seemed to matter to him that the stock had to be doctored, the animals fed, wood gathered, things fixed. Sometimes he didn't even bother getting out of bed. He never talked to Mama and me about anything that mattered."

The words flowed from her without the anger she'd harbored for years.

"It never seemed to matter to him that there might not be enough food, that we had no money. He assumed we'd get by somehow. I tried to get my mother to talk to him. She wouldn't, so I tried. At first he ignored me, but once, when I was bigger, he grabbed me. I think he was drunk that day. He said I wasn't ever to question him again or he wouldn't come home anymore."

She remembered the shocked, fearful, and accusing looks from her mother.

"Mama blamed me when he didn't come home for a long time after that. She said she'd make me go live with her sister in Alabama if I ever questioned him again. She said she couldn't live without Papa. I guess she was right. She died within a year after we heard he got killed. I don't think he hated us. He just didn't care one way or the other."

She guessed that was the hardest part, knowing that no matter what she did, she didn't matter.

"He used to say it was a real disappointment I wasn't pretty. Then he could have taken me to the saloons. Men would have bought him drinks just to talk to me. But men didn't like plain, strong, hardworking women. They wanted pretty women who knew how to have fun. He said I was too plain and dull for any man to marry, that I'd better latch on to the first man who showed any interest in me. I associated looks and charm with all the things my father did that hurt us. You've got so much of both, I was sure you had to be awful. Getting into a gunfight that first day didn't help, either."

"Would it have been better if I'd let them humiliate Ben?"

"I grew up so sure no man would ever marry me, I decided I didn't want to get married. I couldn't believe it when William started to pay attention to me. I thought I was the luckiest girl in the world."

"It's a shame one of your father's bulls didn't gore him to death before you were two."

"Everybody liked him."

"He should have had Cade for a cousin."

"I thought you liked him."

"Only half the time. But whenever I start to get angry with him, I remind myself he saved my life." Owen sat up and got to his feet. "It's about time we got ready for bed. I told Ben and Myrl to be here by daybreak."

"You hired them without talking to me first?"

"A good foreman always hires the crew. It leaves the boss free to think of the important stuff."

"And just what *important stuff* am I supposed to be thinking about?"

He held his hands out to her. She reached up and he pulled her to her feet. She ended up uncomfortably close to him.

"You could stop thinking I'm as terrible as your father."

"I don't. I—"

"You can stop thinking William only wanted to marry you because you were as plain, dull, and boring as he is." He pulled her even closer. "And you can forget every word your father said. You have beautiful eyes. You should always look straight at people. You'd mesmerize them. And you have beautiful hair," he said as he twisted some of it around his finger. "It's long and thick, a rich coffee brown. You should wear it down more often."

"It gets in the way."

"You also have a spectacular figure. I don't blame those cowboys for looking at you with lust in their eyes. I get a little warm myself."

Hetta felt a tremor shoot through her body, but she warned herself not to be foolish. William had never lusted after her body.

"And your skin is flawless. I don't know how you managed to grow up in the brutal Texas sun and not be as brown as a walnut."

"I *am* as brown as a walnut."

"You're a luscious almond color. Ida has moles."

"She calls them beauty spots."

"She'll have hairs growing out of them before she's forty, but your skin will still be perfect."

"I'd better take myself to bed. Much more of your talk and I'll never set foot outside again."

"That would be a shame. You should always be seen in sunlight."

She didn't fully understand it yet, but she hadn't felt so good, so optimistic, in months. Considering how bad things looked, she was either a great fool, or coming back to the ranch was the absolute right thing to do. She hoped she wasn't a fool.

"I'll see about the horses," Owen said. Then he

shocked her by kissing her on the top of her head. "Your father was a fool."

He turned and walked away. Didn't grin at her, chuck her under the chin, or do anything cute and charming. He was downright brotherly. Despite all the compliments, he hadn't flirted with her all night.

It came as something of a surprise when Hetta realized she *wanted* him to flirt with her. She'd gotten used to his compliments. Not the part about her skin or figure. The feeling that he liked her, that she was important to him. He might boss her around and do things without asking her first—just like every other man she'd ever known— but he did it because she was important to him, because he was taking care of her. Maybe that was what she wanted, to feel that someone was taking care of her.

Now Owen was, but she couldn't figure out why.

There was no monetary gain she could see, certainly not if he meant to pay her bills until she could sell her cows. She meant to have a written agreement before she put herself under that kind of obligation. No telling what he might demand in payment. Hetta didn't understand why that thought should cause such a strange sensation— half chill, half pleasurable ache. It was as though she feared and wanted something at the same time.

Owen had turned her life upside down, but she guessed she couldn't blame him. She'd let herself get off course when she decided to marry William. No, she'd gotten off course when she let her father make her believe she was of so little value no one would ever want her. She owed Owen a lot for helping her see she was more than that. Ida and William had helped, too. But for some reason it had taken Owen to make her believe in herself.

It was time for bed. She had work to do tomorrow. She might have two thousand dollars worth of steers out there right now, but if they didn't get the new calves branded, there wouldn't be anything to sell in the future. She didn't have any money to buy more cows. She had to make the most of every one she had.

She made her way into the log room, then waited a moment for her eyes to become adjusted to the darkness. This had been her room, the part of the house nobody wanted. Ironically, it was the only part of the house that had survived untouched. Even her bed was still here.

She expected to find the mattress covered in dust and dirt, but somebody had used it often enough to keep it clear of debris. She spread her bedroll out on the bed. Tomorrow she would start a list of things to buy. She couldn't afford much, only real necessities. As she prepared to crawl inside her bedroll, she decided sheets were a necessity.

"You in bed?" Owen called from somewhere outside her doorway.

"Not yet."

There was no use comparing this to Ida's comfortable bed and cozy bedroom. This was her home from now on. She might as well make up her mind to make the best of it. She sat down on the bed and wiggled down inside the bedroll.

"Are you in bed yet?" Owen called again.

"Yes."

"Good. I'm coming in."

Chapter Eighteen

Hetta's body stiffened. "You can't come in!"

"Of course I can," Owen replied, his body a shadow in the doorway.

He sounded relaxed, almost jovial. She felt tense, almost threatened. There was something about his shadow in the doorway—big, masculine, powerful, *impersonal*—that robbed her of her comfort. She guessed it was knowing she was vulnerable. She told herself this was Owen, that he just wanted to protect her. She felt herself relax, but it was cold comfort to know she was safe because she was so unattractive.

He disappeared into the blackness of a corner of the room. She heard him but couldn't see him. "What are you doing?" she asked when she couldn't stand the suspense any longer.

"Laying out my bedroll."

"The floor is awfully hard. Wouldn't you be more comfortable finding a sandy spot outside?"

His chuckle was soft, unnerving.

"You'd be able to hear better outside," she said.

"I'd also be a better target. Go to sleep."

"I can't."

"Why?"

She didn't know how to tell him her feelings were so contradictory, she couldn't be sure what she felt. "I'm not used to sleeping in a room with a man I don't know well."

"Don't do it. It's extremely dangerous."

"Why isn't it dangerous with you?"

"Because I'm your friend. Besides, I don't get any pleasure from forcing myself on women. I might steal a kiss, but only if I get some encouragement."

"Do women turn you down?"

He was silent for a moment. She wondered if there was some prohibition against asking a man that question, whether she'd crossed some line only another man would see. Women would have discussed every instance in detail.

"I don't ask them for more than they're willing to give."

What were they willing to offer, and how much of it would he take? He gave the impression of being the kind of man who was ready for fun the minute it was offered. In town they saw him as a gambler, a dangerous man of action. But around her he was more likely to tease her or act like a big brother.

The sound of clothing hitting the floor snapped her train of thought. "What are you doing now?"

"Getting ready to crawl into my bedroll. Do you want a step-by-step account?"

"Are you undressing?"

"Of course I am. I don't go to bed with my clothes on."

All the tension came racing back. What did he mean by *undressing*? Her father used to sleep without anything on when it got hot. Tonight it was *very* hot. Did that mean Owen was naked? Her body got warm just thinking about it. She couldn't understand why she was having this kind of reaction to him. Would she have felt this way if it were William?

She knew right away she wouldn't.

Her belly was tight, churning. She felt keyed up, tense, anticipating something. But what? She was making herself crazy. She knew he wasn't going to force himself on her. She knew she didn't want that even though she wished she were attractive enough to cause him to think about it.

Then she realized it was very simple. She was alone with a man she found attractive, personally and physically. She liked him *as a man*. She found him attractive *as a man*. He had touched something inside her that William hadn't. This had nothing to do with dependability or all the other virtues. This was pure animal magnetism. She was no more immune than anyone else.

"How close are you?" she asked.

"You can reach out and touch me if you're afraid."

"I'm not afraid. I just wanted to know where you were. I don't want to stumble over you if I get up."

"I'm a light sleeper."

"Are you between me and the door?"

"Don't worry. Nobody can get to you without going through me."

"I wasn't worried. I just wanted to know."

If she could reach out and touch him, *he could reach out and touch her*. She could practically feel his hands on her arms, her shoulders, her . . . She forced herself to think of the calves she would help brand tomorrow. She hadn't done that in three years. She didn't know if she had the strength or stamina to last a whole day. She needed her sleep. Myrl and Ben would be here soon after daybreak. She turned over, her back to Owen.

"Good night," he said.

"Good night."

She didn't feel the least bit sleepy. She lay there, expectant, waiting for something. "Thank you for coming." She hadn't meant to say anything. She certainly hadn't meant to say that.

"I know you don't want me here."

Now she felt bad. He didn't have to help her. He could easily have turned his back on her.

"It's not that."

"Then what is it?"

"I'm not sure."

"Then go to sleep and don't worry about it. You'll figure it out soon enough."

What if she didn't figure it out? She hadn't been right about William. If Owen hadn't come along, she'd probably have married William and turned into a woman she didn't want to be.

Now she knew she wanted to live on her ranch, not in town, to be free to rope and ride astride. And if she ever did decide to marry, she had enough self-respect to demand that she be treated as an equal. After all, she had great skin, beautiful eyes, and a fabulous figure. Owen had said so, and he ought to know.

But if her skin, eyes, and figure were so great, why didn't it tempt him to take advantage of her?

Hetta decided she must be going a little crazy. In very short order she'd gone from wanting to be engaged to William to realizing she didn't want to marry any man out of gratitude, but Owen's presence was disturbing her more than any of that.

She needed time to get accustomed to her new attitudes. No, to discover what she *really* wanted and to admit and be content with her true feelings, whatever they turned out to be. And one of those true feelings was that she was strongly attracted to Owen. She wasn't considering marriage. She was just talking attraction. That was okay. She smiled in the dark. There'd be something wrong with her if she *weren't* attracted to him.

And she liked him. That was okay. It meant friendship, companionship. It didn't obligate her to anything. That made her feel so much better, the tension gradually left her body.

Owen's breathing had become slow and regular. He didn't waste his time agonizing over everything that happened. He accepted things as they came, dealt with them, then moved on. She'd spent so many years being afraid, she hadn't been able to enjoy what she did have. She made a promise to herself right then and there that she'd never be afraid again. She'd concentrate on what she had rather than what she didn't.

And for the time being, she had Owen.

Hetta awoke to the sound of men's voices. She sat up abruptly, fearful until she remembered she was at her ranch, sleeping in her old bed, and the voices belonged to Owen, Myrl, and Ben Logan. She crawled out of her bedroll and scrambled into her clothes, horrified she had slept so late. The sun must have been up for an hour. She nearly ran into Owen coming through the doorway.

"I was bringing your coffee," he said, holding out a cup.

"Why did you let me sleep so late?"

"You looked so peaceful, I didn't have the heart to disturb you. Do you know how charming you look when you're asleep?"

Of course she didn't, nor did she believe him, but she felt herself blush. "I meant to cook breakfast." The aroma of bacon and fresh bread floated on the cool morning air.

"It turns out Myrl is a genius with coffee beans and young Ben is a pretty good cook. That lets you off the hook at least some of the time."

Why should she feel guilty because she hadn't assumed the woman's role? It was something else her father had drummed into her head. She was doing the work of a man. She was equal to anybody here.

"Thanks for the coffee," she said to Myrl. "It's good."

"Been making it for more than forty years. Ought to have figured out how by now."

She walked through the ruin of her house into the ranch yard. The sun, blazing in a cloudless sky, had already started to heat up the air, but it was invigorating to be out in the open. Birds sang in the trees and scratched among the dry leaves and grass for food. The air felt clean and dry, the pungent scent of sagebrush strong on the slight breeze. The aroma of cooking bacon was so delicious her mouth watered. She took a deep breath and drank it all in. She wondered how she'd managed to spend nearly three whole years living indoors. How could she have forgotten all of this?

Memories flooded back of the days she'd spent in the saddle, the delicious freedom to come and go as she wanted, to spend her day alone or in company, to be dirty and sweaty without offending anyone's sensibilities. Her heart swelled with anticipation. She had finally come back to where she belonged, to who she was.

She was home.

"I'm starved," she said, turning toward Ben. "I hope breakfast tastes as good as it smells."

"It will, ma'am. After I was hurt, cooking was all I could do."

That must have been a blow to his pride. "Owen is expecting you to be in the saddle all day."

"Looking forward to it," he said as he handed her a plate.

She smiled when she saw the bacon, beans, and biscuits heavy with bacon fat. Ida would have cringed. Hetta took her plate, walked over to the shade of a Mexican olive, one her mother had planted, and squatted down on dry leaves. She picked up a piece of bacon, tore off a bite with her teeth, and chewed, a contented sigh escaping her.

"It's good?"

She looked up to see Owen preparing to sit down next to her. She nodded, her mouth too full to speak.

"Cade says it's army food Texas style."

"I'll have to meet your cousin," she said when she'd swallowed.

"You'll love him. He's dependability personified."

"Then it's good he's married. Otherwise you'd be defending him from half the women in Texas."

Owen smiled so brilliantly, Hetta's stomach nearly rose to her throat. "Not quite. I'm much better-looking."

Hetta felt the laugh coming. She tried to hold it back because she knew that was exactly what Owen expected, but it rippled out of her. It wasn't just because Owen was being Owen in a way that was so much like Owen she couldn't help laughing. She was laughing because she was happy. For the first time since her mother had died, she felt her life was going in the right direction, that something good was just around the corner.

"You don't think I'm more handsome than Cade?" Owen said, his smile wide and teasing.

"You assured me you were the most handsome man in Texas," she said with another laugh, "but I bet if I went to San Antonio, I'd find dozens of men better looking than you."

"Have you been to San Antonio?"

"No."

"That accounts for it, then."

"Accounts for what?"

"It's a city of nothing but ugly men. I nearly caused a riot the last time I went."

She could see amusement dancing in his eyes. He was telling a whopper and enjoying it. "Who rioted?"

"The senoritas. I barely escaped with the clothes on my back."

"I can't imagine you in tatters. Even now you look like you're dressed for town."

He wore a pale yellow shirt with a brown vest. His dun-colored pants were indecently tight and unquestionably provocative. He wore a pair of those new boots she'd heard about, the ones with the thin soles and high heels. They looked smart, but they made him walk a little funny. His attire was finished off with a broad-brimmed hat with a flat crown and a blue bandana. Compared to Myrl, he looked like an advertisement in one of those catalogs William got in his store.

"I have a reputation to keep up," Owen said.

Hetta turned back to her breakfast. "Eat up. I'm anxious to see what you look like at the end of the day. I won't look as pretty as you," she said as she forked beans into her mouth. "Mama used to say I looked like I'd been wrestling cows and lost."

"You'll probably need a hot bath to soak your aching muscles."

She nearly choked on her food. "I'll worry about getting clean after I get dirty. Now eat your breakfast and stop trying to make me blush."

"Can I make you blush?"

"You know you can."

"Not in front of Myrl."

"In front of God."

Owen laughed. "Not God. For Him I have a great deal of respect."

That surprised Hetta, but she didn't say so.

"You've got a lot of these trees around," Owen said of the Mexican olive. "I didn't think anything could bloom in this heat."

"Ma liked anything that bloomed. She used to have me bring back any flowering plants I found."

"You can start collecting them again."

She didn't know if she wanted to. Flowers reminded her too much of her mother. She got to her feet. "Time to get started!" she called out. "You men going to sit in the shade all day?"

"Watch out for that calf!" Owen shouted. "He's coming your way."

Hetta struggled to ignore her screaming muscles as she scrambled to cut off a bull calf. She was thankful that her mount—they'd captured some of the horses Manly had used—knew almost as much about handling cows as she did. Her body was so close to the edge of total exhaustion, she didn't think she could have managed on her own. The pony outraced the calf, cut from side to side as the calf made vain attempts to escape, then trotted behind the calf as he decided to return to the herd.

"What do you say we make this the last one for the day?" Owen called out.

"Good idea," Hetta replied. "Ben and Myrl still have to ride back to town."

She should have been the one to decide when to stop, but she wasn't about to call a halt when Owen and Ben still looked strong in the saddle.

But they still had to brand and castrate this calf before anybody could quit.

Every muscle in Hetta's arms and shoulders screamed in protest, but she gritted her teeth, built her loop, and tossed it toward the calf. She sighed with relief when it settled over its head. How could she have forgotten how hard this work could be? Ben got a rope on the calf's hind legs, and he went down in the dust. Owen neutered the calf with swift precision. Myrl trotted up with the hot branding iron that sizzled as it burned through coarse hair into tough skin. The stench of burning hair and scorched skin had been the signature of the day.

Owen handed Myrl the branding iron and got to his feet. "There. You can let him go." Hetta and Ben jiggled their ropes off the stunned calf, who climbed uncertainly to his feet, looked around, and decided to take his anger out on Owen. He lowered his head and charged.

"Look out!" Hetta shouted.

Instead of running away, Owen moved *toward* the calf. At the last moment, he dodged to the side and threw himself on the calf, his hands gripping the small horns, the heels of his boots digging in the dust as he threw his weight against the calf. Seconds later the calf was on the ground, Owen's knee pinning his head to the ground. Owen flashed a big smile at Hetta.

"What the hell do you think you're doing?" Myrl asked.

"Having a little fun," Owen said.

He released the calf and nonchalantly brushed the dust off his clothes, never once looking to see if the calf would charge him again. The dazed animal got to its feet and wandered off toward the brush.

Hetta didn't tell Owen her heart was beating twice as fast as normal, that it had been in her throat when she saw him tackle the calf.

"I'm hungry," Owen said as he turned to his horse and mounted up. "Ben says he'll help you with dinner before he goes back to town. His stomach is growling so loud, I'm surprised you can't hear it."

Hetta was too tired to feel hungry.

"Myrl and I will get the water and the firewood," Owen said. "You got a tub anywhere?"

"What do you need a tub for?"

"To heat water so you can have a bath."

Hetta forgot all about food. "It got burned up in the fire."

"Burned up?"

"Melted out of shape. Ma kept it on the back porch.

That's where the lightning struck. Besides, it was a washtub, not a bathtub."

Owen grinned. "Growing up, I took every bath I ever got in the washtub. Not that I took too many. Nobody cares what you smell like when you live back in a mountain hollow."

She couldn't picture Owen living on a poor dirt farm in the mountains. He seemed like a man who'd been around sophisticated people all his life.

"Nobody cares too much when you live on a poor ranch miles from town," Hetta said, "but I do like a bath."

"That's women's stuff," Myrl said. "No man takes a bath unless somebody makes him."

"You can't get a female to come near you when you smell worse than a week-old carcass," Owen said.

"I don't want no females nosing around me," Myrl said.

"What about you?" Owen asked Ben.

"Nobody cares what a cripple smells like."

"You didn't act like a cripple today," Hetta said. "I never saw a man put in a better day's work."

Ben flushed and looked away. "As long as I don't have to depend on my own legs, I'm okay."

"Looks to me like you're okay, period," Hetta said.

"Sure he is," Owen said. "That's why I hired him. I'm a good judge of character."

Hetta looked from Myrl to Ben and back to Owen. "You picked this crew to hang out with and you call yourself a good judge?" She laughed. "What would your cousin say?"

"He'd say I'd jumped in above my head. Now stop trying to make me feel bad about myself and start talking supper with Ben. My stomach's starting to wonder if my throat's been cut."

The ride back to the ranch was more of the same, joking, poking fun at each other, enjoying the camaraderie that had developed during the day. Hetta had been friends with Ida all her life, but she'd never felt that she really belonged. She didn't know what lay ahead, but she was certain of one thing.

Any desire to marry William was a thing of the past.

The week passed in a blur of flashing cowhide and exhaustion, the reek of sweat and burning hair, the bawling of cows and the shouts of men as they worked the herd. Hetta was relieved to have the branding done. All she wanted to do was go home, crawl into bed, and sleep for at least two days.

"What are you going to do now?" she asked Ben when the work was finished.

"Owen's night patrols." He grinned suddenly. "The ranchers found out it wasn't a lot of fun to stay in the saddle all night, hiding in the brush. They'd rather pay me to do it."

"What about you?" she asked Myrl.

"I'm going with Ben. Somebody's got to keep the kid out of trouble."

Working with her and Owen had done wonders for their self-respect. Myrl hadn't been drunk in more than a week, and Ben had started to take pride in what he was able to accomplish.

"What about you?" Ben asked Owen.

"I'm staying here."

Ben's gaze narrowed. "There's not much to do until spring."

"I figured Hetta might need help rebuilding her house."

"It's too hot for building," Myrl said.

"You don't want Hetta sleeping outside in the winter, do you?"

"She could go back to Ida. She's been moaning all over town about how much she wants her to come back."

"I'm staying here," Hetta said, "with or without a rebuilt house."

"Well, you'd better rebuild soon," Ben said.

"Why?"

"If I'm not mistaken, that's a bathtub sitting in the middle of what used to be your porch. I'd think you'd want some walls around you before you use it."

Hetta whipped around to face Owen. It couldn't have come from anybody else.

"It's your housewarming gift," he said, grinning like the proverbial cat that caught the canary. "It came a little early."

Chapter Nineteen

Ben and Myrl had gone back to town, leaving Hetta and Owen to argue all through dinner.

"I'm not taking a bath in that tub," she said for the dozenth time, "so you can stop wasting your time heating and hauling water."

"Fine," Owen said, "but I'm sick of smelling worse than my horse. I intend to stay in that tub until I've soaked the whole week's grim and sweat off me. I was even considering asking Ida if she'd let me use her bathtub."

"She'd close the door in your face. She's the only woman I know who doesn't turn into a simpering idiot when you smile."

"You don't either."

"That's because I know what a terrible person you are."

"But you like me anyway."

She tried not to look at him. It was impossible to resist his smile. "I must—I let you do things I'd never let any other man do. I still can't figure out why."

"My charm."

She sighed. "I guess I'm as silly as those females who swoon every time you smile."

"I'd be happy if you looked faint just once."

"Stop pretending you want to make love to me. You'd run screaming into the night if I started acting lovey-dovey."

"It would be a surprise, but I'd do my best to hold up my end."

She was talking nonsense to keep from admitting she desperately wanted a bath. Owen had been heating water in every kind of container he could find. The tub was nearly full. The lure was practically impossible to resist, but she couldn't take a bath with nothing between her and the rest of the world.

More to the point, nothing between her and Owen.

He got up, dipped a finger into the water heating over the fire, then poured it into the tub. "This is your last chance," he said.

The temptation was too great. "It's so open. Anybody . . ." She let the sentence die away.

"I'll make sure no one comes near the house."

She looked toward the bath. She could almost feel the magic of the warm water on her body, easing her tired muscles, cleansing her skin, soothing her nerves.

"You've got to promise you won't let anyone come close enough to even suspect I'm taking a bath."

"I promise."

"You, too."

"I've got to stay close in case something happens."

"I'll scream if they do."

"Might be too late. Make up your mind before I get tired of being a gentleman and strip in front of you."

The tantalizing thought of a hot bath was too much for Hetta. She retreated to the safety of the shadows to undress. "What about you?"

"I'll take my bath after you're finished."

*   *   *

The temptation to see Hetta in her bath was more than Owen could withstand. He didn't know what it was about her that continued to attract him. Okay, he'd been annoyed when she told him she didn't like men of his type. He didn't like being considered a *type*. He was an individual, unique, unlike anyone else on earth. He'd never intended to seduce her, but he had intended to change her mind about him.

And he had. But somewhere about the same time, *he* changed his mind about *her*. The problem was he couldn't figure out why.

He'd always judged women by one standard. If they weren't beautiful, they didn't interest him, but something about Hetta had caught and held his interest. She was too straightforward and blunt to have charm. She hadn't the vaguest idea how to flirt or respond to flattery. She preferred simple dresses and hairstyles. She wasn't afraid of getting dirty or sweaty.

And she'd made it absolutely clear she wasn't the slightest bit interested in him.

Yet he *liked* Hetta. He was worried about her. It was one thing to talk a woman out of marrying the wrong man. It was quite another to talk her into giving up what would have been a comfortable and secure future without being able to offer something in its place. But other than helping her get her ranch back on its feet, he didn't know what he could do. As soon as he hanged Laveau, he'd have to leave Texas.

"Do you want me to wash your back?" he called out, making plenty of noise as he approached the bathtub. "You can't do it yourself."

"I've been washing my own back for years, and I've survived quite nicely."

"You survived, but I'm about to show you one of the fun things you missed."

"Go away," Hetta said when he reached her side. She grabbed a cloth to cover her breasts.

"You don't mean that."

"Yes, I do."

"Where's your soap?"

She waited a moment before producing a bar of home-made soap.

"That's liable to take your skin off."

"It's all I have."

"You'll smell like wet leather." He disappeared inside the log room and appeared a moment later with a bar of soap. "This will make you smell very different."

"Where did you get that?"

"San Antonio. I bought it because I liked the smell. I didn't know that I had a use for it then, but I do now."

"I don't want you washing my back, especially not with some expensive soap that smells like perfume."

"Don't condemn it before you try it."

"I ought to scream."

"That would only attract the kind of men you *don't* want to see you in your bath. Now stop complaining and try to enjoy it."

He dipped the soap in the water, got it wet, and worked up a lather.

"What is that fragrance?" she asked.

"Lavender. The saleswoman said it's the favorite scent of English ladies."

"Then it's too fancy for me."

He didn't know what had prompted him to offer to wash Hetta's back. He'd done it only once before, with a woman he wouldn't introduce to his friends, but he'd found it a very erotic experience. Yet the feel of his hands against Hetta's soft skin had a calming effect. It almost made him worry about himself. How could he be touching a woman's bare skin and be calm?

But everything about Hetta was different. *He* was different when he was around her. He'd spent too much of his life feeling on edge. It would be nice to feel that he had nothing to prove. He might even think of hanging around a woman who could make him feel like that.

Hetta had felt her muscles tense when Owen splashed water on her back. Just the knowledge that his hands were about to make contact with her skin was enough to keep her on edge. She didn't know what she expected his touch to be like, but it wasn't what she anticipated. At first it felt strange, but as Owen washed her back, then her shoulders, finally her neck, she started to relax, to enjoy the feel of his hands massaging her sore muscles. His hands moved slowly, gently, seductively over her skin. Odd she should feel so keyed up and so relaxed at the same time. She'd never felt this way around William. Of course, William had never washed her back. She wouldn't have let him.

He wouldn't have offered.

The feel of Owen's strong hands on her back, rubbing, rubbing, rubbing, induced a kind of lethargy. It wasn't as if she were sleepy. It was more as if she was so relaxed she didn't have the energy to care about anything. She could almost imagine they were the only two people in some universe pervaded by the exotic fragrance of lavender. The scent was like a cloud, enveloping her, lifting her, transforming everything around her into a world far from the harsh reality of south Texas.

She felt like a princess in a make-believe world where everything could be exactly as she wished. Where all women were beautiful and all men were handsome and charming. Where a man would do anything within his power to please the lady of his choice.

She opened her eyes and turned her head so she could watch Owen. She never tired of watching his body. The play of powerful muscles under his glistening skin fascinated and intrigued her. He was like the panthers she'd heard about, all sinewy muscled grace. He made a purring sound in his throat that caused something deep inside her body to twitch and stretch until she stirred restlessly.

"Do you want me to wash your hair?"

"I can do it."

"I can do it better."

She doubted that, but she didn't have the energy to argue.

"Okay."

She didn't ask herself why Owen had offered to wash her hair, though she'd never heard of a man doing such a thing. She didn't even ask herself where he'd learned to wash a woman's hair, though the answer might be intriguing. She simply gave herself up to Owen's control.

"Close your eyes and tip your head forward," he said.

He held the back of her head in one hand while he cupped water over her hair with the other.

"I shouldn't be washing my hair so late," she said. "It'll take all night to dry."

"Not if you dry it by the fire. Keep your head forward," he said as he worked the fragrant lather into her hair. "I don't want to get soap in your eyes."

She'd never used scented soap, but she liked the way it made her skin feel, the way it smelled, the feeling she got knowing she smelled so fragrant. It made her feel beautiful even though she knew she wasn't.

"Where did you learn to wash a woman's hair?" Hetta asked.

"I need some fresh water to rinse the soap out. Keep your hair out of the water until I get back."

She sat there, holding her hair atop her head, knowing she'd knocked on a closed door, wondering what secret was hidden behind it.

"This may be a little cool," he said. The water soaked into her hair and ran down her neck, poured over her shoulder in rivulets. After the warm bath, it felt cool and refreshing. And invigorating. It made her feel more alive, more energetic. She hoped it was the effect of the water. She didn't want to think it was the effect of Owen being so close, of his hands touching her body.

"There," Owen said. "The soap's out of your hair. Let me dry it for you."

She didn't want him to dry her hair. She felt terribly vulnerable, anxious now to put an end to this. But she couldn't get out of the tub with Owen hovering around.

He found a cloth from somewhere and began to squeeze the water out of her hair.

"You know you have beautiful hair, don't you?"

"It's brown. What's beautiful about that?" Ida had black hair. Another friend had hair the color of corn silk in late summer.

"It's a rich brown, like the fur I saw on a very wealthy woman once. She said it was mink."

Hetta had never heard of a mink. She hoped it wasn't some kind of rodent.

"Thick and rich," Owen said. "It looks wonderful against your skin."

Every nerve ending in Hetta's arms, back, and shoulders came instantly alive, waiting fearfully—or anxiously—for Owen's touch. She knew his hands were only inches from her skin. She found herself growing tense, waiting for the moment when his fingers would brush against her.

She told herself not to be stupid. He'd touched her before, even kissed her, and she'd survived. But somehow this wasn't like before. She wasn't sure how, but she was absolutely certain his touch wouldn't be the same. As for his kiss . . . if he kissed her now, she was certain she'd faint.

"That's all I can do with this cloth," Owen said. He was sitting on the side of the tub, leaning over her. She could almost feel his breath against her skin. "You need to get dressed and come sit by the fire."

Then he touched her—just a brushing of his fingers as he released her hair and let it fall down her back. The caress felt wonderful; it felt terrible. She didn't know what to make of the conflict.

"You'll have to leave so I can get out of the tub," she said.

"I won't look. Where's your towel?"

He'd broken his promise to stay away. She couldn't trust him.

He'd washed her back *and* her hair. Something maybe a brother might have done for a sister. Not that she knew any brothers who'd do such things. Then she realized why she was so afraid. She was certain she was so plain, so ordinary, so unattractive he didn't *want* to take advantage of her.

"I promise I'll close my eyes."

"Like you promised you'd stay away?"

"I knew you couldn't wash your own back. Since you'd never ask me yourself, I volunteered. Now where is your towel?"

She was certain that even if she sat there until the water went cold, he wouldn't go away. "It's with my nightgown."

"That looks like a bed sheet."

"It is. I don't have any towels."

"Then I really will have to keep my eyes shut."

"You weren't planning to?" She turned around to look into his eyes before she remembered she was still clutching a cloth to her breasts. She turned back quickly, but she'd seen the humor in his eyes.

"Maybe I was planning to take a little peek, but not until after you'd wrapped yourself up. You do have a spectacular body. I'd be lying if I said I didn't enjoy looking at you."

An interesting personality. Pretty eyes. Beautiful hair. Spectacular figure. Why couldn't she have been given the one thing that really mattered, a pretty face? She was a fool to be worried about modesty. She had nothing to tempt Owen to be anything but a perfect gentleman.

"Promise to keep your eyes closed until I get inside the log room."

"Okay."

"If you break this promise, I'll never believe you again." Why hadn't she said she'd never *forgive* him?

"I promise." He picked up the sheet. "You can't dry yourself with this."

"It's all I have."

He shook the sheet and it unfolded. "It's big enough for the two of us."

That was exactly the kind of remark she wished he wouldn't make.

"Just close your eyes."

"I bet you'd act just like this if you'd married William."

She couldn't imagine that William would ever enter any room where she was taking a bath.

"If I were your husband, I'd insist upon drying every bit of you myself."

"Just hold up that sheet and close your eyes."

"What would William do?"

"He wouldn't force me to remain in my bath because he wouldn't close his eyes."

"The man has no imagination. Can you imagine the dull children he'd have given you?"

"Owen!"

"Boys who wouldn't have the gumption to steal a kiss, girls who'd think they ought to run away from boys who wanted to kiss them."

"Not everybody is as free-thinking as you. Though I do know several who'd keep me in the bath by refusing to do as they promised."

"I never break important promises."

She wondered if she'd accidentally stumbled on something. She'd found that the only way to tell when something was significant to Owen was to watch his eyes. They turned a lighter shade of blue, as if the truth were being squeezed out of him, but she didn't dare turn around to look at him.

"You and I never agree on what's important."

"Keeping your trust is important to me."

"But I don't trust you."

"If you didn't, you'd never have spent the last week sleeping with me just a few feet away."

"You didn't give me any choice."

But she *did* trust him. She had almost from the first.

"Okay, I've closed my eyes."

She turned and looked up. He'd closed his eyes, but his shameless grin mocked her modesty.

"I can imagine what you look like," he said. "Do you want me to describe you?"

"No." She stood and reached for the sheet. For two seconds she thought he wouldn't let go. Then he chuckled, released the sheet, and stepped back.

"Then I'll describe you for myself," he said.

It made her feel positively hot all over to think he might ever—even once—have imagined what she looked like at that moment.

"Your skin has a faint almond tint to it. I'm glad it's not pasty white. It makes you look more alive, more eatable."

Hetta wrapped the sheet firmly around herself. She didn't want to imagine what Owen meant by *eatable*.

"You've got long, slender legs," he said. "I like tall women."

Hetta hurried inside the log room. She meant to get into her nightgown as quickly as possible.

"Your neck is long and elegant. It holds your head up

at a proud angle. A short neck would make you look dumpy even with your elegant figure."

She'd never heard of any man talking to a woman like this. She was certain William wouldn't. Couldn't.

"I don't know about your feet," he said. "People went barefoot half the year where I came from," he said. "You couldn't do that here. You'd step on a dozen thorns in less than an hour."

Normal men didn't pay attention to a woman's feet, did they?

"But it's your curves that catch and hold a man's attention. You're tall and slender, but you're not flat."

She was horrified to find her breasts starting to tingle as she dried them. This had never happened. Not like this.

"A man likes to see gently curving hips, high, firm breasts. It makes him—"

"Will you stop!" Every word seemed to attach itself to her body and stir up feelings she didn't know how to control.

"I thought all women liked compliments," he said.

"Not when she's being talked about like a side of beef." She finished drying her legs and reached for the nightgown.

"I never talked about a cow like this."

He sounded so shocked she couldn't help laughing. "I hope not. Your cousin would probably have locked you up in the crazy house."

She tied her nightgown over her breasts, put her feet into her slippers, and sighed with relief. She didn't feel so defenseless anymore. She looked out to see him bending over the fire. "What are you doing?"

"Heating more water."

"Why?"

"So I can take a bath."

"I promise I'll stay inside."

"You can't. I have to finish drying your hair."

Chapter Twenty

Hetta couldn't explain why her feet carried her to where Owen stood waiting for her. She'd had no intention of leaving her room in her bedclothes. She certainly had no intention of letting him dry her hair.

"Sit down close to the fire," he said.

And she did. Just as if she didn't have a mind of her own.

"Turn around and tip your head back."

Maybe her feet knew there was nothing dangerous about sitting with her back to Owen, her head lolling back. Her head would have said it was better to go to bed with wet hair.

"Do you have a brush or a comb?"

She held up a hand that contained both. She didn't even remember picking them up.

"I'll comb it first to get out any tangles."

He carefully worked his way though her hair until the

comb ran smoothly from her scalp to the tip of her hair without pulling or catching.

"Where did you learn to do that?" she asked.

"I had a sister," he said. "My mother was gone by then. There was nobody else to take care of her."

"You never mentioned a sister."

He didn't respond, just continued to run the comb smoothly through her hair.

"Do you have any other brothers or sisters?"

"No."

He put down the comb and picked up the brush. She could feel him brushing her hair in such a way that he pulled the hair well away from her body, then let the brush bristles gradually release it so it would float through the air a few strands at a time and dry much more quickly.

"You've done this a lot, haven't you?"

"Enough."

"Why?"

"I told you, because there was nobody else."

He seemed to be talking more to himself than to her, remembering a past he didn't mean to share. She wondered what chain of events could have produced a man so riddled with contradictions. No one in Pinto Junction would believe that the man who'd beaten Newt Howren in a fistfight would be drying her hair with a gentleness one would have sworn could only belong to a woman.

"Turn around and drop your head down so I can dry the underside of your hair."

She did as he asked.

"You have beautiful hair."

"You told me."

"It's like heavy silk."

"You said it was like mink."

"It has the color and sheen of mink, but it feels like

silk. Why do you keep it braided and coiled under your hat?"

"So it won't get caught in the brush or some tree when I'm chasing a cow. It could break my neck."

"Did I tell you that you have a beautiful neck?"

"Ummm. Long and elegant."

The heat from the fire was making her sleepy. The soothing sound of Owen's voice—he was murmuring now more than talking—was making it difficult to concentrate. She felt as if she wanted to . . . The feel of Owen's lips on the back of her neck brought her out of her lethargy. "What are you doing?"

"Did anyone ever tell you that the nape of your neck was practically irresistible?"

"No."

No sane man extolled the nape of a woman's neck. She was certain William would have bitten his tongue before he would have let such a comment come out of his mouth. As for kissing it . . . well, she couldn't think of any reprimand suitably stern.

"The men of Pinto Junction have a lot to learn if they're going to appreciate their women properly." His kisses didn't stop. His lips traveled from the base of her neck, up the center, to the hairline, down one side and up the other until they came to a stop at an ultra-sensitive spot about an inch above the base of her neck. Hetta wasn't sure what he was doing, but she was certain that if he didn't stop she would simply dissolve.

Summoning all her energy, she pulled away. "I think my hair is dry now."

"I'm not finished," Owen said.

She held out her hand for the brush. "I can do the rest."

"It'll be more fun if I do it."

The old Owen was back, smiling seductively, his eyes dancing with merriment. She had to pull herself together while she still could.

"I'm too tired for fun."

"Are you sure?" His look turned positively roguish.

"I've got to finish drying my hair and get to bed."

"What's your hurry?" He took two pots of hot water off the fire and poured them into the bath.

"I'm tired. Besides, I have to be in bed before you start your bath."

"Why?"

"Decent women don't go around peeping at men while they're taking a bath."

Owen grinned. "You're welcome to look all you want."

"Why do you like to tease me so much? We both know you're not interested in me."

"That's two questions. Which answer do you want first?"

"Neither. I'm going to bed."

"I'll talk really loud."

She stood up. "I already know the answers."

"I like to tease you because you're such a prude," Owen said to her back as she walked to her log room. "You act as if anything physical between a man and a woman is unnatural."

"I don't think it's unnatural," she answered without turning around. "But I do think it's an improper subject of conversation for two people who hardly know each other."

"The first day we met you told me you knew everything about men like me."

She turned and was shocked to see he'd already taken off his shirt. She spun back around. "You're nothing like what I thought you would be," she said, louder than necessary, hoping the sound of her voice would help drive out the image of his broad chest, the muscles in his arms.

"I hope that's good."

"It is."

But was it good for her? The more admirable he became, the harder it was for her to pretend she didn't like him, to pretend she didn't wish he liked her. She was absolutely certain they couldn't successfully live together for the rest of the summer, not to mention a lifetime.

"Don't you want to hear my answer to your other question?"

The thought of spending a lifetime with Owen had rattled her so badly, she couldn't even remember the other question.

"Tell me tomorrow."

"I'd rather tell you tonight."

"Okay, but don't blame me if I'm asleep before you finish."

"I'll blame myself," Owen said. "You're a mass of contradictions. You say you're an independent woman, yet you let what other people expect of you determine what you do. You say you love this ranch more than anything, but as soon as it fell on hard times you turned your back on it and moved into town."

Hetta charged back through the doorway. "I *did not* desert my ranch. In case you haven't noticed, it burned down. Rustlers stole most of my cows. I had to find a job and support myself until I could figure out how to start over."

"I would have expected you to stay and fight."

"How? With what?"

"You're a smart woman. You'd have figured it out."

"That's easy for you to say. You weren't here."

"No. I was helping the Confederacy lose the war about then."

She didn't know which was harder, facing the superior numbers and firepower of the Union army or facing the superior numbers of the rustlers and the firepower of lightning. Maybe it didn't matter. They'd both lost.

"It must have been devastating to lose your father, mother, and the ranch in such a short period of time."

He had sat down to remove his boots. "You must have felt very lonely."

Patrick Gwynne hadn't been a good father, a faithful husband, or an honorable man, but he was her father and she had grieved for him. It was worse when her mother died less than a year later and lightning destroyed her home. She'd felt too helpless and hopeless to attempt to stand on her own, too mentally and emotionally exhausted to figure a way out, but she'd always intended to move back.

"Okay. You retreated, but you've come back. That shows you're strong, with just enough vulnerability to be intriguing."

"Intriguing?"

"A woman without vulnerability is a frightening thing to a man. What could he possibly have to offer her?"

Clad only in his pants, Owen got to his feet. When his fingers moved to the buttons at his waist, Hetta ducked into the log room. There were some things she wasn't strong enough to face.

"But that's only part of what I like about you," Owen continued. "I never know what you're going to do. You're a continual surprise."

Hetta didn't mind being an enigma to Owen, but she didn't like discovering she didn't know herself any better than he did.

"You're smart, too, interested in something besides yourself, your clothes, and your looks."

That wasn't hard since she had no looks, no money, and no life.

"You're not the most beautiful woman in Pinto Junction, but in other ways you've got it over every woman within a hundred miles."

He had to be the only man who thought that.

"You've got the most perfect feminine form I've ever seen."

She wasn't quite sure what he meant by *feminine form*.
Nobody in Pinto Junction used words like that.

"But I've already told you that."

"When did you tell me?" She shouldn't have asked, but
she wanted to know.

"When I told you I couldn't resist kissing the nape of
your neck. If you weren't so standoffish, you'd have a
dozen young cowboys hanging around your door."

"I'm not standoffish."

"You drive men away before they can get to know
you."

"I do not."

"You look at them like they're up to no good."

Most of them were.

"Then you tell them you know all about *men like
them*."

"I never knew anybody who could make up fantastic
stories as fast as you can."

"I'm not making stuff up. You glare at people so they
don't dare look you in the eye."

"I've known these people all my life. I don't—"

"Ben and Myrl say the same thing. If any man so much
as smiled at you, you froze him out or turned your back
on him so often he gave up."

Her father had told her no man could be interested in
her except for the momentary pleasure he could get from
her body.

"Maybe I had a reason," she said in an unsteady voice
that was.

"Maybe you *thought* you had a reason. It's about time
you realized you don't."

"Supposing you're right, what was I supposed to do?"

"Wash my back and I'll tell you."

He couldn't really think she would wash his back. Just
the thought of touching him made her feel weak. She
made up her mind to get in bed and go to sleep, but her

feet didn't move. Her slippers might just as well have been nailed to the floor.

"Are you coming?" he called.

She opened her mouth to refuse, but no sound came out.

"You're afraid, aren't you?"

"No." The choked sound that came out of her mouth made her seem petrified.

"I'm in water up to my chest. There's nothing to embarrass you."

"I don't know what kind of woman you're used to, but I'm not in the habit of bathing men."

"I didn't think you were. I thought I'd show you how much fun you're missing."

"Decent women don't indulge in that kind of *fun*."

"How do you know? Have you asked?"

She felt like an idiot, standing in a dark bedroom, arguing with a man in a bathtub. "Of course I haven't. They'd think I was crazy."

"I wouldn't."

"But you do all kinds of things normal people don't do."

"If you let other people make the rules in your life, you'll be miserable."

"There are some things that people just don't do."

"Because they're afraid."

"I'm not."

"You're afraid that being close to me will cause you to do something you'll regret."

"I am not."

"Prove it."

"I don't have to prove anything to you."

"Prove it to yourself."

Was she afraid she'd lose control? Yes, but not in the way he thought. She was afraid she'd admit she liked Owen so much, she would wish he liked her in return.

She realized now she'd been avoiding him from the very beginning because she was afraid of her reaction to him.

At the same time, something else inside her had recognized a kindred spirit and had refused to be caged any longer. She didn't know why Owen should be the man to make her forget all the promises she'd made to herself, all the warnings she'd repeated until she believed them. If she didn't want to feel like a coward for the rest of her life, she had to face him.

The scene that met her eyes outside seemed unreal: a man sitting in a bathtub in the moonlight. For a moment he was so still he looked as if he'd been carved from marble. Even his blond hair appeared colorless in the pale moonlight. He looked up, saw her, and smiled.

"I thought you weren't coming."

"All of us have to face trials," she said. "It looks like facing you in the bathtub is mine. After this, you'll know I'm not afraid, and maybe leave me alone."

"I'm not sure I want to."

She didn't understand the look he gave her. It wasn't his trademark brilliant smile. There was something almost wistful about it, as though there were something he might like but knew he couldn't have. His eyes seemed to burn with intensity rather than sparkle with merriment. It was a look so unlike him, she could almost believe he was serious. Her unruly heart leapt with excitement. She didn't understand how any part of her could be so stupid as to believe that Owen Wheeler looked on her as a woman and found her to his liking.

True, he'd said some nice things about her, helped her to believe in herself and not be afraid of the future, but he'd done that as a friend. He had this great well of self-confidence, and he didn't understand why others didn't have it, too. He had so much that came to him naturally—looks, charm, ability—he couldn't understand what it was like to be unable to think of oneself as equal to everybody else.

"I've never washed a man's back before," she said as she came toward him. "You'll have to tell me what to do."

"Just work up a lather and scrub."

Her feet slowed as she reached the tub. Once she realized the water that reached almost to Owen's nipples was opaque, her body relaxed, and she took her first deep breath.

"Do you want me to use the same soap?" she asked.

"I see no reason why women should be the only ones to smell nice. I like my horse, but I don't want to smell like him."

She wondered what William would have said. He never smelled like a horse, but she was certain he wouldn't have used perfumed soap. The more she learned about Owen, the less she understood.

He handed her the soap and a scrap of material to use as a washcloth. "I've been looking forward to this all day."

That surprised her. "Do your women always bathe you?"

"No."

"What made you think I'd be different?"

He looked up at her with his old, by now familiar, devilish smile. "I didn't know, but I was hoping."

"Why?" She concentrated on working lather into the washcloth. Looking into Owen's eyes wasn't a good idea. Even in the half dark, they seemed to pull her in, as if she were drowning in something so soft, so wonderful, so necessary, she didn't want to resist.

"It's not much fun to do anything alone. Wasn't it more fun to have me wash your back?"

"It was different." She had been too intensely nervous to call it fun.

"Is that all you can say? I'll have to see if I can do better next time."

"There won't be a next time."

"Are you planning to remain dirty until spring?"

She placed the washcloth on his back and began to scrub. If she imagined it was the kitchen floor, maybe she could get through this. "No. I'll bathe myself from now on."

"If you scrub your back the way you're scrubbing mine, I'm surprised you'd want to."

She stopped immediately. "What's wrong?"

"I'm dirty and sweaty, not a stubborn stain that won't come out."

She stepped back. "If I'm not doing it right—"

He looked up at her, the smile gone, his eyes intense. "What are you so afraid of? Don't tell me you aren't, because I can see you are."

She forced herself to resume washing his back, more gently this time. He turned in the bathtub until he could grip her by the wrist. "I promised I wouldn't let anything happen to you. Don't you believe that?"

He'd half risen out of the water, exposing his muscled abdomen. Hetta was certain that if God had ever created perfect men, one of them had to be Owen.

"I believe you'll protect me," she said, returning his gaze, "but guns and muscles can't protect me against the most dangerous risks."

"Friendship can, and people who care."

"Are you my friend? Do you really care about me?"

Chapter Twenty-one

Hetta was horrified that her thoughts had turned into words, but she had to know. "What have you done because of *me*?"

"I've stayed in Pinto Junction. I've moved out here to protect you."

"You stayed because you want to hang Mr. diViere. You want to protect me because you feel guilty for causing me to have to leave Ida's house."

"Did your father belittle you so much you can't believe that anyone except a man as desperate as yourself could possibly be interested in you?"

Hetta turned away. "I'm not desperate. I'm realistic."

"Who told you that all a man sees in a woman is her face?"

She was angry now. Not only had he belittled her by saying she was desperate, he was now trying to convince her that a man's interest in a woman could extend beyond her physical appearance.

"Haven't you ever seen a handsome man or woman take a spouse who wasn't nearly as attractive?"

"Only my parents." She dipped her cloth in the water and started washing his back again.

"And?"

"I don't know why my father married my mother," she began. "He certainly didn't love or respect her. It may have been because she had a little money. At times he reduced my mother to quivering, sobbing incoherence. I once asked him why he bothered to come back if we disgusted him so much."

"What did he say?"

"Only that we were his responsibility, and he couldn't abandon us even though we deserved it."

"Why did he say that?"

"Do you want me to wash your hair?"

He grasped her wrist. "Tell me what he did to you to make you think no one could ever love you."

She didn't want to tell him. She didn't even want to remember. She jerked her wrist from his grip, threw the washcloth into the water, and moved away from him. "He told me I was ugly." She started to shake just remembering how much her father had enjoyed saying it, enjoyed seeing it hurt her. "He told me no man could look at me without feeling queasy."

"He was lying."

Even his death hadn't taken the sting out of his words. She felt tears gathering at the back of her eyes, but she refused to cry. He wasn't worth it. She was never again going to cry because of him. "I asked my mother a hundred times how she could adore a man who treated her worse than he would a slave. She would only say she would die if he ever left her. And she did."

Hetta would never have believed that a person could make herself die, but her mother had virtually stopped eating. Starvation may have killed her, but she'd died of a broken heart. Hetta had taken an oath that same day that no man would ever have such a hold over her.

"My father was cruel, but what he said was true."

"Then how do you explain that nearly every woman alive, plain or ugly, gets married?"

"They marry out of necessity, not love or caring. I'm not in such need."

"Why would you refuse to believe that anyone could love you?"

"Because it's true."

This was an intellectual discussion to Owen, an effort to prove a point in a debate. It had nothing to do with the reality of her life. Sure, somebody somewhere might fall in love with her—if she could be introduced to every man in the country, she might find one or two—but her choices were confined to a small part of Texas.

"I like you. Ben and Myrl like you as well."

"I'm not talking about friendship."

"Neither am I."

She whirled around to face him. If he wasn't talking about friendship, what was he talking about? "You're not in love with me," she said, her voice not sounding quite like itself. "Don't pretend that you are."

"I've never been in love. Don't know that I can be. In any case, I'd make a lousy husband. Any woman I married would be miserable."

She thought that any woman he married would probably get down on her knees to give thanks at least once a day.

"The water is getting cold. Is there any soap left on my back?"

She pulled herself together. "A little." She hurried to rinse his back. She wanted this evening to end.

"You think you've got everything figured out," he said as he worked lather into his scalp, "all the answers written down so you have only to look at the list and you'll know exactly what to say and do." Some soap lather rolled down his forehead, across the bridge of his nose, and onto his upper lip. He blew it off, sending tiny bubbles into the air. "Not everybody sees you as you see yourself. You're a very attractive woman. I wish you'd stop *trying* to look as plain as possible. With those eyes—"

"You've told me about my eyes. They're round and gray. What's beautiful about that?"

"—your skin, and that magnificent head of hair, you could be the most striking woman in Pinto Junction. And with the right dress to set off your figure, you'd have men lining up at Ida's front door."

"Which would be pointless, because I'm not living with Ida anymore."

Owen got up on his knees to rinse his hair in the bathwater, his entire back and half his bottom exposed to Hetta's view. She wondered how he could stand to expose so much of his body, then realized it wouldn't be difficult if you were certain that everyone would admire what they saw.

"You've made up your mind that nobody can find you attractive enough to fall in love with you," Owen said as he ran his hands though his hair to get rid of the excess water. "You refuse to listen to anything to the contrary."

"When somebody actually *does* fall in love with me, maybe I'll change my mind."

"They won't, because you won't let anybody get close enough to find out what a wonderful person you are."

"For God's sake, Owen, what's so wonderful about me?"

"Lots of things. And as soon as I dry off, I'll tell you."

Before he could stand up, she turned and fled.

Owen asked himself for the hundredth time why he felt he had a right to interfere in Hetta's life, and for the hun-

241

dredth time he couldn't come up with a good answer. He couldn't let her waste herself on a man like William. In all fairness, he guessed he ought to say William would be wasting himself on Hetta, too. Neither would be able to understand or appreciate the true value of the other.

Owen rubbed his shoulders vigorously. The night chill made it uncomfortable to be damp. He pulled a shirt out of his saddlebag and began to dry his hair.

He couldn't give Hetta a man who would cause her to break every vow she'd ever made about letting a man into her heart, but he could make sure she got her ranch back in working order.

But that wasn't the reason he was here. The fact was he liked Hetta more than he'd ever liked any woman; he wanted to do things for her. He'd already promised to help her sell her steers in the spring. Now he was thinking he should do something about the house.

But he shouldn't stay. If he did, he would raise expectations he couldn't fulfill. She might even think he'd fallen in love with her. He'd never managed to remain interested in any woman for more than a few weeks. He couldn't even use the excuse that, like his mother, he wanted to marry somebody rich. He was simply incapable of falling in love.

So how was he going to stay here until next spring, help Hetta gain enough self-confidence that she could believe someone could truly love her, and not cause her to think *he* was falling in love with her?

Maybe he ought to find a husband for her. A quick run-through of the men in Pinto Junction turned up no one he could trust to take care of Hetta.

What the hell was he thinking about? He didn't know anything about husbands, certainly not for a woman like Hetta. She was intelligent, spirited, and aggressively independent. At the same time, her self-esteem had been destroyed. She would never be able to forget her father's words unless she found a husband who understood what it was like to be rejected by a parent, who loved Hetta enough to spend the rest of his life making her feel loved and valued.

He didn't know where she might find such a man. Those weren't exactly the character traits of a successful rancher. And Hetta's husband would have to be a rancher. Owen picked a blossom from a Mexican olive tree. On first sight he would have said the fragile white blossom had nothing to do with Hetta, that a woman of such robust health, height, and aggressiveness could never be compared to a blossom that exploded into great beauty, then faded quickly.

But Owen knew that inside she was as fragile as this blossom, as susceptible to bruising. She wouldn't give her trust easily. But once she gave it, it would be total.

He sat down before the fire and put on a shirt. He didn't know why he should think of it tonight, but he had to decide what to do with his life after he hanged Laveau. He'd spent so much time pursuing that goal, he hadn't given any thought to himself. He didn't want to continue floating through life. He needed to find a purpose, something to do.

He didn't intend to go back to Virginia. Except for his cousin, Cade, nobody in his family cared about him. He might as well stay in Texas.

He looked at the dark hulk of the ruined house. He looked up at a sky filled with millions of stars and a big, bright moon. The glow of the dying embers seemed like a metaphor for the end of a good day. He liked the quiet, the solitude, the feeling of openness. Maybe he ought to buy a spread, become a rancher for real.

The idea appealed to him. He'd learned a lot working for Cade, but he'd thought of it as just something to do until they could find and hang Laveau. He'd especially enjoyed working with Hetta. It was hot, hard, and occasionally dangerous, but he liked the feeling of accomplishment. He also liked the camaraderie that had developed among the four of them. He felt that he belonged here even more than at Cade's ranch. Maybe it was because no one knew him here. He could start over without any baggage from the past.

"Why are you still up?"

Hetta stood in the doorway of the log room.

"Thinking about my future." He'd never shared that kind of information with anyone, not even Cade.

"I thought you'd already figured that out."

"So did I."

It was too dark for him to see her expression, but he sensed that she had tensed.

"Did you come to any conclusions?"

"Yes."

Another pause.

"Does that mean you're leaving?"

"Do you want me to stay?" Another question he hadn't meant to ask, an answer he didn't want to hear. "Don't answer that. It was unfair."

"Would what I want make any difference?"

Now she was asking the unfair question. "I've already promised to stay until you sell your steers."

"That's not what I asked."

He didn't really have to be here. He could hire Myrl and Ben to stay at the ranch. She couldn't object to an old man and a cripple she'd known all her life. She probably wouldn't think twice about having them around. Besides, it would help keep Myrl out of the saloons and give Ben something to do besides think about his crippled leg. It would be good for all three of them.

But if she asked him to leave town, what would he do then?

"It would make a difference," he said.

She was silent a moment before going back inside the

log room. Her voice came out of the dark interior. "Then I want you to stay."

Hetta stared at the pile of lumber before her. It looked like far more than she needed, far more than she could pay for. She recognized the boards that would be used for the roof, sides, and flooring. She could even tell which would be used to frame the house and which were the joists for the floor and roof. But some of the pieces looked like beams for a foundation. None of the old support beams had been damaged. Why would she need new ones? Then there were the mortar, nails, and tin for the roof. And windows and doors.

"Did I order all this?" she asked William. "Are you sure you didn't mix my order up with someone else's?"

"There's nobody else around here who can afford to build a wood-frame house. If you have any questions, ask Owen. He's the one you asked to make out the list of materials."

"He's not here. It's his turn to be on the rustler patrol."

"Do you mean he left you here by yourself?"

She bridled immediately. "I can take care of myself."

"No woman can take care of herself," William said. "A woman's nature is too gentle, too trusting, too unworldly to know the terrible things that can happen."

"Then it's a good thing she's got us to protect her."

William turned to see Ben appear from the log room. "Us?"

"Myrl's asleep," Ben said. "We was on the rustler patrol last night."

"A cripple and a drunk," William said scornfully. "How much protection can you be?"

"My trigger finger ain't crippled," Ben said. "And Myrl ain't been this sober since before he was weaned. Owen'll be back in an hour or two."

Hetta was flattered that Ben would take protecting her

245

so seriously, but she didn't need protecting from William. She did need to find out how much she owed him.

"Go wake Myrl," she said to Ben. "Tell him it's his turn to collect wood."

"You shouldn't be cooking over an open fire," William said. "Ida told me to beg you to come back. She—"

"I'm not cooking over an open fire," she told William. "The stove survived the fire."

"Myrl and me fixed it up just fine," Ben said, pointing with pride to the stove, which now looked remarkably like Hetta remembered it.

"You still shouldn't be out here," William said. "Never a day passes that Ida doesn't beg me to bring you back to town."

"Tell Ida I'm fine and happy to be back in my home." She drew William away from the house. "You haven't said anything about how much I owe you," she said in a half whisper. "I don't know that I can pay you everything now, but—"

"You already paid for it."

Hetta knew she wasn't losing her mind, but she had to wonder if maybe William was.

"I wouldn't order that much stuff unless it was paid for. Though if you'd asked me, I wouldn't have advised you to turn all your money over to Owen."

It was obvious that William thought she was a gullible female without enough sense to know how to take care of herself.

"I know he's been helping you," William said, "but you ought to give your money to Ida's uncle."

Except for the little bit she'd been forced to spend for food, Ida's uncle already had her money. Neighbors had been leaving fresh vegetables and an occasional chunk of bacon. She hadn't even had to buy seed for the garden she'd planted.

"I guess I just forgot how much I ordered."

"You forgot?"

"We've been really busy. I've got more stock than I thought."

"I thought the rustlers had cleaned you out."

"So did I, but I was wrong. Owen's going to get his cousin to take my steers to St. Louis."

"That's crazy! There are bands of thieves all along the Shawnee trail just waiting to steal whole herds. Then there are farmers who'll shoot any cow before they let it cross the border. You'd be better advised to sell any steers you have to the tallow factories."

"Owen says his cousin can get me ten times what I'll get from the tallow factories."

"Ida thinks you're putting too much trust in that man. We don't really know him. He could be a criminal out to gain your confidence. We don't—"

"How can you say that?" she demanded. She had been feeling mortified and angry that Owen had paid for the building materials without letting her know. But she forgot everything in the face of William's attack on Owen's character. "He's done more for Pinto Junction in the short time he's been here than anybody else. He stopped Newt Howren and his friends from terrorizing people. He organized a patrol that's kept the rustlers at bay ever since. Neither of which anybody else could do. And he hasn't asked for as much as a *thank you*."

"I don't say he hasn't done some good things, but that doesn't mean you ought to go trusting him like you do. Ida says—"

"I'm sick of *Ida says!*" Hetta snapped.

William looked hurt. "She worries about you."

"Tell her to stop. From now on, when she starts to tell you how worried she is about me, talk to her about money. She pretends she's not interested, but she's petrified she'll go broke. She wouldn't know what to do without it."

"That's her uncle's business."

"Owen says he and your father are behind the times, that you're the only one with enough foresight to know what to do and enough gumption to do it."

"Mr. Wheeler said that about me?" William said after a moment of shocked surprise.

"Yes, so I do hope you'll talk to Ida about her money."

"As a matter of fact, I have been," William confessed a bit sheepishly. "I've spent several evenings assuring her that her investments are perfectly safe. In fact," he said in a confidential manner, "I've been trying to talk her into making new ones. With everything changing so quickly, I don't think it's wise to—"

"You shouldn't tell me anything you've discussed with Ida. You'd better head back to town or you'll be late for dinner. I see Owen coming. I've got some things I have to discuss with him immediately."

Chapter Twenty-two

Even before he dismounted, Owen knew he was in real trouble. When Hetta talked to him about morals or proper behavior, she got that prim, schoolmarm look. Now she looked just plain mad.

"I see the lumber got here." He walked over to see if he'd gotten everything he'd ordered. Hetta followed.

"It's a bit more than I expected," she said.

"We'll need all of it."

"I guess we'll find out, won't we?"

She had no intention of telling him what was bothering her. She was waiting for him to walk into her trap. Okay, he'd play her game. She was going to get him anyway. "Did William bring it himself?"

"He came with two men to deliver it. Maybe I'll hire them to do the work."

"Better to hire me, Ben, and Myrl."

"Why?"

She was getting her back up again. "Because we're

cheap. Since we work for you and will be inside the house often, we'll want to do a particularly good job. Nothing like being face to face with your shortcomings every day."

"I suppose you would know a lot about that."

Ouch! She was working up to something big. He wished one of the boys were here to tell him what he'd done. He couldn't come right out and ask what it was. A woman could accept a man's intentionally doing something he knew she wouldn't like. Men did that all the time. But to have committed a grave sin and be totally unaware of it . . . well, there was no excuse for that.

"That depends," he said. "Not everybody looks at things the same way."

"I never realized how true that was until you forced your way into my life."

She'd accused him of a lot, but *forcing his way into her life* was something she'd added since yesterday.

"Did he leave a bill of lading?"

"Why should he do that?"

"So I'll know if I got everything I ordered."

"I told him I didn't need it."

He felt the net closing but still didn't know the reason. "Why?"

"Everything is here and paid for."

Aha! So that was it. He would deal with blabbermouth Tidwell later, but right now he had to get his head out of the noose.

"You want to know why I did that, don't you?"

"What makes you think that?"

"The murderous look in your eyes."

"You must see that a lot."

"Women are usually happy to have me around. I make it a point to leave before I wear out my welcome."

"You miscalculated this time. Why did you pay for everything?"

"William wouldn't have ordered all that stuff otherwise."

"Then you should have told me."

"You weren't there. It was easier to do it myself."

"That's not the real reason."

"When did you start being able to see inside my head?"

"I could always see inside the head of men like you. You like to control women. You can't bear the thought that a woman could succeed without a man. If we do, we'll threaten your position in the world, your view of yourselves as indispensable. Your—"

Owen couldn't stand it any longer. "You've been wrong before, but you haven't said anything stupid."

"I'm not stupid!"

"No, you aren't, so stop saying stupid things, and before you tell me any more of what I *think*, let me tell you what I *know*. I saw my mother manipulate one man after another. They would do anything to keep her happy. Control works both ways. It depends on who's got the stronger hand and how ruthlessly they're willing to play it."

"You—"

"Let me finish before you take another bite out of me. During the war I saw women running farms and businesses without their husbands, brothers, fathers, or sons. And they did a damned good job of it. They kept the food and supplies coming. They performed more individual acts of courage than my whole troop. I *know* women can succeed without men. And you know something else? That has never threatened me, because I've never wanted to prove myself indispensable to any woman."

He hadn't meant to say that much, but he was tired of being branded an unprincipled rogue just because he was good-looking. For the first time in his life he'd done something for someone else with no ulterior motives, and she was trying to saddle him with a load of guilt.

"Is it so hard to believe I did it just because I wanted to help?" he asked.

"Yes."

"Why?"

"Nobody does anything without a reason."

"Can't you believe I might actually be able to do something without expecting something in return?"

"Maybe you're doing this to relieve your conscience about something else you did, or didn't do."

A sudden vision of Rachelle Ginter's blood-strained body lying in the orchard grass flashed though Owen's mind. He was pursuing Laveau because of Rachelle, but could that also be the reason he was helping Hetta? She was right. People didn't do things without a reason, but that didn't mean the reason had to be bad.

"You forced me to realize I was marrying William out of fear. That was pretty hard to take. I don't like that realization any more now than I did in the beginning, but I accept it. Maybe you're hiding from something."

"What makes you say that?"

"Because there's no reason why, out of all the women you must have known, you should have picked me to help."

"You don't believe it's because I like you?"

"Not enough to do all the things you have done."

"Well, you're wrong. I do like you enough. I may not know all the reasons *why*, but I do." He realized that wasn't very flattering, but he decided that nothing but the naked truth had any hope of puncturing Hetta's iron-clad belief that no one could possibly like her for herself. "A lot of people like you enough to take an interest in your welfare. You may not believe that, but it's true. And we're not going to stop liking you and trying to do things for you just because you don't know how to say *thank you*."

"But why?"

"You haven't believed a word I've said since I got here. I don't know why I should think you'd believe me now." On a sudden impulse he grabbed her and kissed her, hard. "Do you understand that? I kiss women I like. Other men do, too. It doesn't mean anything earth-shaking. It's just another way of saying I like you."

She looked stunned but not overwhelmed. "That doesn't make sense."

He gave up. "Just mark it up as one of those things people do that defies explanation. Right now I'm in desperate need of lots of coffee and food. Then we have to get to work on your house."

"I don't need any more space," Hetta said. "The house was big enough before."

Owen just kept shaping the stones for Myrl to carry to Ben, who laid them in the foundation. They'd been arguing about this for three days. Owen had stopped answering her. He probably couldn't hear her over the sound of the mallet and chisel on the stone.

There were times when she wondered how she managed to keep her mind on her work. She wasn't used to men working without a shirt on. Not Myrl and Ben. Owen. He said pounding stone caused him to work up a sweat. He didn't have to tell her that. She could see the moisture glistening on his body. She felt as if the temperature had gone up at least ten degrees.

Maybe fifteen.

What was it about the sight of his body that affected her so strongly? She could be a dozen yards away, yet she felt as though she were touching him, as though she could feel the heat and texture of his skin. No matter how long she kept her gaze averted, or how determined she was to divert her thoughts, she couldn't get away from this feeling of closeness, the sense that he was only inches from her fingertips.

She liked Owen far more than she wanted to admit, and this nerve-racking response to his presence made her feel vulnerable. A woman wasn't in danger from a man she could ignore, but Hetta had reached the point where she couldn't ignore Owen, not even in her sleep. Erotic dreams she blushed to remember interrupted her slumber every night.

"You can take all the extra material back to William. I'm sure he can find someone to buy it," Owen said.

"What am I going to do with all the extra space?" she asked.

Owen had told her she would need it for the family she was going to have one day. He'd said it was pointless not to build the extra rooms while they were at it. Besides, Texas was so devastated by the war and Reconstruction, building materials were cheaper now than they would be in the future. People were willing to sell just about anything for cash money.

He still refused to take any money for the building materials. She thought she'd outmaneuvered him when she went to the bank and asked Ida's uncle Fred to transfer the money to Owen's account, but Owen didn't have an account.

"You need to stop working," she said to Owen. "It'll soon be time for bed. Mryl and Ben have left for town."

"Good," Owen said. "My muscles are sore."

They didn't look sore. They looked wonderful. She wondered if it was proper for a woman to have such thoughts about a man. Her mother had never talked about her feelings for her husband. Ida had only scorn for women who were unable to control their physical reactions to a man, but Hetta couldn't stop the shivers that raced up and down her spine.

Hetta handed him the towel he'd used earlier to wipe

the sweat off his body. He'd thrown it over a bush to dry. "It's been a hot day," she commented.

"You look cool," he said. He'd buried his face in the towel.

"I'm not. The stove is hot." They'd reframed the old part of the house and put up joists for a second floor.

"It gives your cheeks a becoming flush," Owen said.

"That's not what my father called it."

Owen lowered his towel and hooked her with his gaze. "It's time you put everything your father ever said out of your mind. The man was so jealous of you, he couldn't stand it."

"Why on earth would he be jealous of me?" The idea was so preposterous, it left her breathless.

"Because he knew you were stronger than he was. You didn't need him, and he knew it, so he tried to tear you down."

"That's impossible. That's—" She couldn't think of a word that would show just how absurd she found the idea.

Owen tossed the towel back on the bush. "Will you massage my shoulders? Three days of shaping stones have made my muscles really stiff."

His request caught her off guard. Impulse almost caused her to refuse, but he'd kept his distance since the night he'd washed her back. She wanted to massage his back. Just the thought of touching him made her feel deliciously weak.

"You don't have to do it for long," he said coaxingly. "Just long enough to work the knots out."

"Okay." Did her voice sound uncertain to him?

He sat down in front of her and turned his back. "Did your mother ever say the kind of things your father said?"

"Of course not. She loved me."

He turned, and his gaze met hers. "I think he hated you."

Something in his expression, some tiny shadow that flitted across his face and was gone as quickly as it came, made her pause. "What made you say that?"

He took her hand and placed it on his shoulder. "The muscles right across the top," he said. "My father hated my sister."

As her hands began a slow kneading of his muscles, he spoke softly.

"She wasn't my father's child. He let her live in his house, but he wouldn't look at her. My ma hadn't wanted another child, especially one as plain as my mother was beautiful. There was no one but me to take care of her."

He didn't have to tell Hetta that the more his sister was mistreated, the more he tried to protect her.

"Where is she now?" Hetta asked.

"She died of scarlet fever the year before the war. My father refused to come to the funeral. I sent my mother a message, but she had a new husband by then. She didn't want any connection with her past."

"I'm so sorry." She couldn't think of anything else to say. "It's a terrible thing to die so young."

"It can be worse living and knowing your parents don't love you."

Her hands moved on their own, momentarily detached from her thoughts. Did Owen really believe no one could love him? Could that be the reason behind his need to prove himself irresistible to every woman he met? She felt his muscles swell under her fingertips, sensed the power in his upper arms.

How could a man so big and powerful, so capable and self-confident, be vulnerable the same way she was, feel vulnerable?

For the first time in her life she realized that men needed the same kind of emotional support women needed. They might not use it the same way—they certainly didn't express their need in the same way—but they were just as dependent on other human beings to make them feel needed, to feel whole.

With that realization, a wall somewhere inside her crumbled and fell. Men were no longer the enemy, the all-powerful. They didn't just *want* women. They *needed* them.

She was aware that her hands were no longer massaging Owen's shoulders and arms. They were *caressing* them. The change had come with her realization of the change in their roles. She needed comfort, but she could give it as well.

And that made her feel very powerful.

Owen seemed to have been aware of the change. He'd gone very still. Even when her hands moved from his shoulders to his back, he neither moved nor spoke. She enjoyed touching him, not because of his muscles or because of his size, but because it gave her a feeling of connection to him.

Owen turned without warning. "Let me do your back. You'll have to turn around," he said when she didn't move. "And slip your dress off your shoulders," he said after she had turned.

She wouldn't be nearly as exposed as she had been in the bath, and he wouldn't be doing anything she hadn't already done to him, but it seemed different, as though she'd be giving up a little more ground. *Or handing it over.*

"Back in a moment." Owen was on his feet and striding toward the log room before she'd finished unbuttoning the front of her dress. She had it off her shoulders, her eyes turned away from him, by the time he returned.

"I have something that will make it feel better," he said.

"What?"

"Rose-scented oil."

She'd never heard of such a thing.

"I bought it for a lady in San Antonio."

The drops were cold on her hot skin, but she loved the subtle fragrance. She was certain Owen's San Antonio friend was no *lady*, but if this oil was an example, maybe she could learn a few things from her.

She had expected that the feel of Owen's hands on her back would cause her to clutch her dress tightly against her breasts. Instead, she felt the tension leave her body, her muscles relax, her hold on her dress loosen. Maybe she had stopped being afraid of her own reaction to him.

Lassitude caused her to let her head drop. It was simply too heavy to hold up. Even when Owen kissed the nape of her neck. *Especially* then. She moved to give him more room when he started to kiss her shoulders. She wondered why William had never wanted to kiss her, why Ida said she didn't want men slobbering over her. Neither of them knew what they were missing.

She didn't object when Owen shifted his position so he could kiss her lips. She hadn't forgotten the kiss in Ida's parlor, the kiss that had changed her life. He'd kissed her twice to prove a point. She had wondered if he'd ever kiss her just because he wanted to kiss her. Now he had, and she gave herself up to enjoying it.

But the kiss that began so gently, a mere brushing of lips, quickly turned hot and impatient. She responded without restraint. She'd waited a lifetime for this, had never thought it would happen. Abandoning her hold on her dress, she threw her arms around Owen's neck and returned his kiss with the pent-up fervor of years of longing. The feel of her nipples brushing against his chest, then pressed hard against it, only served to heighten her need. She wanted to take her fill of this moment in case it never came again.

The feel of Owen's hand on her breast startled her. Not because of what he did, but because of how it affected her. Nothing she'd ever experienced had come so close to overturning her senses. It was as though she were suddenly cut adrift from the world around her. But even that didn't compare to the feel of Owen's lips on her breast.

She felt as if she would explode.

She never knew that men wanted to do anything like this. She never suspected that women would let them. She was certain she wouldn't. If she'd been able to conceive of it in the first place. But it was happening to her, and she knew she'd never feel fully alive until it happened again.

Her body arched against Owen—it did it on its own—and a soft moan escaped her. Forces beyond her imagination controlled her body. They appeared to know what they wanted, what she *needed*.

But when Owen's hand moved down her side, along her thigh, and lifted her dress, she felt herself stiffen.

"I won't hurt you," he whispered. "I'd never hurt you."

She'd reacted from shock rather than fear, just plain not knowing what was going to happen next. Her muscles seemed paralyzed, unable to respond to orders from her mind. Even when his hand moved under her dress and up her inner thigh, she couldn't move. She waited, wondering, fearing.

"I'll stop if you want me to," Owen said.

Her mind screamed *yes*, yet she shook her head.

Owen's lips turned their attention to her breasts, but she couldn't think of anything except his hand as it moved along her thigh.

"Open for me," he said.

She knew she couldn't move, that her knees would remain pressed together for the rest of her life, yet she did relax, she did open for him.

The shock when his hand entered her was profound. After everything else that had happened to her, she was certain she wouldn't be able to endure it. She was even more helpless to resist the waves of sensation that consumed her, that robbed her of strength and will. She'd

never experienced anything so powerful in her entire life.
She heard moan after moan. They seemed far away but
they must have come from herself. She wanted to stop,
but she couldn't. Her whole body moaned in an attempt
to give voice to what was happening. And the message
was clear.

More was not enough.

As though in answer to her unspoken plea, a wave
swept through her that nearly obliterated consciousness.
She hung on, determined she wouldn't miss even the
smallest sensation. For a moment she feared she
wouldn't be able to retain her grip. Each sensation
pushed her closer to the edge. Just when she was certain
she couldn't endure any longer, the waves crested in an
exquisite peak and tension flowed from her like water
over the rim a pond.

She was exhausted, yet completely reborn.

Hetta lay awake, unable to sleep. What had happened
still astonished her. She'd never imagined it was possible
to have such a powerful physical response to a man, any
man, for any reason. It staggered her to think her body
was capable of such explosive feelings. It was like discovering she had a whole other self about which she had
known absolutely nothing. But having discovered it, she
knew it would be impossible to abandon it. She had
crossed a kind of barrier, completed a rite of passage,
had reached a dividing point in her life. But as astound-
ing as this was, what she couldn't understand was why
she'd allowed Owen to do as he wanted with her body.

Okay, curiosity could have been part of it, but she'd
never before given in to curiosity. It couldn't be rebellion.
Nobody had put any restraints on her. She was a grown
woman, free to do as she wished.

She hadn't been trying to attract Owen or encourage
him. If that had been her aim, this could have happened

the very day she'd met him. That left only one possibility.

She had wanted it to happen.

She looked over at Owen sleeping in his bedroll only a few feet away. Was she so strongly attracted to him that she couldn't have resisted? Maybe, but she didn't think so. She was certain she hadn't done it in hopes of getting him to marry her. Neither one of them wanted that. Was she testing to see if what he said could exist between a man and woman was true?

It was probably a little bit of everything. Owen had changed the way she looked at the relationship between a man and a woman. She was no longer afraid of his physical presence. And with the loss of fear had come a feeling—no, a certainty—that there was something she'd missed. She'd wanted to know what it was.

Though her curiosity hadn't been fully satisfied, she didn't want Owen to think he owed her anything, that he had to do it again. She intended to be the one to decide if she wanted things to change.

"Myrl thinks we ought to make the house bigger," Owen said to Hetta as they entered the kitchen. Ben had provided the table they used for meals, Myrl the chairs, dishes, and eating utensils, saying he was spending so much time on the ranch, he didn't need those things in town.

"What for?" Hetta asked.

"He thinks we all ought to move out here. It would save a lot of time traveling back and forth."

"I said, *might as well build us a bunkhouse*," Myrl contradicted. "I didn't say nothing about moving into no house with a woman."

"Myrl's afraid some female will trick him into marrying her," Ben said.

"Ain't no female in her right mind going to marry me,"

Myrl said. "Now, if it was young Ben or Owen we was talking about, that'd be a different story."

"Ain't nobody looking to marry a cripple," Ben said, "so that leaves Owen." He winked at Hetta. "It wouldn't surprise me none to find out he's helping you with your ranch just so he can keep away from the women chasing after him."

"Any woman who marries a man just for his looks and money deserves all the unhappiness she gets," Owen said.

"I don't think she'd be unhappy if the man was rich and good-looking enough," Ben said.

"Hell, no," Myrl added. "If you're rich enough, nothing matters as long as you're not so ugly you scare the children."

"I'll probably have women making all kinds of excuses to come visit me once the house is done," Hetta said.

"My ma says there's at least a dozen gals who've had their eye on Owen ever since he came to town," Ben said. "She says they were standoffish at first, but now they're trying to figure out how to pry him away from you."

"Me!"

"Who else has he been hanging around?" Ben asked.

"He isn't *hanging around* me."

"I hate to interrupt this fascinating discussion," Owen said, taking his place at the table, "but I'm hungry. I've got a big pile of stones to shape this afternoon, and I need food if I'm going to do it."

"Those women would be more than happy to feed you," Ben said. He turned to Hetta. "Ma says there'll be so many, you won't have to do any more cooking."

"Don't go discouraging Hetta just yet," Myrl said, an anxious frown on his face. "If they're trying to catch Owen, they won't be looking to feed us."

"Don't worry," Hetta said. "I'll see you're fed even if every single woman within fifty miles shows up."

"I don't think there'll be that many," Ben said, "but we got one coming now."

Owen didn't even glance up. "Send her home."

"Don't you even want to know what she looks like?"

"Nope. Pass the beans. This ham smells mighty good."

She passed the ham to Owen but couldn't take her eyes off the approaching visitor. No woman had ever come out to the ranch on a social visit. She was curious who it could be.

And irritated. This was her ranch, her territory. No one should come without an invitation. In the past she'd have welcomed virtually all visitors, but she didn't intend to let any woman use her ranch to prey on Owen. Or Ben or Myrl. Nobody had appreciated them before. Now that they'd proven themselves, she meant to see that any woman who wanted to marry one of them was worthy. She intended to protect her men.

Protect her men!

When had she started to feel like that? They were adults, fully capable of taking care of themselves. Maybe. Ben was a nice young man, handsome, cheerful most of the time, and a hard worker, but he thought of himself as a cripple. He could be very successful in the right profession. He could also be practically enslaved by some unscrupulous female.

Myrl needed his freedom. Marriage would make him miserable.

Then there was Owen. Even though he seemed a confirmed bachelor, one who would visit many flowers but pick none, she couldn't help feeling he was in more danger than the others. He wouldn't have built up such a formidable defense if not to protect a weakness.

But she didn't have to worry about the men just yet. The woman pulling up in the buggy was Ida.

"You've got to return to town immediately," Ida said the moment Hetta approached the buggy. "It's a matter of life and death."

Chapter Twenty-three

"William is going crazy worrying about you," Ida said. "I'm afraid he'll lose his mind."

Hetta couldn't imagine why William would worry about her so much that it would threaten the balance of his mind. She'd been too involved in rebuilding her house to wonder whether he was disappointed that she had broken off their engagement. But it was clear that Ida was upset. Hetta had never seen her so flushed and agitated. What a ridiculous circle—William worrying about Hetta and Ida worrying about William. Hetta felt almost guilty for not having worried more about either of them.

"Come out of the sun," Hetta said, drawing Ida toward the unfinished house. "You shouldn't have come out in the heat of the day."

"I couldn't put it off any longer," Ida said.

Hetta glanced at the three men sitting around the table. From the looks on their faces, not one of them believed William could be as upset as Ida said. Hetta hoped they wouldn't say so.

"It's about time we got back to work," Owen said, getting to his feet.

Hetta knew Ida was profoundly upset when after watching the three men move off, Ben limping and Myrl moving awkwardly because of his mistreated body, she didn't make a comment about Hetta depending on a stranger and two broken-down cowboys.

"William would be upset with me if he knew I'd come."

"Okay, what's going on?" Hetta asked. She drew Ida toward the table and offered her a cup of coffee, which she refused.

"He's pining after you. You should see him. Even his mother is worried about him."

Though he'd never been sick a day in his life, Mrs. Tidwell was convinced that William's health was so fragile he might be struck down at any moment.

"Is he not eating? Is he slighting his work?" Hetta asked.

"William would let his health suffer before he would shirk so much as the smallest responsibility," Ida said, obviously indignant that Hetta would even suggest such a possibility.

Hetta had no trouble believing that. The hardware store had always come first. "Everybody knows that," she said. "It's one of the things I most liked about him."

"He says you told him you're not in love with him, that marrying him would be a big mistake for both of you."

"That's right."

"How can you say that?" Ida asked with an intensity that startled Hetta. "There's not a woman in all of Pinto Junction he admires more than you."

Maybe that had been their problem. They both thought admiration and respect were enough. But that had been before Owen arrived in Pinto Junction.

"William has never been one to talk about his feelings."

"Oh, he hasn't said anything," Ida assured her, "but you only have to look at him to know he's suffering."

"Maybe it's a sour stomach. His mother's a horrible cook, but she's too miserly to hire someone to cook for her."

"I've tried to convince her to eat at the restaurant, but she insists she has to cook for her family, that it's the only time they spend together."

"She'll never change. Now let me pour you some coffee, and you can tell me what's been happing in town since I left."

"William has been going out of his mind," Ida snapped. "That's what's been happening."

"Owen says business hasn't been good lately. Maybe that's why William's looking worried. Tell him Owen says things will pick up as soon as ranchers find a better-paying market for their cows. He says—"

"It has nothing to do with business, though I don't know how Owen Wheeler can think he knows so much about it."

"Maybe it's his father's health."

"It's not his father, either."

"How do you know?"

"Because he told me. He's come over to my house every night since you left."

Hetta was surprised. William had never wanted to see *her* every night. She didn't see any reason for Ida to start blushing and looking miserably uncomfortable. It wasn't her fault that William wasn't man enough to accept the end of their *understanding* without needing a shoulder to cry on.

"He pretends to come to talk business," Ida said. "But he really comes to talk about you. He doesn't understand why you want to live in this ruin." Ida's glance took in the partially rebuilt house and the hot and dusty ranch yard with its neglected corrals and outbuildings.

"It won't be a ruin much longer," Hetta said, bristling. "The house will be finished soon. Then I'll see about getting everything else repaired."

"Why are you building such a big house? William says you bought twice as much lumber as you need."

It seemed that William hadn't confined all his conversation to business and how much he missed Hetta. "Owen says it's cheaper now than it will be when things return to normal."

"William's worried you'll have nothing left for the ranch."

Hetta was beginning to be irritated at William for discussing her affairs with Ida.

"Tell William I'm not out of money yet."

"But you can't possibly get enough money for your few cows to pay for everything."

"Owen's taking my steers to St. Louis. He says I can get ten times what I can at the tallow factories."

Ida lowered her gaze. "William is worried you might be depending too much on Owen's advice. He's been very helpful in some ways, but we still know so little about him."

"He's just helping me with my ranch. I'm not planning to marry him."

"You're not interested in him in that way?"

Hetta couldn't imagine where Ida got the notion she might want to marry Owen. But what confused Hetta was that Ida looked almost hopeful.

"Whatever possessed you to think either of us was interested in getting married? He's not looking to settle down."

"He's spent so much time helping you. People in town are beginning to whisper. Nothing bad," she hastened to assure Hetta, "but you can't expect to live out here with three men and not cause speculation."

"And just what are they *speculating*?"

"Everybody says Owen's been different since he set up the rustler patrol. He doesn't gamble anymore, and he spends all his time helping you. They're saying he's showing all the signs of getting ready to settle down."

"And they think he's going to settle down with me?"

"You're the only woman he's been seeing."

"Owen's not *seeing* me. We work together. As soon as everything is fixed, I expect he'll move on."

"That's what worries William. He's afraid you'll set your heart on marrying Owen, only to end up heartbroken."

William wasn't the kind of man to think in terms of broken hearts. That was Ida. Hetta appreciated her friend's concern, but it also made her impatient.

"I haven't set my heart on anything except getting my ranch back in working order," Hetta said.

Hetta knew the words were untrue as soon as she said them. She knew Owen wouldn't marry her, but she was finding that it became a little bit harder each day to imagine her life without him. She hadn't wanted him in her life. She'd done everything she could to drive him away, but she'd come to depend on him in a way she'd never depended on William.

"You can't run this place by yourself," Ida said.

"Once I sell my steers, I'll have money to hire help."

"William says you don't have enough cows for that. He says you still have to worry about rustlers."

"William has said an awful lot. He must spend a lot of time with you."

Ida flushed red. "I've told him not to come so often, but he has no one else to talk with about you. He really is worried sick about you."

"Well, tell him not to be. I'm happier than I've been in a long time. Now tell me all about yourself. What are you doing? Is there any gossip worth repeating?"

"Nobody's talking about much of anything but how bad business is, the rustlers, and the dance coming up in about a month."

"What dance?"

"The merchants decided we needed something to take our minds off our troubles, so they organized a community dance. You'll have to come. You can stay with me. We'll dress up in our fanciest clothes, and you'll stun William by how beautiful you look."

"I doubt I'll have time. There's so much work to do here."

"If you put off having fun until everything's finished, you'll never have fun." Ida glanced uncertainly at Ben, who'd come up to the house with a bucket of mortar. Myrl followed with a load of stones. "Where's Owen?" Ida asked.

"He pulls the stones from an outcropping and shapes them," Hetta said.

"There's no end to his talents."

"He can do just about anything."

"You sure you're not going soft on him?"

Hetta laughed, but it didn't come easily. "If you mean do I like him more than I did in the beginning, yes. If you mean am I hoping to marry him, no. A man like Owen isn't going to marry an ugly woman."

"You're not ugly. Your face has character. You'll be striking one day."

She laughed again, and this time it definitely wasn't easy. "Go back to town and assure William I'm not in the least bit of trouble. How could I be with three men looking after me?"

Ida opened her mouth—Hetta was certain she meant to point out Ben and Myrl's defects—then closed it again. "Remember, you're welcome to move back with me any time. If anything changes—"

"You'll be the first to know. Now it's time for me to go to work." She could hear the muffled sound of Owen's hammer striking stone and the thump of Ben's trowel as he set a stone in place.

Ida got to her feet. "I used to think I understood you."

"I used to think I did, too, but I was trying to be somebody I wasn't."

"Did you tell William that?"

"Yes, but you know men. I couldn't possibly be right as long as my opinion differed from his."

"Are you *really* happy out here?" Ida asked.

"Yes, I am. I'm a rancher's daughter, Ida. I don't really know *how* to live anywhere else. William should be glad I discovered that before I agreed to a marriage that would have made both of us miserable."

Ida looked very uncomfortable. "Don't you want to get married?"

"I don't know. Right now I can't think of anything except my ranch."

Ida left looking even more unhappy than when she'd arrived.

"You ought to think about what she said," Ben said.

Hetta had forgotten that Ben was close enough to overhear their conversation.

"About moving back to town?"

"About getting married. Ranching ain't no job for a woman."

Hetta grinned. "Are you trying to propose to me?"

She was sorry she'd teased him when she saw how badly he blushed. "Even if you was foolish enough to develop a hankering after me, you don't need a cripple for a husband."

"Then who did you have in mind?"

Ben focused his gaze on his work. "Owen."

Hetta couldn't describe the feeling that swept over her.

It was as though she'd suddenly sensed danger; every hair on her body stood on end.

"Did Myrl put you up to this?" she asked.

Ben put down his trowel and looked up. "Nobody put me up to nothing. I see the way you two look at each other. It's obvious you were meant to be together. Seems everybody in Pinto Junction knows it, too."

If Ida's words had surprised Hetta, Ben's stunned her. "Why would you think that?"

"Because you're in love with him."

She experienced that strange feeling again. "You're wrong. Besides, he's not interested in me."

"Have you seen him pay a minute's attention to any other female?" Myrl asked. He'd come up with a load of stones in time to hear Hetta's words.

"No, but—"

"Neither has anybody else. He's followed you around like a calf after its ma, working like a field hand and paying the bills, too. If that ain't a man in love, I never seen one."

"He doesn't even like me sometimes."

Myrl rolled his eyes. "Owen is clever enough with his tongue when it don't mean nothing. But if he likes a woman, you'll know it by his actions, not by anything he says."

"I don't understand. You can't mean—"

"There's some things a man can't hide," Myrl said. "Now I'd better stop jawing or he's going to want to know what I've been doing with my time."

Both men had obviously said all they intended to say, but they had set Hetta's mind and emotions into a turmoil. Could Owen like her enough to want to marry her? Did she like him well enough?

She'd hardly formed the last question before the answer came hurtling back with the speed of a bolt of lightning. Yes, she did like him enough to consider marrying him.

That realization shocked her so badly she had to sit down. Surely she couldn't have fallen in love with a man and not have known it. When you felt that strongly about someone, you *had* to know it. How could she have been so unaware of her own feelings?

She moved through the routine of putting away food and washing up without giving a thought to what her hands were doing.

They'd started off on the wrong foot. She'd assumed she knew everything about him, that he was just as bad as her father, and sooner or later he'd prove it. Then she'd gotten angry when he tried to make her feel better about herself. She'd been certain he was a flirt, a man who toyed with women's feelings for his own amusement.

Then he'd attacked William, first saying William was unworthy of her and finally that she didn't love William. She'd fought him tooth and nail on that score, but in the end she'd had to admit he was right.

She'd been furious with him for causing her to have to move out of Ida's house, for insisting on moving out to the ranch, for helping her, for paying for the materials, for deciding she needed a bigger house.

She'd spent so long being angry at what he was doing, she'd never stopped to figure out how she felt about him. She almost laughed aloud. She'd been trying to get rid of him, and *all the time she wanted to marry him*.

That accounted for *her* actions, but why had he stayed despite her strenuous efforts to drive him away? Surely a man didn't do all the things he'd done just to prove she'd judged him unfairly. Was it possible he did like her enough to think about wanting to marry her?

That thought scared her as nothing ever had.

It made her vulnerable in a way that nothing else

could. She had spent her whole life building a defense around her emotions, preparing to be unloved, accepting it, convincing herself she didn't want love. She could have married William and been safe. There was nothing safe about Owen. He'd spent weeks trying to build her self-confidence. If she admitted she loved him, she would be defenseless.

But she couldn't deny that hope had taken root. Ben had only put into words what she'd been feeling but wouldn't let herself believe.

She had to make sure she hadn't mistaken love for gratitude or even friendship. The idea that she might again consider marriage for the wrong reason gave her a cramp in the pit of her stomach. But she got a worse cramp when she thought of missing out on love because she was too afraid to believe it could happen. She would have to study Owen, view his actions in a different light. She would have to be absolutely certain she wasn't making a mistake.

But she had to do one thing more. She had to let him make love to her. She knew that the physical was an important part of any relationship. She didn't know exactly how it would fit into the responsibility and dependability she valued so highly, but she knew it was important to Owen. Ida would say she shouldn't do this, but then Ida would probably think of the physical relationship only in terms of having children or satisfying her husband's needs.

Hetta wasn't going into marriage if every aspect of it didn't offer her the same satisfaction and chance for happiness it offered her husband. She had to know, and the sooner the better.

Owen was certain that Hetta was looking at him differently. It had started just after Ida's visit. She must have said something to make Hetta suspicious, but what?

273

"Have you ever built a house before?" Hetta asked him.

They'd eaten supper, cleaned up, and were sitting on the front porch, something else he had insisted she must add to her house. He couldn't imagine a house without a front porch. It was the way you welcomed the world, where you sat as you contemplated what to do next.

"A few," he replied. "My pa was a carpenter. It's hard to make a living in the mountains just farming."

He was looking up at the sky—they hadn't put up the railing or the roof—still unable after more than a year in Texas to get accustomed to its vastness. He grew up seeing the sky through breaks in the trees. He always had the feeling of being closed in. But here the sky was so huge, so enormous, it seemed to wrap around you. And much to his surprise, that was comforting.

"It was my way out of the valley and away from parents who hated each other, their children, and probably themselves."

"I expect you were a success."

He'd measured his success by the women he could attract rather than the quality of his work. After a lifetime of being powerless to affect the dynamics within his family, to protect his sister, he'd enjoyed his power over women. Maybe Cade was right when he said Owen found power intoxicating. It had taken hold of him and wouldn't let go.

"Do you miss it?" she asked.

"No."

If the war hadn't come along, he'd have been in a comfortable position that would have given him the time and means to pursue the women who had become his passion.

But the war changed everything.

He met his cousin, became part of a group of men who took honesty and dependability as the basic ingredients of life, men who were willing to give their lives for what they believed. For each other. It had been a revelation to him. And though he'd ridiculed their creed at first, he was drawn into it. Yet the more he was drawn to it, the more he hated himself and what he'd become.

Then he'd met Hetta and everything changed again.

"You've never been a rancher," Hetta said. "How will you know when you find the right place?"

"It will feel right."

"Suppose the owner won't sell?"

"Then I'll marry the daughter of the family and take over." He didn't know why he'd said that. The only way for a man to have a successful marriage would be never to allow himself to develop any feeling for his wife, never to allow her any chance to betray him.

"Actually, I don't plan to get married," he said. He flashed what he hoped was his most disarming smile. "I couldn't give up all the women in the world for just one."

"From what Myrl says, people in town think you already have."

"They must have realized you're the pick of the women in Pinto Junction."

"They don't realize any such thing. They're wondering about your intentions."

"Are you?"

"Of course I am. You come to town and set yourself up as a gambler and a lady's man. Next thing I know, you're defending Ben and Myrl, taking on Newt and the rustlers, and setting yourself up as my guardian angel. If you were any other man, I'd think you were courting me. Since I know you *don't* want to marry me, I have to assume you're working up to asking if I'll have an affair with you."

Owen was glad they were talking in near darkness. He was certain this was one time his poker face would have failed utterly. "Would you?" His voice sounded unnatural even to himself.

"No."

Odd. He felt both disappointment and relief. He wondered what it meant.

"But I might go to bed with you under certain conditions."

The tension returned, increased many times. "Such as?" He tried to see her face, but she'd turned away from him.

"You said men kissed friends. Do they ever . . . have relations with friends?"

"Sometimes."

"It would have to be like that. Just friends. It might be once. It might be more."

"But you wouldn't expect me to fall in love with you?"

"No. We'd have to be just friends."

"I don't understand why you're doing this."

"I'm not sure, either. I just know it's something I want to do." She turned to face him. "Are you saying you don't want to?"

"No. I just want you to be sure."

"I am."

The silence between them was awkward.

"You want to try it tonight?" she asked.

"Do you?"

"If you want."

"Okay."

Silence fell again. After a few moments she stood. "I'll go into the bedroom. You can come in when you're ready."

Owen had never felt so strange in his life. Many women had invited him into their bedrooms, but never like this. He did want to go to bed with Hetta, but he wasn't sure he liked the way she was going at it. He'd always gone to bed with women purely for physical enjoyment, but he didn't want it to be that way with Hetta. He'd imagined something quite different.

He'd imagined making love to her.

For the first time he'd be making love to a woman he respected, admired, liked a great deal. It wouldn't be simply an exercise in physical pleasure. It would be an extension of what he felt for her, how he'd come to regard her during these past weeks. He wanted to feel some connection to her, some sense of sharing, the sense that there was something more between them than mutual pleasure.

He couldn't shake his vague feeling of uneasiness. Despite what he'd told her, he couldn't imagine how friends could be lovers. He'd never been friends with a woman, never stayed around any woman as long as he'd been around Hetta, never waited this long for a woman to agree to sleep with him.

The whole situation was a first for him. Was that why he was disappointed? Because this was the first time he'd felt close to a woman and *didn't* feel he had to go to bed with her, and she'd proposed it to him? Somehow he felt he'd lost something.

He was powerfully attracted to Hetta, so why did he feel so conflicted? Maybe he would know afterwards. He didn't want to keep Hetta waiting. She might think he didn't want to make love to her.

And that was very far from the truth.

Chapter Twenty-four

Hetta sat on the side of the bed, her hands folded in her lap, her gaze on the doorway Owen would walk through. She had made her decision. All she could do now was wait. She hoped she was doing the right thing.

She had fallen in love with Owen. That was the first and most important thing to know. The second was that he didn't want to marry her. Of that she was certain. William might have been negligent in not mentioning marriage, but Owen had avoided it. Marriage wasn't in his future. Women were.

Did she want to marry him? Not as things stood now. So why did she want to make love to a man she wasn't going to marry, something she would never have contemplated even days ago?

Was it because this was all she would ever have of him, and she wanted all she could get before he left? Because she'd never love anyone else, and this was as close as she'd ever come to a loving relationship with another man? Because he'd taught her there was a physical side to marriage that was wonderful and powerful in and of itself and she wanted to discover it with him?

Probably all of those things. She wondered if this was how her mother had felt, but decided it wasn't. If the man she married cheated on her, she'd attack him with a branding iron. Besides, she didn't think Owen could love any woman enough to be faithful. So she was going to take what life offered her. She wouldn't be satisfied, but she would have had a taste of what might have been. And a taste was better than nothing.

A shadow in the doorway shattered her thoughts. She would never stop being surprised at how big he was.

"Are you sure?" he asked.

"Have you decided I'm not attractive after all?"

He crossed the room quickly, dropped down next to her on the bed. He unclasped her hands and took them to his lips. "I find you even more attractive than at first," he said in between dropping kisses on her knuckles. "I just want to make sure you're not doing this for me."

A wry chuckle escaped her. "This is entirely for me. I imagine you've already had more than your share."

But he didn't know what it was like to make love to the woman he loved. She would have something he didn't. Might never have.

"If you're sure?"

"Kiss me and judge for yourself."

To be held in his arms was wonderful. To be kissed as well was bliss. She wondered if William would have ever learned to hold her like this. Not tenderly as if she were something precious that might break, but roughly, as if he couldn't get enough of her. She was certain he would never have kissed her like Owen kissed her.

Owen attacked her as if she were a luscious fruit and he was famished. There was nothing gentle about his kisses. They were hungry, sloppy, even noisy. Ida would have been horrified. Hetta loved it. She needed to feel he wanted her so much he couldn't control himself. She didn't want manners. She didn't want decorum. She didn't want sensible. She'd had that all her life. She'd made a conscious decision to cast them aside for tonight. If this was to be her one time, she wanted to experience everything.

She threw her arms around Owen and kissed him back with a wildness that surprised her. She had spent so many years denying the physical, telling herself she would never have a relationship such as this, didn't want it, and wouldn't miss it, that she hadn't realized she had such a physical nature, such a deep, flowing need. She was certain it was a legacy from her father. She would never let it control her, but tonight she intended to give it free rein. She wanted to experience everything in the arms of the man she loved.

She was surprised how good her decision made her feel. She knew he didn't love her, that he would never be her husband, but none of that could destroy the happiness that infused her with a sense of well-being. She loved! And it had made her a more whole woman.

They lay down together, their arms still around each other. Hetta had always considered herself a big woman—especially next to petite Ida—but she didn't feel big next to Owen. She could barely get her arms around him. She felt small, vulnerable, and she discovered that wasn't half bad. It was nice to feel she had someone bigger and stronger to protect her.

Feeling the muscles as they moved across his back provided a kind of erotic pleasure she found impossible to explain. Maybe it tied into the feeling of being the weaker of the two, of needing his strength to protect her and being assured it was sufficient. She only knew she gained pleasure from the feel of his strong arms around her, the certainty that his body could overpower her at any moment. The sensation was almost as powerful as his kisses.

But not quite.

His kisses were wonderful. She especially liked it when he kissed her eyes, her nose, her hair, any part of her he could reach. It made her feel he wanted her so badly he couldn't kiss her fast enough, often enough, deeply enough. Then he would kiss her on the lips and his tongue would thrust into her mouth begging for more of her. She fought back, her tongue launching its own invasion, countering the attack, locked in such fierce combat that her breath came hot and heavy. They fell back to regroup.

But while she lay breathless, drained by the force of the emotions that filled her, Owen's hands moved restlessly, insistently, inquisitively over her body. After exploring every part of her back, arms, and sides, they moved to the buttons of her dress. A cascade of sensation followed the movement of his fingers from neckline to waist as he undid the buttons and slipped her dress over her shoulders. A repeat with the buttons of her shift raised her temperature further.

She anticipated his touch on her breasts. She knew it would come, knew it would send hot currents along her nerves, alerting other parts of her body, bringing them to a fever pitch of anticipation. She could already feel his touch, imagine its impact.

Yet when it came it was even greater than she'd anticipated. The moment the tip of his tongue touched her nipple, she practically rose off the bed. When his teeth tugged gently, she did rise, her back arching and a long, shuddering moan escaping her parted lips. He cupped her other breast with his hand, gently kneading it, teasing, torturing her nipple with his thumb and fingertip. She tried to pull him away from her breasts, to pull his lips

281

to her own, but he was like a starving man who would not leave what sustained him.

She ran her fingers back and forth through his hair, the movement of her hands becoming more rapid, more unpredictable, as his assault on her body intensified. She felt she had to push him away, yet she pressed him hard against her, arched her body against him.

"Lift your hips," he whispered.

Her body stilled when his hands moved her clothes down and off her body. In a matter of seconds, she lay naked beside him.

"You, too," she urged, knowing she wouldn't feel so vulnerable if he weren't still fully clothed.

If she'd thought he would have to leave her alone while he removed his clothes, she was mistaken. He seemed to have twice as many hands as he ought. They were everywhere. On her breast, unbuttoning his shirt, exploring her body, removing his clothes. It was almost like magic. Soon he lay next to her, as naked and vulnerable as she.

Hetta had never imagined what it would be like to lie next to a man completely stripped of his clothing. She'd never imagined what he would look like, feel like, act like. She never tried to imagine it because she didn't want to, wasn't supposed to, was afraid to. Now she felt she was about to explode from the force of the sensations that rocketed through her body. With trepidation, she reached out to touch him.

His skin was soft. Somehow she'd expected it to be leathery, even hard. Heat radiated from him like from a stove in winter. His body trembled under her touch. Did she affect him as strongly as he affected her? She moved her hand down his side and over until she touched his bottom. She felt brazen—maybe too brazen—but she received her reward when Owen groaned softly.

"That feels good."

Emboldened, she squeezed gently. He responded by pressing against her until she could feel his arousal against her side. At the same time, his hand moved over her hips and between her legs. The double shock sent her body into a frenzy.

"Don't be afraid," Owen whispered. "I won't hurt you."

She didn't think he would. Her muscles relaxed, and she felt Owen's fingers part her flesh. Determined to be equally bold, she reached out and took hold of him.

"Touch me anywhere but there," Owen said.

"Why?"

"I'll explode if you don't remove your hand."

She didn't understand. She felt like *she* was exploding, and he didn't remove *his* hand.

"Why?" she asked.

"Women build slowly, men all at once."

She didn't feel like anything was happening to her slowly.

Owen's fingers entered her, found the spot that caused her body to shudder with ecstasy. She felt the waves beating within her, the heat churning in her belly, the tiny pinpoints of fire racing along the pathways of every nerve in her body.

But as Owen continued to massage gently that magic spot, to tease and torment her breast with his teeth, lips, and tongue, she had less and less thought to give to him. Everything centered on her own body, on the myriad of sensations bombarding her. She felt surrounded by them, helpless in their thrall. She moved against him. She moved away from him. She wanted to escape. She never wanted to be without his touch. The heat in her belly grew more intense, began to spread to the rest of her body like a heavy liquid.

"Now." She heard herself say the word but had no idea what she meant. She only knew she wanted the delicious torture to end, to release her from its grip. But the intensity continued to grow until she thought she couldn't stand it. Then her body shuddered in release and liquid heat flowed from her like lava.

She felt herself begin to cool, to relax, her breathing to become less ragged, her muscles to release their tension. Owen moved above her, and she felt something large and hot enter her, filling her until she thought her body could stretch no more.

Her mouth formed into a round "O" as he began to move slowly inside her. Even as she adjusted to the knowledge that she was truly joined with Owen, the waves within her began to build and heat again. Everything that had happened before was happening again, only faster. Through the enveloping layers of sensation that surrounded her, she became aware that Owen's breath was coming in gulps, his movements faster and deeper. His body became taut, the muscles hard.

She felt they were caught in the same waves, enveloped in the same steamy cloud. Her body rose to meet him, fell away, rose again, trying to force him deeper and deeper inside her toward the need that seemed to remain just out of reach. She heard herself calling his name over and over, pleading with him not to hold back, to plunge deep within her.

She locked her arms around his neck, kissed him with all the urgency of the need that held her in its grip. His breath was coming faster, his body even more rigid, but his movements inside her had slowed to a deliberate rhythm. Contrary to her expectation, it increased the tension until it peaked and she threw herself against him.

Owen made a few quick, hard thrusts and his body went rigid as tremors shook him from head to toe.

For one splendid moment they melded, were as one. They began the gradual descent together, then into themselves.

*   *   *

Hetta lay awake, unable to sleep despite the comfort of Owen's regular breathing. He had been asleep for more than an hour, but she was still too keyed up to close her eyes.

She tried to make sense of her feelings. She should have been angry that she'd just experienced something wonderful which she'd probably never have again, even angrier that the man she loved didn't love her or want to marry her. Yet she felt a kind of peace she'd never felt before. It was almost as though she'd found an answer to a question she hadn't asked.

She decided to accept everything without question. She wouldn't have what she wanted, but this time she wouldn't go away empty-handed. She had a small part of Owen to keep with her.

Always.

Owen told himself not to take his anger out on the wood and nails. It wasn't their fault he was a fool. Why had he slept with Hetta? The question had nothing to do with physical gratification. Anybody but an idiot could have seen it. *He* had seen it. And he'd plunged ahead anyway.

Would he always give in to his need for women without considering the consequences? Only this time the consequences appeared to be more serious for him. Hetta acted as though nothing had happened. She hadn't referred to that night since. She'd continued to work with him, be around him, relate to him as she always had. She hadn't remarked on the fact that he was keeping his distance, that when he went on rustler patrols he chose his shift so she would be asleep when he returned.

He was supposed to enjoy making love to one woman after another, to feel no guilt, to look forward to the next time. Now he felt guilty as sin, called himself a selfish bastard at least a dozen times a day, and couldn't even think of touching Hetta again. She had asked him to make love to her, but she was an innocent. He wasn't. How could he call himself a friend when he'd taken advantage of her innocence? He was nothing but a selfish son of a bitch, just like Cade said, out for himself and never thinking of others.

Well, that wasn't entirely true this time. He couldn't think of anybody but Hetta. He'd racked his brain for a way to repair the damage he'd done, but he could only come up with one answer. Two, really.

He could marry her or leave Pinto Junction immediately and forever.

The first was impossible. Just the thought of marriage made him begin to sweat. He would never allow himself to be put into a position like his father's. He'd do something violent.

But as soon as he thought of leaving Pinto Junction, he thought of several reasons he had to stay. He hadn't finished Hetta's house. She would need someone to help her rebuild the other buildings, get the ranch running again, brand the spring calves, round up the steers, take them to market, protect her from rustlers. The longer he thought, the longer the list grew.

And that didn't include the fact that he didn't want to leave.

He was starting to like Pinto Junction, beginning to feel comfortable. He definitely liked working on the ranch, working with Hetta, with Ben and Myrl. He could even like Ida and William as long as they left Hetta alone.

Then there was Hetta herself. He'd never found a woman he liked so much, enjoyed being around, felt so comfortable with until he let his lust get out of hand. How could he be comfortable with that between them? He'd finally been able to forge a relationship with a woman that wasn't purely physical, where there was no commitment, no danger of betrayal. They could each do what they wanted without hurting the other, and could still enjoy a relationship that was closer than that of most married couples.

He wanted it back. He wanted to be able to brush against her, touch her, even kiss her without feeling she expected him to do more, without feeling the *need* to do more. There was a tension between them now that hadn't been there before. So many subjects were off limits. He didn't feel free to be himself. But that wasn't what bothered him the most.

He was afraid he might be falling in love with Hetta.

That would only make things worse. He had tried to deny it, but there were too many signs. He'd practically forgotten about Laveau. He's started to like Pinto Junction. He was helping Hetta rebuild her house and paying for the privilege! He hadn't even thought about what he'd do if she couldn't pay him back.

He knew enough about falling in love to know that when a man starts doing all he can to stop a woman from marrying another man, there's a distinct possibility he's hoping she'll marry him. Could he have been foolish enough to fall into that trap without even knowing? Was he working so hard on this house because he wanted it to become *his* house?

He *was* falling in love with Hetta. That was the only conclusion a sensible man could reach. And unless he was badly mistaken, she'd reached the same conclusion and wasn't thrilled about it, either.

Hell! He'd better do something fast, or he'd lose the best friend he'd ever had.

"That's it," Owen announced as he drove in the last nail on the porch roof. "The house is finished."

Hetta stepped back to get a better view. It was hard to believe her three-room cabin had been replaced by an eight-room house with four bedrooms upstairs, a kitchen, parlor, and dining room downstairs. She had a porch on the back and one in front.

"I'd see about getting some furniture," Myrl said. "That place is as empty as a barn."

No one was more acutely aware of that than Hetta.

She had intentionally put off getting furniture, fearing it would put even more distance between her and Owen. As it was, he'd stayed in the log room after she moved into one of the new bedrooms. She hadn't wanted to, but he'd said the mistress of the house had to have the best room. He had threatened to buy the furniture himself if she didn't.

"I'll wait on the furniture," Hetta said to Myrl. "I don't have much money left."

Mr. diViere hadn't sent anyone to replace Tom Manly. She didn't know if he meant to, but it might be better if he didn't.

"I think we ought to have a party to celebrate finishing the house," Myrl said.

Ben agreed. "Ma's been talking about one for nearly a month," he said. "She's offered to bring anything you want."

Mrs. Logan gave Hetta all the credit for Ben's recovery from his depression. Hetta told her it was all Owen's doing, but Mrs. Logan said no man had ever had the sensitivity to understand Ben, not even his own father and brothers. She even credited Hetta with the fact that a nice young woman had started to show an interest in Ben.

"I have a better idea," Hetta said. "How about celebrating at the dance? I'll treat everybody to dinner. Afterwards we can go to the dance and not come home until dawn."

"Will there be whiskey?" Myrl asked.

"Has there ever been a dance in Pinto Junction without whiskey?"

Myrl gave a shout and threw his hat into the air. "It's

been six weeks since I had a drop. I'm going to enjoy myself."

"How about you?" she asked Ben.

"I'll go if you teach me how to dance," he said. "But I think we ought to make Owen stay here. If he gets all slicked up, the rest of us won't stand a chance."

Owen hadn't come down from the porch roof. Hetta glanced up to find him looking unusually bleak. That surprised her. Owen's good humor and unflagging energy had kept them all going through the long days of hard work. She had expected he would be the first to welcome the notion of a celebratory dinner and dance. Except for taking his turn on the rustler watch and going into town for supplies, he hadn't left the ranch.

"Maybe we can bundle him off to San Antonio," Ben said.

"I say we get him drunk and lock him in his room," Myrl said.

"You don't have to worry about me," Owen said. "I'm not going."

"Why not?" Hetta asked. "You've been tied up here for ages. You deserve some fun."

"My friends were counting on me to find Laveau, and I've let them down. It's about time I got back to the job that brought me here."

He'd been mentioning Laveau more and more often recently. Hetta had an uneasy feeling he was getting ready to leave.

"It won't be the same without you," Ben said.

"What'll be the fun of bragging about what we've done if you're not there?" Myrl asked. "You know we couldn't have done it without you."

"It's been the four of us from the beginning," Hetta said. "It ought to be the four of us celebrating, too."

"I need to talk to my cousin. I never did ask him about taking your steers with him. And I owe my friends an explanation about why I didn't do what I set out to do."

In the two months they'd lived at the ranch, it had become inextricably identified with him in her mind. The new house belonged to her, but it was his creation. He was responsible for the ranch being in operating shape again. He had decided which of the outbuildings to repair and which to tear down.

Now he was threatening to leave. She had the terrible feeling that if he left, he'd never come back.

She knew he was afraid of marriage because his parents' relationship had been so horrible. She knew he didn't think much of women because he despised his mother. She also knew he didn't think much of himself because he believed he was like his mother—fickle, irresponsible, valuing beauty above substance, and avoiding any relationship that might require anything of him.

But in the last month she'd watched him change into a completely different man. No one could question his sense of responsibility or fairness. He'd shouldered responsibility for the rustler watch and had helped Myrl and Ben find reasons to feel like men again. But more importantly to her, he'd taught her to believe in herself, in her own worth.

At first she hadn't understood his insistence that she have such a big house. She didn't need a home that Pinto Junction's wealthiest citizens would have been proud to own. She had watched the hours he'd spent making sure every detail was right, pulling things apart and doing them over again until he was satisfied. She'd listened to him argue with William when he wasn't satisfied with the quality of the materials. It had puzzled her until she realized Owen wasn't building this house just for her. He was building the house he would have wanted for himself.

She wouldn't let him leave before she forced him to admit what he'd tried to hide even from himself. He might never get married, might never have a family, but she didn't want it to be because he had been afraid to try. Even worse, she didn't want it to be because he'd convinced himself he didn't deserve it.

"You *are* going to the dance, Owen Wheeler," Hetta said. "We're going to get dressed in our fanciest clothes and have the time of our lives. Don't argue. This is my ranch, and I'm the boss. You *will* be at that dance and you *will* have a good time. Understand?"

Owen flashed a wintry smile that wrung her heart. "Yes, boss. I understand."

Only she knew he didn't understand at all.

"You can't wear that dress," Ida said.

"What's wrong with it?" Hetta asked. It was a brown gingham she'd just bought.

"You've got to make yourself as pretty as you can to convince William to talk his mother into announcing your engagement."

Hetta had planned to stay at the hotel, but Ida had descended on her before she'd dismounted. She insisted she wouldn't be able to hold her head up if Hetta stayed anywhere but at her house.

"I'm not going to marry William. I don't love him and he doesn't love me."

"Of course he does," Ida said, more tense than Hetta had ever seen her. "I told you he talks about you every time he comes here."

"I don't know why. He disapproves of everything I do."

That was a wonderful thing about Owen. Nothing she did upset him. She could ride astride, handle a rope, even climb on the roof to bring him more nails, and he only encouraged her to be even more adventurous.

"He's just worried about you trying to work your own cattle and build your own house," Ida said. "As for staying out there with Owen, well . . ."

"Owen is helping me with the ranch."

"People in town know how much that ranch means to you, but they didn't like the idea of you staying out there alone with Owen. So they asked Ben and Myrl to keep an eye on you."

"Who are *they*?" Hetta asked.

"Well, everybody. Goodness, they've known you ever since you were born, Henrietta Gwynne. Everybody wanted to make sure nothing happened to you."

"Everybody?"

"Yes. Even William's mother asked about you. Twice."

Hetta found it hard to believe that anyone in Pinto Junction had been worried about her. She'd never felt that anybody paid her any attention.

"I can take care of myself," Hetta said, surprised to hear a catch in her voice.

"We know, but we still worry."

Hetta had known Ida her whole life, but she'd never felt truly her equal until now. She walked over and gave her friend a big hug.

"Thank you," she said. "It's nice to know somebody cares about me."

"We always have," Ida said, hugging her back. "That's why I'm determined you should look beautiful for William."

Hetta stood back from her friend. "You know I can't look beautiful."

"Wait until you see the party dress I got for you."

"You shouldn't be buying dresses for me."

But even as the words left Hetta's mouth, she felt excitement begin to build inside her. Was it possible she could actually look pretty? Was there something she could do that would make Owen see her as something other than his tall, hardworking, plain female friend? She wasn't a beauty, but if she could cause Owen to set aside his plans for several months, then there had to be something more to her than a plain face and a plain way of speaking. She didn't have the least idea what it was, but Owen liked it. The question was, did he like it enough to stay in Pinto Junction?

She wished she had Ida's ability to flirt. Still, Owen didn't go in for pretense. He'd been ruthless in pulling down her defenses. She didn't know if she believed Ben's assertion that lots of men would have talked to her if she hadn't been so brusque and standoffish, but she did know she hadn't given any man a chance.

"What does the dress look like?" Hetta asked.

"Close your eyes," Ida said, her own eyes sparkling with excitement. "It'll only take a minute."

Hetta closed her eyes and tried not to drive herself nuts trying to understand all the little sounds Ida was making.

"Okay, you can open your eyes," Ida said.

Hetta opened her eyes, and shock ripped through her from head to toe. "I can't wear that! It's red." The dress had a tight-fitting bodice, full skirt, and puffed sleeves trimmed with a blood-red floss fringe.

"Nobody else could wear it, but it will look fabulous with your almond skin and dark hair."

"Not with this face."

"Wait until you see what else I have." Ida reached for a case on her dresser and opened it.

"That's face paint!" Hetta exclaimed.

"It's called cosmetics," Ida said, "and women everywhere use it to make themselves more attractive. When I get through with you, William won't even know you."

But Hetta wasn't thinking about William. She was wondering what Owen would say if he saw her in this dress and Ida's cosmetics. Under normal circumstances she would never have considered the dress or the cosmetics, but she had to convince Owen to stay until she had a chance to make him believe he deserved love. If this dress would do that, she'd wear it.

"What are you going to wear?" Hetta asked Ida.

"I don't know," Ida said, suddenly turning away. "I haven't made up my mind."

Hetta knew Ida never stepped out of the house without spending half an hour deciding what to wear. For a dance, she normally couldn't think of anything else for at least a week. Hetta realized Ida hadn't been acting like herself for some time. She'd put it down to Ida's worry that she might lose her money, but Ida was proud. She'd wear her best dress to a dance even if it cost her her last dime.

"Ida, what's bothering you?"

"Nothing. I'm just worried about you and William."

"No, you're not." She didn't know why she was suddenly so sure that something more serious was wrong. "Have you lost your money? Owen said times are bad."

"I haven't lost my money," Ida said.

"Then what is it?"

"I'm just worried about you and William. He's pining away for you. He's—"

"He wasn't pining the last time he was at the ranch. He hardly paid me any attention."

"He feels unsure of himself around Owen."

"Why?"

"Owen's so big and handsome and good at everything he does, he makes William feel insignificant. I've tried to tell William everybody admires him as a businessman, even Owen, but he thinks you broke your engagement because Owen makes him look dull."

"We never had an engagement to break," Hetta said. "Besides, he knows good and well that I . . ." She broke off. The truth hit her all at once. "I know what's wrong! You're in love with William yourself."

With a terrible wail, Ida threw herself onto the bed, sobbing.

Chapter Twenty-five

"It's all right," Hetta said to Ida for the twenty-first time. "I don't love William."

"But he was your fiancé," Ida wailed. "I'm your best friend. And I tried to steal him from you. I should be shot."

"You've done everything you could to throw us together. That ought to prove to you we're not right for each other."

"But William still talks about you."

"Would you let him in the door if he came courting you?"

"Of course not. What kind of friend do you think I am?" With that, she let out another wail. "I'm no friend. I'm a cheater, a double-crosser, a snake in your bosom."

The image nearly made Hetta giggle. "You're just a beautiful young woman who's fallen in love for the first time in her life."

Ida sat up, her eyes filled with tears. "I tried not to like him. I told myself I was memorizing his good points so I could convince you to marry him."

"You're both just as foolish as I was," Hetta said. "William jabbering about me so he could come sit with you, you letting him because you felt guilty about liking him."

"I think it's very honorable of him."

"What good does it do to be stuffed full of honor if you're miserable? I nearly married William for the wrong reasons. Now you're *not* marrying him for the wrong reason."

"William has never even hinted at marriage."

"Then it's up to you to put on your prettiest dress, use some of your cosmetics, and be so beautiful, charming, and absolutely adorable, he won't be able to help himself."

"Do you really think he's been coming here to see me? He really does talk about you."

"I wouldn't be surprised if William liked you best from the first, that he only paid attention to me because he thought he'd never attract someone as beautiful as you. Tonight you have to let William know it's all right to start courting you."

"I couldn't do that."

"Well, I can, so that's taken care of. Now what are you going to wear?"

"Don't you feel just a little upset about this?"

"No."

"Why not?"

"Because I'm going to wear that beautiful dress you bought me and use some of your cosmetics. I intend to convince a certain man he has a right to be loved."

"I'm not going," Owen told Ben at the hotel.

"Hetta won't like it."

"She probably won't even know. Within fifteen

minutes she'll have a dozen men fighting to dance with her."

Hetta had looked terrific when she came down to supper. She was wearing an ordinary brown gingham dress, but everything about her seemed more alive, more vibrant, more exciting. She wasn't attractive in the fragile way Ida was. She looked strong and healthy. Happy. And fine. That was it. Fine.

It wasn't that she ignored him. On the contrary, she hadn't stopped telling him how much she appreciated what he'd done, how she could never have done it without him. It sounded as if she was getting ready to tell him he'd exhausted his usefulness, and it was time to move on. Maybe this was her idea of letting him down easy. If it was, it wasn't working.

He was taking the idea of leaving very hard.

"It's you she wants to dance with," Ben said.

"I don't believe in stretching things out. We both know it's time for me to leave."

"What have you got to do that's so important?"

None of it seemed important now, not even finding Laveau. "I've made promises I haven't kept."

"So you're going to keep other promises by breaking one to Hetta?"

"It won't matter. You saw how happy she was at supper. She didn't stop talking about the dance."

"She didn't stop talking about how much she appreciated what you'd done, how she couldn't have done it on her own."

"Hetta's indomitable. She'd have gotten it done."

"How about Myrl and me? Would we have *gotten it done* without you?"

Owen felt irritable. He didn't like people thanking him.

"Would we have put together the rustler watch without you?"

"You could have done all that without me," Owen said,

beginning to be really irritated. "There's always a rough period after a war. It takes people time to settle again, but they do."

"And you'd know all about that, having survived so many wars yourself," Myrl said.

"Things *don't* always settle down by themselves," Ben said. "It takes people willing to stand up for what's right. I don't know why you didn't go home, but the whole town is glad you came here."

"I don't give a damn about the town." He hadn't meant to say that, but Ben was making him angry.

"But you give a lot of damns about Hetta."

"Everybody likes Hetta."

"Nobody likes her the way you do." Ben hobbled to a chair and sat down. "I don't know what it is about being in town, but as soon as I get here, I'm too weak to stand on this leg."

"Then get yourself a job on a ranch."

"I intend to as soon as you buy the ranch you've been talking about buying ever since you got here."

"That was a cover."

"Maybe, but I know you want one. I even know which one you want."

"How can you know when I don't?"

"You know, but you won't admit it. You want Hetta's ranch. And you want Hetta along with it."

Owen didn't know whether to be more dismayed that he'd finally admitted his feelings to himself or that they were so obvious Ben had picked up on them. He hoped Hetta hadn't.

"Hetta's a great woman, but I'm not the marrying kind."

"But you love Hetta."

"Like I said, she's a great woman."

"So you wouldn't want to make her unhappy."

"No."

Ben stood. "Then get dressed and go to that dance. I think she's in love with you."

"You're crazy."

"Maybe. But if I'm right, the worst thing you could do to her would be to disappear without a word. Maybe you're not the marrying kind, but if you don't let Hetta know how you feel about her, you'll hurt her more than anyone has in her life. If she knows you don't love her, it will hurt, but she'll get over it. If you go away without telling her, she'll always wonder."

"You really think she's in love with me?"

"Yeah. So does Myrl. Now I've got to be going. It takes me a lot longer to get all duded up than it used to."

The last thing Owen wanted to know was that Hetta loved him. He didn't trust his own feelings to remain true. They might change as soon as he found himself around another woman. They always had before. But knowing there was a possibility Hetta loved him changed everything.

He'd never allowed himself to think of a wife, home, or family. His family had been miserable, and he wanted no part of another. When loneliness threatened to overwhelm him, he'd channeled his energies into seduction. Later, the war and his hatred of Laveau had consumed most of his energies. But unbeknownst to him, the friendships of the war had given him the family he'd never had, a feeling of belonging he'd never known. It had engendered in him a need for companionship of the soul and spirit rather than just a union of the body. He'd never kidded himself that he was happy with his superficial existence, but he'd told himself it was all he could have. But now the possibility of more, slim as it was, was being held out to him. Could he resist reaching for it?

Falling in love had been the farthest thing from his mind when he came to Pinto Junction. He'd thought he was spending time with Hetta just to prove she'd been wrong about him. But somewhere along the line he started to like her. And the more he liked her, the more he wanted to help her. Then desire had complicated the picture still more.

Nothing had gone right since he'd come here. The best thing he could do was to leave as soon as possible. Ben and Myrl would soon forget him. It might take Hetta longer, but she wasn't the kind of woman to lose her heart to someone like Owen Wheeler.

Ben was wrong. It would be better for everyone if he just disappeared.

"Have you seen Owen?" Hetta asked Myrl.

The dance had been under way for nearly an hour. A string of partners, mostly young men too tongue-tied to say much, had kept her on the dance floor. Ida said she was so pretty she'd knocked what little sense they had out of their heads. Hetta knew there was only so much a pretty dress and cosmetics could accomplish, but apparently it was enough. Even William looked at her with new eyes.

"I haven't seen him since supper," Myrl said.

"Did he say when he'd get here?"

"Nope."

Even though he'd been at his most charming and entertaining during supper, she'd gotten the feeling he wasn't coming. She couldn't be around a man she loved for weeks on end and not learn to see the shifts in mood, the slightly too loud laugh, the smile that was too broad, the gaze that moved constantly. Most important of all, he hadn't eaten all his food. Owen wasn't a big eater, but he always ate every speck he put on his plate. Myrl kidded him that his plate was so clean it didn't need washing. She guessed that came from growing up poor.

"Would you go look for him?" she asked.

"If he's coming, he don't need my help," Myrl replied.

"And if he ain't, I ain't going to change his mind."

Myrl was in a querulous mood. He wasn't drinking, either. Ben had been dancing with a young woman who seemed undeterred by his bad leg and shuffling gait. But Hetta had no trouble interpreting the glances he threw in her direction from time to time. He was worried, too.

"What's wrong with your friend?" Myrl asked Hetta. A nod of his head indicated Ida.

"She's not having a good time."

"Why? Every man in the place has stood in line to dance with her."

Except William.

"I can't explain without betraying a confidence."

"You can't betray what everybody knows," Myrl scoffed. "It's plain as the nose on a newborn calf, she's mooning over that fella you was mooning over a while back. Looks like he's stuck on her, too."

Hetta didn't know why she'd thought Ida's feelings could have remained secret when hers hadn't.

"Just look at them, staring at each other. The moment the other stares back, they turn away so fast it's got to scramble their brains. Won't have any sense at all if this keeps up much longer."

"Then I guess I'll have to do something about it." Hetta walked over to where Ida stood talking to two young men. "Please excuse us," she said. "I've got to talk to Ida." Hetta drew her into a corner. "What did you tell William? Why is he avoiding you?"

"I don't know what you mean."

"I mean you're looking at him like you're starving and he's the only food that can keep you alive. And he's doing the same."

"Now you're being ridiculous," Ida said. "But I suppose this is the way you talk around Owen."

"What I do around Owen isn't the point. William's crazy about you. Even Myrl has seen it."

301

Ida's expression turned to that of a hunted animal. "How can that old man know? I haven't looked at William all evening."

"Yes, you have, and people are noticing. What did you tell William to make him stay away?"

"I told him he had to do everything he could to win you back." With that, she clamped her mouth shut and started to go back to the men waiting for her. Hetta reached out and caught her arm.

"What else did you say?"

Ida looked mulish.

"Out with it. If you don't tell me, I'll corner William. And you know he can never keep his mouth shut."

"If you must know, I told him he had to stop coming to see me. People might think I was trying to steal him from you, and I'd never do anything like that even if I had to die an old maid. There. I hope you're happy."

"Why did you do something so stupid?"

"Because I won't steal him from you. I couldn't stand myself if I did."

"You're not stealing him. We've been through that already."

Ida turned and walked off. Hetta let her go because she understood that Ida was truly upset. It was up to Hetta to make sure this love-crossed couple got past their various inhibitions.

The musicians were turning up their instruments in preparation for the next dance. Hetta hurried over to William. "Dance with me," she said. "I've got to talk to you."

Hetta wondered why she'd never noticed that William was a terrible dancer. Neither of his feet seemed to know or care what the other was doing. Or where hers might be. He trod on her toes as readily as on the planks of the dance floor.

"I understand your house is finished," William said.

"We finished yesterday," Hetta said.

"People say it's just about the biggest house in Pinto Junction."

"That's not what I want to talk about."

"People are wondering why you built such a big place and where you got the money to pay for it."

"Let them. It'll give them something to talk about besides the war, the Yankees, and the rustlers. Now I—"

"There's been a lot of speculation about Owen staying out there."

"Stop blathering and listen to me."

"Ida has been worried sick about you."

"You finally got something half right. Ida *has* been worried sick, but not about me. She's so in love with you she can't see straight. And don't try to tell me you're not in love with her."

William came to an abrupt stop, his left foot planted squarely on the toes of her right foot.

"Don't stop dancing. And get off my foot before you break my toes."

William started dancing again, but his coordination was worse than ever. Hetta decided her feet wouldn't last long enough for her to convince him he had to take the initiative if he and Ida were to achieve happiness.

"Let's walk," she said.

Dozens of pairs of questioning eyes followed them as they left the dance floor.

"What makes you think Ida is in love with me?" William asked as soon as they were clear of the light coming from the lanterns suspended around the dance floor.

"She told me so."

William fell silent.

"You don't have to clam up. I don't want you to be in love with me. Ida's just horrified she's fallen in love with a man who's supposed to be in love with her best friend. I can't get it through her head that I don't love you and you don't love me. It's up to you to do that."

303

"I've been trying to tell her for the last month," William said. "But every time I try to talk about anything but you or business, she says it's time for me to leave."

"That's just guilt. What she needs is for you to convince her you're so in love with her, you can't live without her."

"She won't talk to me."

"For God's sake, William, be a man! You've got to pay her as much attention as you pay your business. Think of her as a business opportunity. She has reservations about whether it's in her best interest to be your partner, but you know it'll be the best thing that could happen to the two of you. Think of all the logical reasons why you'd be happy together, but don't forget to tell her you love her. That nothing else matters as long as she loves you."

"Do you really think that will work?"

It wouldn't work for her, but she figured it was the only way William was ever going to stop quivering in his boots. "You're a nice man, William. You'll take very good care of Ida."

"But she's so beautiful. And even my pa says I look like the hind end of a calf."

"She thinks you're very handsome."

"I'm not rich."

"You will be. Owen says you're the only one in this town with any business sense."

Hetta felt sorry for William. It was obvious he didn't have any better opinion of himself than she used to have of herself. On impulse, she kissed him on the lips. She laughed when he reacted as if he'd been shot.

"I bet nobody's ever kissed you before," she said.

He shook his head.

She hooked her arm in his and headed back to the dance floor. "Don't hesitate," she told him. "As soon as we get back, I want you to march right up to Ida," she said. "Don't wait for the next dance. Cut in."

"I can't do that."

She laughed. Why did some people fight so hard against what they wanted? "Of course you can. It's easy."

As soon as they reached the dance floor, she pushed him in Ida's direction. He hesitated only a moment before striding up to Ida and tapping her partner on the shoulder. Ida tried to protest, but William took her in his arms and proceeded to dance around the floor, systematically treading on all her toes.

Pleased with herself, Hetta turned, only to find herself face to face with Owen. Before the smile of welcome could curve her lips, his look of wild anger froze her.

"What in hell do you mean by painting yourself up like a whore?" he demanded.

305

Chapter Twenty-six

Owen knew he was kidding himself when he decided he couldn't leave without saying goodbye. He was really looking for a reason to stay. For more than an hour he'd remained in his hotel room staring at a bottle of whiskey, but whiskey couldn't help what ailed him.

He wouldn't say anything to her about falling in love with her, not when he couldn't be sure himself. No point mentioning something that might be infatuation, fascination, fantasy, intoxication. All were unstable states of mind that didn't endure. No, he'd just repeat that he had this duty to his friends which he couldn't ignore any longer. She didn't need him anymore. Once her steers went to market, she wouldn't need him ever again.

Seeing Hetta leave the dance floor with William shocked him. They were in earnest conversation, each absorbed in what the other was saying. He couldn't get close enough to hear what they were saying, but it was clear that Hetta was pressing William to do something. It was equally clear that William wanted to do it even though he was fearful.

Was Hetta pressing him to get his mother to announce their engagement?

It was an open secret that William had been afraid to approach her. Myrl said that was probably why Hetta had given up on him and turned to Owen.

Owen had been convinced that Hetta had given up on William because she'd realized she didn't love him. But now he couldn't help wondering. Hetta had her house, her ranch, her independence. She didn't need Owen anymore. Could she be turning back to William? Marrying him would secure her future, both financially and socially.

It was exactly what his mother would have done.

But Hetta wasn't like his mother. He didn't know what she was doing, but it had to be something else.

Then Hetta kissed William, and Owen felt sick to his stomach. How could she do that if she didn't like him? He tried to convince himself he'd misinterpreted her actions. But it wasn't easy to remain convinced when Hetta hooked her arm in William's, turned him around, and started back to the dance floor looking immensely pleased with herself. She leaned on him, smiled, even laughed as she talked earnestly to him. She presented the general impression of a woman who'd just secured a happy future for herself.

Owen knew the sensible thing to do was turn around and ride straight out of town, but no one in his family had ever been sensible. They'd responded to events around them like a weather vane, turning whichever way the wind blew. He had to confront Hetta with her treachery before he turned his back on her forever. She had caused him to let down his defenses long enough to glimpse a dream. Now she'd closed the door with a sharp bang. He had to know why.

He didn't need an explanation of why Hetta pushed William in Ida's direction the moment they reached the dance floor. Ida had been her general. Who better to help her celebrate her victory? He approached Hetta and spun her around to face him. Only then did he see she'd made herself up to look like someone he didn't know. Her appearance reminded him so much of his mother, he could practically visualize her in Hetta's place.

"What did you say?" Hetta demanded, her face reflecting disbelief.

"Why did you paint yourself like a strumpet?"

"I didn't *paint* myself. As for looking like a strumpet, I've never seen one, so I'll have to rely on your expertise to judge."

"You did it for him," he said, not even bothering to indicate William. "You needn't bother denying it. I saw you."

"I don't know what you saw, but—"

"I saw you kiss him, your arm linked in his."

"Good Lord, is that all you're upset about?"

"It was a very clever strategy. It took courage. I don't know of another woman except my mother who could have brought it off."

Hetta's expression hardened. "Exactly what strategy did I pull off so brilliantly?"

"Everybody knew William was afraid to tackle his mother about the engagement. You used me to bring him up to the mark. In the meantime, you got me to brand your cattle and build your house. Now that you don't need me anymore, you've got your hooks back into William." He took her face in his hands and pressed his thumbs against her deep red lips. Then he slowly pulled his thumbs down to smear the lipstick across her cheek. "Why did you do this to yourself? You were perfect just like you were."

Hetta knocked his hands aside. "Apparently I wasn't

308

perfect enough, or I would have snared William the first time."

She looked furious. But he got the feeling she was even more hurt than angry.

"A woman has to reach down into her arsenal for anything she can use to catch her man. Your mama should have taught you that." She practically spat the words at him.

"If you were my woman, I'd never let you out of the house looking like that."

"Why? Would you be afraid I'd go looking for someone better looking and richer?"

That was exactly what he'd be thinking.

"I'll never be your woman. But if I were, I'd step out of the house dressed any way I wanted. But just for your information, if I ever did agree to be your woman, I'd be your woman forever. Once I make a promise, I keep it. And once I believe in a person, I don't change my mind because of something somebody else did years ago."

"It's not just my mother. It's all the women I've known."

"Then you should keep better company."

"They couldn't help themselves, but I thought you were different."

"Am I so plain and ordinary I have to be different from every other woman?"

"I liked you the way you were."

"Well, I didn't. I'm tired of being the ugliest woman in the room."

"I won't let you do this to yourself."

Hetta looked at him as if he'd lost his mind. "You won't *let* me?"

He was getting this all wrong. All he wanted to do was tell her she didn't have to change herself, that he'd always liked her, had always been attracted to her. "I keep my promises, too, and there's one I've ignored for too long."

Leigh Greenwood

She seemed to go still. "Is this your way of saying good-bye?" She gestured at the lipstick he'd smeared across her cheeks.

"You shouldn't have done that."

"What I *shouldn't have done*, Owen Wheeler, was think a fancy man like you could turn into a decent human being. I should have realized that with your looks and money and women falling over themselves to please you, you'd never have a real interest in someone like me. I was just a challenge for you. It must have been fun to try to convince me a man could find me attractive. Well, congratulations, you did it. Only I went a step too far, didn't I? I started to believe I was attractive. But that wasn't what you wanted. You wanted me needing *you* so I could believe in myself. You wanted me to depend on you so much I'd do anything you wanted. You even paid for my house so I'd feel obliged to you. Well, it won't work. I'm grateful for what you've done, for me and for the ranch. I can't repay you for helping to rebuild my self-confidence, but I can and will pay you for your work at the ranch and on the house."

"I don't want your damned money!"

"Now you'd better go. I'm sure your promises are weighing heavily on your conscience. I'll be staying in town tonight. That will give you time to leave the ranch before I return."

He couldn't let her go like this, thinking she had to paint herself or buy expensive gowns to be attractive, that she had to have a pretty face or nothing else mattered. What she was inside had transformed what she thought was an ordinary face into something special, something unique, something that reached out to him as sheer beauty never had.

He stretched out a hand to bring her back, but someone knocked his arm away.

"Let her go."

It was Myrl. He looked stone cold sober. And angry. And just behind him Ben approached, an equally angry expression on his face. That was when Owen saw at least a dozen people staring at him, their expressions ranging from curious to bewildered to angry.

"I was just trying to convince her she didn't need to paint herself to be attractive."

"And you think telling her she needs you to control her was the way to do that?" Myrl said.

"I don't want to control her."

"Yes, you do," Ben said. "You want to control everybody around you. You did something for me I couldn't have done for myself. I'll always be grateful, but you expected us to pretty much abandon our lives and do what you wanted."

"You told us to be part of the rustler's patrol, and we did it," Myrl said. "I even stopped drinking."

"You told us to help build Hetta's house, and we did it," Ben said. "We stayed at the ranch when you wanted, slept in town when you wanted. You forced Hetta to let you brand her cows. You built her a house she didn't want. Now you want to tell her how to dress."

"Who convinced her she didn't love William, that she shouldn't marry him?" Myrl asked.

"I won't apologize for that."

"Nobody's asking you to," Ben said. "Our lives were out of shape. You came along and bent them back into shape, but you're not responsible for us anymore."

Owen had never felt responsible for them but nor did he feel they were a burden. He'd finally been able to do something for someone other than himself, finally begun to *think* of someone other than himself, and here it was being thrown back in his face.

"I didn't do anything expecting gratitude."

"We know that. We wouldn't have said anything if you hadn't said what you did to Hetta."

311

They didn't understand. It was different with Hetta. Ben just needed time for his injury to heal. Myrl just needed a job, but Hetta had been about to do something that would have ruined her life.

"What did you expect me to do? She's going back to William." Owen pointed to where William and Ida were talking excitedly. "She told him to give the good news to Ida. I expect they're already planning the wedding."

Ben turned to where Hetta had disappeared. "I don't think you're reading this one right," Ben said.

"There's one thing I'm reading right," Owen said. "She told me to be gone before she gets back to the ranch."

Owen turned away. Without thinking, he found his feet carrying him in the direction Hetta had gone. The moment he realized what he was doing, he stopped. There was no point in following her. They'd said all there was to say. He should have left after they'd finished the branding.

He'd told her he'd leave when he took her steers north to market, but somehow he'd taken it for granted he would return. He would have to pay her, help her decide whether to buy extra cows, make sure she wasn't being hit by rustlers. He'd hadn't accepted that there had to be a final break. He had started thinking she belonged in his life.

Yet the break had come, and he'd be a fool not to recognize it. It wasn't the way he'd imagined, but maybe it was best. It was sharp and painful. There could be no question about coming back to help her. When he rode out tomorrow, it would be final. He turned and headed to the hotel to collect his horse and saddlebags.

It was like walking into a head wind. He had to fight his feet to make them move. His body wanted something his mind knew he couldn't have. She didn't want him and had told him so. She'd told him so many times before.

It was time he believed her.

*   *   *

Hetta's eyes were so filled with tears, she couldn't tell where she was going as she left the dance hall. How could she have been so foolish as to let herself fall in love with Owen? She had known from the first what he was like. But he'd behaved so differently from her father, she'd decided he was an exception.

New rule: There are no exceptions. No, it was an old rule. She'd just forgotten it.

What could have made her think a man like Owen would marry anyone like her or settle down if he did? When she'd broken off with William, she'd even decided she didn't want to be married. She couldn't imagine what had caused everything to change.

That wasn't true. There was something wonderful about being in love. Days were sunnier. Problems weren't nearly so difficult to solve or hard to face. And no matter what happened, there was the feeling that everything would turn out right in the end.

Which was an object lesson. When things seemed to be going too well, they probably were. Any sensible woman would have been looking over her shoulder, watching for signs of the approaching disaster.

She hadn't, and it had caught her unaware.

Laveau diViere kept to the shadows, his curses silent on moving lips. What in hell was Owen Wheeler doing in Pinto Junction? The man should have been a hundred miles to the north living like a fat, lazy bastard on a ranch he'd helped his cousin steal from Laveau. He cursed again. He'd spent a year trying to get over the humiliation of having to jump through a window to keep from being captured by Cade Wheeler. He knew they'd try to hang him if they got their hands on him, but he'd spent the last year building contacts with the Union troops. By bribing the men of an army troop to go around with him to back up his story, he'd been able to convince people in towns like Pinto Junction that he could protect them from the army and rustlers alike.

They didn't know the army wasn't anxious to travel very far from the coast, but he did. That suited his plans well. He'd used Hetta Gwynne's ranch, along with two others, as holding stations for cattle he rustled farther north. He'd been furious when he heard Tom Manly had been killed and the town had started a rustler patrol.

He breathed a sigh of relief when Hetta walked away from Owen. Maybe he could salvage the situation yet. He followed her and caught up.

"Miss Gwynne."

Hetta slowed down but didn't stop. The voice was familiar, but she couldn't place it. She attempted to dry her eyes.

"Miss Gwynne."

Hetta turned to see the handsome face of Mr. Laveau diViere staring back at her. Surprise momentarily kept her silent.

"Don't you remember me?" he asked.

"Yes. I just hadn't expected to see you."

"Business has kept me away. Why are you leaving the dance?"

"I have a headache. I thought a little quiet might help it go away."

"I'll accompany you. We have things to talk about."

Hetta didn't feel entirely comfortable with diViere accompanying her, but she didn't have a reason to refuse.

"You did get my payment, didn't you?" he asked.

"Yes. Thank you."

"It's about time for another one."

"You haven't used my ranch for months."

"I leased the right to use it. That means I have to pay you even if I don't use it."

Hetta didn't know why that made her uneasy. It was a

perfectly good business concept. She guessed she was letting what Owen had told her about diViere influence her thinking. It made her skin crawl to think she was alone with a man who could cold-bloodedly betray his friends.

"This isn't a very good time," she said.

"I promise I won't take long."

"Then we can talk here."

"I never discuss business in public," diViere said. "I'll feel much better in your parlor."

She gave in gracefully. DiViere was very careful to observe the proprieties. He waited outside until she had lighted the lamps.

"Now what do you want to discuss?" she asked when he'd seated himself.

"I noticed you were talking to Owen Wheeler."

"I didn't see you at the dance."

"I had just arrived, but I overheard some of what you were saying. You're wise to tell him to leave."

Hetta controlled her impulse to defend Owen. "Do you know him?"

"Not well, but he doesn't have a good reputation."

"What has he done?"

"He's something of a lady's man. He picks out a victim and charms her out of her good sense. I've heard it said he always manages to walk away with a fat wallet."

"How could he do that?"

"Maybe the families of these impressionable young women pay him to leave."

She didn't doubt that Owen would attempt to dazzle any attractive female he met, but she couldn't imagine him taking money. DiViere was up to something, and she wanted to know what it was.

"He may have a poor character, but I need his help at the ranch."

"I'm willing to continue our relationship. Isn't that help enough?"

"I still need to rebuild my ranch. You won't always want to use my land, and I have to be able to support myself."

"Surely you can find more dependable men."

"Owen Wheeler is the best worker I've ever had."

DiViere looked thoughtful, as if he was trying to make up his mind what to say next.

"Have you thought that he might have an ulterior motive?"

"What?"

"He could be establishing one kind of character to act as a cover for what he is really doing."

She forced herself to laugh. "He tried to pass himself off as a gambler when he came here, even a gunman, but it didn't work."

"Why?"

"He rescued an old cowhand from drinking himself to death, gave a handicapped ex-soldier a chance to prove he could still do a good day's work, and helped a woman with no self-respect realize she was worth something after all."

"That's exactly what I meant, building a character to cover what he is really doing."

"What could that be?"

"Rustling. I'm told hundreds of steers have been stolen in the last two months. More than before he arrived."

Owen was right. DiViere was a liar. "I don't know who told you that," she said with as much wide-eyed wonder as she could muster. "Owen organized a rustler watch a month ago. We haven't had more than a dozen head go missing since."

DiViere's smile was slow and showed no trace of chagrin. "An all-around good Samaritan. I appear to have underestimated Owen."

"War does change people, though not always for the better."

She thought she detected a tightening of his expression, a flash of some strong, violent emotion.

"Do you mean something in particular by that?"

A little voice told her to shut up, but a rebellious streak told her she ought to stand up to him. She'd been running from things all her life. This was her chance to decide just how much of a stake she wanted to have in her community. She could stand up for what she thought was right, or she could turn her head and let someone else do it.

The way the people of Pinto Junction had done before Owen arrived.

"Owen says you're behind the rustling, that he followed you from San Antonio. He says you wanted my ranch to hold stolen cattle until you could drive them to Mexico."

"Is that all your very opinionated friend said?"

"That's all that affects me."

"And do you believe him?"

"That depends on what you tell me."

"I assume he told you I betrayed his troop."

She nodded in assent. She was surprised when he started laughing very softly, so softly it was almost sinister. "It's a real shame he and his cousin weren't killed when their troop was ambushed."

What kind of man was diViere to be able to laugh and wish men dead at the same time?

"If the fool had gone in like I told him, no one would have escaped. But he couldn't possibly take advice from a traitorous Johnny Reb. I drank a toast when I heard he'd been killed."

Hetta had thought her father was evil, but now she realized Owen was right when he said Patrick Gwynne had been just mean and jealous. DiViere was evil.

"It's easy to take the steers," diViere said. "Some of the fools haven't branded their stock. All I have to do is run them off and place my brand on them. The rest are too afraid of the Indians or the bandits to come after me."

Hetta couldn't believe he was sitting there calmly telling her he was a rustler and describing how he did it.

"When Owen finds out you're here, he'll arrest you."

There was that smile again. She didn't trust it.

"I think you'll find he'll be the one who's in danger of being arrested."

"Why?"

"Let me worry about that. You should concentrate on continuing our relationship. I'm expanding my operation, and I need to buy your ranch."

"I'm not selling my ranch to anyone. What's more, I plan to tell the sheriff you're behind the rustling."

He was laughing again. She was beginning to hate that.

"Foolish girl. Do you think I would have told you what I did if I thought you or Owen could harm me?"

"He says he can prove you're the rustler."

"The army would have me out of jail and this town under its heel in less than a week."

"They'll believe me."

"Not after I show them receipts for stolen cattle with your signature on them."

Chapter Twenty-seven

He couldn't possibly have any such receipts. She'd never rustled any cattle. She wouldn't know where to sell them if she had.

"How . . . ?"

"You signed the agreement between us," he reminded her. "It was easy enough to find someone who could copy your signature."

"People here have known me all their lives."

"Don't they find it odd that none of your cows have been stolen in the last few months?"

"But no rustler would sign anything." It had never occurred to her that she would need to protect herself from this man. Everyone except Owen trusted him.

"I've learned to protect my back," he said.

"If you stopped rustling, you wouldn't have to."

His expression turned ugly again. "If Cade Wheeler hadn't stolen my ranch, I wouldn't have to rustle."

From what Owen had said of his cousin, she didn't

think Cade Wheeler had ever stolen so much as a dime in his entire life. "What do you want from me?"

"To continue our arrangement. It might work out even better if people think you're rebuilding your herd. You've got so much land, no one will notice my cows."

Hetta got to her feet. "It's pointless to continue this discussion. You can't use my land anymore. What's more, if rustling around here starts again, I'll go to the sheriff and tell him you're responsible."

Without getting up, diViere regarded her with something akin to amusement. "I like a woman with spirit. Is that what Owen sees in you?"

"That's none of your business."

"I'm curious how a woman whose face is unremarkable—but I feel compelled to add that the rest of your attractions are very remarkable—has captivated a man famous for his addiction to beautiful women."

"I haven't captivated Owen."

"He's spent months building your house . . . and paying for it. I find that most interesting of all."

Hetta felt her skin burn, and it made her furious. "I borrowed the money."

"I'd be most interested to know how you intend to repay such a loan."

Hetta marched across the room and threw open the parlor door. "We have nothing further to say to each other."

DiViere got to his feet with a languid slowness that was an insult in itself. "I hope that's not the case." He reached inside his coat and withdrew his wallet. He took out several papers, one of which he handed to Hetta. "Let me leave this with you. I think you'll find it very interesting."

Hetta took the paper without looking at it. "I'll give it my closest attention. Now leave."

"I'll be back to see you tomorrow."

"I won't see you."

His hateful smile appeared again. "I believe you will."

Hetta followed him to the front door. She didn't take a deep breath until she had locked the door behind him.

The paper seemed to burn in her hand. It contained nothing of any significance except the signature. *Her* signature. It wouldn't do any good to destroy it. She was certain diViere had more. She believed she could convince the sheriff she was innocent, but the longer she stared at the signature, the more uneasy she became. No one would condemn her publicly, but she was afraid many would have doubts. And if diViere could get people to forge signatures for him, he might be able to manipulate the rustling as well. Maybe he was laying another trap for her, one she couldn't see yet.

She had to talk to Owen. He would know what to do. She was going to see him because he was the only one who understood how truly evil diViere was. No one else would believe her.

She was certain everyone in town would welcome diViere. And once that happened, he would be back demanding to use her ranch. He might even attempt to force her to sell it to him. She couldn't allow that. The ranch was the only thing in the world she truly loved, the only thing she couldn't do without.

Somewhere in her heart a tiny voice whispered *Owen*, but she wouldn't listen. She had to learn to live without him. After what he'd said tonight, she had no choice.

Owen gazed at the house that rose up before him, a dark shape against the star-filled sky. Like hundreds of other houses, it was nothing more than a collection of wood and stone. Better than most, not as good as some. There was nothing special about its exterior. There was nothing elaborate about its interior. Yet it was part of him.

"You took care of that tonight," he said aloud to himself.

He'd begun the ride from town determined to pack up and be gone before dawn, but each step his horse took seemed to diminish the anger that filled him, his need to put distance between himself and the only woman he'd ever believed he could trust. By the time he'd reached the ranch, he was wondering where everything had gone off course.

He couldn't remember when he'd stopped lumping Hetta with all other women, when he'd decided she was someone he wanted to help, to get to know. It probably began the moment he decided to improve her self-image. His sister was the sweetest, kindest person he'd ever known, but no matter how hard he worked to build her self-confidence, their father's indifference and their mother's selfishness tore it down again.

Hetta was stronger than his sister. All she needed was someone to believe in her, to convince her to believe in herself.

He believed in her, too.

But he hadn't been able to believe in her tonight. He'd taken one look at her and William together—the image of her kissing him still burned in his memory—and all rational thought had left him. Anger such as he hadn't known in years had consumed him; he'd said things he didn't mean. He'd just wanted to lash out, to hurt her as much as he'd been hurt.

Had he been hurt? Disappointed, betrayed, and used, but hurt? You had to be emotionally involved to be hurt. You had to have let someone inside your defenses, let them come to mean something to you. But if he hadn't been hurt, why was he feeling as if he'd lost something of great value he could never replace?

He looked up at the house again. The feeling that he belonged here wouldn't go away. Somehow it had become a part of him. It probably came from his having been the one to build it. He'd helped build houses before, but he'd never felt this attachment. There was a feeling of permanency, constancy, but why should he have found it here?

Because of Hetta.

He'd have to be a fool not to recognize that truth. But it was the nature and the extent of the connection that surprised and upset him. He'd sworn he'd never get emotionally involved with anyone.

He'd failed.

He'd also sworn he'd never let anything control him.

He'd failed at that, too.

And that meant he had to leave before he lost the last shred of pretense that he was in control of his life.

Yet he couldn't leave without seeing Hetta again. He had to tell her he hoped she would be happy with William. He'd been wrong to try to separate them. If she wanted William badly enough to wear a fancy dress and cover her face with cosmetics, she ought to have him.

But even as he made this resolution, he knew it would be the hardest thing he'd ever do. He didn't want her to marry William. He wanted her to want him instead.

Okay, he'd finally admitted the truth. He wanted Hetta for himself. But that didn't help. He didn't want to get married. Just the thought of being tied down made him jittery. Besides, he wasn't marriage material. Neither of his parents were nice people.

The sound of hoofbeats intruded on his thoughts. It was probably Myrl or Ben, but he didn't want to see them. He walked over to his horse, picked up the reins, started to lead the animal into the trees. Maybe whoever it was would decide he'd gone somewhere else and go back to town.

But he changed his mind. He'd been running from things his whole life. First his mother, then his father, his sister, and finally himself. It was time to face what he was and come to terms with it. He wanted to go off somewhere and see if he could discover who he really was. But before he did, he had to see Hetta one last time.

Hetta had rehearsed what she meant to say to Owen, but the moment he materialized from the shadows, the words went straight out of her head. How could she think of diViere or rustling when the man she loved stared at her as though his worst nightmare had just materialized before his eyes?

"I had to come," she said, determined to speak before he did. "I had to tell you—"

He cut her off. "I was going to come see you in the morning."

"Then you know?"

"I didn't know until tonight, but if you really want to marry William, I hope you'll be happy."

"I don't want to marry William," she said, forgetting all about diViere.

"But I saw you kissing him."

"He and Ida are in love with each other. I couldn't get Ida to listen, so I was trying to build up his courage to talk to Ida despite her resistance."

He looked as if he didn't believe her, *couldn't* believe her.

"It was a kiss of friendship. You told me that friends kiss each other, remember?"

He still looked doubtful.

"I couldn't be in love with him, not now that I've fallen in love with someone else."

He looked shocked. Then he turned stiff; his face became wooden.

"I'm sorry for what I said," he began. "I should have told you that you looked very pretty tonight, but you reminded me of my mother. And when I thought you'd just used me . . ."

"You were angry and wanted to get back at me."

He didn't say anything, but she didn't need words. Pain had caused him to strike back at her. She felt hope surge within her. The more she had hurt him, the greater the possibility he was in love with her.

"I don't know who you're in love with," he said, "but I hope it's somebody who can make you happy."

"I'm sure he can, but I don't know if he will."

That startled the stiffness out of him. "Is he crazy?"

"I don't think he knows I'm in love with him."

"That's not surprising. You haven't been off the ranch enough in the last two months for him to know you're interested."

"He knows, but he's determined not to fall in love. He doesn't trust it. He doesn't trust women. But mainly he doesn't trust himself."

He turned suddenly still. "Why?"

"Because he thinks he's like his mother. And though he would deny it with his last breath, he loved his mother very much. He had to, or she couldn't have hurt him so much."

He looked as though he'd been turned to stone. "You're in love with me?"

She smiled at the look of disbelief on his face. "Couldn't you tell? Everyone else could."

He came toward her, stumbling at first, then more quickly. She didn't wait for him to reach her. She threw herself out of the saddle into his arms.

The feel of his arms closing around her was like the fragmented parts of her life finally coming together. She was where she belonged, where she wanted to be.

"You shouldn't love me," Owen said after he broke the kiss. "I'm the last person in the world to be able to give you what you need."

"I don't know what I need or what I want."

"You deserve a husband who will be faithful to you, who will think nothing in his day is more important than coming home to you and going to sleep with his arms around you. You deserve a man who has an unblemished reputation, who is respected by your friends. Most of all you deserve a man who thinks you're the most wonderful woman in the world."

"I'll settle for a man who's not quite such a paragon," she said, trying to keep from crying. "I don't want to feel as if he's doing me a favor by marrying me."

"No one could feel like that, especially not anyone who knows you."

"Then it's fortunate I fell in love with you. There's nobody who knows me better.' "

He stiffened. "But I'm not the man for you."

"Do you like me?"

"More than I can say."

"Let's forget all this talk about husbands, and you can concentrate on telling me what you like about me. Don't worry about it being more than you can say. I've got nothing else planned for tonight."

He held her away from him. "I'm being serious."

"So am I. No one has ever told me what they like about me."

"I've told you."

"Tell me again. I have a terrible memory."

"I can't *be* what you deserve."

"Then let's enjoy the moment. If it's all we have, I don't want to waste it."

"Do you know what you're saying?"

"Yes."

Did she really know what she was doing? She couldn't be sure, but she couldn't stop herself. She'd been holding herself in reserve her entire life. She hoped she could penetrate Owen's defenses, get him to let down his guard far enough to discover how he felt about her. She might fail. It hadn't been easy for her to overcome years of thinking herself worthless. She was certain it would be even harder for him.

"Why are you doing this?" he asked.

"You've restored my faith in myself. I want to do the same for you."

"Why?"

"Because if you can believe in yourself, you can believe in love." He didn't appear to be convinced. She caressed his cheek with her hand. "You have a lot to give, Owen Wheeler."

"I'm not making any promises."

"I'm not asking for any. Now, are you going to kiss me again, or do I have to show you how?"

He didn't need any more encouragement. For a fleeting moment Hetta was sorry Ida would never know the pleasure of kisses such as Owen could give. He picked her up and carried her to the house. She was pleased when he headed to the log room. When he took her inside, she felt she had come home.

He sat down on the bed with her in his lap. She knew she was too big for that, but she liked the feeling. She rested her forearms on his shoulders and intertwined her fingers behind his head. She could barely see his face in the dim light coming through the window, but she didn't need light. She'd memorized every part of his face weeks ago.

"What made you think I had gone back to William?" she asked.

"Stupidity."

"You're not stupid. There must be a reason."

"Will jealousy do, with a little anger thrown in?"

"I don't know. Nobody's ever been jealous of me before."

"That's because you never let anybody think they had a right to be jealous."

"You're not telling me everything."

327

"I've told you many times how attractive you are."

"You've said I had a fantastic shape, beautiful hair, and striking eyes. You haven't said they placed you under some kind of spell."

"You want to dig out every secret I have, don't you?"

"I just want to know how you feel about me. And I don't want any descriptions of my skin."

"I like you in a way I've never liked another woman. I thought you were different, that you couldn't be influenced by money and position the way my mother was. That's why I had to convince you that you didn't love William. You deserve so much more than the tepid kind of love he can give you." He reached up, took her hands in his, gripped them tightly. "Good God, Hetta, you have no idea what kind of passion can exist between a man and a woman."

"I thought that's what love was supposed to teach me."

"I've never been in love, but liking, respect, and strong physical attraction can stir up passions from deep in the soul."

"You never acted as if you were strongly attracted to me."

"After Rachelle, I swore I'd never do that again, even if it meant I'd never live with a woman."

"Will you feel guilty about me?"

"Everything will be different with you."

"Why? What caught your interest?" She needed to know that she meant more to him than just another conquest.

"I couldn't stand to see you being grateful to Ida just because she treated you like a human being. You're special, and I had to make you see that."

"So you talked me into breaking off my not-quite-engagement, branded my calves, and built my house. There must have been an easier way."

"I thought of one, but I was afraid to try."

She chuckled. "I can't believe you've ever been afraid of any woman."

"I was afraid that if I went too far, you'd expect more than I could give. And if you felt I'd betrayed your trust, you'd never trust any man again."

"And that was important?"

"More important than anything."

It wasn't the declaration of love she'd hoped for, but if she could keep him in Pinto Junction a little longer, she'd find a way to make him realize she was more important to him than he suspected. She knew he would go on refusing to admit he was in love because it made him feel vulnerable. She'd spent years building her defenses, but Owen had stormed her barricades and torn them down. Now she had to find a way to do that for him.

"I didn't wear that dress or use cosmetics for William. I did it for you."

"Why?" He sounded as though he couldn't believe her.

"The whole time we've been working on this house, I was certain your feelings for me were growing stronger, but you gradually put more and more distance between us. You even stopped telling me I was attractive. When you asked Ben and Myrl to start sleeping here rather than going back to town every night, I knew you liked me more than you would admit. I was desperate to find some way to break your control."

"And all you had to do was appear to be interested in William again. I did break rather badly, didn't I?"

"Right in front of everybody, so you'll never be able to deny it."

"I don't want to deny it."

"What do you want to do?"

"I'd rather show you you're right."

329

Chapter Twenty-eight

Hetta didn't have any way to compare Owen's kisses, but she didn't need to kiss anybody else to know he was special. He had to be because he made her feel special.

His kisses were gentle, like butterflies brushing her lips. Yet his kisses were satisfying. Clearly, kisses could vary with the mood or what you wanted your partner to feel. It was an entirely new and exciting language, one that had an unlimited number of wonderful messages to whisper as soon as she learned to understand what it meant.

But just now she didn't need to know much more than that Owen was holding her, kissing her, running his hands up and down her arms, causing goose bumps to pop out all over her. How could she have guessed the touch of the man she loved could cause such a reaction? Was this the reason her mother had said she couldn't turn against her husband, no matter what he did? Hetta tried to put her parents out of her mind, but she couldn't stop wondering if she would feel the same way about

Owen as her mother had felt about her husband.

As important as that question was, Hetta was losing her ability to think logically. The feel of Owen's lips on her mouth, neck, and shoulders, the feel of his hands as they caressed her from shoulder to wrist, the feeling of his body shifting and swelling under her as she sat in his lap—it was all acting on her like an electric charge. She remembered one night after a terrible electric storm when she was a child, the air had seemed so charged with energy the small hairs on her body stood on end.

That was how she felt now, as if every part of her was waking up, beginning to tingle with excitement, to hum with contentment, to warm with desire.

"You . . . taste . . . so . . . good," Owen said.

His words were disjointed because he was planting kisses all over her, but it wasn't important. They were communicating on a level where words were unnecessary, maybe even unwanted, certainly inadequate. She marveled that things could have changed so quickly for her, that she had asked Owen to make love to her when just a few weeks ago she wouldn't have let a man touch her, much less kiss her.

But Owen could do anything to her he wanted.

She hoped he would.

Owen woke to find Hetta lying beside him and a guilty conscience working overtime. He'd taken his pleasure of her without promising anything for the future. Again. She didn't ask it of him, but he knew he ought to give something.

He *wanted* to give something, but the old fear wouldn't go away. Marriage wouldn't work if you were really in love. It would only hurt you. Hetta didn't trust love any more than he did, probably less, but knowing that still didn't satisfy him. And this morning he finally knew why.

He was in love with Hetta.

A few months ago that thought would have scared him so badly, he'd have jumped into his pants and ridden out as soon as he could saddle his horse. Now he felt a great sense of relief. He was in love, truly, honestly, completely in love, and he was happy about it. He knew it made him vulnerable. He'd never had a serious or sustained relationship in his life. He looked for the worst in people and didn't believe in the best. Settling down in one place had always been something he couldn't do.

But now he *wanted* to be in one place. He *wanted* to put down roots, to become part of a community, to have a family, to build a life that had meaning rather than being filled only with moments of satisfaction masquerading as happiness.

He looked at Hetta lying beside him and wondered again how anyone could think she was plain. Hers wasn't the kind of beauty that would fade with age or be compromised by children and hard work. It would only grow more lustrous through the years. After so many misspent years, he didn't deserve such a wife.

But would she marry him?

He'd behaved like a fool at the dance. Even though she loved him, she wouldn't be able to forget how quick he'd been to think the worst.

It might take a little time to learn to think and behave differently, but he could do it. He *had* to do it if he was to achieve the happiness he wanted.

He slipped out of bed without waking her. He dressed and left the log room. He liked the early morning. The air always felt cool and crisp. It looked clear, undisturbed by the activity of the day. Even the industrious birds didn't spoil the peacefulness. But the two riders coming up the trail did. It took just a moment to realize that even though the riders looked familiar, they weren't Ben and Myrl. A smile began to spread slowly over his face.

Broc and Nate. It would be good to see his old friends after so many months.

The smile vanished abruptly. Broc and Nate wouldn't be interested in anything except the whereabouts of Laveau. Owen hadn't done his part. Even worse, he had spent last night in Hetta's arms rather than going to town to chase down Laveau. She had told him about Laveau after they'd made love. Broc wasn't going to like that. Nate would hate it.

But the two men rode up with smiles on their faces. "I told you," Broc said to Nate. "Now pay up."

"Not until I make sure you're right."

"What are you two doing here?" Owen asked as the men dismounted.

"Coming to see what you've been up to," Broc said. "You've been suspiciously quiet for a long time."

"Broc said you'd probably found yourself a comfortable nest with a pretty young widow and forgotten all about us."

Broc gave the house an appreciative look. "Looks like a real good nest to me."

"A really good nest," Nate echoed. "What does the owner look like?"

"She looks like me."

Hetta had heard what they'd said.

"I tried to get away from these brutes," Owen said, determined to put the best face he could on a terrible situation, "but they followed me."

"I'm sorry for anything I said, ma'am," Nate said, having the decency to look abashed. "Just giving Owen a hard time. We didn't mean anything by it."

"He's a good man." Broc's seconding of Nate's opinion was feeble.

Hetta just smiled. "I don't know your names, but since you appear to be his friends, I'll invite you in for breakfast."

"We don't want to put you out, ma'am," Nate said.

"You won't if you stop calling me ma'am. My name's Hetta Gwynne."

"I'm Nate Dolan from Arkansas," Nate said.

"Broc Kincaid from Tennessee," Broc said.

"We were in the same troop during the war," Owen explained. "The army didn't care what kind of riffraff they let in."

"They must be very good," Hetta said. "They kept you alive."

Broc and Nate looked at each other, smirks on their faces. "I think he's met his match," Broc said.

"I hope so," Nate said.

"Owen will show you where to put your horses." Hetta smiled prettily, a smile Owen knew meant trouble. "What caused you boys to turn up just now? It couldn't be you've been pining for Owen's company."

Nate's expression changed immediately. "We've been following Laveau," he said to Owen. "He's brought a herd of rustled cattle down this way."

"Where is he?" Owen asked.

"We don't know. We were late getting the news. Then a couple of rains washed out any trace of him. We were hoping you could tell us."

"You can discuss it over breakfast," Hetta said. "Then we can go into town. Laveau is supposed to be back sometime tonight."

Hetta disappeared into the house.

"Is she . . . ? Are you—" Nate started.

"Don't ask," Broc said.

"If you're asking if I'm in love with her, the answer is yes," Owen said. "If you're asking is she in love with me, I want her to be."

"Well, I'll be damned," Nate said.

"Me, too," Broc added.

334

"I never thought you'd fall for anybody who wasn't . . ." Nate's voice died away.

"Beautiful?" Owen added for him.

"Well, yeah. You always were so damned particular."

"A lot of things have changed since I took the road south," Owen said.

"That's obvious," Broc said. "I want to hear every detail."

So while they unsaddled their horses, rubbed them down, and staked them out to graze, Owen related the events of the past few months.

"Are you going to marry her?" Nate asked.

"I don't know if she'll agree after this morning."

"Hey, we're sorry about that," Broc said.

"At least she's still talking to you," Nate said.

"Women always talk to him," Broc said. "How can we help?"

"Catch Laveau. At least she'll know I was telling the truth about something. Now when we go inside, see if you can say something good about me."

"I don't remember anything," Broc said, "but I'll make up something."

"You don't remember because there isn't anything," Nate said.

"I should have taken a shotgun to you two the minute I recognized you," Owen said.

"And have to capture Laveau all by yourself?"

"It would be easier than putting up with you two."

Owen hadn't realized how much he'd missed his friends. He must be getting sentimental.

Hetta had prepared a large breakfast. "I know how men eat," she said.

The men helped themselves to seconds.

"We had to take care of ourselves during the war," Broc explained.

"Your wife will appreciate it," Hetta said.

"I'm not likely to get one with this face."

Broc usually mentioned his face to set people at ease. The scars were impossible to ignore.

"Very often external scars are easier to live with than internal ones," Hetta said.

"She's just the woman you need," Nate said to Broc. "Want me to help you steal her away from Owen?"

"She's not anybody's woman," Owen said. "But if you think you're getting in line ahead of me, you've been eating loco weed."

"Go ahead and fight over me," Hetta said with a teasing smile. "Nobody's ever done that."

"Are all the men in this town blind?" Broc asked.

"They see all too well," Hetta said, "but it was sweet of you to say that."

"That's Broc for you," Owen said, feeling an unaccustomed twinge of jealousy, "sweet as can be."

Hetta got up. "While I wash up, you can decide what to do about Mr. diViere. But you'll do well to remember he's practically a hero in Pinto Junction. Convincing people he's a deserter and a rustler won't be easy."

For the next twenty minutes the men discussed possible courses of action. In the end they came to the conclusion they'd have to play it by ear. As long as the Union army remained in Texas, Laveau had a formidable protector. If they took things into their own hands, they would immediately become outlaws.

"I think you ought to let me help," Hetta said.

"Why?" Nate asked.

"He has forged papers which make it look like I've been rustling. He thinks he's got me backed into a corner, and he won't be on his guard with me."

"I don't like it," Owen said.

"What do you have in mind?" Nate asked Hetta.

"Send him a message saying I want to talk to him. When he comes to the house, you can be here."

"No," Owen said.

"It sounds perfect," Nate said.

"I don't want Hetta in the same room with Laveau."

"She can make an excuse to leave before we move in," Broc said.

Owen still didn't like it.

"Let's head for town," Hetta said.

"It's not decided," Owen said.

"We had an understanding, remember? I have no control over you, and you have none over me."

"I was a fool to agree to that," Owen said.

"Amen," Broc said.

"I don't want you to do this," Owen said after Nate and Broc left the room. "I don't trust Laveau."

"You'll be in the house before he arrives. What could go wrong?"

"Anything. Everything."

"Okay, Owen, what is it you're not saying?"

He guessed it was now or never. He had to tell her at this moment, or she'd never believe him. "I love you. I couldn't stand it if you got hurt."

She looked at him as if he'd started speaking a foreign language and she didn't understand a word.

"I've never felt this way about anyone, and it scares me to death."

"When did you fall in love with me?" Her voice was almost disembodied.

"I don't know, but I realized it this morning when I was sitting on the bed watching you sleep."

"Why didn't you tell me?"

"Because I was afraid you'd say you didn't love me."

"I told you I did a long time ago."

"I don't mean it like that. I mean I love you like I want us to build a life together, have children, become part of the community."

"You're saying you want to marry me?"

337

"Is that so hard to believe?"

"I didn't think you wanted to marry anybody."

"I didn't until I met you."

"What changed your mind?"

"You did. I was determined to uncover the wonderful, vital person that's the real you. I liked what I found so much I fell in love with you."

Hetta just stared at him.

"Say something," he said.

"I'm thinking."

"Say something else."

"I've got to do a lot of thinking. In the meantime, we have to catch Mr. diViere."

"I'm not letting you go."

Hetta had started toward the door, but she turned. "You don't control me. Not now, not ever. We ride as equals or we don't ride at all."

"Hell, you sound like Cade. He was always ordering me around, too."

"Neither of us will give orders. We come up with them together. You think that's possible?"

"No, but I'm willing to give it a try."

"You can't go downtown," Ida said to Hetta. "The sheriff says he's going to lock you up."

"Nobody's locking her up," Owen said. They had planned to keep out of sight in Ida's house until they captured Laveau.

"He's looking for you, too," William said. "He figures Hetta couldn't have done this by herself."

"Everybody knows my own stock was rustled, my house struck by lightning and burned, and that I lived with you while Mr. diViere used my ranch."

"He says it was a ruse, that you fooled him, too," William said.

"People are asking where you got the money to build

that big house," William said. He dropped his gaze to the floor. "I didn't tell them Owen paid for it."

"That's not important now," Hetta said. "What can I do to prove my innocence?"

"Produce Laveau with the stolen cattle," Owen said.

"I agree," Broc said.

"I'll get Myrl," Owen said. "He knows this area better than anyone."

"You can't," William said. "The sheriff's got Myrl and Ben down at the jail. He thinks they have been helping you and Hetta."

"We have to get them out," Hetta said. "I won't have two innocent men in jail just because they worked for me."

"What should we do?" Broc asked.

Owen didn't like the plan they settled on, but Hetta was insistent.

"They're in jail because of me. It's only fair that I take a small risk to get them out."

"I don't call being put in jail a small risk."

"You just make sure you get Myrl and Ben out."

The plan was to have Hetta go to Fred Moody's office. She would go through the middle of town, telling people she would explain everything at the bank. With luck, that would draw the people off the street, the sheriff out of his office, and give them a chance to break Myrl and Ben out of jail.

"You make sure nothing happens to her," Owen said to William.

"Nothing will happen to Hetta," Ida said, her eyes filling with moisture. "I owe her everything."

Owen was afraid he was going to be forced to endure one of those tearful displays females indulged in which so completely mystified him.

"Don't you start crying," Hetta said to Ida. "You've got to look indignant, even fierce, and that's hard with tears

339

running down your face. Now let's get going. The sooner we get Ben and Myrl out of jail, the sooner we can go after the rustled herd."

"You aren't planning to go, are you?" William asked Hetta.

"Of course I am. It's my reputation that's on the line."

Poor William. He never would have understood Hetta even if he'd been married to her twenty years. Owen wasn't sure he understood her, but he sure as hell approved of her. She was the most woman God had ever put into one skin. He had made up his mind he wouldn't be satisfied until she agreed to marry him.

"I think you're actually enjoying this," Ida said to Hetta.

"In a way I am." They had already encountered about a dozen people, who were amazed Hetta would appear in public. Curious to hear what she had to say, the crowd following her grew until it seemed the entire population of Pinto Junction was on its way to the bank.

"I don't understand you," Ida said.

"I didn't understand myself until recently."

"Until Owen showed up."

"Yes. It was about then."

"Are you going to marry him?" William asked.

"Has he asked you to marry him?" Ida asked, astonished.

"Yes."

"What did you say?"

"She probably said she would," one woman snapped.

"*I'd* marry him if he asked me," a young woman walking nearby said.

"But he's a rustler!" the first woman exclaimed.

"He's too handsome to be a rustler," the young woman replied.

"Straw," the first woman declared. "That's what you've got for brains."

"How many cows did you rustle?" an angry man asked Hetta.

"Are you going to believe a stranger over a woman you've known all your life?" Ida demanded.

"But diViere's got proof."

"Have you seen it?" Hetta asked.

"No, but—"

"Then you don't know what he has."

"Then where did you get the money for that big house?" the man asked.

"I'll answer all your questions when we reach the bank," Hetta said.

She kept wondering if Owen had been able to get to the sheriff's office. She hadn't heard any shots or shouts for help. Mr. diViere had gotten everybody so worked up, they were liable to act first and think later.

She hoped Owen wasn't worrying so much about her that he didn't pay attention to what he was doing. It was nice having somebody worry about her. She told herself to go slowly. She didn't doubt that Owen loved her, but marrying him meant a whole different kind of love. She wasn't certain she trusted herself not to turn into her mother. Owen was the kind of man it would be so very easy to love to the exclusion of common sense.

She would go to her grave alone before she turned into her mother.

And Owen was so much like her father in some ways, it gave her cold chills.

"All of you can't come inside." Fred Moody had met the crowd at the bank door.

"There's only room for about a dozen."

"We're all coming inside," the woman said, "even if it means some of us have to stand on your desk."

It took a while for everybody to get settled, but Hetta didn't mind. And the more noise they made, the less likely they were to hear any sounds from the street. Once they were quiet, the sheriff turned to Hetta. "I have evidence that shows you have been rustling cattle for nearly a year. What have you got to say for yourself?"

Chapter Twenty-nine

"This is almost like the war," Broc said.

"Except it's daylight," Nate added.

"And it's our own people who'll put our necks in a noose if we're caught," Owen said.

"We're depending on your silver tongue to protect us," Broc said.

"You'd better depend on Hetta."

"Are you going to marry her?" Nate asked.

"If she'll have me."

"I never thought I'd see the day a female would refuse you," Broc said.

"Well, you've seen it. Now stop picking at me and concentrate on getting to the jail without being caught."

"We don't have to worry," Nate said. "Nobody knows us."

"Yeah. We can just melt away and leave you to fend for yourself."

They had been making their way through the brush that grew along the edge of town.

"Do you think he'll have anybody guarding your friends?" Nate asked Owen.

"I don't know."

When they arrived at the jail, they found two deputies inside. "What do we do now?" Nate asked.

"You've got to get their attention," Owen said. "Give them some tale about following rustlers and wanting their help."

"Which has the virtue of being true," Broc pointed out.

"See if you can get them to go with you. If you can't, distract them long enough for me to get in through the back. Whatever you do, don't create a ruckus. If they find out I'm involved, Hetta will be in danger."

"You really are serious about her."

"Yes."

"Wait until Cade hears. He won't believe it."

"He'll have to when he's invited to the wedding. Now get going."

If there was a wedding, Owen thought as he watched Broc and Nate make their way to the main street. Hetta hadn't acted the least bit anxious to marry him. Maybe after almost marrying the wrong man, she had cold feet. He'd just have to convince her to change her mind.

The back door of the jail was locked, but the lock was so old-fashioned it didn't present any problem to a man who had taken apart and repaired locks when he was helping his father build houses. It wasn't really a jail. It was a house where the sheriff lived. Owen could hear his wife moving about upstairs. Two iron cells had been built in one of the rooms to serve as the jail. He would need keys to open them.

"What are you doing here?" Myrl asked the moment he saw Owen.

"You've got to get out of town," Ben said. "The sheriff is talking about hanging you."

"I'm getting you two out so we can find the rustlers and clear our names," Owen said. "Where are the keys?"

"The sheriff took them off a hook on the wall in the next room."

When he approached the door to the front room, Owen could hear Broc's sonorous voice—he'd been trained to act on a stage—through the wall. The responses of the other men were faint by comparison.

"Careful," Ben warned. "The deputy's lost nearly his whole herd. He's determined to make you pay for it."

Owen eased the door open enough to see that Broc and Nate had the two deputies in conversation, their backs turned to Owen. He could also see the keys hanging on a hook practically behind Herman Meyer, a hot-head with a habit of blaming his failures on someone else.

Owen eased the door open and slipped into the room. He knew he couldn't reach the keys without being discovered, but he wanted to get as close as he could. Broc helped by talking still louder to Meyer. Nate moved in so close, the other man couldn't do anything but gaze back. Owen had nearly reached the keys when some instinct warned Meyer to turn around.

"What the—" Meyer had his gun halfway out of the holster when Broc brought the butt of his own gun down on the back of Meyer's head. The man crumpled into a heap on the floor.

"The sheriff will come after you," the other man said, no fear showing in his eyes.

"I'm just collecting my friends so we can find the real rustlers," Owen said. "When we do, we'll bring them and the cows back." He took the keys off the hook.

"The sheriff says diViere has proof you and Hetta are the rustlers," the man said.

"He has forgeries," Owen said. "Now, I hate to do this, but I have to lock you and Herman up so you can't sound the alarm before we get out of town."

"Do you know who's been doing the rustling?" the man asked.

"Some of it. Maybe most."

"And you'll bring him in?"

"Yes."

The man walked willingly into the cage after Owen had released Ben and Myrl. "I'll make sure Herman keeps quiet," he said.

"What makes you believe me?" Owen asked.

"No rustler would do what you did for Ben and Myrl."

It was nice to know that some people believed in him despite Laveau's evidence. "I wish more people felt like that."

"You'd be surprised how many don't think you're the rustler. The sheriff didn't have any choice, not after di-Viere showed him those signed papers."

"Let's get going," Broc said. "You can chat with your neighbors later."

"Get your horses and meet me at the ranch," Owen said to Ben and Myrl.

"Where are you going?" Ben asked.

"To get Hetta."

"What do you want us to do?" Nate asked Owen as Ben and Myrl hurried out the back.

"Mix with the crowd at the bank. Find out what's happening."

"Where will you be?"

"Right here. Remember, no matter what happens, you're not to let anybody lay a hand on Hetta."

He wished he were the one to make sure Hetta was safe, but he knew he was the one person who would endanger her. He had to trust in Hetta's ingenuity and his friends' loyalty, but he swore he'd never let anything like this happen to her again.

"I don't care how many pieces of paper you have," Hetta said to the sheriff. "I didn't sign any of them."

"Then why would Mr. diViere say you had?"

"Because he's the rustler."

"Mr. diViere is a valued customer who has a substantial account with my bank," Fred Moody said.

"You've known me all my life," Hetta said. "Has any one of you ever known me to tell a lie?"

More than one person squirmed under her gaze.

"No," a man in the crowd said. "Nobody here has ever heard you lie."

"Maybe we haven't asked the right questions," a woman said.

"What questions would you like to ask, Alva?" Hetta said, turning to face the woman who'd heckled her on the way to the bank.

"Where'd you get the money to build that big house?"

"I borrowed it."

"Where? Fred didn't lend it to you."

"I borrowed it from Owen Wheeler."

"And just how do you propose to pay him back?"

The implication was obvious, but Hetta refused to blush. "By selling every steer I own in the spring."

"You could sell your whole herd and you wouldn't get enough money to pay for that house."

"Owen's cousin is taking my steers to St. Louis this spring. He says I can get at least thirty dollars a head."

A babble of voices erupted, all wanting to know if she really could get thirty dollars for one steer, when Owen's cousin meant to leave, and would he take some of their steers.

"I don't believe a word," Alva said. "You're just trying to get folks so excited they'll forget about your rustling."

"What I am trying to do is get folks to believe I had nothing to do with the rustling. I mean to prove it by going after the rustlers myself. I know some of you think I ought to be arrested right now—"

"You got that right," Alva said.

"—but that won't help stop it."

"It will if you're doing the rustling," Alva said.

"What are you proposing?" someone asked Hetta.

"You give me and my men a week to bring the rustlers in."

"I can't let you go," the sheriff said.

"Suppose I leave the deed to my ranch as collateral? Everybody knows I own the best graze and the only permanent water source in the county."

"You could be out of Texas by then," Alva said.

"If I don't come back, you can sell the ranch to the highest bidder and distribute the proceeds to everyone who's lost cows."

"I say we let her do it," someone yelled.

"I could use the cash," someone else said. The chorus of agreement grew.

"I just hope Owen was able to get Ben and Myrl out of jail," Hetta whispered to Ida. The words were hardly out of her mouth when she recognized Broc squeezing his way into the room. A wink told her all she needed to know.

"If you don't find the rustled cows, I'll buy your ranch and give it back to you," Ida said. "You've given me far more than a ranch."

William looked uncomfortable.

"I never had him," Hetta said. "Now get your uncle to talk the sheriff into letting me go. We've got some rustlers to catch."

And after that, she had to decide what to do about Owen's offer of marriage.

*   *   *

"I can't believe you put your ranch up as security," Owen said for the hundredth time.

"It was the only way to make everybody believe I was serious," Hetta replied.

"You realize Laveau could already have taken the herd Nate and Broc were tracking to Mexico."

"You'd better hope not. Or you'll never get back the money you loaned me."

"I don't care about the money."

"I do. Now stop arguing and try to figure out where those cows could be."

The six of them had been over every corner of the county without finding a trace of the herd. Laveau wouldn't have had time to take the cows out in small groups. They were still in the area. The question was where.

"Okay," Owen said to the men gathered around the campfire on the fifth night of their search, "they have to be here. Think. We can't allow Laveau to outsmart us."

Owen was feeling desperate. He would be responsible if Hetta lost her ranch. If he hadn't been so intent on proving that Hetta couldn't resist him, he could have driven Laveau so far away he would never have come back to bother Hetta. But as usual, his ego had gotten in the way. Every time he thought he'd finally proved he was different from his mother, he did something to prove he would never escape his heritage.

If he really loved Hetta, the best thing he could do would be to leave and let her find someone who could be the kind of husband she wanted. God knows he had tried to be different. But every time he made a little headway, something came along to push him right back where he started.

But he wasn't about to give up Hetta. He had never believed he would be loved. Now the possibility was within reach, and he didn't mean to let it go.

But if Hetta lost her ranch, she'd never marry him. She was more likely to get a few cows and homestead part of the creek where it ran through her land. The ranch was so big, a new owner would never notice, or try to drive her out if he did.

He sat up as if he'd been stuck with a pin. He was a fool! Why hadn't he thought of that before?

"I know where they are," he announced.

"Where?" Hetta asked.

"The only place within fifty miles we haven't searched."

"But we *have* searched everywhere," Ben said.

"We forgot Hetta's ranch."

"But . . ." Myrl started to speak, then stopped.

"Laveau didn't bring the herd in," Owen said. "Somebody else did it, and where did they always take the cows?"

"My ranch," Hetta said.

"Laveau always planned to use your land. He intended to use those forged papers to keep you quiet if you tried to refuse. And if by chance someone did discover the herd, it would be proof you were a rustler. He had you in a tighter corner than you knew."

"I say we go after them first thing in the morning," Ben said.

"We go tonight," Owen said.

"We outnumber them," Hetta said.

"We don't know how many are on guard," Owen said.

He had found the rustled cattle in a basin where the water course fanned out and provided enough grass to support a herd of around two hundred for up to a month. Two men lay asleep in their bedrolls near the embers of a nearly dead campfire, but Owen was certain there was at least one more man out there somewhere.

"Do you recognize either of them?" Owen asked Ben and Myrl.

Both shook their heads.

"Then there has to be at least one other man," Owen said, "someone who can go into town for supplies without arousing suspicion."

"Who would that be?" Broc asked.

"Newt Howren."

"He won't be alone," Myrl warned.

Broc took out his binoculars and slowly surveyed the area. "I don't see anybody," he said. "Not even horses."

"He's here," Owen repeated.

"Then he's got some sort of hideout," Broc said.

"How are we going to flush them out when we can't see them?" Nate asked.

"We could stampede the herd," Broc suggested.

"But that would wake up the two who're sleeping," Owen said.

"Then we have to draw them out of their hiding place," Hetta said.

"Got any ideas?" Nate asked.

"Yes, and I think it'll work."

Even before Hetta started to explain her plan, Owen knew he wouldn't like it. "Don't put yourself in danger again," he warned.

"I'm the only one who's *not* in danger," Hetta assured him. "Newt won't know I suspect anything. He'll just think I'm assuming he's taken over from Tom Manly."

"He'll want to know what you're doing out here in the middle of the night."

"I'll tell him Mr. diViere sent me with a message."

"What message?"

"Not to do anything until he hears from him. That people in town will be suspicious of any herd they see moving south."

"Sounds like excellent strategy," Broc said.

"I agree," Nate added.

"I won't let you do it," Owen said.

Hetta's reaction was all the more unnerving because it was slow and deliberate. "Since this is my ranch and my reputation that's at stake, I have the right to decide what to do and who does it."

"We agreed I would be in charge of this search," Owen said.

"That was when we were wandering all over the county. We're on my land now."

"Somebody has to handle the two men at the campfire," Owen said, conceding defeat. "Myrl, you and Ben do that."

"Be careful," Owen said to Hetta. "I didn't go through everything to lose you now."

"What did he go through?" Nate asked.

"Not nearly enough," Hetta said. She removed her hat and let her hair fall down over her shoulders.

"What are you doing?" Owen said.

"Making sure they know I'm a woman," Hetta said. "And I'm going to sing. I can't carry a tune, but they'll know I'm coming."

"I still don't want you to do this," Owen said.

"You'd better get used to it," Broc said. "I suspect this is just the first of a lot of things she's going to do you won't like."

"It's not the first," Owen snapped.

Broc laughed softly. "I thought I'd never live to see this day. If only Cade was here."

"I'm riding out," Hetta said.

It was all Owen could do to keep from reaching out and pulling her back. If Newt or his pals so much as laid a finger on her, he'd hunt them down and feed their carcasses to the coyotes.

"You sure you want to marry her?" Broc asked, a laugh in his voice. "She seems a trifle strong-minded to me."

"She's hardheaded as a mule," Owen said, "and I'm going to marry her if it's the last thing I do."

"That woman will eat you alive," Nate said, his face wreathed in smiles.

"I can see it now," Broc said. "Hetta'll be sitting on the porch after dinner smoking a thin cigar while Owen cleans up in the kitchen. What kind of apron do you want me to give you for Christmas?"

Owen punched Broc so hard he fell over, still laughing.

"Make sure the kids are tucked in," Nate said in a high falsetto. "It's chilly tonight." He dodged Owen's fist. "I think I'd like pork chops for dinner tomorrow."

Owen tackled Nate and they went down on the ground. But Nate was laughing so hard he couldn't fight back. Owen let him go in disgust. "My turn will come," he said. "And by God, I'm not going to miss it."

"Of course you can't go to the saloon," Broc said, imitating Nate's falsetto. "You have to stay with the children. You know I have a stockholders meeting."

Owen aimed a kick at Broc's behind, but the sound of Hetta's unsteady and very out-of-tune singing robbed it of any force. He grabbed Broc's glasses. Hetta was walking her horse toward the herd, singing softly. Five minutes passed and no one appeared. She was so far away, Owen knew they wouldn't be of any help if there was trouble. He handed the binoculars to Broc and headed for his horse.

"I can't leave her out there by herself. I'm going to follow through the brush."

Hetta hoped she didn't sound as nervous as she felt. Though she didn't think her singing could be any worse if she'd been shaking with fear. She was surprised the cattle didn't stampede, but they only turned their heads as she passed, apparently as tone deaf as she was.

She looked from side to side as she rode, but she

couldn't see the men she felt certain were watching her every move. Her plan hadn't seemed dangerous when she'd proposed it with five men surrounding her, but now she was out here by herself and every step was taking her farther away from Owen. She hated to admit it, but she'd give just about anything to have him at her side right now. She might even marry him.

That possibility kept teasing her. She wouldn't marry him until she felt certain he loved her enough to remain faithful. She knew she couldn't endure a repeat of what her mother had lived through. This was all or nothing.

She switched to a hymn she'd heard in church, hoping she could come closer to singing a recognizable tune. She wondered if Owen could carry a tune. He probably had a beautiful singing voice. It seemed every lady's man could sing as well as dance.

She'd just started on a second hymn when she heard something stir in the brush about thirty yards away. Moments later, Newt Howren emerged on horseback, followed by two men whose appearance made her wish even more ardently that Owen was at her side.

"What are you doing out here all by yourself?" Newt asked. She could tell from the tone of his voice, he'd already decided she was trouble.

Chapter Thirty

"Mr. diViere sent me," Hetta said. "I have a message for you."

"He wouldn't send you," Newt said. "You're hooked up with Wheeler."

"I'm not *hooked up* with Owen Wheeler," Hetta said. "He just works for me."

"Wheeler makes plenty gambling. He doesn't need to work for you."

"He's trying to convince me to sell to him," Hetta said.

"What would he want with a ranch here?" Newt asked.

"I don't care why," one of the other men said. "I just hope I get a chance to fill his hide with lead."

Hetta had to bite her tongue to keep from responding. She hoped Owen had noticed she'd drawn Newt out into the open. She didn't know how long she could hold him.

"How long have you boys been here?" she asked.

"About a week," one of the men said.

"I didn't see you come in," she said.

"We came in from the south. DiViere didn't want—"

"Shut up," Newt growled. "You talk too much."

"She said diViere sent her."

"Maybe he did, maybe he didn't. I ain't so sure."

"He came by a few nights ago to renew his lease," Hetta said.

"He said you threatened to turn him in to the sheriff."

"I got angry when he tried to bully me with some papers he'd forged." She hoped Owen would hurry up. She wasn't used to making up lies every time she opened her mouth.

"I told him that wouldn't work. Everybody knows you're close as peas in a pod with Ida Moody," Newt said.

"Ida's been my friend for years, but being her friend doesn't pay the bills. Mr. diViere's rent money will."

"He paid you?"

"It's the only reason I agreed to come out here," she said. "You could have taken me for one of the rustler patrol and shot me."

"Can't nobody take you for a man, not even in the dark," one of the men said.

"You sure are a lousy singer," the other man said.

"What's diViere's message?" Newt asked.

Hetta didn't hear anything to make her think Owen was about to come to her rescue. She had said she could do this on her own, and it looked like she was about to get the chance to prove it.

"He said you were to wait to move the herd until you heard from him," she said. "A couple of men from a ranch near San Antonio are in town. They'd recognize some of the brands."

"We always go out the south," one of the men said. "Ain't nobody watching down there."

"I told you to shut up," Newt said.

"It makes no difference to me where you go or when," Hetta said. "I'm just telling you what Mr. diViere said."

She started to turn her horse but the men moved closer on either side.

"Where do you think you're going?" Newt asked.

"Home. I've delivered the message."

"I don't think you delivered the right one."

"I told you exactly what Mr. diViere said."

"I don't think he sent you out here with any message."

"Then what would I be doing out here in the middle of the night?"

"Spying on us so you can tell your boyfriend where we are."

"I knew where you were. Why didn't I tell him earlier?"

That stopped Newt for a moment, but only a short moment.

"DiViere told us Owen Wheeler was looking for us. He said you were with Wheeler. He said we were to stay in hiding."

"Then you ought to tell your men not to sleep in the open."

"He said we were to kill you if we saw you."

"The sheriff would hang you."

"DiViere said it would be blamed on the rustlers. He says we're not using this place anymore, so we can kill anybody we want."

"I don't know what Mr. diViere may have told you earlier, but he came to my house tonight. He said things had changed and I was to bring you this message. Now I've told you what he said. If you don't want to believe it, that's your choice."

She dug her heels into her horse's flanks and pulled back on the reins at the same time. The animal reared, its forelegs pawing the air dangerously close to Newt's head. When the men pulled their mounts back a safe distance, Hetta turned her horse and spurred him into a full gallop. She had to reach Owen before Newt got her. A bullet whistled by.

"Don't shoot," she heard one of the men shout. "We can get rid of her afterwards."

Hetta spurred her horse harder, but the rustlers had faster horses. She looked over her shoulder. Newt's horse was outrunning the others. He would catch her before she could reach Owen. Her only chance was to lose him in a tangle of brush. But no sooner had she turned her horse toward the closest thicket than she noticed a horseman moving inside the thicket coming toward her. Newt had even more men than they had guessed.

She jerked her horse's head away from the thicket.

"Hetta, it's me!"

She'd never been happier to hear the sound of Owen's voice. She turned her horse just in time to avoid being caught by Newt and plunged into the thicket. It proved to be a narrow band, and she soon found herself on the other side, but Newt came crashing through behind her. Owen met him with a fist to the jaw that sent Newt tumbling to the ground.

Owen dropped from the saddle, and he and Newt were soon rolling around on the rocky ground. Deciding it wasn't fair to leave Owen to handle Newt on his own, Hetta slid out of her saddle. She punched Newt several times, but that didn't seem to make any impression on him. She kicked him, but that only elicited a grunt. Hetta pulled a small pear cactus up by the roots and flung it on Newt's back, then stomped on it with her booted foot.

Newt's screams shattered the night. He threw himself off Owen, but he landed on his back, driving the thorns in even deeper. Owen wasted no time in tying Newt hand and foot.

Owen threw his arms around Hetta and held her so tightly, she was certain he'd cracked a rib. "If you ever do anything like this again, I swear I'll lock you inside your house and not let you out until you're too old to ride."

"There are two more men behind me," she said as she tried to avoid Owen's efforts to kiss her into silence.

"Let Broc and Nate have them. We can't deprive them of all the fun."

"I didn't see them."

"They're experts at not being seen. Do you hear anybody coming after you?"

There was silence. "No."

"Now forget everything and promise me you'll never do anything like this again."

"How can I make promises with Newt howling like a yard dog?" But it was much easier to ignore Newt than she suspected. Being in Owen's arms, having him act as if she were the most important person in the world, as if he would go crazy if anything happened to her, well, what woman wouldn't ignore a little squalling for that?

Broc and Nate came crashing through the brush. "You're supposed to capture the enemy," Broc said with a wide grin. "She's on our side."

Owen didn't loosen his hold on Hetta. "We did, but he won't stop howling."

"I'd hate to fall on something like that," Nate said when he saw the cactus attached to Newt's back.

"He didn't fall. Hetta hit him with it, then drove it deeper with her foot."

Broc and Nate turned their gazes to Hetta.

"Are you sure you want to marry her?" Broc asked. "If you ever get into a fight, she'll turn you into a pincushion."

Owen turned back to Hetta. "I'll just have to make sure I don't give her a reason."

Nate turned to Broc. "I'll bet you fifty dollars he doesn't make it through the first year."

"Make it six months," Broc said, "and I'll raise you twenty-five."

* * *

It was an impressive procession that rode into town early that morning. Owen and Hetta led in the five rustlers, their hands bound, their feet tied beneath their mount's bellies, followed by Nate, Broc, Myrl, and Ben driving the stolen herd. They were surprised that although nearly everybody in the town appeared to be on the street, nobody rushed over to find out why five men were tied up and two hundred steers were milling in the streets.

"Something must have happened," Hetta said, looking around. Most of the people seemed to be gathered outside the bank.

"They're probably auctioning off your ranch."

"They wouldn't do that. Ida promised . . ." She broke off when Owen gripped her arm. "What?"

"That's Cade and Pilar. What are they doing here?"

"Where?"

"In front of the hotel. Broc, what's Cade doing here?"

"I'll find out."

"I want to talk to him," Hetta said. "I've been wanting to meet him for ages."

"I've got to get these men to the jail," Owen said.

But when they reached the jail, the sheriff wasn't there.

"He's over at the bank," the deputy said. "What am I supposed to do with those fellas?"

"Put them in jail," Owen said. "We caught them red-handed with rustled steers."

"Hot damn! I been wanting to put a rope around Newt's neck for a long time."

Cade and Pilar were on the boardwalk in deep conversation with Hetta when Owen came out of the jail.

"Mr. diViere robbed Fred Moody and shot William," Hetta told him. "I've got to go to Ida."

"I'll come, too."

"At least say hello first," Pilar said. "And congratulate me."

It took Owen a moment to realize that Pilar's figure

had assumed a very different shape. "You're going to have a baby?"

"Two of them, from the looks of me," Pilar said, laughing and disappearing into Owen's hug.

"I hope it's a boy," Cade said. "Her grandmother has already decided it will be my fault if it's a girl."

"Maybe it'll be twins and you'll have one of each. Then everybody will be happy."

"Except me," Pilar said. "I'll be huge."

"Hetta was telling us about all the things you've done since you got here," Cade said.

"Hetta's a little prejudiced."

"I noticed." Pilar winked.

"Your friends back her up," Broc said. "According to them, Owen has just about transformed this town."

"They're going to try to make him mayor."

"There's nothing to be mayor of," Owen said, feeling acutely uncomfortable. "What are you doing here, and why did you bring Pilar when she's . . . like this?"

"It's called pregnant," Pilar said.

"Since I hadn't heard from you, I thought I'd see if you still had a whole hide."

"I can take care of myself."

"We can talk later. You'd better get over to the bank. Your friends need you."

The scene that met Owen's eyes at the bank was unexpected. William lay on the floor, his mother bent over him, emitting ear-splitting wails while the doctor attempted to bandage him up. Fred Moody lay sprawled in a chair, his wife fanning him furiously, demanding to know exactly how much money had been stolen. Ida clung to Hetta, pouring out her story in between sobs.

"What happened?" Owen asked the sheriff.

"It seems Mr. diViere went to the Moodys house before the bank opened to ask Fred for enough money to meet a payroll for a herd he had coming in. Not suspecting anything, Fred came over here by himself. Young William reached the house a few minutes after Fred had left. He said he wasn't comfortable with the idea of Fred being alone with Mr. diViere in the bank, that Hetta didn't trust him. He arrived in time to hear diViere tell Fred to empty the safe. William's entry into the office rattled diViere. He pulled a gun, shot William, then shot Fred and escaped."

"When did this happen?"

"About two hours ago. Most people were just getting dressed, so it was a few minutes before anybody got into the street. By that time diViere was gone."

Once again they had come so close, yet Laveau had escaped.

"Will William—"

"He's not badly hurt. The bullet struck a rib, traveled around, and went out the back. It's painful, but he'll be all right."

"What about Fred?"

"He has a hole in his coat, but not in his skin. He'll be okay once his wife leaves him alone," he added in a whisper.

Owen thought briefly about getting Broc and Nate to go after Laveau but changed his mind. With a two-hour head start, they'd never catch him before he reached one of the friendly army units that would protect him. No, they'd have to save Laveau for another day. Right now he wanted to talk to Hetta.

"I'm taking Ida home," Hetta said to him. "As soon as William is home and comfortable, she'll go sit with him."

"I'm coming, too," Owen said. He didn't look forward to hearing Ida tearfully repeat over and over how heroic it was of William to save her uncle, but if it was the price he had to pay to be with Hetta, he'd pay it.

*　　*　　*

"You seem to have created quite a stir," Cade was saying to Owen. They were sitting in Ida's parlor. She had gone to sit with William. Owen had nothing left to do but convince Hetta to marry him. But Cade and Pilar had been here for a couple of hours and didn't show any signs of leaving.

"I wouldn't have if it hadn't been for the rustlers. Nobody paid me much attention otherwise."

"Once he stopped gambling and taking everybody's money," Hetta said.

"Up to your old tricks again?" Pilar asked.

"It was just a cover. I never won much."

"Are you going back with us?" Cade asked.

"I thought I'd stick around. I offered to take some of Hetta's steers with us to St. Louis."

"Is that okay?" Hetta asked.

"Sure."

"Then we'll look for you before long," Pilar said. "The boys miss you. There's nobody better when it comes to attracting beautiful women," she said to Hetta. "I think the men use him as bait."

What was Pilar doing? Owen wondered in dismay. He'd thought she liked him.

"Even my grandmother, who dislikes all Anglos on principle," Pilar said, "doesn't dislike him quite as much."

She was up to something, but it was clear that even Cade didn't know what.

"I'm glad to know he didn't cause you and your friend Ida to fall out over him." Pilar sighed. "I've warned him over and over again to be careful, but he's a hopeless flirt. I'm sure you'll be relieved to send him north with the steers. You've had to put up with him long enough."

"I haven't suffered all that much."

"It's sweet of you to defend him." Pilar stood. "Women always do. But I like you, so I'll keep him away from you. We have to go," she said to her husband. "If Grandmother

363

finds out I didn't take my nap, you won't have any peace until the baby is born."

She kissed Hetta on the cheek and hurried her husband from the room.

"What in hell were you trying to do back there?" Cade asked the moment they reached the street. "Owen wants to marry that woman."

Pilar took Cade's arm as they started toward the hotel. "She wants to marry him, too, but something is holding her back. Nothing makes a woman want to defend her man more than criticism from another woman."

Cade wrinkled his brow. "So you were really trying to help him?"

"I liked Hetta from the moment I met her. She'll make him a perfect wife. And he's crazy about her. What time is it?"

"A quarter after two."

"I expect we'll see him before five o'clock. If not, we'll have to come back. We can't leave until they're engaged."

"What do you plan to do, lock them in a room together?"

"I expect they'll have a small wedding. She doesn't strike me as a woman who wants a lot of fuss. You know we'll have to stay."

"For what?"

"For the wedding. I expect they'll get married the day after tomorrow."

"I'll never understand women," Cade said. "Never."

She looked at his creased brow and smiled. "You're not supposed to."

"I thought you said she liked you," Hetta said to Owen.

"She's only telling you the truth."

"I think she's jealous you're better looking than her husband."

"Pilar never cared about anybody but Cade."

"I don't think you ought to go back with them. I like your cousin, but—"

Owen grabbed Hetta and kissed her hard.

"Pilar's probably a fine woman . . ." Hetta began the moment her lips were free.

Owen's next kiss was a lot longer. He didn't end it until he felt Hetta melt against him.

"Now it's my turn to talk," he said before she could recover. "I love you. I want to marry you. I want to stay here with you, *always*. I don't want to go back with them. I don't want to attract any ladies anywhere. I only want to attract you. Do you think you can possibly love me enough to give it a try?"

"You said you weren't the marrying type."

"Maybe I should have said I wasn't the marrying type until I found just the right woman for me. Now I've found her."

"You promise not to try to tell me what to do?"

"Of course I'll try, but you won't listen."

"You won't mind living in Pinto Junction?"

"I'd hate living in Pinto Junction. We'll live on your ranch."

"You promise to wash my back?"

"Every night." Owen slipped from the sofa and down on his knees. "Will you marry me?"

"Get up."

"Not until you say you'll marry me. I'll lie on the floor until Ida comes home."

Hetta laughed. "I'll marry you on one condition."

"What is that?" He didn't like conditions. Sooner or later they caused trouble.

"You're never to tell me I'm beautiful."

"Never?"

"Well, at least not for twenty or thirty years."

"I can't make that promise," Owen said, "but there is

one I will make." He took Hetta's hands and pressed them against his cheeks. "I may not tell you you're beautiful, but I promise to make you *feel* beautiful."

It took several kisses to seal their promises. When they'd finally leaned back against the sofa, still holding hands, Hetta asked, "When do you think we ought to get married?"

"Tonight."

Hetta laughed. "We can't do it that quickly."

"Then how about tomorrow?"

"I think the day after would be better."

"I don't think I can wait that long."

"I have to have time to find a dress."

"Wear the one you wore to the dance."

"I can't get married in a red dress!"

"Why not?"

Hetta sighed happily. "I'm glad there's at least one thing you don't understand about women. No man should know everything."

WYOMING *Wildfire*

Leigh Greenwood

With the inheritance of half her uncle's Wyoming spread, Sybil Cameron feels she's gained her independence at last. Then she meeets her partner, Burch Randall–a man who believes a woman has no business running a ranch. She vows to keep her cool no matter what. Yet as Burch's muscular arms close around her, a deliciously hot feeling courses through her body.

To Burch, Sybil is a wild filly: spirited, headstrong, and in need of a man's brand. But he soon learns this is one woman not to be tamed.   In fact, he finds he glories in her passionate abandon, revels in her raw courage, and wants only to take her and set the prairie ablaze in a Wyoming wildfire.

Wicked Wyoming Nights
Leigh Greenwood

When Eliza Smallwood first meets Cord Stedman, he personifies the devil himself. The famed cattle rancher chases Eliza and her homesteader uncle off his land, but instead of harming them, the blue-eyed cowman protects them from attack. Eliza can't help but picture herself as the heroine of exotic daydreams starring the mysterious rancher.

Cord Stedman commands respect, but no one sees him laugh until he meets Eliza. Cord soon finds himself saving the beauty at every opportunity, including the time her unscrupulous uncle forces Eliza to sing at his new saloon. But Cord quickly realizes that the chaste enchantress has liberated something of his, as well . . . his heart.

LEIGH GREENWOOD
The Cowboys

The freedom of the range, the bawling of the longhorns, the lonesome night watch beneath a vast, starry sky–they got into a man's blood until he knew there was nothing better than the life of a cowboy . . . except the love of a good woman.

___Jake	4593-1	$5.99 US/$6.99 CAN
___Ward	4299-1	$5.99 US/$7.99 CAN
___Buck	4592-3	$5.99 US/$6.99 CAN
___Chet	4594-X	$5.99 US/$6.99 CAN
___Sean	4490-0	$5.99 US/$6.99 CAN
___Pete	4562-1	$5.99 US/$6.99 CAN
___Drew	4714-4	$5.99 US/$6.99 CAN
___Luke	4804-3	$5.99 US/$6.99 CAN
___Matt	4877-9	$5.99 US/$7.99 CAN

Dorchester Publishing Co., Inc.
P.O. Box 6640
Wayne, PA 19087-8640
Please add $2.50 for shipping and handling for the first book and $.75 for each book thereafter. NY and PA residents, please add appropriate sales tax. No cash, stamps, or C.O.D.s. Prices and availability subject to change.
Canadian orders require $2.00 extra postage and must be paid in U.S. dollars through a U.S. banking facility.

Name _____

Address _____

City_____ State_____ Zip _____

E-mail _____

I have enclosed $_____ in payment for the checked book(s).

Payment <u>must</u> accompany all orders. ❑ Please send a free catalog.

CHECK OUT OUR WEBSITE! www.dorchesterpub.com

CHASE THE WIND
CINDY HOLBY

From the moment he sets eyes on Faith, Ian Duncan knows she is the only girl for him. But her unbreakable betrothal to his employer's vicious son forces him to steal his love away on the very eve of her marriage. Faith and Ian are married clandestinely, their only possessions a magnificent horse, a family Bible, a wedding-ring quilt and their unshakable belief in each other. While their homestead waits to be carved out of the Iowa wilderness, Faith presents Ian with the most precious gift of all: a son and a daughter, born of the winter snows into the spring of their lives. The golden years are still ahead, their dream is coming true, but this is just the beginning. . . .

HANNAH'S HALF-BREED
HEIDI BETTS

Wounded and in desperate need of help, David Walker has survived the treacherous journey to reach the blue-eyed, blond-haired girl of his memories. And in Hannah's arms he discovers Heaven. But torn between the white man's world and his Indian heritage, David wonders if he's been saved or damned.

The man who calls himself Spirit Walker bears little resemblance to the boy who comforted Hannah during her darkest hours at the orphanage. There is nothing safe about the powerful half-breed who needs her assistance. Still, the schoolteacher will risk everything to save him, for their love is strong enough to overcome any challenge.
